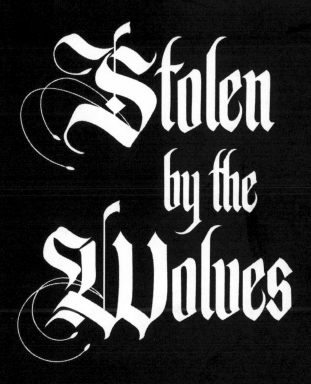

Stolen by the Wolves

Book 1 in the
VIKING OMEGAVERSE

LYX ROBINSON

Book 1 in the
VIKING OMEGAVERSE

LYX ROBINSON

Published & illustrated by Lyx Robinson
www.lyxrobinson.com

CONTENT WARNINGS

In this book there are graphic depictions of violence, battles, sexual situations and strong language. This is a slow burn "why choose" series, therefore as the series progresses, the main romance will involve more than just one love interest. If you'd like to remain spoiler-free regarding the specifics, please turn this page.

.

.

.

A more detailed list of content warnings:

- *Arranged marriage*
- *Sexual assault (not by the hero, but by the antagonist. The scene does not involve any penetrative sexual acts, and the characters remain clothed.)*
- *Self-flagellation*
- *Religious trauma*
- *Ritualised human sacrifice*

VIKING INVASIONS IN BRITANNIA ◆ 870 ◆ A.D.

Kingdom of the Northern Isles

Kingdom of the Southern Isles

ALBA

Dal Riata

Strathclyde

Northumbria

Northern Uí Néill

Connacht

Mide

Dublin

Leinster

Munster

The Dane Law

Gwynedd

Mercia

Wessex

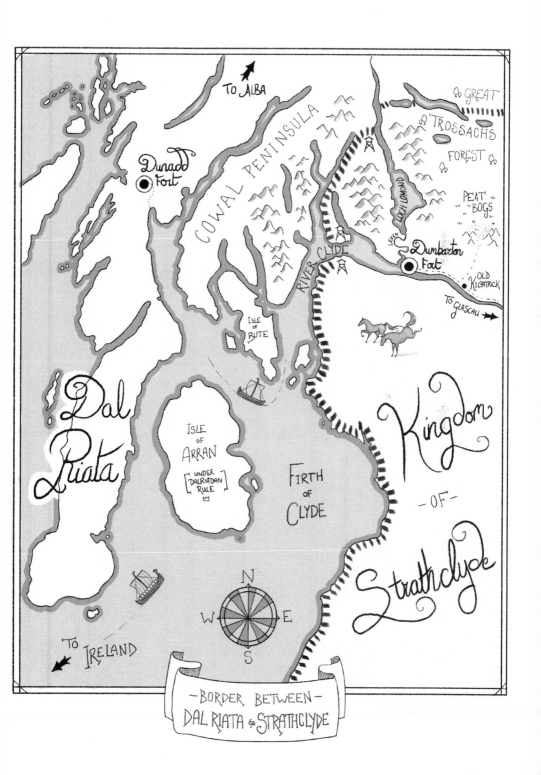

TO ALBA

GREAT

TROSSACHS

FOREST

Dunadd Fort

COWAL PENINSULA

LOCH LOMOND

PEAT BOGS

Dumbarton Fort

RIVER CLYDE

OLD KILPATRICK

TO GLASCAU

ISLE OF BUTE

Dal Riata

ISLE OF ARRAN

[UNDER DALRIADAN RULE]

FIRTH OF CLYDE

Kingdom

-OF-

Strathclyde

N
W   E
S

TO IRELAND

-BORDER BETWEEN-
DAL RIATA & STRATHCLYDE

GLOSSARY

In this series, the Old Norse language includes some modern Icelandic phrases (which is the closest modern language to Old Norse), for anything I didn't find in my Old Norse ressources.

As for the extinct Brittonic language of Strathclyde, I borrowed from its sister-languages and descendants to recreate it, namely: Welsh (modern and medieval), and Breton (modern).

Brittonic

Ankou - Death (from Breton)

Calan Mai - May Day festivities (from Welsh)

Gall-Goídil - Norse-Irish settlers (from Old Gaelic)

Glascau - Older form of Glasgow, lit. "blue/green hollow" (from Welsh)

Yec'hed mat - A drinking toast (from Breton)

Old Norse

Blòd - Blood

Fljùga - Fly

Hleypa - Gallop

Hvarfa - Walk

Skàl - A drinking toast

Varg - Wolf, the term they use for Alphas

Vyrgen - Plural of Varg

Vanirdottir - Daughter of the Vanir, the term they use for Omegas

Vanirdøtur - Plural of Vanirdottir

Prologue

SHE STANDS AT the entrance to the great hall, her slight shoulders wrapped in white fur. Underneath the white cape, she wears nothing.

The niece of a Briton king. Standing in the great hall of a Jarl.

There are no shackles around her ankles now. She is here by her own will. She no longer wears the grooves of her captivity, nor the haunted look in her eye.

She chose this path. She chose me. We are inexorably tied together by virtue of what she *is*.

A rare descendant of the Vanir. A jewel from a jealously-guarded land.

Whatever terms she uses for it – that I am cursed by her horned devil, that she is no less innocent in the eyes of her Almighty for bearing the desires that she does – no amount of philosophy can deny what ties us together.

She can feel it just as keenly as I can. I can see it in the way she holds herself so very still in a room full of slavering Vyrgen men. I can sense it in the tension she holds within her.

I can smell it in the sweetness of her scent.

The moon is full; she is in heat.

Sitting in my high chair, I lift a hand. "Princess Tamsin of Strathclyde," I intone in her harsh Brittonic tongue. Ivar and Olaf jeer from either side of me, pulling a cheerful uproar from the others at the sound of that language on my tongue. "Welcome to the great winter feast of Illskarheim."

It's a signal for her to come forward. The other Vanirdøtur maidens are already at my feet, similarly attired in furs and fineries that Tamsin helped prepare for the feast.

It is their initiation night. Most of them already have their sights on the Vyrgen they wish to claim. Just as the roasted pheasants and mead-lathered boar will sweeten their tongues, so my ever-faithful karls will labour to earn their favour. Tonight, those men who endeavour to show their quality may at last, if their courtship has been successful, earn themselves their pair-bond.

But no one touches her.

My beloved spouse. My pale princess.

If I invite her to enter this way, it is only to show them what true power is.

Only a true Varg leader could keep a hall full of rutting males still as a flushed Vanirdottir walks down the aisle, cutting a clear path in the middle of them all.

A few of the drunkards, Orm and Armod especially, growl with barely contained lust as she passes by them. They get pulled back and yelled at cheerfully by those who have not yet dampened their self-control with mead.

I watch her come towards my brothers and I. She is a vision, all in white with a crown of winter berries around her head. That familiar surge of possessiveness shoots down to my groin, tightening my abdomen. Hot blood throbs through me as I imagine the night to come.

One of my karls watches her jealously as she passes him, his eyes flashing in the firelight. A low growl rumbles in his throat, dampening the general hilarity of the pre-feast mood.

All it takes is one look from me, and his contestation withers away. He tears his eyes from my pale princess, though it visibly pains him to do so.

The Briton girl is *mine*.

She's trembling by the time she sinks her bare feet into my sheepskin rugs. She smiles nervously at her kinswomen, then meets my gaze. Once she stops in front of me, she slides her hand into mine.

Her lips are parted, her eyes glazed as she holds herself before me. As I lace my fingers through hers, her intoxicating scent only grows stronger. The touch of my hand ignites something deepseated and ancient within her; that delicious essence that she tries so hard to deny.

Not just a Vanirdottir, but a princess of royal blood. She is too fine to belong to a mere Jarl. I understand this as I gaze at her pink lips, her translucent skin, her fine red-gold hair. She is a gift fit for kings.

But I will never let her go.

Chapter 1

THRAIN

YEAR 870

WAXING MOON OF MAY

T HE WAXING MOON hangs low in the sky, a golden crescent in the deepening sunset. Our longboats follow the shredded coast of Dál Riata, drums beating the pace, men grunting as they plunge the oars to and fro. I stand at the prow of my ship, my brothers manning the others, all of us watching the glitter of metal along the clifftops as Lord Aedan's men line up to greet us.

"Archers on the cliffs!"

Olaf's cry spans our small fleet. Our men work their oars with growls of disdain, keeping us at a safe distance from the coastline while we progress towards the beach.

An army is waiting for us there.

I lay a hand on the axe at my belt.

I had anticipated this. Olaf and Ivar believed their father's word, that the King of all Alba could be trusted, that his vassals would not protest the alliance between Alban and Viking kings. But I have never trusted men who wear golden circlets upon their heads.

The Lord of Dál Riata stands at a high vantage point overlooking the beach, astride his horse. His disapproval of his king's decision rings loud and clear in the form of hundreds of soldiers brandishing shields and halberds.

I grit my teeth as I take a rough count of his numbers. We tried to be as unthreatening as possible, but of course, there was always a risk that he would turn our decision against us. We travelled before the full moon with only a small party of men – and now he greets us with these massive numbers as though we had dragged an entire army to his shores.

How foolish we were. Showing respect to a lord who does not respect us in the slightest.

So. He seeks to take advantage of us while we are *unthreatening*. Perhaps he knows that even in small numbers we still pose a very real threat. There is a smidgeon of respect there, at least.

Hot blood thuds through my body as the sky darkens. The moon might not be full, but my anger more than makes up for it. I glance over at my brothers, finding them already sliding their weapon from their belts. Many of our men had been expecting a fight, eager to test the mettle of our supposed allies. We've faced worse odds than this and prevailed – they're all but chomping at the bit to be loosened on Dálriadan shores.

Fwizzzz.

Splosh.

I glance around at the source of the sound. An arrow has been loosened at our ship, but we're still out of range – it's fallen into the waves, leaving a sad little ripple in its wake.

Confused, we all look up, my men grabbing instinctively at their shields. A yelled order from some commander on the clifftop echoes across the distance that separates us. No other arrows come – they would never reach us, as the commander doubtlessly knows.

"Ha!" laughs one of my karls. "What clear aim! What skill! No doubt that one is being praised for his talents."

I smirk as others begin to jeer and bark their loud, mocking laughter, surely audible from the clifftops. It was probably a mistake, a rookie fiddling and firing out of sheer terror. But more present in my mind is the very *idea* that Lord Aedan's men might be trying to intimidate us. Telling us not to approach or expect a deluge of arrows.

Fury crawls up my spine. I did not slay the High King of Ireland to come here and be treated like some common bandit.

"Armod!" I call, and my faithful karl comes to stand by me. "Give me your spear."

He proffers it. "Thrain, shouldn't we wait to see what they have to say?"

My lip curls as I stare up at that rider on the high rise overlooking the beach. Lord Aedan's blue cape billows in the wind as he stares coolly back at us.

"I think their message is very clear already," I growl at Armod, curling my hand around his spear and turning to squint up at the clifftop.

Armod stands back. "At this distance?" he mutters in wonder.

"He has made his statement. Let us make one in return."

I throw the spear with all my strength.

The long spiked pole flies high into the air, metal singing as it slices through the wind. A murmur rises from the boats as many eyes follow its flight.

It strikes the offending archer so hard in the face that it throws him back with the full force of my throw.

My men howl in delight at the opening of hostilities. Arrows pelt back at us, losing themselves in the water and then thunking against the flanks of our ships as we draw closer.

"SHIELDS!" comes Ivar's cry as we all creep into range. Olaf repeats it; my crew need no direction as they're already covering their heads. Annoyance at finding myself caught in Lord Aedan's trap makes me snarl as I hold up my own shield.

We're close now – our ships are gliding towards the sand. Once we arrive on the beach I know they'll send their mad Vyrgen out first – that is the custom in these lands. They are sent out to perch themselves on our spears and blunt our advance for the main army.

Arrows zip through the air, clunking into our shields, slamming into the decks of our ships to form small forests. I hold myself still, my pounding blood silvered by the sight of the waiting troops.

I could not say I hadn't been looking forward to this outcome.

Let us be rid of the lordling, then – we only need his fort, the great stone castle of Dunadd, as our outpost on these shores. We don't need him. The King of all Alba could not fault us for defending ourselves – in fact he would owe us an apology for this inconvenience.

The ships drag across shallow water. With a rallying yell, I leap from my ship and splash into the thigh-high waves. My brothers follow me, and the three of us lead our men up the beach to meet our would-be hosts.

Their mad Vyrgen come at us, half-dressed, barely wearing any metal. Axe meets bone, blades clatter against tattered chainmail. Their front lines are no match for us – these Vyrgen are untrained, uneducated, little more than frothing beasts chucked at the front to do the work of guard dogs. Gofraid told us they were prisoners and criminals, men who would be missed by no one. To think a kingdom would treat its Vyrgen like this – it sickens me. It is a mercy to dispatch them. I send them to the next world, axe bloody, hoping to give them back some dignity in death.

My brothers and I open the way into the enemy's messy formations, cleaving through with relish. None of us are thinking about politics anymore. Sheer delight fills me to see how strong and united we are even without the full moon to bolster us. We must make a sight for those watching from the clifftops. The taste of blood in my mouth reminds me of my last moon-craze, the havoc we wrought on those Irish battlefields, and I'm growling and panting like a beast as I crunch across the corpse-strewn ground.

The main Dálriadan army decides our advance is not quite as blunted as they had hoped. Their so-called front lines are scattered across the bloodied sand in a grotesque spectacle. Shouts and yells ring in the evening air as their defensive formations splinter.

They've decided to flee.

Olaf and Ivar stand on either side of me, shields spattered with blood, both wearing the eager smiles of wolves on the hunt. Our men take chase, throwing jeers and whetted steel at the backs of the Dálriadans.

This is insane. They have us wildly outnumbered and yet

they choose to run? They cannot hold any loyalty towards their lordling if they defect so easily. How humiliating for him! We are completely surrounded and yet Lord Aedan's men stand down, either fleeing or refusing to fight, throwing their weapons down.

Good. Let him lose all his credibility and rue the day he dared to insult us.

I glance up at the lordling, still perched up there on his cliff, though he's looking far less confident now. Feral excitement surges up in me as I realise he's within my range, if I could only find a spear—

"Thrain!" Ivar calls, staring at something off to the left. Immediately he yells to our men, "Stop, *stop!* A rider comes, a woman! STOP!"

Olaf sees what it is and joins him, both of them turning to our masses of excitable men and yelling commands. It is no easy task to bring them to heel – if the moon had been full it would've been near impossible. Those who emerge first from the heat of battle help their Jarls to subdue those who do not immediately rise to clarity.

I strain to see over the many heaving bodies.

A white horse bearing a graceful rider gallops across the beach towards us. Long golden hair streams out behind her. She is neither armed nor armoured – she wears naught but a flowing white gown.

With many a growl and rough shoving of shields, I help Ivar and Olaf to subdue our warriors as she approaches. When at last she comes close enough for us to see her face, I can only be glad that our men are free of the silvery lust that the full moon would've instilled in them.

She has all the bearings of a royal lady. Beautiful, aged, wise-looking. If she comes to us in this way, it can only be to plead for peace. Perhaps it was the sight of her white gown that made the Dálriadans stand down. As disappointing as it is to stop our gleeful massacre, we are still here for political reasons, though I suspect many of our men have forgotten all about them.

"Go, Thrain," Olaf huffs at me as he restrains one of the more difficult blood-spattered karls. I nod at him. One of us has to step forward and show authority to the pack – show them they must stay behind their pack leaders.

I march out to meet her, my shield still firmly in hand in case Lord Aedan decides to task his remaining archers with more treachery. Hoofbeats muted in the sand, the great grey stallion comes to a halt with a snort. The rider gazes down at me, then beyond at our men, at the longboats rearing up out of bloody water, and the Dálriadans scattered in pieces across the ravaged landing spot.

Her eyes are wide with horror. She's panting as she holds herself there in front of me, absolutely helpless before us all if not for the radiance of her royal rearing.

She locks eyes with mine again. I have to commend her for keeping her wits in front of such a bloodbath and facing me head-on.

"Who among you are the three lords of Dublin?" she asks faintly.

"I am one of them," I tell her in her Gaelic tongue, my voice still hoarse and deep from the combative growl that has not quite left my chest. "Thrain Mordsson. And my brothers are with me – Ivar and Olaf Gofraidsson." I gesture behind me in their general direction. "My lady, this is no place for a woman."

"I am Lord Aedan's mother," she says, trying to recover a more authoritative tone. "Lady Catriona. Sister to the King of all Alba. Please listen to me. It was never our plan to come here and try to repel you. My son – he acted of his own accord, and I was foolish enough not to predict it. Our agreement with your King Gofraid still holds, you must believe me. My son made a decision he had no right to make. Please – I would ask you to respect the terms of our agreement, and stand down."

Respect. She asks respect of me, a bloodied and insulted Varg chieftain still haggard with bloodlust.

But she's here, risking her life for the sake of her son. She's not quite foolhardy enough to get down from her horse and stand level with me, but she's still putting herself in grave danger by being here at all. With my enraged pack behind me, I would not ask a woman to observe the usual courtesies of humility and pardon – she's already standing far too close for her own safety.

I lift my chin and give her a pointed look. "If my men are provoked again, I cannot guarantee your son's safety, nor that of his men."

"You will not be provoked," she says. "I swear it. You have my word. You are our allies as per the terms of our alliance. My king will not stand for this, I promise you, he will punish Lord Aedan very severely when he hears of this. Dunadd fort has already been prepared for you – please, let us put a stop to all this. Will you meet Lord Aedan with me?"

ᚦᚱᛏᛁᚻ

Lady Catriona signals the clifftop commanders to bring down their archers. Incredibly, they obey her. Lines of men march down to join us in the gullet between the cliffs, longbows slung over their shoulders.

My brothers and I watch as she effortlessly takes over military command. Aedan himself disappears from his high rise. I smirk as I realise even he is answering his mother's summons.

Interesting. So the mother wields more authority here than the lordling himself.

As the sun's dying rays of light illuminate the horizon, my brothers and I meet with the rebellious lordling.

He is a small and scrawny man once he has dismounted from his horse. He all but wades in the ceremonial breastplate and chainmail he wears. I observe him, quelling the growl in my chest at the sight of this boy, this *boy* who thought he could intimidate us.

Beyond the insult of his welcome committee, he did not join in the fight either. No wonder his men fled and stood down at the first signal. There isn't an ounce of bravery in him. Even as he stands before us, his fear is plain on his face.

His mother glowers at him.

"By order of King Causantin, ruler of all the lands and tribes of Alba, we are joined in alliance with the kingdom of the Southern Isles and the three lords of Dublin," Lady Catriona intones. "I ask that the pledge be given again for consolidation. Aedan, you will show deference to these men and accept them as your allies."

It is castigation of the best kind. The lordling quakes with fury at the mere idea of having to abase himself like this in front of his men. He was humiliated already by the mass defection of his own army – now his mother is forcing him to take a final, perhaps fatal blow to his own standing.

I take off my helmet, tuck it under one arm so he can see my face. Then I step forward, not bothering to hide my smile as I hold out a hand to him.

He glares at me. Then he divests himself of his own helmet and comes to meet me, clapping his hand into mine.

My smile widens to uncover my teeth.

Allies, then. He's lucky to be alive.

Chapter 2

TAMSIN
FULL MOON OF MAY

RHUN RIDES AHEAD of me. He picks his way through the foliage, pushing aside heavy-laden branches that sag with spring blossoms. The forests of Dumbartonshire are bursting with colour at this time of year, bringing to mind many previous springs, many sweet memories of the childhood we will soon be leaving behind.

Rhun has his back to me, his short ginger hair scruffy as always, his leaf-green cape sweeping down from his shoulders to pool over his horse's back. I wonder whether this will be the last image I have of my twin brother: out for an afternoon ride, the sun dappling his hair, his face bright and happy as though nothing could possibly be wrong.

How often will I think back on this moment after I lose him?

If I lose him, as he keeps reminding me. *If.*

"God's *bones,* these branches!" He glances at me over his shoulder, leaning suddenly to the right. "Ach – Tam, look out!"

The low-hanging branches escape his grasp. I only have half a second to duck before they burst out at me, whipping my dress and sending my horse halfway across the path.

"*Rhun!*" I shout at him while he laughs. Sitting back, I focus on calming my mount so he might stop twisting around like an excited pup. Eventually, he calms enough for me to fix my posture – I had been hanging on by barely a thigh.

"There, boy," I grunt as I hoist myself back into position with fistfuls of his mane. "There you go. Nothing's going to hurt you."

"You all right back there?" calls Rhun. "Still on your horse?"

"I am, no thanks to you!"

"Don't blame me. If that horse were any more skittish, he'd jump out of his own skin," Rhun says. "You should leave him here. Surely your future husband has a well-bred colt already waiting for you as a wedding gift."

I scowl at him. He says it as though it were something to look forward to, when he knows I don't care for any of it – neither the future husband nor the well-bred wedding gift.

"I am *not* leaving Cynan here," I huff at him. "And what horses do they have in Dál Riata? Their stock has always been ungainly and temperamental."

Rhun snorts. "Right. Definitely a step down from that scrubbrush you're riding right now."

I would flick a branch at him if it wouldn't scare Cynan again. Instead I ignore my brother's goading and focus on reassuring my mount, whose ears are pricked towards me.

Since my old greying Galloway mare got too old to ride, I've been working with this strange little Nordic stallion, undertaking the challenge of making him rideable. Bareback is all he'll stand for now, but he doesn't make it comfortable. Even if I manage to find a spot to perch on his plank-like back, his nervous attitude makes it difficult to work with him.

Truth be told, he's a welcome challenge. In a fortnight's time, under June's new moon, I'm to finally meet the man I have been betrothed to nearly all my life. It has been a long betrothal, breaking off with every war, only to be consolidated again following the frayed diplomacy between our kingdoms. Strathclyde and Alba have always been at war, so for a long time I was sure that I would never meet him, that to be 'promised' protected me from actual marriage. As long as King Arthgal treated me and my cousin

Eormen like white flags of truce, we would not have to actually meet our husbands, nor suffer the courtship of anybody else. We knew we would be at war with Alba again in a blink, so we could keep our freedom as promised princesses indeterminately.

But now… with the Viking threat on the horizon, everything is accelerating.

In a fortnight's time, our royal family will finally welcome Prince Domnall of Alba and Lord Aedan of Dál Riata for our formal courtships. They will stay with us in Dumbarton fort, dine with us in our halls, and consolidate our alliance once and for all so that we might present a united front against the Viking threat.

At least, that is what Uncle Arthgal hopes. The Albans have always been treacherous bastards, hiding a knife up their sleeve even as they promise friendship with us. But we have no other choice of ally. And Uncle Arthgal hopes that the consummation of our betrothals might be a grand enough gesture to win their loyalty. After all, girls like Eormen and I have never been sent outside of the borders of Strathclyde.

This kingdom has always been a sanctuary for girls of our kind. But in the face of war, the doors of our sanctuary must open. And we must go willingly into the beds of strange men.

If I can forget all about my betrothal while I work with Cynan, then I'll gladly put up with his moods.

"You're losing your touch," Rhun teases me as I reach his side. He towers over me on his beautiful jet-black Galloway mare. "I remember a time when you could gentle a moody old nag like him in a day."

I glare at him. "I might have some things on my mind."

Rhun cocks an eyebrow at me. "It's a poor horsewoman who brings her issues with her in the saddle."

"I don't have a saddle."

"Well then maybe you need one!"

Annoyed, I cluck my tongue and trot ahead of him under the low-hanging canopy.

I'll show my brother. Cynan has an extra gait, a four-beat pace called the tölt – it's a particularity of his breed that piqued our interest when we first found him at Dumbartonshire's annual foaling festival. The horse dealer promised us he was an old Viking warhorse, scraped off the battlefield and still full of fire. Rhun gave up on him once he saw the stallion's temperament, but I know Cynan's strange gaits still fascinate him.

"Come on, boy," I mutter, and ask Cynan for the tölt. He snorts and chucks his head as he gives me a disjointed trot instead. For a moment I wonder if he's just going to keep fighting me – but he picks up his hooves at long last, sliding elegantly into the four-beat gait. The quick succession of steps gives us a burst of speed, and we eat up the ground, leaving Rhun in the dust. He laughs in surprise and canters to catch up.

We make a race of it until we turn into a straight, flat path between flowering fields.

"Come on then!" Rhun shouts. "Show me what that stubborn old thing can really do."

I glance at him wryly. He just wants to see me fall, that much is obvious from the wide mischievous grin he's wearing.

Breathing out, I try to imagine myself as the Viking who owned Cynan before me. Axe at my belt, helmet on my head. A chill runs through me as I remember the tall Danes I've seen milling around the ports of Gwynedd, and the longboats we've glimpsed on our trips over the Firth of Clyde. I tuck in my chin, staring ahead at a fixed point.

Overpowered. Unstoppable. Bloodthirsty. I paint the image over myself, growing into it, a thrill of confidence filling my body and straightening my posture.

"*Hleypa*," I tell Cynan, the Norse word rolling off my tongue, courtesy of the horse dealer. *One must speak the proper language if one desires to be understood.*

Cynan tosses his head and plunges into the path at a canter.

I imagine forty pounds of chainmail weighing me down, laced leather shoes heavy with blood and muck. The weight of the weapons I bear. Though he is my enemy, the Viking I embody has something that I never will, and that I'll always envy.

Power. Control. Raw strength and an iron will that commands respect.

I lean back, hunched into imaginary armour, and give Cynan

more leg.

I glide into his movements. My hips follow his every stride, rocking as though we were physically joint. Laughing, I grab hold of his mane and dare the command—

"*Fljùga!*"

And he flies. He widens his stride until he's galloping along the path. My hair whips back behind me, cloak streaming out, Cynan's mane covering my forearms as he pounds across the forest road.

"Look at you!" Rhun cries out gleefully. "A Briton shield-maiden!"

ᛏᚼᛘᚤᛥᛁᚼ

We make it back into the winding forest path without further incident. Rhun's got a proud tilt to his chin as he gives me his opinion of my posture, and I find myself glowing at his compliments.

He's the one who taught me to ride – I used to be afraid of horses, and he couldn't stand the idea that his own twin sister might not love what he loved. ("A *Briton* princess, afraid of horses? Unacceptable.") He's always been a merciless teacher, always finding the faults in my technique. Except for these past few weeks – he's been suspiciously nice to me as soon as I push myself even just a little.

I know he's trying to make me feel better about what's coming. But I don't have the heart to goad him for it. My betrothal might be looming in the near future, but he has his own trial that he must face too. And it's far deadlier than mine. Much as we might've tried to outrun our fates, they're catching up to us, and his is breathing down his neck.

Tonight. His fate awaits him tonight. Once the Hunter's Moon rises, his trial will begin.

We've had plenty of opportunities to talk about my betrothal. But we've carefully avoided the subject of his own fate. We both know we're going to have to talk about it at some point.

Just… not now. Not when the sun is so gloriously warm

and the forests so welcoming. We tacked up our horses and left Dumbarton fort without making a fuss, pretending we didn't have the imperative to return before sunset, pretending the future might still be an open road lying under our horses' hooves.

For now we'll enjoy one last ride, one last taste of freedom while we still have it.

ᛏᚾᛊᚣᛉᛁᚾ

We arrive at the top of a hill. In the centre of the clearing are two young trees growing together, one ash and one rowan, white flowers bursting like stars between their entwined branches. Around them stands a circle of mossy stones. Ahead, beyond the fronds of the trees, the river Clyde glitters in the late afternoon sun.

We come to a halt, falling quiet. Rhun dismounts first and I follow suit, both of us leaving our horses to graze while we stand before our trees.

For a while, neither of us says a thing.

There can be no chatter when we're standing here in this place of memories. We both decided to come here without mentioning what it meant to both of us.

Our father planted those trees. Ash for me, rowan for Rhun. This is where we buried his ancestral torc, so we would have a piece of him for ourselves without having to go to the family barrows. The tree roots must be twined around it by now.

I watch Rhun step into the stone circle and go to his tree, laying a hand on the bark. It towers over him now, about twenty feet tall. Wind whispers through the branches as though they were welcoming us both.

It's the last time we'll be free to come here together.

A ball forms in my throat. I try to make myself step into the circle, but I can't.

Rhun looks over at me, his teasing expression gone. Slanting sunlight catches the ginger curls that tumble over his forehead. He nods at me.

"Come on."

I shake my head.

"Come on, Tam."

"If he knew," I mutter. "If he knew—"

"What?" Rhun asks. "If he knew who you were marrying, he'd disown you? Is that what you believe?"

I grimace. Rhun always knows what lurks in the darker corners of my mind; he knows me better than I know myself.

He steps over the stones and takes my hand so he can drag me into the circle. "Father would do no such thing. It's not like you've got any say in who marries you, is it?"

We stand together before our trees, staring up at the gently swaying branches overhead.

"He'd probably still be set on you marrying that lord from down in sheep country," Rhun says. "Remember? That one from when we were six?"

I manage to smile as I remember him. The little lord had waddled into our court with his parents, chubby and red-faced with a lick of wispy blond hair on his head. He looked so much like an oversized baby that I had whined and whined to my parents to break off the betrothal. I hadn't understood much of the politics at the time – nor did I have much of a concept of marriage. I only knew I didn't want to sit next to that drooling boy who smelled of sheep.

"I'll bet he's a right charmer now," I say.

"I'm sure he is. Maybe you'll meet him one day and kick yourself over such a missed opportunity."

"What missed opportunity? It's sheep country. And that whole fief was swallowed into its neighbour ages ago. He might not even have any claim on the inheritance now."

"I didn't mean his fief. You don't come across a good-looking lordly match every day."

"Please! Like that matters."

Rhun grins at me. "Oh right, sorry. I'll pretend you don't mind marrying any old toad that King Arthgal chooses for you."

"I do mind," I say. "I mind marrying. I mind *marriage*. At least you don't have to—"

I stop myself, horrified by what I was about to say, the

selfishness of it. Rhun goes on smiling, indifferent to my blunder.

"I *am* happy that I'm exempt from it," he says quite cheerfully.

I groan. "If I could come and be a Cavalier with you instead, I'd do it in a heartbeat."

He barks a laugh. "I'd like to see you in a fencing match, *Princess* Tamsin. You'd be begging for your bridal gown in minutes."

"Shut up," I grumble. "I'd be good."

"Sure. With some practice, maybe. And maybe if your adversary was blind and deaf—"

"Shut up!"

"All right, all right. If you're so sure then maybe we could switch places. We've got the same face. Just chop off your hair, wear my clothes and sit in my place tonight, and no one will be the wiser."

"Oh, and you're perfectly happy getting into bed with the lord of Dál Riata?"

Rhun cocks an eyebrow at me. "I could make it work. How hard can it be? Lie back and count to ten?"

"Yes, Rhun, that's exactly how it goes," I tell him, laughing. "And maybe if he's blind and deaf, he won't realise the pretty maiden is no maiden at all."

"You're just jealous. You know I'm prettier than you," he says, grabbing me and poking me in the ribs so that I double over. I wouldn't have thought I could laugh until my sides hurt, not today, not here. But Rhun is adamant on tormenting me until we've fallen in the grass, knees stained green, panting as we recover from our mock-fight.

"See? You're a terrible fighter," he laughs as he holds both my wrists in one hand. I wrench away from him, face burning with shame and frustration at my own weakness.

"I'm just out of *practice*," I snap back, but he only laughs more.

It's remarkable how Rhun can keep a cool head on a day like this. I gaze at his freckly face as he leans back against his tree, keeping an eye on our horses whose ears are pricked curiously towards us.

So much talk about my betrothal when the situation he's facing is far worse than mine.

"You aren't scared about tonight?" I ask him at long last.

Rhun stares thoughtfully at the horses a moment longer.

"No," he says.

"But... but what if—"

"There are no what-ifs," he says firmly. "I'm going to be a Cavalier."

I bite back my retort. He'll only be a Cavalier if he passes his trial. He doesn't mention what might happen to him if he fails.

At least he will know by tonight whether he passes or not. I wish my betrothal could be over and done with as quickly as that. How does one navigate being married to the enemy? Surely the prospect of violent death follows each and every misstep. Having to win your man's favour day after day sounds like a tedious drawn-out sentence, not much more merciful than the knife that waits to bite into Rhun's throat.

We sit there against our trees for a little longer. Our fates feel too heavy, too tragic, too enormous to consider seriously.

"You know what Father would've done?" I say at long last. "He would've fought Mother and Uncle Arthgal on all of it, and he would've taken us far away from here."

Rhun frowns at the horses without answering.

"We could still make a run for it," I insist. "Right now. We've got our horses and waterskins. I've got some gold on me."

He gives me a deadpan look. It's not the first time we've discussed running – we've had this conversation countless times.

"No," he says.

"It's our last chance."

"No. I told you. I'm not putting you in danger."

"You think I won't be in danger in Dál Riata?"

"They've made arrangements for you over there," he says. "I can't protect you, Tam. I can't even protect myself, so how do you think either of us would fare on the road with no one to look after us?"

I grit my teeth. He's right, as always. I hate how helpless we both are. I *hate* it – I hate it so much. I rip at the grass, trying to hold my anger in.

He wraps an arm around my shoulders. "Hey. It'll be all right."

"But what if you fail?" I ask in a small voice.

"I won't fail. I'll become a famous Cavalier, and I'll visit you up there once Alba and Strathclyde are firm allies. If we're lucky I can even get assigned as your personal guard. And then we'll be together again. It'll be fine, you'll see."

I close my eyes and see Rhun clattering into a distant stone courtyard, hailing my Dálriadan husband. How many children will I have by then? What changes will I have gone through? Perhaps he won't even recognise me. Perhaps I won't even be fit to call myself his sister any more.

My heart pounds harder as I consider my strange future self, the ghoul with the litter of children. To have no control over what I might become – it's enough to stopper my throat and shorten my breath. And Rhun... he might not even be a part of my future at all. His trial will determine that.

"We should've run," I mutter. "We should've run a long time ago."

Rhun's hand tightens on my shoulder. This time, he doesn't find anything to say.

Chapter 3

THRAIN

FULL MOON OF MAY

"CLEAR THE WAY!"

Ivar's shout disperses the kitchen servants, leaving us room to manoeuvre our way to the main workspace. Our afternoon's catch is slung over my shoulder. The servant girls stare as I heave it onto the emptiest table.

Crash.

The stag carcass splays out onto the wooden tabletop. Its forelegs and hind legs are tied together, its huge body rising in a hill of tawny fur. One shoulder bears a bloody red wound. Ivar's arrow pierced it right through the heart – a quick and clean death.

"No!" one of the girls wails, rushing over to us. "Please, not on the table! Mugain will have our skins – please, my lord, pick it up—"

I ignore her, eyes on the open doorway that leads to the ovens. I know the head cook can't be far. There's a feast to prepare tonight – she's been badgering us about what an imposition on her time it all makes, what a waste of precious resources it is when my Dubliners and I are already pilfering the pantries of Dunadd fort.

When Mugain arrives, I grin at her. All the blood drains from her face when she sees the gigantic stag taking up her entire workspace.

"What is that!" she cries. "What is *that!* Get it off the table – it's not even been gutted!"

"Large enough?" I ask her, and she gives me a withering glare.

"*Off.* The table. Unless you want the rest of your feast to taste of forest rot and offal!"

"You forget who you're addressing, woman," Ivar growls, but it's no use. Mugain's already marched over to the other side of the room, leaning into another doorway to shout, *"Butcher!* Come up here!"

"She talks like that to everyone," I tell Ivar. "She'd talk like that to the King of all Alba."

He snorts. "I'd like to see that." Turning, he nods towards the exit. "Come on, let's go. She'll have the butcher hang you up by your feet right next to the stag if we stay here."

I shrug the stag back onto my shoulder. "You go," I wheeze out. "I'll help them with it."

Ivar raises his eyebrows at me. "You? In the kitchens?" Then he smirks. "You're leaving me to deal with the lordling. Again."

"Surely you don't need my help to handle the boy."

He meets my gaze, black eyes hooded with understanding. "Don't try to flatter your way out of this. You're always avoiding him."

He cuts a stark figure in this room, lean body wrapped in black, tattoos blooming on the shaved sides of his skull, long dark hair braided in a crest to show them off. He's used to intimidating people into doing his bidding. But he can't intimidate me.

"I'd rather a face-full of stag intestines than a meeting with that man. At least I'm at full liberty to cut this up," I add, patting the great bulk of the animal.

Ivar snorts and then shakes his head in defeat. "I allow you far too many liberties. You'll owe me for this." He jabs a finger at my chest. "You had better be there to greet the Southern Isle Jarls. I won't be making excuses for you to Gofraid if you aren't."

"Yes, yes, I know."

"I'll send someone to drag you out of the servant quarters if you don't—"

I laugh. "*Go.* I'll be there."

ᚦᚱᚨᛁᚾ

The gutting and butchery is meticulous work. It allows me to focus on keeping my hands steady even as the sun sinks to the horizon, announcing the coming nightfall.

This is the first full moon we'll be spending in Dál Riata. Lord Aedan knows full well that certain conditions must be met if we're to cohabitate. These full moon feasts are a necessity that he and his staff are still not very well inclined to accept.

But they do not have a choice in the matter.

When we first arrived, Lady Catriona had prepared Dunadd fort for us as per the directives of King Gofraid of the Southern Isles, our Viking leader with whom she and her royal brother have allied themselves. Food and women filled the great hall, nervous servants held themselves at the ready for us. Gofraid himself welcomed us to the high table with open arms, eclipsing the wary Dunadd councilmen. We were polite enough – at least, as polite as a Varg pack fresh from battle can be. We observed the courtesies expected of political allies, washed, feasted, and took our time to enjoy what our new allies willingly offered. The servants warmed to us, at least – the councilmen, perhaps a little less.

No matter. We had the lady as hostess. They bowed when she told them to, just as the lordling had.

Fresh from his defeat, and thus bearing the angry air of a whipped servant boy, Aedan had avoided us as much as he could that first evening. He would not accept his humiliation. We were all on our guard, knowing only too well that a man in his position could act in anger and further deteriorate our relationship.

As it happened, my brothers and I were not the targets he chose.

In the days following our arrival, Lady Catriona became conspicuously absent. Eventually she returned to sit in on the Dunadd council meetings and our military gatherings with

Gofraid, where we spoke at length of our plans for Strathclyde and the Albans' extensive knowledge of the place. But she had difficulty walking, and was surrounded by blue-clad guards who helped to prop her up. Her face was scratched and bruised, her eyes rimmed with tender pink skin, though she powdered herself to hide it.

One of her eyes had gone white. That, she could not hide.

My brothers and I learned from the servants that Aedan had done it. Struck his own mother in his rage. Blinded her in one eye. I could not bring myself to stand in the same room as him when I learned of it, afraid of what I might do to a man who would abuse the women of his own line in such a way.

Incredibly, Lady Catriona did not punish him. She did nothing. Simply stood back and allowed him to take back the mantel of lord of Dál Riata while she recovered from her injuries. She told anyone who asked that she had suffered a bad fall from her horse.

Nobody believed her. But social etiquette demanded that we go along with the lie.

With his mother beaten down from her position of authority, Aedan has grown proud again, fully invested in his role. His servants are not happy, and neither are his councilmen, nor even the villagers who come for an audience with him in his great hall. They all come expecting the lady and leave again, disappointed to have missed her.

They all dislike him. Even beaten and blinded as she is, Lady Catriona still holds the hearts and loyalties of her people. I can only wonder how long this has been going on for – how long the lordling has beaten his mother back for being a far more effective and respected ruler than he is.

I hack at the stag's sack of guts, taking it from inside the carcass, careful not to pierce it. It is more difficult than I could've imagined, bearing a political alliance with people who do not think like us, whose actions would have me drag them to the village square to exact bloody retribution. I must still my hand for the sake of politics, and it aggravates me to let Aedan's actions slide. My brothers know I have issues controlling my anger when it comes to beaten women – they have let me avoid the lordling whenever possible, but I know I cannot avoid him forever.

Now Ivar has gone to kindly inform Aedan that he and his councilmen must vacate the great hall so that we might invade it for our full moon feast. It's easy to imagine the look on Aedan's face, the prude outrage lighting his features as well as his advisors'. I see them skulking away indignantly to the safety of the west wing, where they will be safe from our chaotic merriment. No doubt the lordling will barricade himself in his quarters for the next seven days while he allows a horde of Vikings to sate their rut under his roof.

He too must accept repugnant things for the sake of politics.

As I hack through the stag's hip joints with the butcher's axe, I see him again on that high rise when we first alighted on his shores. A pale little weasel in his rich robes. Incredible what kind of man passes as *lord* in these lands. I should've thrown that spear when I had the chance.

Now I must respect the truce. And he must, also. We both know the King of all Alba sanctioned our presence here. Aedan can do nothing but tuck in his tail and obey his royal uncle. While we wait for Causantin to arrive in Dunadd and direct our plans regarding Strathclyde, we can do nothing but try and keep our alliance intact.

One day I will plant steel in Aedan's guts. One day. For now I must be content to enjoy his hospitality, made only sweeter by how begrudgingly it is given.

However much he detests us, we will dine in his halls tonight.

ᚦᚱᚨᚾᚼ

I help the butcher carry the meat into the kitchen again once it's cut and cleaned and ready to be cooked. Mugain is ordering her girls around, arms coated in flour, her headscarf askew over her greying pinned-back braids.

Some things never change, regardless of where you go. Wherever food is being prepared, there always seems to be this stout old woman with a bark-like voice, extending her hand and shouting *why isn't that done yet?*

I'm smiling to myself as I let her order us around. She is the only one in this whole fort who speaks like that to me, and for the sheer temerity of it, I allow her to. The butcher and I slap down the meat onto the workspace she designates, and servant girls crowd around us to take the pieces wherever they're destined. Almost feels like home.

"Thrain Mordsson in my kitchen," she grumbles to herself as she bustles up to me. "You take up enough room for at least three men with those shoulders of yours. Can't even get around you."

It's obvious she wants something from me — she never comes close to me unless it's to forcefully subtract a favour.

"I'll take my leave," I assure her, still grinning. "Just as soon as you ask whatever it is you're burning to ask me."

"Hrmph." She supervises her girls for a moment as they clatter around with pots and plates, arranging the meat portions on each. Mugain helps them hand it all out to the passing oven workers, giving instructions. *That one to the fire. Those ones for pie. Oh — someone get that leg to the ovens before the dog steals it!*

I lay my axe on the cutting board, waiting, secretly pleased to be among all this bustle and activity. Homesickness sparks in the pit of my belly as I watch them busying themselves, not even sparing time to be afraid of me. In fact some girls show surprising familiarity in their attitude towards me. Some of them blush whenever our eyes cross.

I know they must have families and friends in the Southern Isles — the coastlines closest to Dál Riata were ceded to Gofraid not so long ago, after all. Perhaps they already know what our full moon feasts entail.

At long last, Mugain turns back to me and gives me a pan of dirty water to wash my hands in. I do so while she leans closer to talk.

"So. Tonight. Your Viking *feast,*" she grumbles. "Lady Catriona has informed me of… what is to take place."

"Good."

"I understand we're to keep serving until about midnight?"

"Yes."

She mutters something in such an archaic form of Gaelic that I barely catch any of it.

"My girls," she huffs. "Lady Catriona said that if they wear white aprons, they'll be safe from you. Can we count on that?"

"You can."

"I want your *word*, Thrain Mordsson, that they won't get roped into your... your..."

"I can guarantee you, as long as they keep their aprons on, we won't touch them," I tell her. "The girls who wish to involve themselves in our feast may choose to take their aprons off. Otherwise—"

Mugain scoffs. "How will I know it ain't your lot that's doing the undressing?"

"These feasts have rules. Any undressing that happens is strictly on the terms of the young woman who chooses to do so."

"My girls ain't like that," Mugain says, shaking her head.

It takes a single glance across the room to find Mugain's girls all bending their heads over their tasks, suddenly extremely interested in the broths and vegetables they're preparing.

"I know your kind," Mugain goes on. "Lying and manipulating to get your ways. Sly lot, you are. If I find a single one of you has touched a girl you shouldn't have – I'm going to Lady Catriona to see about it."

I bite back a laugh. The lord of the fort has such little credibility that even his kitchen staff go to his mother rather than him.

"I'm sure your girls are glad to have such a strict overseer," I tell her. "You can come and see me, too, if you hear something. I don't abide rule-breaking. Any one of my men who oversteps his boundaries must answer to me."

Her wrinkled face turns up to me as she considers this. That she can stare me so plainly in the face without flinching, without fearing the mere sight of me... this is why I love erring in the servant quarters. These bitter old women don't care who's in power as long as they can take care of their brood.

Feels almost too much like home.

"All right," she barks. "Now if you would kindly get out, my lord. I need space to move around, and you surely have better things to do than pester an old woman."

"Indeed. Good luck."

ᚦᚱᚨᛁᚾ

The full moon is slowly rising. It pulls at my blood, raises my senses to full alertness. I meet Ivar in the stone courtyard of the fort so that we may join Gofraid in welcoming his travelling Jarls. Olaf is not with us – this time he's the one that Gofraid complains about.

While Gofraid leads us all back into the fort with many a boisterous laugh through his great white beard, I share a glance with Ivar. He's wearing a worried look. Reluctant as I am to forsake the rich scents of food wafting down from the great hall, I nod at him, excuse myself and break away from them. We both know where Olaf must be hiding.

I head up to the battlements of the fort.

Sure enough, he's sought refuge up here under the stars. I can pick out his outline in the moonlight, his cropped white-blond hair and beard almost ghostly silver, his cape brooch and silver belt buckles glimmering. Back in Dublin, he spent many a feast night staring out at the night sky, letting the cold breeze cool his ardours. It looks like he's out to drink ale by himself and reminisce again, waiting for the spell to pass.

I drift over to him, observing the view. In daylight, we can see all the way down to the loch where we docked our longboats, after our rocky arrival. In the darkness we see only the lights of the port village, throwing golden glitter over the black water.

The masts of our longboats rise up in the torchlight one after the other until they're sunk into darkness. Beyond, sky and sea join into a great black canvas.

Strathclyde is somewhere out there.

Soon… with Causantin's help, we'll sail out to discover it.

Olaf gives a disgusted groan. "Oof. You smell of fresh tripe. Were you in the kitchens or something?"

I smirk. "Sorry to spoil your moment."

"Ah, you're not spoiling anything." He hands me his horn. I

take it, sniff the contents. He's brought a small barrel up with him, apparently determined not to even set foot in the great hall. "I heard you and Ivar had a fruitful hunt."

"We did, yes." Taking a sip, I grimace at the stale taste. "They call this ale? Do they even use grain or do they sweep their barn dust into a barrel of water?"

Olaf laughs. "I take what's available. At least it's potent barn dust."

I hand him back his horn. "I only hope those pot-lickers we left in Dublin won't have drunk all our good reserves by the time we get back."

He hums thoughtfully at that. When he drinks, he lifts his chin, baring his throat to the moonlight. The circular bite mark has faded to a white scar now, but it's still visible.

I know mentioning Dublin isn't tactful of me. Not on a feast night. If he's drinking out here alone, it's for good reason. But I can't just let him continually wallow like this.

"Have enough of that ale for two? Or should I bring something up?"

The way he glances at me tells me he knows exactly what I'm doing. "Don't miss the feast on my account. Though you might want to wash before you go and mingle."

"I can stay out here with you. The night's clear."

"Thrain." He grins. "Ivar would have a difficult time handling the feast alone. You know Gofraid prefers to retreat to his chamber for his own revelry. So stop mothering me. The men are the ones who need mothering tonight."

I laugh. "Yes, that's precisely my role isn't it."

"You're the one who chose it. When Kætilví isn't around, you step into her boots."

"Mmm." Now it's my turn to wish he had kept his mouth shut. Worry prickles at my fingertips as I think of my mother, all alone in the great halls of Dublin.

Olaf places a paw on my shoulder. "If anyone can keep Dublin from becoming a shambles while we're out here, it's your mother," he tells me. "You see? If you stay with me you'll just start worrying about things you can't change. Get down there, find better ale, enjoy yourself."

"Olaf—"

"I'll be fine."

ᚦᚱᛆᛁᚾ

By the time I've washed the stink off me and emerged from my quarters with fresh clothes, the feast is properly underway. Loud voices clang around the main hall, laughter and conversations punctuated by fists pounding wood, mead pouring thickly into cups, and the tinkle of tableware being moved about. Norse and Gaelic and other dialects merge until it is all senseless noise.

I take a deep breath. The air is thick with the scents of hundreds of Vyrgen men. The night is young yet – their rut is only beginning, coming to the surface in the form of rambunctious behaviour and a desire to touch, bite, chew, smell as many different savours as possible.

I can feel it in my own body. A tremor is running down my hands as the moon calls me to action, lures me towards the place where all those delicious scents are coming from. Walking out into the great hall, I find Vikings and Dálriadan villagers alike feasting together in the merry light of the lit hearths.

It is tame yet. Women from the fort and the port village are straying around the colonnaded walkway that encircles the hall, peeking between wooden pillars, giggling together at the very idea of having come here. I expect many of them must be frustrated wives, coming under cover of darkness to experience something other than the boredom of their marital bed. Others wear looks of utmost outrage, but their presence here belies their eagerness to involve themselves in what they would deem sinful.

Surely word must've got out that Viking feasts are quite... convivial. Mugain's girls are flitting around the hall still putting out jugs and platters, some of them quite pink in the face as they move around this sea of roaring men, their white aprons still firmly fixed upon them.

I traverse the walkway until I can enter the hall near the topmost table. Ivar is there with the best of our men as well as the Southern Isle Jarls. Already he has his hand on the thigh of the young man sitting next to him, both of them leaning close enough to announce how they're intending to end the meal.

When he sees me, he straightens and holds out an arm to me.

"There he is!" he says with a smile. "You're late, Thrain! Come, there's a seat for you."

The Jarls around the table greet me, lifting their goblets as I sit among them.

"It's a great honour to sit with the wolves of Dublin," says one Southern Isle man, leaning to pour mead for me from a jug. "But tell me – I thought there were three of you? Where is the third?"

"Aurvandill has only just arrived," Ivar tells me. "He doesn't know yet that Olaf is an old churl who dislikes noise and merriment."

This Aurvandill fellow laughs and talks down the table at someone to ascertain the truth of Olaf's reputation. Ivar leans into me, expecting an explanation.

"He's up there. Drinking."

Ivar sighs. "And reminiscing about his late wife, no doubt."

"It's barely been a year, Ivar."

"I know, I know. But still. If he wants to stay faithful to the dead, that's his business. Only, I would appreciate it if he at least showed his face while it's still early."

"I wouldn't count on it."

Again Ivar sighs heavily. "Well, at least you're here."

I grin at him. "Of course. You know I can't leave you unsupervised. I might wake tomorrow and find a hole where the fort used to stand."

With a smile, he clinks his goblet against mine. "Always good to hear you have such confidence in your right-hand man. *Skàl.*"

He drinks; I follow suit, then turn so that I might bring the whole table into the toast.

"*Skàl!*"

Chapter 4

TAMSIN

FULL MOON OF MAY

I STARE SULLENLY out of my bedroom window. The moon is rising just over the horizon, full and round, a golden coin shining between the boughs of the trees.

Rhun was so afraid of arriving late to the fort. He tried not to show it, but as the sun sank further towards the horizon, he started to sweat and tighten his hands on his reins. He's always been good at keeping his symptoms in check. But he must brave his trial regardless, just like all the other cursed boys.

I left him at the doors of the great hall where Cavaliers and priests were waiting to greet him. They ushered him inside quickly, eyes on the darkening sky. I could only grasp his hands briefly until he broke away from me. We shared a long look before the priests closed the doors again and advised me to get away from there before the cursed boys could scent me.

I scrambled up the east stairway and into my room so I could get ready before Mother could find me. Everywhere in Dumbarton fort, everyone is preparing for the Hunter's Moon Festival. My royal cousins titter excitedly in the corridors like it's just another festival to pretty themselves up for.

I bite back my anger at the sound of their laughter. They're still innocent. They don't know what this festival means. After all, when I was their age I used to love it, too.

Back then my lady mother took me out into the grounds where we'd mingle with the townswomen and help prepare the festivities. I didn't understand then, the purpose of bringing out pots of wolfsbane for the priests to handle. I loved watching them brew their potions with the dark purple petals. The fort grounds hosted a great crackling fire where all the unwed girls from Dumbartonshire danced and played. I thought it was just for fun.

The older boys would sit all around the fire, not allowed to move as we danced around them. It was a game that I loved to play. My royal cousins held my hands as we danced barefoot in the tall grass to the sound of flutes and drums.

Then, as I grew older, I started asking my mother questions. Why did big groups of boys leave after the Hunter's Moon? She always told me that they went off to become men and go on perilous adventures.

But once I was old enough, she knew those explanations didn't hold.

She sat me down one night and told me. There are some men, she said, who bear a terrible curse. They were born with the mark of the devil seared onto their hearts. It is a lust for violence and all things carnal, a relentless thirst for chaos that manifests at each full moon.

Those are the boys who are sat around the fire. The cursed boys. Their affliction becomes noticeable as they grow from childhood into adolescence. It starts with their sense of smell, much more refined than any other. Then, it shows in their impulsiveness, their cravings, and finally, their increasingly violent behaviour.

The curse can be monitored and controlled while they are still young. During the full moon, their families send them to the chapels and fields so they might be worked to the bone, exhausting their energies through hard manual labour. But come their eighteenth year, manual labour isn't enough to appease them. They can no longer be considered safe. Upon the advent of the Hunter's Moon, they must pass the test to see where their destiny lies.

Each year, Uncle Arthgal and his lords hold festivals across the land of Strathclyde to put the cursed boys to the test. They all sit around great bonfires and suffer the judgment of the wolfsbane flower.

If they drink the sedative and remain impassible to the dancing girls, then they are sent to become Cavaliers, the knightly order that protects our borders and the royal family.

If the sedative does nothing to calm their ardours... then they must be taken out to the bogs, as per the ancient custom.

This year, Rhun turned eighteen. He'll sit by the fire like the rest.

And he'll be judged.

"Tamsin! Don't you look a fright!"

I turn away from my bedroom window. Hilda is in the doorway wearing a lovely spring dress, embroidered by her own hand. Mother prefers that she dress in the type of matronly clothes that befit her position – but for special occasions she can get away with some colours. Tonight she's even woven pink ribbons into her greying plaits. I force a smile, not wanting her to worry over me as she always does.

The precaution is useless. Coming closer, her expression crumples into a frown. "Don't you give me that smile, lass."

My mouth flattens again. She knows me better than my own mother – she practically raised Rhun and I alongside her own children.

"It'll be all right," she says, rubbing my arm.

"You can't know that," I say miserably.

"Ah, but I do know it!" she says. "Rhun's a good boy. I don't see why he wouldn't pass the test, good strong lad like him. He'll make an excellent Cavalier." With a twinkle in her eye, she adds, "And Clota watches over you both, doesn't she? All will be well."

The reminder makes me glance down at my bare wrist. I used to wear a beautiful bronze torc there, tipped with twin horse heads. Rhun wore an identical one. On the night of our eighteenth birthday, Hilda took us down to the old canals of the river Clyde so we could give them both as offerings to our revered ancestor, as per the old tradition.

For luck.

"Your bath's ready," she tells me. "Come along now, pet."

I follow her to the water closet. It's close and stuffy in there. Hilda's drawn a hot bath in the copper tub. White mist dances on the surface of the water, inviting me in. I tug at the laces holding together my dress while Hilda fusses over the festival gown she's prepared for me.

"See that?" she says, holding out a sleeve. "Proper luxurious, isn't it? Look at the needlework there. And how the black thread shines!"

I indulge her, glancing at it. I can't deny the richness of the embroidery. It'll be the most expensive dress I own.

All I can think of is how I won't be able to run in it, skirt the walls, climb the castle grounds. Mother sent me this as a bribe, a consolation prize after forcing me to attend the festival. She wants me to accept my role tonight and hold myself up straight and dignified.

"I caught Cinnie trying it on earlier," Hilda says, giving me a wink as she folds it carefully over a chair. "Almost cracked it around her bosom."

I manage a faint smile. Hilda's daughter must've looked stunning in it with her curves and streaming black hair. "She can have it after tonight," I tell my old nursemaid.

"No, child, no! I wouldn't let Cinnie dance around in a dress that's worth ten years' wages! And besides. It's yours."

"She'd probably wear it far better than me," I say. "And I'm sure she'd love to parade it in front of Rhun."

"You have a point there." Hilda laughs as she takes over unlacing my dress, batting my hands away. "Poor child. Falling in love with a Cavalier-to-be! She's heard one too many love ballads, that one."

I smile as she begins to hum a popular tune. She's so confident about Rhun's fate. She's probably just as worried as me, but she knows what I need to hear. There are scant few people in this fort who truly feel like family to me, and with the festival looming tonight… I'm achingly glad for her company.

She's done with my laces – I lift my arms so she can pull the gown off me, leaving me in naught but my shift. My arms fall back down, suddenly sluggish. I realise abruptly that my body is beginning to feel heavy. Hilda leads me to the bath and reaches for her scented soap pots, asking which perfume I'd like, but I'm distracted. I turn to stare at the black window.

Something's shifting. Outside the moon must be rising steadily, darkness overtaking the earlier sunset colours. My heart races as I feel a familiar red heat thrumming through my veins.

The full moon governs me, too. I bear a curse just like my brother.

The priests tell us that all curses come with gifts. The men marked by the devil have the gift of preternatural strength and heightened senses. We women marked by Clota have the gift of heat cycles, which heightens our chances of fertility, and spares us the dangers and discomforts of regular conception.

But upon the rising of the full moon, both of us develop an appetite for chaos. Regardless of our education, we turn lustful, greedy, destructive. It is a constant battle to hold onto who we truly are beneath what the curse dictates.

"I'm clean enough," I tell Hilda. "No need for the full bath. A glove will do."

"Really?" Hilda snorts. "You were out riding with Rhun all day, girl. You smell of horse. You're getting in even if I have to hold you under."

A pang rings through me as I think of Rhun in that packed hall, fenced in by grim-faced Cavaliers. If I'm starting to feel the effects of the full moon, then he must be too.

"Your lady mother would give me an earful if I let you wear all this sweat and grime to the festival," Hilda goes on. "If not for your own comfort then you still must be scrubbed to merit the fineries she prepared for you. Red wool dyed in Carolingian fashion! Not even Princess Eormen has a gown like that."

And she's off, gossiping about fabrics and sewing and servant gossip about who's wearing what tonight. Normally I'd listen in, eager to pick up bits and pieces of know-how to use once I'm far away in Dál Riata.

But tonight I can't concentrate. My condition is clouding my mind, my heart too heavy to indulge in any more gossip. I know she's only trying to put me at ease – she heard me argue with my lady mother to see if Rhun could be spared the trial. She heard how my arguments fell flat.

She might lose him too tonight. She raised him like a son after all. She's just good at trying to distract herself.

My thin linen shift is beginning to stick to my skin in the damp air. I shiver as the folds embrace my curves.

"Come, child," Hilda says gently. "Lift your arms now, there's a girl."

I look at her, frowning, hating that my condition might manifest even tonight when my brother's life is at stake. She nods wisely, understanding. She is a normal woman, free of any curse, but she's well used to tending the needs of a daughter of Clota.

"We'll be quick about it," she promises.

I let her tug my shift artlessly over my head so that I'm left naked. With no further protest, I climb into the tub.

The water is blessedly hot against my skin. Despite the gentle summer night outside, the chill of last winter clings to every nook and cranny of the fort. Even the curtains and carpeting that dress the place aren't enough to chase away the cold. I melt into the tub.

God almighty. What warmth. The sweet scents of flowers and soap drift around me tantalizingly. My body comes alight as I lay there, and I blush with shame.

The priests trust the daughters of Clota to correct ourselves when in full flush of our heat. Unlike the men, we retain our conscience during the full moon and therefore can be trusted not to stray from God's path.

I think hard of the flogger that lies in the trunk at the foot of my bed. I miss its leather-bound handle and long, knotted leather strips. I concentrate on the memory of my last lashing, the purifying pain of it.

The priests may say that the desires of men cannot be corrected like the desires of women can. That men are made dangerous by lust, whilst we may suffer it with dignity.

But by God, sometimes I swear the flush is so strong that I would let the devil himself take me.

The night is still young, thankfully. I dig my nails into my own palms as I sit in the bath, hunched over while Hilda scrubs my back. Warm water laps at my skin like a lover's fingertips, seeps between my legs like a long seeking tongue.

My nails bite deeper and deeper. Blood wells up, drifts through the water in red curls.

I sigh as the shimmering layer of pain drapes over the sinful yearn.

Clota, I pray as I wrap my bloody palm around my bare wrist again. *Let Rhun be spared the bogs. Please save him, please… you have to save him for me.*

Chapter 5

TAMSIN

FULL MOON OF MAY

DUMBARTON FORT IS perched on a steep rock overlooking the River Clyde. To the west, the water curls around its rocky foundations, waves rising up to batter against it in bad weather. To the south, a gentle grassy slope stretches between our outer wall and the borders of Dumbartonshire. We call it the King's Garden, for that is where Uncle Arthgal holds the year's festivals – last harvest, All Soul's, and the reaping of young cursed men.

An old stone amphitheatre is carved into the slope, overlooking the grassy plain. At the foot of it is a round slab, hosting the ancestral table where priests have prepared their wolfsbane potion for centuries.

Everyone has their proper place. At the beginning of the evening, the royal family heads to the great stone table, led by Uncle Arthgal and the anointed priests who've travelled up from Glascau for the occasion.

We unwed daughters of Clota are to sit in the amphitheatre until the dances begin. We wear our crimson gowns and cloaks, all of us clumped together, ladies and princesses and peasant girls sitting side by side along the stone benches.

Ahead on the grassy slope, the great bonfire steadily grows fatter as Cavaliers and townsmen throw kindling into its glowing maws. Several townswomen prepare long tables and cooking stands around the outskirts of the dancing grounds. In the orange glow of the bonfire, they all look as smudged and ethereal as fae flitting about the grounds.

The Hunter's Moon dithers near the horizon, slowly rising. It drags our sensibilities away behind it with every inch of sky it gains. My pulse is pounding at a steady rhythm, not quite wild enough to scare me, but loud enough to let me know what's coming. Knuckles knock against a door in my chest, the Other Tamsin waiting to be let in, wearing a wide inhuman grin.

We all sit in our red cloaks and pretend we don't feel it, this giddy rising of our blood. All of us hold ourselves still as stone whilst our deep nature begins to dance within us.

As we wait for the cursed boys to arrive, we watch the townspeople below busying themselves with their preparations. They've got a feast to cook up and many neighbours to greet. As per the rules of the festival, they'll stay seated and look on while the cursed boys pass their test and we cursed girls dance around them. Only once the boys have been led back to the fort will the townsfolk mingle with us on the grass.

Hilda and her daughters are out there. I try to take comfort in that fact as I sit on my cold stone bench, fiddling with the hem of my cloak.

It'll be all right. Just like Hilda said, there's no reason why Rhun wouldn't pass the test. He'll stand up once it's over and open his arms to me. I'll run and hug him, and then we'll turn to wave at Hilda and her girls.

I close my eyes, frowning as I hold onto Hilda's words of comfort.

All will be well.

ᛏᚻᚷᚣᛋᛁᚻ

Drums announce the arrival of the cursed boys. I turn my head so fast I hear my neck crick.

The heavy iron gates that cut an opening in the fort's outer wall spit out a procession of Cavaliers, all wearing their usual blacks and golds. Wedged within their formation, the line of cursed boys walks.

Rhun's right there at the front. I stand when I see him, drawing grumbles from the girls around me.

He's apart from the others, walking between two familiar Cavaliers. Emrys and Kelwynn. They grew up with us – they're both barely older than us. Emrys is wearing that smug, self-satisfied air of a Cavalier wielding his freshly-obtained authority.

Anger surges through me at the sight of them. They lead my brother towards the bonfire like they themselves didn't cheat death only last year!

Uncle Arthgal holds out his arms to the boys. He's booming some words of welcome for the sake of the townspeople. As he speaks, Emrys and Kelwynn turn and lead Rhun away from the main line, heading for the royal family.

They're coming towards us.

I hop down from my seat. Girls complain as I push between them and step on their hands. My cousin Eormen is on the last step, and she glares at me as I wedge a foot down between her and one of her sisters.

"What are you doing?" she hisses, but I pay her no heed.

The general clamour that the girls are making attracts the eyes of the royal family. Mother glares at me and makes urgent shooing motions with her hand to remind me of my place.

I don't care what any of them think. I have to go to Rhun. His Cavaliers step closer to him as I scramble up onto the platform, both of them eyeing me uneasily. They don't know whether they have the permission to apprehend a daughter of Clota while the moon is rising.

Rhun sees me and breaks away from them. We meet at last, arms wrapping around one another. His grasp is strong and unwavering. He must've waited for so long in the great hall, prey to the mounting tension of the evening – but he's still just as confident as he was in the forest earlier.

Both Cavaliers try to separate us, but Uncle Arthgal calls them off. A murmur rises from the townspeople beyond. They must take some entertainment from the fact that a prince is attending tonight. Annoyance fizzles through me, making me clamp my teeth. Uncle Arthgal is only allowing us this rule-breaking because it'll make him seem compassionate to the townspeople. Like he isn't the one orchestrating this whole ordeal.

I break away from Rhun, slick his scruffy ginger locks from his face. He smiles boldly at me, eyes downcast as he stares at my dress. His smile is too wide. He must be scared – he just doesn't want me to see it.

"You look pretty," he says.

"How are you feeling?"

"I'm fantastic. Never better."

"Good." I wonder for a moment if I should break his confidence or not. But he should be prepared. "Listen. Arienh is here."

His smile falters. "What? But she lives way down south now."

"She must've come up to keep her Dumbartonshire friends company." Seeing his crestfallen face, I add fiercely, "She knows what's at stake. She'll leave you alone. I'll make sure of it."

He's lost his smile completely now. The mention of his old paramour seems to have well and truly broken what precious confidence he'd managed to build up. They were together a long time before Mother found out about it and forced Rhun to break things off. Arienh never forgave him.

"I wasn't sure whether to tell you," I stammer. "But I saw her up in the amphitheatre."

He nods, staring sightlessly ahead. "I'm glad you told me."

"Rhun, my lad," comes Uncle Arthgal's rumbling voice, summoning us to him. Reluctantly, we both turn to look up at our king's great bloated figure. Our hands stay clasped together as we step towards him. Uncle Arthgal claps a great palm on Rhun's shoulder and says, "Are you ready for your trial?"

Rhun bows his head. "Yes, Uncle."

It's custom for the king's family to oversee the preparation of the wolfsbane potion. Uncle Arthgal allows us to stay beside him while the priests bend over the great table, revealing their process to us. They mix organic matter into ethanol, adding crushed leaves, honey, and holy water taken from the chapel at Glascau. The wolfsbane flower sits in its pot in the middle of the table. They take from it with gloved hands, crushing stems and mixing purple flowers into the potion.

Uncle Arthgal must make sure that the priests don't add a toxic dose. From what I understand, the other ingredients counteract the toxicity of the wolfsbane so that it might cool the ardours of a cursed man without killing him.

As a prince of royal blood is present at the festival this year, the king's oversight is all the more crucial.

It doesn't smell as bad as I would've anticipated. Rhun stands next to me, his hand still locked in mine. His breathing is somewhat laboured, as it always is during the full moon. He's impervious to me at least – one small mercy of the devil's curse is that it turns a boy's head firmly away from the women of his own family. Here on the platform at least, he's safe from temptation.

Finally, the potion is ready. The priests place a droplet of it in each of the cups that they've prepared for the two-hundred boys who will be tested tonight. Uncle Arthgal pours wine into one of the cups before turning back to Rhun.

"It's a very brave thing you're doing tonight, Rhun," he says slowly, as though my brother were a small child. "You're giving the example to the townsfolk. Everyone must make sacrifices to ensure the survival of this kingdom, even the royal family. With your involvement, they're reminded of just how crucial this night is."

"Yes, Uncle."

"Say your goodbyes, now."

Diligently, Rhun accepts a kiss from Aunt Beatha and then our mother. She takes his ginger head in her hands, brushes her pursed lips against his forehead and hands him swiftly back to Uncle Arthgal. She can't seem to look at him.

The king gives his nephew the cup. Rhun takes it, his face pale as a ghost's. I want to knock the cup out of Rhun's hands, drag him away from this damned platform, saddle up our horses and ride far away from here. We should've gone from this place a long time ago. I should have persuaded him, God, I should've forced his hand if all else failed. We wasted so much time hoping and dreaming that things would get better, that our lives here would become more bearable, that surely the trials ahead of us wouldn't be so bad. They were far away, we told ourselves, too far away to touch us.

We should've gone. He wanted to protect me so much that he ended up endangering his own life.

Rhun glances at me. The somber expression he's wearing tells me he knows exactly what I'm thinking. I must look ready to grab him and run – because he shakes his head at me, denying me the fantasy.

He lifts the cup to his lips and drinks the sedative.

Beyond, the Cavaliers are sitting the boys down around the bonfire. Uncle Arthgal wastes no time steering Rhun down the slope so he might personally lead his nephew down to the stone benches.

Rhun lets go of my hand.

My brother, my best friend, marches towards his fate straight-backed as though he had no fear in the world. Or at least, he's trying to give the impression.

We all watch in silence as the Cavaliers shackle the remaining cursed boys to the benches around the bonfire. Rhun is the last to be seated. Uncle Arthgal shackles him there for all to see whilst the Cavaliers step back, marking a perimeter around the boys.

They all look like criminals as they sit there with iron around their wrists. Shackled like so many thieves lined up for a hanging.

I want to cry. Rhun holds his chin up defiantly as he sits there, all alone.

The priests file down to the cursed boys, each of them bearing a tray-load of cups. They each stop by a boy, hand him a cup so that he can pour the potion down his throat.

Then it is done. They all sit, the sedative curdling in their bellies, diffusing inside them.

And the music begins.

Chapter 6

TAMSIN
FULL MOON OF MAY

ALL AROUND THE bonfire, the unwed daughters of Clota run onto the grass and form wide rings. They dance together, red gowns billowing around their legs. Some are laughing, careless and happy. Others look more solemn. It's easy to pick out which girls stand to lose someone tonight.

I have never been so averse to the mere idea of merry-making. It's a ruse to draw out the devil in these poor boys. Why would any of us want to do that?

Eormen bumps into me on the way down from the amphitheatre and gives me a hard look. Her sisters all stop and wait for her as she pins me to the spot.

"You coming?"

Her words are cold. To her this is our duty, regardless of the fact that many of these boys will be sentenced to death tonight. To her, nothing is more sacrosanct than her father's bidding. God himself speaks through King Arthgal's mouth, so if he bids us to dance then we should dance, no questions asked.

I glare at the arrogant tilt of her head, the perfect fall of her blond hair, the lofty call to duty that her whole posture evokes.

We daughters of Clota should not disgrace ourselves by showing our feelings, especially during the full moon when they bubble so close to the surface. That's what she believes.

My nails bite into my palms as I keep my mouth shut.

"You're such a child," she mutters. Her gaze flicks to Emrys. He steps closer to me, answering the summons of the king's eldest daughter. She nods at him and then leads her sisters to the grass, all of them holding hands.

"You have to dance," Emrys tells me as I dither by the edge of the platform. "Don't make me drag you down there."

He's really enjoying his new-found authority far too much. Sighing, I step down from the platform beside him. We march down the slope together, heading for the rollicking rings of revellers.

"It wasn't so long ago that you sat down there by the fire, was it?" I ask him. "How can you stand there and watch this happen?"

"I would rather watch this happen than have our kingdom overrun by the savagery of cursed men."

His well-practiced words make me see red. Already he's placed himself above his fellows, like he's determined to forget his own trial ever happened.

"All of these boys grew up in good Briton families," I snap at him. "If we taught them to behave, if we didn't act like it might be so inevitable for them to fall for the slightest provocation, then—"

"Stop it," Emrys snaps back. "You've been playing that tune for years, Tamsin. You should know better. It's not because Rhun can behave himself now that he can be considered safe." He looks hard at the bonfire, his face taut with annoyance. "Without the wolfsbane, cursed men are unpredictable. That includes your brother. You should not trust him as blindly as you do. Even after a man earns his Cavalier's robes, you should always keep in mind what he's capable of."

"Yeah," I snarl at him. "And so should you. You're just like him, Emrys. But for the wolfsbane, you'd be shaking and sweating like a dog right now. So you can stop acting all high and mighty."

He clenches his jaw and hooks his fingers in his belt just

beside the flask that hangs there. His own dose of wolfsbane is contained within. Like the other Cavaliers, he'll be adding drops to his wine every night of the full moon to sedate himself.

"Your affliction makes you forget yourself," he says, his voice gruff. "I have to display the authority vested in me by the Church of Glascau—"

"My *affliction* has nothing to do with it," I growl. "You've always been arrogant and in love with yourself."

He seems to understand something as I insult him. Instead of going on with his lordly tone, he smirks. Just the sight of that face makes me realise what I sound like.

"You always knew I was unavailable," he mutters. "You can't still be angry at me for leaving and fulfilling my duties."

My face goes red. "None of this has anything to do with – with that!" I blurt out. "See! I'm angry about two hundred boys being provoked into damnation – and still you think it's somehow secretly about you!"

Emrys shakes his head, but thankfully drops the subject of whatever childish relationship we might've had years ago. "For the last time, the devil does not wait for provocation," he says. "Wolfsbane is the only shield we have to protect ourselves from what he would make us into. Rhun knows that. Rhun understands the fear of losing control and becoming a rampant beast. Don't presume to know what's best for him when you have no idea what that feels like."

I want to bark at him that I do know, that every single daughter of Clota feels that visceral fear, too. Just because our curse pushes us to lustful abandon rather than violence doesn't mean we can't be afraid of ourselves. But I don't want to imagine my brother in such a beastly state. I don't want to think about it.

We've reached the revellers. Wide drums echo in the night, giving a throbbing pulse to the darkness. My royal cousins laugh together, holding hands as they weave through the steps of a three-beat dance.

Emrys is walking close enough beside me to submerge me in his scent. Woodsmoke and leather. Mindlessly, I want to lean into it. His allusion to our past is bringing up buried memories,

waking my heat in earnest. Images of him at Calan Mai three
years ago come unbidden to my mind. The taste of his lips, the
strength in his grip when he pulled me against him that night...
my body grows hot and languid at the mere thought of it as we
walk together under the rising moon.

I wrap my arms around myself, shaking away the memories.
Not for the first time, I envy him his potion. If only there could be
a suppressant for the daughters of Clota, too! That way we might
not feel such absurdities at the most inappropriate moments.

Eormen's circle shifts and reveals Rhun to us. He's sitting
still as a bunch of pretty merchants' daughters dance near him,
tempting the evil out of him. It's agony to watch every little
twitch he has, waiting for him to betray himself.

"Go on then. Dance," Emrys commands.

"I *can't*."

He sighs and pushes me into Eormen's circle.

Small hands grab mine and whisk me into the dance. The
flute players keep up their repetitive theme, dictating our steps.
I shuffle after the others, looking over the blond heads of my
cousins for Rhun.

So far he's holding up quite well. Each glimpse I get of him
shows me his straight-backed posture, hands in his lap, head
tilted up in concentration.

He'll be fine. I've got to believe it.

Lute-players enter and launch into a familiar five-beat tune.
Some girls keep their rings intact whilst others pull away in pairs.
In the shifting of the dance, Eormen has somehow reached my
side. Before I can protest, she takes my hand and fits us between
two other couples.

The Hunter's Moon watches over us as we concentrate on the
steps. I'm so wound up with anxiety and stiff self-control that I
can barely get my feet to follow correctly. Eormen on the other
hand moves around me with all the grace one would expect of
Strathclyde's darling.

She leads me better than anyone I've danced with before.
The pent-up frustration of the heat expresses itself through our
movements, all our twirling and foot-stamping making us sweat

out its wild fancies.

Some childish part of me is awed to be dancing with my dazzling cousin. But she's rarely extended her friendship to me before. I know she's only doing it now because our lives will soon become tangled together.

After a while, Eormen seems adamant on capturing my attention. I try to ignore her, waiting for the switching segment of the song to pull us apart again.

"I'm sorry about Rhun," she tells me at last. "I wish he didn't have to sit out there. I know it must be hard."

"Shut up. Don't do that."

"What? What did I do?"

"You always know what to say, but you never actually mean it."

She sounds genuinely abashed. "Is that what you think of me?"

We march ahead, our movements rigid. A pang of guilt rings through me. I'm still angry about Emrys, angry about the king, angry about everything. She's only trying to be nice to me. But I'm in too foul a mood to retract my words.

"Well it's true, isn't it? You never liked Rhun or me."

"You never exactly let me get close, Tamsin. But you're still family. So of course I hope Rhun passes the test."

Thankfully the switching segment arrives at last. I twirl away from her, heart pounding with guilt as I let another girl catch me. Eormen finds another dance partner, and I try to tell myself she deserved my spite as I watch her spin away.

One glance at Rhun calms me somewhat. He's still sitting there, eyes closed, shackled hands relaxed in his lap.

The moon hasn't risen to the apex yet. The hardest part is yet to come.

ᛏᚾᚣᛋᛁᚾ

Like the other girls, I quickly become one small figure in a field of red billowing gowns. Dance partners shift with every new song. I try to grasp the girls whose dancing styles fit mine, keeping an eye out for Arienh.

Slowly the physicality of the dances, the repetitive steps, the leaning to and fro… it lures my mind away from rigid etiquette. I find myself relaxing, my body warming with the exercise.

We stamp our way through another circle dance. I sweep by Emrys, who's standing among the circle of Cavaliers that guard us against the cursed boys. He's wearing a small smile as he watches me. The sight of him manages to distract me, as does the crowd that presses all around me.

I haven't seen Emrys smile like that since he came back from his training. When my next partner pulls me against her for the couples' dance, I let my body curl around hers a little too close.

I'm smiling now too. There is a snake writhing in my belly, and the familiar warmth of it is loosening my self-control.

The touch of my partner's soft hand sends shivers down my spine. She's so pretty with those full lips and those flowers in her hair. She steps closer to me as per the movements of the dance. Her thigh presses between mine, encouraging me to back away as she leads me between the other couples.

My pulse throbs between my legs as she keeps pressing me there. The contact isn't overly insistent and yet I feel drunk with it. Her eyes darken as she realises how pliant I am in her arms.

It's such cruelty to have to ignore her. They make us dance together, thinking that as long as men aren't among us, we won't feel desire. But this girl, whoever she is – she could pull me away right now into the darkness and I'd follow her gladly.

She throws out her arm, spinning me away from her. My loose hair whips around me, the heights of the heat and the spinning motion making my mind swim. Then I spiral towards her again until my back fits against her ample bosom.

I hear her sigh as I lean against her. I imagine myself loosening her plait, digging my fingers into the softness of her chestnut hair. I imagine how her smooth plump lips must feel against my fingertips. I see myself tugging away the red cloak that drapes her shoulders so that I may bare her collarbones.

Her hands slide down my body and settle on my waist. The caress sends a bolt of desire through me. I bite my lip as she holds me against her, her grip almost possessive.

Then the dance forces us apart. She breaks away from me, gathered up immediately by another girl, leaving me breathless and aching for contact.

"You missed a step," comes Emrys's voice.

He's right beside me. I must've staggered out of the line of paired dancers and ended up in front of him again. Looking up, I find him devouring me with his eyes. I should throw him off – but instead I turn to face him, daring him to follow where his thoughts are headed.

"Does the wolfsbane truly make you impervious to this?" I ask him, playful now with the languor of the dance and his obvious interest.

Something about the way he looks at me makes my insides tie themselves into knots.

"Your Grace. Don't play with me."

"So you aren't impervious."

"I am," he says. Then he leans closer. "You should be careful, princess. Your scent is becoming… quite overpowering."

I glance at him. His words rip me out of my heat-stupor.

No. No, what am I doing? I can't let myself enjoy this.

I look around wildly and glimpse my brother between the dancers.

Oh, God.

He's hunched low, hands writhing against his shackles as he stares at one of the groups of girls. Other boys have already succumbed – there are empty benches, boys being wrestled to the ground by Cavaliers.

I can't quite sense it like the Cavaliers and cursed boys can. But from the amount of red-clad girls on the grass, I can imagine that the bouquet of scents must be intoxicating. That, mingled with the warm night air and the smoky smell of burnt wood… no wonder so many of them seem to be having trouble holding themselves together.

Rhun's whole body is turned towards that circle of girls, fixed upon it like a bloodhound. His face is strangely intense, eyes glazed, mouth parted. His wrists twist in their shackles, bruised and bloody with his struggling. My heart stills as I realise who he's staring at.

Arienh. She's there.

I have to go to him. He's so focussed on her that he's hurting himself, growling and hissing as the shackles bite into his wrists. Then he hunches again, burying his face in his hands as though trying to regain control.

I step forward – but Emrys grabs me by the arm and snaps, "No. Leave him."

"He's in pain, Emrys! Look at him."

Emrys does as I say. There is empathy in the way his grasp softens.

"Pain is his salvation," he says. "If he doesn't learn to embrace it then he is lost."

That group of girls comes dangerously close to him. Arienh is staring right at him. Ice clunks in my stomach as I realise I can't stop her, I'm too far to intervene in time.

I watch as Rhun lifts his head. It's like the scent of her has pulled his attention up rather than the sight of her. When he does look at her, Arienh smiles coolly at him and reaches out a hand as though to invite him.

The cruelty of it! She knows what awaits him if he breaks – she's doing it on purpose. I want to howl at her, wrench her away from my brother.

But the damage is done.

He tilts his head to the side. His eyes flash, his lips retract, every bit a snarling animal. I watch, paralyzed with horror, as he brings his chest forward, pitting his weight against the chain that holds him down.

The iron bracket breaks off the bench.

He pushes himself up, bent over like a wolf as he aims straight for Arienh.

"*NO!*" I shout, but it's too late. Emrys holds me back, and I watch as the waiting Cavaliers catch Rhun, containing his wild defiance and yanking him to the ground.

It's over. Just like that, it's over.

He failed the trial.

Chapter 7

Thrain
Full Moon of May

I SIT IN MY high chair, a cup of mead in one hand, observing the scene before me.

At every table, the food has been devoured, empty jugs pushed aside. Fur pelts have been strewn over rough wooden surfaces so that men and women may hold one another in comfort.

The hall is divided by decorative wooden panels – some seek privacy and drag their partners away behind them to consummate their desires. In one corner, musicians strike wide drums and sing songs, giving rhythm and refrain to the pandemonium.

The moon has risen to the apex. Like the howling of wolves, cries of passion fill the hall. My blood burns through me as I hold myself apart from it, the pain of inaction crippling my limbs, shortening my breath.

It is a familiar pain. I know Olaf must be feeling it, too, though alcohol numbs it somewhat. There are many things that men of our kind can take to lessen it – plants, potions, concoctions. But all taste foul and none are truly, entirely effective.

It is best to take none and practice self-mastery. That is why I push myself to hold back for as long as I can before indulging any carnal desires. Relying on external sources for self-control only allows that fundamental weakness to remain. That is what I was always taught. That is the behaviour I encourage in my men.

Of course, they are not all as adept at mastering themselves. Especially on the first night of the full moon.

This is the worst hour. I'm tense with anticipation, eyes roving over the sweating backs and crooked legs that crowd the tables. I'm waiting for the inevitable cry, the struggles of a girl pulled down unwillingly into the embrace of my men.

It comes as it always does. It's muffled and feeble, but my senses are so strained tonight that I could hear the buzz of a fly on the other side of the hall.

I push myself to my feet.

My body weighs as much as a boulder. Unfulfilled desire drags through my veins as though I had drunk molten iron. But the promise of coming violence lights my steps, sparking eagerness in the pit of my stomach as I stride through the roiling mass of bodies, into the depths of the hall.

A dishevelled Varg is pulling at one of Mugain's girls. It's past midnight; she's one of those who has taken off her apron. He has her by the wrist, grinning at her, his eyes red with lust. But she is already involved with another – she's straddling Nýr, a handsome young man whose clean-shaven jaw and tied chestnut hair is understandably preferable to the other one's haggard state.

Nýr is growling a deep-throated growl, but has not risen as it would dislodge her from his lap. Others around them have noticed the struggle and call out to the intruder in Norse.

"Vegard, you ugly bastard, can't you see she doesn't want you—"

"You stink, man, you can't expect to be invited—"

"You mind your own fucking business," Vegard growls, and yanks harder at her wrist.

Nýr's growl is infecting those near him, drawing answering rumbles from the men. I can feel my own hackles rising as I observe the scene. Words will not work on that wretch, seeing how far he's gone in his moon-craze.

I step into the fray, trap Vegard in a choke-hold. He immediately releases the girl and lets out a strangled snarl of surprise as I wrench him back. We stagger around until the backs of my thighs hit a bench. Vegard twists and slips from my grasp, his elbow colliding with my face. I backhand him in return, grab him by his tunic and slam him down against the bench.

He's dazed as he blinks up at me, as though realising for the first time that he's fighting with his pack leader. My own growl blooms deep and deadly in my chest as I loom over him.

"You really want to do this?" I ask him. "I am not half as spent as you are."

He looks at me. The potency of my growl seems to have dragged him out of the moon-craze. Now at least, he can comprehend words again.

"Forgive me, Thrain," he pants. "I was…"

"Yes. I saw." I gaze down at his shamed face and say quietly, "You were out of control. You will calm yourself. Keep to the pack for tonight."

He tucks in his chin. He is one of those men who retains shame at the very idea of bedding another man, though every full moon sees us all growing rather familiar with one another. Some men turn to one another out of sheer necessity – others find pleasure there and have a keen preference for men. With Vegard however, his true desires are difficult to guess, tangled in games of pride as they are.

I yank him up to his feet. Many faces have turned towards us as we finish our spat, some cheering the victor. Brawls have already broken out and been subdued throughout the night – the moon adds a delicious edge to violence, making it one more pleasure to sample.

"Go and wash yourself," I command Vegard, "and for the love of Freya, get those bits of chicken out of your hair before you come back." This draws laughter from a few of the surrounding men, though most have gone back to their pairs and groups. I pat him on the back, letting him know it is all in good faith.

Once he's gone, I turn to see whether Nýr's maiden needs any further assistance. They both seem quite unconcerned by their surroundings. The sight of violence has clearly ignited Nýr, who has drawn up her skirts and holds her hips in a tight grip, encouraging her movements as she rides him. Her forehead is pressed against his, mewling softly as she grinds upon him.

The sight of them sends hot blood to my groin. I take it as a prolongation of the exercise, willing my body to move away. It is excessively difficult to do so, especially when Nýr glances over her shoulder and looks straight at me. Breathing out, I turn away, ignoring how heavy my erection feels as it throbs against my thigh.

"Wait," Nýr calls after me.

I go very still. Mugain's girl is looking over at me now, too. Her face is a picture of ecstasy as she meets my gaze.

"Come, Thrain," purrs Nýr. "She wants you to join us."

My mouth parts as the words rile up my rut. I take in the girl's bared thighs, the bunched black hemp around her hips, the bodice that is half unlaced so that her shoulders peek out. Her apron lays on the bench beside them like the discarded flag of her prude Christian upbringing. Her hair is a tumble of blond strands brushing her naked skin.

Though she does not ask me herself, her whole posture is an eloquent picture of her hunger.

I step towards them. It's getting very late indeed. Surely by now... I have earned a reprieve from self-control.

I brush the blond strands from the girl's neck. She tilts her head, groaning shamelessly as Nýr bucks his hips against her, burying himself to the hilt.

"What's your name?" I ask her.

"Eithne," she sighs.

From this angle, it is all too easy to slide my fingers down past her shoulder and into the cleavage of her dress. "You aren't afraid to take two of us?"

I squeeze her naked breast beneath the fabric. She only arches her back in a request for more.

"No," she whispers. "But, please... don't tell Mugain."

Her shamelessness sends desire surging through me. I lean down to kiss her, unlacing my breeches with my free hand.

"Eithne," I purr against her mouth. "Your secrets are safe with us."

ᚦᚱᛏᛁᚾ

We divest her of her dress, leaning over her so that we may bite and lick her ample bosom. I let her relieve my wound-up desire with her mouth while Nýr pummels into her, his movements growing more desperate as he nears climax.

At last Nýr gives a great thrust and spends himself inside her, pulling her hips against his. Eithne moans around my erection as he handles her as roughly as he likes. He keeps his knot outside of her, grinding it against her. Candlelight glimmers on the heavy reddish ball, swollen to the proportions of an overripe apple. He closes a hand around it to get himself through the thick of orgasm, but we both know it is nothing like the pleasure of knotting. His climax burns itself out quickly and he slides out of her, drawing a trickle of seed down her thigh.

We give her a moment's respite. Bravely she tries to pretend she isn't tired, but her body is covered in a sheen of sweat, her limbs falling limply around us. We feed her a little honeyed duck, a few apple slices. I know she will not last long enough to satisfy me. I should tell her to get back home to rest, but she has a hold of my arm, heavily-lidded eyes fixed on me as though she knows what I'm thinking and is defying me, daring me to test her limits.

I flip her around, bend her over the tabletop. She screams with delight as I penetrate her. Each thrust coats my cock in the thick glop of Nýr's expenditure. The base of my erection is swelling, the veiny knot slowly growing as I press it against her. It's still relatively small, but she insists on backing up against it, the pressure sending shivers down my thighs.

"I can take it," she murmurs, her voice hoarse. "Please, I can take it."

"No you can't," I growl. But she only grinds harder against me.

"Please," she insists. "It – *ngh*… it feels so good."

I bite my lip. My knot only swells more at the outrageousness of her words, a shiny throbbing mass lodged in the folds of her sex. There is no kind way of telling her that it is completely inappropriate for her to ask a stranger such a thing. I cannot fault her for it — she does not know our Varg customs. The act of knotting is tantamount to a sacred mating ritual, just as potent as a marriage proposal — not some weightless act to perform solely for pleasure's sake.

Nýr is watching us, eyes fixed on the point of our joining where his own seed coats us both. Curiosity lights his face as he watches me hesitate.

I decide to be pragmatic: "It'll hurt you."

"No it won't. I've seen your Viking women manage it just fine."

"That's because they lay with their spouses," I tell her. "You need to know someone intimately before you can share something like that without pain."

She says nothing for a moment. She's almost sulking. Her disrespectful insistence is boiling my blood, pulling me into recklessness. I lean over her, press a hand down on her back to flatten her against the bench.

"I'll show you, then," I growl. Breathing in, I begin to push my knot inside her. The tightness of her makes my eyes roll back, a choked moan falling from my lips. I never allow myself to do this — the sensation is almost too good to bear. The knot is barely at half its full size and already she tenses, gasping, thighs trembling as the knot stretches her obscenely.

"Stop," she gasps, her voice pressed with pain.

I pull out of her. She pants against the tabletop, nails digging into the wood. I bend to kiss her shoulder and observe her face, looking for traces of pain. I know it would've been more of a mercy to tell her outright rather than letting our bodies encounter the limits of this joining. But at least this way I don't have to utter any harsh words that may break the enchantment of the evening for her.

You are nothing to me. I am nothing to you. We cannot share anything more than this.

She breathes for a moment, recovering. From her silence, I gather that she understands. When I bring my hand down to her cleft to check for soreness, she mewls, rubbing against my fingers, clearly eager again.

"Shall we continue as before?" I murmur.

She nods.

ᚦᚱᛜᛁᚾ

Eithne is the first. Others join us after her, women and men and our Vyrgen brothers, all hungry-eyed and slack-mouthed with sexual intent. Skin skids against skin, fingers delve into curly tufts of hair, teeth skim tender places. If an artist were to sit in a corner and weave it all into a tapestry, she would accomplish the most intricate knotwork imaginable.

I am never frenzied, never quite out of control, but the hunger leads me on. Abstaining from knotting my partners pushes me to excess, grabbing drunkenly at the first who eyes me favourably, multiplying my conquests until I cannot remember their names, the proper make-up of their features. Again and again, climax bursts and wanes in a ghostly imitation of the real thing.

The night wears on. Hours pass before I begin to feel spent – not satisfied, but tired enough to stop clawing at the nearest body. Many women have gone by then. Most of the Vyrgen have collapsed on the tables and benches to sleep off their deep sexual exhaustion.

The ones who continue are the most passionate, the spouses and lovers who always choose one another on feast nights, the ones who want to make the most of the full moon's potency.

It is quieter now, the music more audible as the last groups and couples take their time and prolong their pleasure. I watch their bodies curl together, their faces creased in ecstasy, nails riding hard over heaving backs, leaving long red trails in their wake.

As always after the madness of my moon-craze has passed, I find myself wondering how absurd it is to be so violently propelled towards strangers like this. I lie panting in the fur pelts, someone's leg slung across my thighs, another's long hair tickling my shoulder, staring up at the ceiling. So many conquests and yet it is all just empty chaos, leaving me craving something more. Something real.

A woman's voice rings out as her partner brings her to

climax. My eye is drawn to them by the sound. They're seated at a table, the woman riding her man, her head thrown back. Both their necks are marked – the woman wears metal in her mouth, silver canines glinting in the candlelight. The Varg's own natural elongated canines rest against his lower lip as he snarls his pleasure. She's knotted to him – her thighs tense around him, her body hunching over his as she comes down from the high.

I let my eyes rest on them a moment. There is such intimacy in their gestures, in the way they press their foreheads together and gaze lovingly at one another.

I have never known it. The bliss of being knotted with a partner. A moment of deep communion truly shared with another person.

I have to remind myself again firmly as I gaze at them – that is a path I refused a long time ago. I cannot let myself be distracted. I know that to take a spouse would dull the importance of my choices, make me question the long path towards vengeance that I have been walking for many years now.

I break away from them.

Not only would it be an unnecessary distraction, it would be dangerous too. Olaf... losing his spouse dealt him an almost fatal blow. In his state, I wouldn't be useful to anyone.

No. It is better to walk alone. Keep my focus sharpened.

Be satisfied by chaos for the time being.

ᛒᚱᛏᛁᚼ

Ivar finds me at the brink of dawn. I'm leaning against a table, pouring mead for myself. He smells overwhelmingly of sex as he reaches me. There's deep satisfaction in his hooded black eyes, the dishevelled state of his long black hair. It's undone – usually he keeps it in that crested braid, but now it falls on one side, reaching past his shoulders.

"Where were you, then?" I ask him.

"Hmm. Tucked away somewhere private." He tilts a horn at me so I might serve him mead. I do so with a smirk.

"Let me guess. That priest you had your eye on?"

"There is nobody quite as pent-up as a man of God, let me tell you that," he says, making me snort. "Speaking of pent-up. Did you see Olaf at all tonight?"

A pang goes through me at the reminder. I pick up the most intact loaf of bread I can find and gesture at the walkway. "Let's go and see how he's faring."

ᚦᚱᚨᛁᚾ

Morning light dances along the parapets, announcing the end of the madness. Olaf is snoring away, wrapped up in his woollen cape and a fur pelt he brought up. All around him are empty barrels of ale.

Ivar and I grin at one another. I can tell Ivar is thinking of a dozen malicious ways to wake his brother. But the pink sunrise on the loch beyond is too beautiful to ignore. We let Olaf sleep, drifting to the parapets instead.

We lean on the stone bricks, staring out at the loch below and its quaint fishing village. The glittering waves are hypnotising to watch. When I next glance at Ivar, his expression has turned thoughtful.

"I wonder what you'll do," he says at last.

I frown. "What?"

Ivar turns to me, black eyes glinting. "If the Vanirdøtur are real. If we get to Strathclyde and find them there."

I lean against my parapet. "What do you mean, what will I do? Whether the women in Strathclyde are what you hope they are or not, it doesn't change our plans. We will take the kingdom regardless. It is a worthy prize in and of itself."

He's wearing a wicked grin now. "But if we *did* find them there... would it not change your resolve entirely?"

"What resolve?"

"Freya. Was the night so good that you lost all your wits?" he says, his smile sharp as ever. I shake my head, trying to repress the urge to hit him. "I meant your resolve to go back up north after this is all done. These isles are warm and green and fertile. If we found the Vanirdøtur down here... would you not want to stay?"

I rake my long blond hair out of my eyes, slicking it back with a sigh. "You know what I think of your theories," I tell him.

"You still don't believe we'll find them out there?"

I give him an exasperated look.

"I think it's useless to speculate until we're directly faced with the issue," I tell him. "And either way, the answer is no. You know I would not change my resolve for anyone."

He grins as he stares out at the loch again.

"I suppose we'll just have to see," he says.

Olaf gives a great snort of a snore. We both turn to find him blinking blearily up at us.

"You what?" he slurs. "Is it morning?"

Ivar laughs. "Glad your eyes still work well enough after five barrels of ale." He bends over his brother, hoisting him up by the armpits. "Come. You've brooded long enough. Let's get you cleaned up."

Chapter 8

TAMSIN

DAY 1 OF THE WANING MOON OF MAY

"Y OU CAN'T DO this! It was a trick, Arienh tempted him, if it hadn't been for her—"

"That is the very nature of the test, you know that just as well as I do," my lady mother says. Her tone is glacial, as it always is. She sits there in the stark morning light that floods her bed chamber, her face set. I know where to look for the emotion she is repressing – it shows in the pallor of her skin, the tightly clenched muscles in her jaw.

It's not enough for me to keep from hating her.

I'm shouting. I never shout at my mother. But just looking at her face makes me want to break things.

"He's your son! Don't you care? Don't you *care* about us—"

"Don't argue uselessly, child." Her voice is dagger-sharp. "Of course I care about you. I'm your mother."

"Oh, grand words they are! But you would still send Rhun to the bogs without so much as pleading for his life? You would send your son to die and your daughter to rot in the enemy's bed—"

"I have prepared for this moment ever since I first held him in my arms." Her eyes are shining as she says it. "And you have always known your duty to the kingdom. It is the same as Eormen's and the other princesses. Don't you dare say I don't care for either of you. What do you think awaits you when you have children of your own? You'll be faced with the same dilemmas as I."

"I won't have children," I snap at her. "If motherhood turns me into the same cold monster as you then I refuse to do it."

She looks at me as though she can't believe what I just said. Grief finally breaks through the strict composure of her face. I can only watch in horror as she dissolves into tears.

"You think it isn't hard for me?" she asks. "You think I haven't dreaded this moment all my life? I have done everything I can to give both of you the life you deserved. To give you all the freedom and education you deserved. I don't want this to happen any more than you do, Tamsin. I love you. Both of you. But I don't suppose you care to hear it."

I don't know what's more horrifying, to see my mother cry for the first time, or to feel so utterly empty at the sight of it. I should feel terrible that I made my mother cry. I frown, trying to take in her words, ashamed of my selfish reaction.

It... it must be hard for her. For all those mothers of cursed boys who are forced to conform to the custom. I hadn't thought of her perspective before.

Guilt at having called her a monster washes over me. She's in so much pain, more than me in fact. I'm losing a brother – she'll lose both of her children this year.

I carefully place an arm around her and she leans against me, clutching at me with those claws of hers. I listen to the gravelly sobs heaving from her chest. Each minute that passes adds a layer of horror and delirium, as though I still can't believe this is really happening.

"I do care," I mutter, throat tight. "I'm... I'm sorry, Mother."

She pats my hands as her sobs slowly subside. "Your tutors taught you the necessity of the custom, didn't they?" she asks when she's recovered enough to speak. "Even kings must be deposed if they are found to bear the devil's curse. By virtue of what you are, daughter, you should understand that better than most." She grasps my hands in her knobbly fingers. "Clota herself founded this kingdom so we could be free from the violence of cursed men. So her daughters could thrive. Tell me, when was the last time a king of Strathclyde fell in battle?"

I know where this is going.

"None ever did," I answer her.

"The Northumbrians, when did they last push back our borders?"

"They never did."

"And the Picts?"

"I know what you're doing, Mother—"

"No. I want you to tell me." Her fingers are steel claws biting into mine. "Tell me what sustains this kingdom."

The continuation of our sacrifice. That's what she wants me to say. We sacrifice those touched by the devil, just as Clota taught us to do, and God rewards us for it by protecting us. The whole kingdom of Strathclyde is a sanctuary whose foundations are built on the bones of the damned. No invading army has ever known victory once inside our borders.

If we were to let the cursed live among us rather than sacrifice them, then we would lose God's favour. We would doom ourselves to the fates of our neighbours – ever-shifting, war-ravaged territories that have never known peace. That is what my tutors taught me.

The Northumbrians are jealous of our prosperity. Centuries of internal warfare have made it difficult for them to spare any of their sons. They send their cursed to the front lines and pray for salvation, but it is not enough. Wars rage on, women are captured left and right, and they come knocking on our door to steal our own.

The Picts of Alba do not all embrace our Lord God. In many places, their pagan roots are still very close to the surface. The kingdom pushes its cursed out to those tribes that would still accept them, and closes its eyes to the problem entirely.

But they are not the worst. The worst, by far, are the Vikings.

Since childhood, those wild savages have haunted my imagination. Rhun would tell me as I cowered in my bed, how the Vikings elect their cursed as chieftains or kings. And by their ungodly strength, they have ravaged the coastlines of Ireland, Alba and Northumbria for decades, reaping bloodier victories every year.

We have always been surrounded by enemies, but the slow progression of the Vikings is the most terrifying of all. Their Great Heathen Army marches ever closer as it wreaks devastation across all of Northumbria. Only four years ago, the city of York fell to their grasping hands. Even now I still have nightmares about Lindisfarne and the thirty altars of the church of York. I see the walls of God's chapels dripping red with the blood of the innocent.

They are happy to do the devil's work. They revel in it. And they are coming closer to us with each passing of the seasons.

If we do not have God on our side, then how are we meant to resist them?

"Tell me, Tamsin," Mother insists. "What sustains this kingdom?"

I hang my head.

"The continuation of our sacrifice," I whisper.

She draws me against her in a rare embrace. Relief floods through me that she might've forgiven me my slight. She never holds me like this. I can only marvel at what it feels like to be held by my mother, how I might've won this privilege.

"Rhun is in the dungeons with the other boys if you want to see him."

"How long does he have?"

"Seven days. Until the moon's last quarter." She takes my face in her hands. "Promise me you won't do anything rash. God's will must be done."

She looks down at me expectantly. I can only nod and tell her what she wants to hear.

"I promise."

ᛏᛣᛦᛋᛁᛏ

Once I regain my room, I'm alone.

I sit staring out of the window for what feels like a long time.

I feel so strange and empty. I share this room – I *used to* share this room with Rhun, so the knowledge that he'll be gone soon… it makes the place feel so huge and unfriendly, bloated with unoccupied space.

Hilda and Cinnie eventually appear at the door. I push off of my bed and drift towards them. Hilda tries to smile at me but her blotchy face tells me just how hard the trial hit her.

"You all right, love?" she asks in a choked voice. My heart twists to hear how much of an effort she's making to speak normally. I go to her, gather her up in a hug. Hilda makes a little strangled noise as she hugs me back. Cinnie wraps her arms around us so that we're tightly cocooned together.

Hilda's usual cooing and fussing is all broken up by her tight throat. Poor Cinnie is holding onto me so tight that I can feel her every tremor.

"I was so sure," Hilda squeezes out. "I was so sure – good boy like Rhun – I can't believe it."

"It's not fair," Cinnie seethes. "He barely moved a finger until that girl arrived!"

I cling onto them, achingly glad for the familiarity they bring with them.

"We can still go see him, can't we?" Cinnie asks.

"No, child," Hilda says. "Princess Tamsin, maybe, but we won't be allowed down in the dungeons."

"But it's Rhun!"

"I know, love. This is how it is."

I break away from them. The rage is back in full force. Why should I be allowed to see him but not them? Formal ranks seem like such a ridiculous obstacle when they're losing a loved one, too.

"I'll take you with me," I tell them. Cinnie looks up at me hopefully, but Hilda only tuts.

"You can't, lass. There's about forty of those boys down there. I doubt the guards will let two young women in the dungeons when they've proven to be dangerous."

I shake my head. "We can still try."

ᛏᛉᚢᛋᛁᚽ

Hilda refuses to come, but she decides to take on Cinnie's tasks for the evening so she might have her chance to see Rhun. We make our way down the spiral staircase to the dungeons, torch held high in front of us. The sound of many chattering voices grows steadily as we approach the dimly-lit and ominous stone corridor.

It's not fair that those boys might've been dragged down here like criminals when most of them have done nothing wrong. They lived among us for eighteen years, breaking bread with us, growing up with us. And now they are all set aside from us as a preventative measure, though most have never harmed a soul and never would.

How can we be expected to cast away our loved ones, curse or no? I know there is a wealth of history behind this custom. But now that I'm out of Mother's clutches, I'm realising how empty her words were, how her grief changed strictly nothing about the situation. I can't find it within myself to forgive her or even Uncle Arthgal for doing this – perpetuating this gruesome custom, justifying it even as they lump the innocent in with the guilty.

Surely God is benevolent enough to allow exceptions. Surely He would understand that I can't just let my brother go.

I can't do it. I *won't*.

"Ah, princess. Right on time."

The voice drifts through the corridor before I see the one who uttered it. Emrys steps out of the shadows, draped in the smart black wools and leathers of the Cavaliers.

I frown up at him. "What are you doing down here?"

"Your mother mentioned you'd be paying a visit." He gestures at my companion. "Sorry, Cinnie. Relatives only."

"Well that's bollocks," I growl at him. "She wants to see him."

He cocks an eyebrow at my crass language. "I'm sorry but that can't happen."

I try to barrel past him, shoving my shoulder against his. "She's coming with me, Emrys."

Emrys resists me easily. Hands on my shoulders, he holds me there as though I weighed as little as a child.

"She can wait here while I bring you inside."

Cinnie steps in just as I open my mouth to shout.

"Don't," she begs me timidly. "Tamsin, will you tell him I… I'm sorry for him? Here, take this."

She reaches to pull the pink ribbon from her braid. I frown at her, so she wiggles it at me until I take it.

"Give him a kiss from me," she says thickly.

I look at her, hating the situation, hating that a stupid question of rank and blood might deny her a proper goodbye. She stands by a torch bracket, draws her woollen shawl closer over her shoulders and gives me a stiff nod. I nod back and turn to follow Emrys.

He leads me through a door and into the dungeons at last. Other Cavaliers are there, gaolers, sitting and playing with die at grubby, beer-stained tables. They ignore the shouts and groans of the cursed who are piled in the different cells around them.

As I step between the tables, looking around at the cells, something shifts in the atmosphere. There is a sudden quiet. The guards glance up. Two of them immediately get up from their table, knocking over one of the chairs in their haste.

"What are you doing?" the bald one growls at Emrys. "Why would you bring her down here?"

"She wants to see her brother."

"She reeks of the heat." The guard grabs my arm none too gently. "Get her back upstairs before we have a riot on our hands."

My heart is banging in my chest as the noises from within the cells erupt again. The men trapped behind the bars are yelling slurs at me, outright growling and snapping like a pack of dogs.

"Get the bitch away from here!"

"Didn't you torture us enough at the festival?"

"No, don't let her get away! She came all the way down. Invite her in!"

Some sound less than apologetic about their condition. I baulk at their rowdiness. Some are staring at me with a pure, slavering hunger that I've only ever seen in the eyes of our hunting dogs.

Emrys takes a firm step between me and the guard who grabbed me. The guard lets me go upon the insistent glare of his brother-in-arms.

"I'll take the boy out of there. They can speak in the interrogation rooms."

ᛏᚼᚤᛋᛁᚼ

I wait in the dim light of the room they thrust me into. The table in front of me is stained with brown aureolae and long black streaks. Old blood, surely. The walls feel like they're closing in on me as I imagine the pain that this room has contained over the centuries.

When Emrys comes in with my brother, I leap to my feet. Rhun seems remarkably quiet as he sits facing me. He is beyond fear now – he has progressed to a mute sort of panic.

I sit and reach across the table so I can take his hands in mine. Emrys stands by the door and labours to make himself invisible as I focus on my brother.

"Are you alright? Did they give you food and water in there?"

"Some, yes."

"I'm so sorry. It's all my fault." Tears well as I think of the bonfire, the impossibility of rewinding time. "I saw Arienh too late. I should've been paying more attention."

Rhun's shaking his head. "It's not your fault. She was determined to avenge herself."

"I swear to you, when I find her, I'm going to ruin her entire life."

"Tam. Don't." His hands squeeze mine. God, his grasp is so limp and shaky. "Please."

I realise quite suddenly that he might not have the energy to think about Arienh at all when he has to face death itself. I have some idea of how he feels – the prospect of being swept off into my marriage feels similar. Like entering an unknown realm from which there can be no return.

"I'm not going to let them take you to the bogs," I mutter. "I promise you."

He looks at me, a tentative spark of interest lighting in his eyes.

"Princess, if I may," Emrys interrupts. "You shouldn't give him false hopes."

I glare at him. He clears his throat and exits our conversation by way of fixing his eyes on the wall ahead, giving us what privacy he can. I turn back to my brother.

"I know what to do. I'll have the priests brew another potion. Perhaps you just need a stronger dose, that's all. Then you can go into training with the Order and come back to the castle as a Cavalier."

"It doesn't work that way. The priests give us the strongest dose they can. Any stronger and it kills us."

My sweaty fingers fumble with his. "All right. Well, we can think of a better plan. We've got a few days."

"Tamsin," Rhun says on a sigh. "Emrys is right. There is no escaping this, so please. Stop trying to save me."

He's never sounded more like Father. Laying there on his deathbed after our last brush-up against the Albans, he'd accepted the dark fate that awaited him. He'd been grim and wise with the anticipation of it.

I know then as I gaze at the set lines of my brother's face, that there can be no persuading him of better options either. Still, I have to try.

"Well – what about exile? That way you could at least escape the bogs. I could get you out, and then when the Albans arrive, I could convince them to help you. We could organise safe passage for you to the more remote islands of Dál Riata."

"You and your mad schemes." He's smiling wearily now. "I told you before, I don't want you to put yourself in danger for my sake. This is how it must be."

Restlessness stirs in my chest. I feel like I'm speaking to a wall. Now that he's moving towards his doom, he seems to have become immune to any other authority than the inevitable crush of fate.

"You're wrong," I say desperately. "There would be no danger. The Alban royals only want to secure their precious alliance with us. What do they care if I bring unexpected cargo with me?"

"They will care if they discover that cargo bears the mark of the devil."

"How will they discover that? Once the moon wanes to the last quarter, you won't even show any signs of it. We can say you are my Cavalier. And Emrys—" I turn, find him clearly biting his tongue as he keeps his eyes on the opposite wall. "Emrys can vouch for you."

Emrys shakes his head. A small smile forms on his lips. "Remarkable that you might assume I would help you betray your king."

"You're sworn to protect the royal family," I tell him. "It wouldn't go against your vows to help me."

He raises his eyebrows but says nothing more.

"Tam. You're being naïve," says Rhun. "Our alliance with the kingdom of Alba can only ever be fragile, seeing our past history. It would be stupid to do anything that might provoke them. And," he adds with another helpless smile, "you're forgetting one important thing."

"What?"

"You can't break me out of the dungeons. Even if you enlist Emrys's help, the guards watch us day and night."

"I'll find a way."

"Stop it. You're a princess of royal blood. You can't just do what you want, we aren't children anymore. It's your duty to do your king's bidding, as it is mine."

"Even if that duty is to *die?*"

He stares miserably at the table between us. He can't say the words. He might be pretending to be brave but he can't push the lie as far as that.

I sit there like a fool, staring at the boy I grew up with, hearing a stranger's words in his mouth. He sounds a lot like a Cavalier. Too much, in fact. He's hiding himself behind tall words and wise adages he's heard better men say. I know he's scared, but it still stings that he would find the moral high ground a better refuge than what I can promise him.

I turn away from him, trying to hide the tears that are prickling my eyes.

"When is it that you take us to the bogs?" Rhun asks.

"The morning of the last quarter," Emrys tells him quietly.

His words sink into my mind like lead. Seven days from now, my brother will be gone forever. And if I can't persuade him to fight for his own life, how can I hope to save him?

I stand up, skirting around the table so I can sit beside him. The way he looks at me tells me he isn't ready at all. Of course he isn't – he's barely eighteen, still a child in so many ways. His brow crumples as he looks down at my lap, his brave façade vanished at last.

I show him the dark pink ribbon from Cinnie. He manages a smile as I tie it around his wrist.

"Emrys wouldn't let her in," I tell him. "I threatened to kick in the doors but she stopped me just in time."

He chokes out a laugh. "She's always been your voice of reason."

"Oh, she wanted me to give you this, too," I add, leaning to kiss him on the cheek.

Wordlessly, he accepts the kiss. He's always taken Cinnie's affections lightly, as though they haven't evolved past the childish awe she's always held towards him. Tonight though, his expression is difficult to decipher. He turns his wrist over as though realising that this is the last gift he'll ever receive from her.

He'll never see her again. Neither her nor Hilda.

"Tam," he whispers. "I'm scared."

I wrap my arms around him, frowning against his shoulder. I didn't think I could hurt so much without receiving any physical blow. It's like each word from Rhun's mouth lashes me across the heart.

"I'll do what I can," I whisper. "I promise. I'll get you out of here. Whatever it takes."

His fingers crook into my dress, holding me so tight I hear the seams crack.

Emrys steps forward, a cue for me to get up. I peel away from Rhun, feeling delirious that I must obey, that Emrys expects me to leave my brother down here to die. As I watch Rhun wipe tears from his cheeks I feel like I could mount an attack against all the dungeon guards by myself.

We get up. Emrys leads us out of the interrogation room, and then Rhun is abruptly pulled from me by another guard. We barely share a parting glance before they shove his head down and push him into a cell.

The other cursed men are already wreaking havoc again. I can only numbly follow Emrys, dry eyes wide open, trying my hardest to keep the howling grief tucked away in my chest.

He leads the way down the corridor back to Cinnie. She's huddled there next to the torch bracket, looking almost expectant, like she was hoping that I might appear with Rhun trailing behind me. I can't help feeling like I've failed her somehow by leaving him behind.

"Ladies." Emrys walks ahead to lead us back up the stairs. Cinnie tucks in her chin, trying to hide her shining eyes. I take her hand and pull her after me. Together we march up the spiral stairway in silence.

My feet feel heavier and heavier with each step. I promised Rhun I'd save him, but what can I even do? I have no authority. No one will listen to the king's niece. No one cares.

Before I know it, I'm leaning against the cold stone wall of the stairway, staring sightlessly ahead. The truth of the situation feels so heavy. I feel drenched in it, too drenched to even move.

Cinnie wraps an arm around my shoulders, but I can barely summon a response.

Powerless. That's what I've always been. That's why Emrys didn't even try to interrupt me and bring me to reason in that dingy room.

He knows I am completely and utterly powerless to do anything.

Chapter 9

THRAIN

DAY 6 OF THE WANING MOON OF MAY

"I SEE IT! I see the fort!"

Olaf's cry rouses us from our drinking and idle chatter. Ivar pushes himself up first, grinning with excitement. I stand beside him, and together we march across the planking to meet Olaf at the prow of the Dálriadan ship.

Olaf stands there with his hand shielding his eyes from the sun as we navigate down the River Clyde, flanked by our escorts. It's still bizarre to see him dressed in the brown burlap of a Christian monk. All three of us wear the robes, so as not to arouse suspicion. The Britons are expecting a party of Albans to arrive for the princesses' courtship; they must certainly not appear to be accompanied by three Viking lords.

All around us, hilly coastlines rise from the rolling waves. We've left behind the shredded cliffs of Dál Riata. Here the land is stamped down unevenly as though walked over by a giant. Dumbarton fort juts out ahead, the only high place on the north bank of the river.

It is magnificent. It rises from its river-bound rock like a jagged stone crown. The outer walls are stone rather than wood

– the inner sanctum seems similarly ringed with crenelated walls and high towers.

I have seen the feudal mounds of Mide in central Ireland, hilltops mounted with impressive fortifications. But most were wood and mortar easily corroded by flame. Once we amassed enough allies to break apart the strength of the High King of Ireland, the taking of those forts was unlike anything I have tasted before.

But this, this impressive stone fort and its jealously walled-in lands… I have never seen anything like it.

It will require a full siege.

I chance a look at my brothers' faces. Olaf and Ivar are smiling with wordless awe as they look upon the approaching fort.

"Lives up to expectations then, does it?" I ask them. Ivar scoffs.

"Yes. Yes it does."

"Now we must only find out how to pierce stone walls thick as five fathoms," I say lightly. "Just a small matter. Nothing impossible."

"Don't you start with your doomsaying," Olaf rails. "The courtship will give us ample time to learn how to avoid the issue altogether."

The three Alban royals we are travelling with drift out of the ship's forecastle to survey the lands. They stand at the prow with us, two black-haired men and one fair lady. Ivar turns to address them, switching from Norse to their Gaelic tongue.

"Where does that river lead?" He points at the canal that branches off at the foot of the fort. Prince Domnall, the thickset older man, leans over the bulwark to see it clearer.

"That's the Leven. It leads up to another loch," he says. "This whole place is infested with them. Swamplands and bogs and wide lochs. It's enough to sink any army that marches in from the north without proper knowledge of its wetlands."

Prince Domnall has been here before several times, sword in hand, riding hard across torn battlefields. Lady Catriona has only come once to sign a peace treaty alongside her kingly brother. Lord Aedan has never been here, but he faces the sights with a similarly grim face. All three of them speak of the Briton king as one does of a bitter rival, a long-standing enemy who inspires only frustration and the grudging desire to return again and again, until old debts and heartaches are settled.

But the three Albans' constant complaining hasn't been enough to dampen Olaf and Ivar's excitement. They have been in a frenzy about this place ever since they first heard of it. Ireland holds many myths and legends, and in our countless raids, we heard of fabled creatures we thought had been lost to time. The whispers and warnings of a Briton kingdom due East ignited them until they could no longer stand still and savour our Irish victories.

The kingdom of Strathclyde has been all they've spoken about for months.

The kingdom we have just sailed into.

Irish shepherds and fishwives alike speak of rare and precious womenfolk that have been guarded here for centuries. Even the Albans nod and go quiet when we ask about them.

Much as I might've argued against leaving Dublin to come here and chase mysteries, my brothers were persuaded. Here, they fancied they would find their treasures at last.

The lost daughters of Freya. The Vanirdøtur.

Every Northman knows the story. Not all are mad enough to chase its mysteries. But as we pass into these lands, there is something about the abundance of watchtowers, this extravagant fortress, and the bursting green fields around it…

There is no doubt they are guarding something.

All around us, the wind seems to be shifting. We all fall quiet as we approach the mouth of the Leven. Water rushes against the ship's hull, the waves glittering as they bear us forth. Voices carry from the riverbanks as we are sighted.

A faint rumbling draws my eye to a field on the north bank. Out of a thicket bursts a herd of tall dark horses galloping across the grass, following our progress. My mouth parts as I watch them run, their movements far too graceful to be real.

I smile in wonder as our men labour to bring us to their main port. I can't help feeling as though the land itself has welcomed our arrival. Awe pricks my skin as those horses tilt their heads up towards us, whinnying and snorting in our direction as they watch us pass.

An ancient magic lingers in this place. I can feel it. If we were to find the Vanirdøtur anywhere… this kingdom may not be an entirely unreasonable place to look.

ᚦᚱᚨᛁᚾ

My brothers and I set foot upon Briton soil, wrapped up in our scratchy brown burlap. Hoods up, we shuffle behind the Alban royals into the crowded River Leven port.

Lady Catriona told us that Vyrgen men are not welcome here, so we wear dried herbs sewn into our burlap, confusing the scent that would make our nature recognisable to others. Domnall and Aedan precede us, bearing forth their own bland scent of normal men.

A welcoming party greets us amidst the bustle of fishermen and merchants.

"Well met, Your Graces!" calls a man dressed in fine black leathers. His Gaelic is encrusted with strange accents. They must come from the tongue I hear the curious onlookers mumble at one another – utterly inscrutable. The man comes flanked by armed guards, all wearing black tabards inscribed with some type of purple flower.

It seems overly cautious, even insulting, to crowd the port with so many men just to welcome three Alban royals and their small contingent of Dálriadan guards. Especially as all of these men are Vyrgen – I can smell it on them, though their scents are laced with a strange acrid perfume. I'm surprised to find men of my ilk here after what the lady told us. Do they try to hide what they are, too? Is that why their scent is so peculiar? Instinctively I reach for my belt before realising there is only a monk's rope wound around my waist.

We're attracting quite the crowd. I breathe in and out, calming myself. I know the potency of our own deterrents. They cannot detect us.

"We weren't expecting you before the new moon!" the guard calls.

"The weather was fair enough to allow the journey," Lady

Catriona says, taking over the conversation with her usual poise and elegance. "We were informed that it might not hold for much longer. We preferred to arrive early than to delay." She curtseys. "Apologies if this is an unwelcome imposition."

"Oh, it's no imposition, my lady," the head of the guard tells her. He seems cowed by her manners, as most men are. "A runner has already been sent to inform the king. He'll send an escort down for you as soon as possible. While you wait, please – come."

The guard escorts us around the inns and taverns of the port until we reach their towering outpost. From behind my hood, I can't help noticing the sheer amount of those flower-boasting tabards moving around the civilian crowds. Clearly no stranger could alight in that port without being immediately apprehended.

It's a relief to exit the riverfront and its pungent odours of fish. Once we've stepped into their outpost, it becomes easier to sort between the strange scents that surround us. There is some sweetness here that I cannot quite identify. Before I can try to make sense of it, it's cluttered again by the scents of hay and horse as we approach their outpost stables.

The guards fetch us a group of those tall black horses. Up close, they're even more impressive. Their powerful necks take root in deep chests, bodies thickset and sturdy. Lady Catriona is keeping the head of the guard busy with polite chatter, so I allow myself to observe my own steed.

"What breed is this?" I ask Prince Domnall. "I've not seen them in your own lands."

"They're Galloways," he says. His voice is edged with annoyance, as always when speaking of something the Britons own which he does not. "Hybrids. Cross-bred between feral stock and old Roman warhorses." Here he gives me a glance. "The Britons are horse-lords, as I mentioned. They're very protective of their herds."

"I can see why." I trail my hand over my mare's withers and down her front legs, feeling the powerful musculature and sturdy bones beneath. She turns her gracefully arched head, gazes at me with wise eyes.

The siege is far from being organised, much less won. But I

can't suppress the delight that jolts through me at the idea that this land holds many more unexpected treasures just waiting to be discovered.

We mount our steeds and let the guards lead the way out. A paved highway cuts through the farmsteads and climbs the slope towards the fort's entrance.

I sit back and enjoy my mare's comfortable gait, eyes full of the ancient stonework that holds together the legendary fort of the Britons.

This will be an interesting stay.

ᚦᚱᛅᛁᚾ

The road takes us all around the great spur of volcanic rock upon which the fort is perched. It is unscalable; the ledges of rock look treacherous, the whole façade crowded with rowan trees that glitter with their bounty of red seeds.

Once through the forested village that curves around the rock, we emerge upon a great plain; the King's Garden, our guides tell us. Beyond is the single piece of the fort's outer wall that is at ground level. At its feet, a deep ditch is carved into the ground, drawbridge lowered over it. That piece of wall protects the cleft in the great rock that allows passage upward. Our horses' hooves toe the wooden planks of the drawbridge, every step scrutinized by the flower-clad watchmen up there on the crenels.

It's a steep, winding way up to the heart of the fort. My heart is pounding with anticipation as we're allowed into the inner sanctum of such a heavily guarded place. So the armoured prey reveals its heart to the hunter, trusting him to stay his knife.

Finally the last set of heavy iron-wrought gates opens. A vast paved street greets us. On either side are roundhouses and stone structures of varying purposes. Curious onlookers mill about again, interrupting their tasks to stare up at us and mutter in their garbled tongue. We ride along until a new escort of guards greet us, armed to the teeth and wearing too much gold to be anything but the king's guard themselves.

"Your Graces!" they trumpet at us. "Welcome to Dumbarton

Castle, royal fort and home of the king of Strathclyde. You will surrender your arms to us before you meet the king."

We dismount and do as they say. The Alban men give up their swords, while Lady Catriona slips a dagger from her shoe and presents it in good faith. We three Vyrgen have next to nothing under our monk's garb – we submit to their hurried patting, arms and legs out like fools.

I can tell Ivar is trying to catch my eye. I ignore him. It's crucial that we stick to our roles.

And there is something… something ahead of us. That sweetness again, unsullied this time by parasitic scents.

The king's guard leads us to a great wide courtyard surrounded by trees. A stone stairway leads away from it to the entrance of the royal castle. In the middle of the courtyard stand the Briton royals. The king, his crown prince by his side, several other richly attired men and…

Gods.

The women.

I cannot deny the deep-seated yearn that pulls at my guts as we step into their vicinity. I've never felt something like this before, not in plain daylight, not so incredibly strong. Sweet notes of honey and something otherworldly drift around us in that shaded place. Lady Catriona opens her arms to begin the introductions, both Alban princes following her. My brothers and I linger by the king's guard, stiff and staring.

Those Briton women all seem to have stepped straight out of the halls of Vanaheimr. They trail its perfumes of eternal spring, their beauty ethereal and almost difficult to look upon. I try to keep my monk's hood down and not openly stare.

The two youngest are pushed forward by their elders so they might meet their betrothed. One has flowing blond hair, the other a wild mane of ginger curls somehow tamed into a thick crown braid. Even in daylight, their scents are so potent.

My mouth goes dry as I watch the fiery-haired one drop into a polite curtsey, her every movement delicate as though she were an elf freshly tumbled into this world.

It can't be.

It *can't* be.

Perhaps it is just a perfume they wear. Perhaps these royal women are of such fine lineage that their beauty reflects their high birth.

Olaf and Ivar cannot be right. The Vanirdøtur are only a legend. Unless the Clyde bore us into another plane entirely, I refuse to believe it.

My brothers are sending one another urgent glances. They try to catch my attention again, but I can't rip my eyes off of that girl with the fiery hair. The one that Aedan is staring at.

The one that Aedan is betrothed to.

The realisation sinks into my mind as I watch them interact. If she is indeed what my brothers think she is… then we would be sanctioning the marriage of a daughter of the gods to this undeserving wretch.

I swallow hard. I need to rally Ivar and Olaf for an urgent talk. But for now we can do nothing but stare, frozen in our roles.

I only accepted to come here on the incentive of claiming a powerful inland kingdom. Strathclyde is one of the last to have held out against the invading Danes so far, but it is so much more than just a military stronghold. If we were to take over successfully then we could shake hands with the sons of Ragnar Loðbrok, creating an alliance that would span the entire island. Then we would have such numbers that even the likes of Harald Fairhair could not face us down and win.

But if we must do it at the expense of the Vanirdøtur themselves… if we must treat them like we treat the rest of our war prisoners — tear them from their families, slap shackles around their wrists, drag them in a long chained line so we might ship them to wherever they're destined…

I hear Ivar's mocking tone in my ear again. *Would it not change your resolve entirely?*

The girl's freckled face pulls into a polite smile. It does not reach her eyes.

I grit my teeth as I watch her step back among her peers.

I should've anticipated this instead of laughing off the idea entirely. Olaf and Ivar's wild treasure hunt happened to line up with my own goals, and so we set sail to Strathclyde with the expectation of viewing what would soon be ours.

A fort, a town, a kingdom – those things, I can imagine wresting from the enemy. But that girl, that woman who wears the perfume of Vanaheimr...

How can a mortal man ever hope to claim her as his own?

Chapter 10

TAMSIN
DAY 6 OF THE WANING MOON OF MAY

THE ALBAN ROYALS come to visit us on the eve of my brother's
sacrifice. Their imminent arrival is trumpeted through the
castle by our look-outs.

They've come early. They were meant to arrive after it all; after
our heat was over and the boys gone. But they are here now, so
we must greet them despite the gloom that hangs over the whole
fort.

My mother and Queen Beatha make sure that Eormen and I
are appropriately dressed, then march us to the castle courtyard
to wait for their arrival. I've yelled so much at my mother over
Rhun that we're both rigid as ice sculptures as we stand next to
one another. She won't even look at me.

While we wait, Queen Beatha reminds us of the importance
of this day. It's a historic event that we might invite the royal
Alban family into our home. There is an age-old feud between
us that was never officially pardoned. They came to us for an
alliance two hundred years ago, when Domnall Brecc sought to
build an inland kingdom independent from Ireland and its High
King. But he was too greedy and we were forced to shatter his

budding power.

After that defeat, his line recovered, and their inland territories gradually merged with the Picts. The erstwhile kingdom of Dál Riata was engulfed into the mighty new kingdom of Alba, where Picts and Dálriadans break bread together. The descendants of Domnall Brecc now sit on the throne of Alba, and they have never forgiven us for our slight. As long as I've lived they have harassed our borders, promising peace only to turn around and stab us in the back.

But now we're faced with a common enemy. The Great Heathen Army advances in the East, the Gall-Goídil Vikings in the West. The Albans have had to suffer settlers in many of their isles. If we do nothing, if we cannot stand together, then we will all fall before the onslaught of those cursed masses.

Mother says it has pained Uncle Arthgal a great deal to even trust that such an alliance might be upheld. But we know we need one another to face the Vikings, whether we like it or not.

ᛏᚼᚤᛍᛁᚼ

When they arrive in the courtyard, there is palpable tension as they dismount from their borrowed horses. A contingent of armed Cavaliers as well as three burlap-clad monks have come with them. The solemn crowd oversees our meeting as we stand before one another.

The only woman of their party, a beautiful gold-clad lady in a flowing gown, steps before them all. She bows to us and offers us a wan smile. With a jolt I realise her eyes are mismatched - one is eerily white, spoiling the friendliness of her manner.

"May God bless our meeting," she says in their Gaelic tongue. "Your Graces, King Arthgal, Queen Beatha. Thank you for welcoming us into your beautiful lands. I am Lady Catriona, sister to the King of all Alba. Please, allow me to present my family to you."

A handsome man with thick black hair and beard steps forward to bow. She introduces him as Prince Domnall, son of the king and heir to all Alba. He wears a rich blue cape with a cut of fur around the shoulders and white flowers embroidered along the hems. His tunic boasts a riot of Celtic needlework, and his girdle is gleaming with gemstones. He is Eormen's betrothed.

She bows to him, her cheeks pink as they are finally introduced to one another. Then Uncle Arthgal steps up to him and they embrace one another, as though they had never faced one another on the battlefield. Both say in the Gaelic tongue, "Well met, my friend."

It's strange to hear them speak that tongue. To me, Gaelic has always been the language of the Irish merchants who come to our lands for the summer markets. The Albans speak a slightly different form of it, but they're still thankfully understandable. I try to line up my own greeting in my head, heart banging as Eormen steps back again.

It's my turn.

Lady Catriona introduces Lord Aedan, her son and lord of Dál Riata. He comes forward, peering down his nose at me. His receding hairline tells me he must be older than me, though it's difficult to guess his age. His black hair is cut short and slicked back over his skull with tallow. As for his face, I would never have expected such a sickly demeanour, his worm-like lips contrasting vividly against pale spotty skin. The only attractive thing about him is his cape, blue as Prince Domnall's and freckled with tiny embroidered birds. His attire is otherwise far more austere than his cousin's, as though he did not deem it necessary to preen himself for a courtship.

It's bizarre to think they both sprouted from the same bloodline. Where Domnall reminds me of a friendly kind of bear, Aedan has everything of the balding ferret. For a fully grown man he is strangely gangly, his shoulders narrow, his clothing tucked around a flat, bony body.

He's staring at me like he's drawing similarly negative conclusions about me. For a moment I'm insulted by his disappointment – clearly I've tried ten times harder than he has to be presentable. Mother spent all morning twisting my hair up, painting my face and cinching my dress closer around my curves to make sure it was all on show. But he's looking at me like I'm some hag freshly emerged from the bogs.

Then I realise what the sight of me evokes in him.

Dunblane. The battle that fatally injured both his father and mine.

As the story goes, they fell on one another's swords. I've always regarded it as having lost my father to the battle itself, not any specific man – but clearly Aedan does not feel the same.

I hold up my chin and try to endure his gaze. I always knew this would be difficult, but I stayed, I'm here, I'm doing this. I've swallowed my emotions. Surely he should accept his position and do the same instead of flaunting his disdain so openly.

Emulating Eormen's quiet dignity, I pluck up my skirts and give him the low curtsey he is owed.

"I'm honoured to meet you at last, Lord Aedan," I tell him.

A cold, unnerving smile curls his lips as he watches me defer to him. At last he bows back.

"The honour is mine."

ᛏᚹᛅᚯᛋᛁᛏ

My family is well used to luncheons with men who would just as gladly stick knives in our guts as share wine with us. We sit through an endless lunch where the men speak liberally about the Viking threat. The desire to meet with my brother in the darkness of deserted corridors to rag about our guests brings me so low that I'm barely present in the courtly conversations.

Tomorrow morning. My brother's going to the bogs *tomorrow morning* and I'm here, entertaining our guests, making an impression. It all seems so staggeringly unimportant and I feel I'm going mad, turning my face around and nodding at our guests as though any of their opinions mattered.

In the afternoon, Eormen and I are to take our fiancés out into the grounds for a ride while Uncle Arthgal arranges how to shift his responsibilities, now that they've arrived early. Mother and Queen Beatha accompany us, as do several of Uncle Arthgal's sons.

We all file out into the castle courtyard. The three tall monks are just arriving too. Domnall asks Queen Beatha if they could be permitted to come with us. He raves about our chapel at Glascau and how his Alban monks aspire to make a pilgrimage to that holiest of sites.

"We're not going all the way out to Glascau today," Queen Beatha warns him. "I'm thinking perhaps of taking you down to Old Kilpatrick on the hunters' road. There's a small chapel there that was built in Saint Patrick's name – would they be interested to see that?"

"Oh yes. I should think so."

Stable-hands file out of the fort stables, leading a line of tacked-up Galloway horses. They're all regal and well-behaved, their shining coats varying from inky black to blood bay. With a wince I notice the odd one out – Cynan is apart from the others, scruffy and ill-tempered as he wriggles around and fights his stable-hand's grip. His creamy palomino coat is matted with sweat.

I gasp as I see the saddle on his back. Somehow the hand managed to get it on him and now he's doing his best to buck it off.

I break away from my station at Aedan's side and rush to my horse.

"How did you get that on him?" I ask the hand, a scared-looking teenage boy.

"Lunged him," he admits. "He was tired enough not to notice it at first. The king's runner said they had to be ready right after lunch so I thought – if I tired him out, then—"

"It's all right. Here, I'll take him."

Thankfully Cynan's wearing a halter and rope underneath his bridle. I unpick the knot in the rope until it's long and loose in my hands, then send him out in a circle.

He trots, snorting in disbelief that I would ask even more effort from him. I sink into our circle, blotting out everything beyond it. Never mind that he's snorted mucus all over my dress – Aedan doesn't care what I look like, so I don't care either.

"Here, boy," I coo at him. "Calm down, you're fine. I'm going to take it off you. Here, now, shh. Give me a nice walk."

The others are busying themselves with their mounts – I can hear Mother trying to laugh off my behaviour, mentioning my "softness for lost causes". She can't hear me. I ask Cynan to switch gaits in Norse, and he grudgingly starts responding to my cues. We settle at a calm walk at last, and when I stop he mirrors me, muscles twitching nervously.

"There now," I murmur as I approach him side-on. "Good boy. You're a good boy."

As soon as I'm within reach I grab the girth and slip it loose of its buckles. He realises I'm not about to climb on, so he lets me do it. Finally I can face his flank and pull down the heavy Briton saddle.

"Your Grace," says the stable-hand, marching up to me again now that Cynan's stopped being chaotic. He immediately pulls the saddle from my arms. "I apologise, it was silly of me. Shall I tack up Rhun's—?"

"No." I can't bear the idea of facing Rhun's mare now. I've been exercising her in his absence and her low spirits do nothing to appease mine. "We'll be fine like this. Thank you."

The others are all astride their mounts, Queen Beatha leading them ahead. Cavaliers walk alongside them, summoned there to guard us for our ride. Eormen and Prince Domnall are side by side, talking primly together. My mother is riding beside Aedan and Lady Catriona, her eyes bulging out of her head as she glares at me to hurry up. Behind them my royal cousins are all clumped together, chatting and glancing my way with amused expressions.

The three tall monks bring up the rear. Their hooded heads are turned my way. Blushing at the sudden realisation that everyone was waiting for me, I grasp Cynan's mane and heave myself up onto his bare back.

"Don't you dare buck me off," I mutter to him as I straighten up.

We trot to catch up to the monks. Cynan slows to match their walking pace, and for a moment I allow it, trying to quell my embarrassment.

"That's not a native breed," says a deep, accented voice.

I turn to face the monk who's spoken. I can't see much of him in the shadow of his hood beyond a well-trimmed blond beard.

I wonder whether to take him up on the obvious conversation starter. Mother and Aedan are still ahead, clip-clopping side by side, apparently having found some topic to discuss. A shiver of reluctance runs through me as I imagine having to bear their company again.

Why should I make an effort? Aedan clearly isn't interested. He hasn't spoken a single word to me since this morning. Whatever plans I may have had about using him to save my brother seem childish now that I've met him. The effort of forcing him to acknowledge me seems insurmountable, like my own feet are trapped in the peat bogs.

Right, then. I'll just linger at the rear with these quiet monks until Mother drags me back to Aedan. He probably won't even notice my absence.

"He's not native, no," I tell the bearded monk. "I know he stands out a bit."

"Indeed. I didn't think I'd see any Nordic horses out here."

"Well, I got him a few years ago from an Irish horse merchant," I tell him. It's an easy topic to settle on. Might as well while away the afternoon somehow. "We hold a foaling festival here in early summer. Folk from all the different kingdoms of Ireland come, as well as Gwynedd and Cornwall down south. The dealers all bring the year's foals, but also brood mares and sires and the odd rescue they take in from the battlefields."

"Interesting. So which category does that one fit into?"

"He was a rescue first, then used as a sire. He was too broken to ride." I stroke Cynan's mane, speaking quieter so he might not hear the details. "According to the dealer, they found him wandering around a battlefield in Mide. Apparently it was an absolute bloodbath. His dead rider's leg was tangled in the stirrup strap, and he'd been dragging the man around for days."

The monk is strangely quiet as he listens to this. His brothers glance at one another. I wonder if he's breaking any kind of protocol by talking to me. Or perhaps I'm being too grim.

"That's why he won't accept the saddle?" the monk asks at last.

"Yes."

"And knowing all this, you still bought him."

There's amusement in his tone. For the first time that day, I find myself smiling.

"Well, I like a challenge. And he's beautiful," I tell him. "And like you say, we don't see many of these horses here. I was curious about them, these warhorses who come from way up north. They can withstand the world's coldest winters. I think they're very interesting to work with."

"Mmm."

The monk seems fascinated as I go on about scruffy little Cynan, making him out to be a fierce warhorse when he's really more of a grumpy old pony.

Quietly, the monk asks: "Is it the Irish dealer who taught you to speak Norse?"

"Oh, I only know a few words," I say quickly. "The dealer told me he wouldn't respond to anything else. I know walk, canter and fly, and that's it."

The monk's smiling now too. "I heard your walk command. Perfectly on point. How would you say the others?"

I stare at him. Wouldn't he revile the language, as an Alban whose territories are steadily getting encroached upon? Then again, they and the Vikings must share close quarters. It must be inevitable for their languages to seep into one another.

I say the words to him, and he nods, correcting me on slight inflections. His own accent seems impeccable.

"I wonder how your king feels about you harbouring a Viking warhorse in his stable," he says.

"King Arthgal has more pressing things to think about," I say. "I don't think he has a problem with it. He's always said it's useful to know the enemy more intimately."

"Indeed," he says, his voice full of quiet curiosity.

Chapter 11

THRAIN
DAY 6 OF THE WANING MOON OF MAY

ONCE WE'RE OUT in the village, the girl's mother calls her back up to the front of the line. She nods at the three of us and we stare like three lovestruck fools at her freckled heart-shaped face, that impossible smile she gives us. Then she trots away on her Nordic stallion, effortlessly moving with him though she has neither saddle nor stirrups to support her.

Ivar leans towards me as I gaze after her.

"Thrain. What are you doing."

I turn to him. We haven't been alone even once; we were settled into our sleeping quarters in one of the many roundhouses, and then shown around by villagers while the royals lunched together. We had to scramble to try and involve ourselves in their affairs again. Now our horses plod behind, leaving space between us and the rest of the trail. I can finally speak to them both.

Or at least, I try to speak.

"She is – they are all—"

I can't even say it. It is too implausible.

A wide pleased smile stretches Ivar's mouth. "You noticed, did you?"

Olaf seems similarly pleased with the turn of events. Both of them have been hoping for this, expecting this. The existence of the Vanirdøtur has always factored seriously in their plans. But not only do the Vanirdøtur exist – they are *alive*, real women of flesh and blood, their voices expressing discordant opinions, their desires wholly their own.

They live in this world of ours, this same world with its war-torn territories and blank-faced victims. They speak its many languages. They are buffeted by its merciless politics.

I wonder if Ivar and Olaf factored those particular details in, when they plotted to lay their hands on these goddess-touched women.

"Yes, they are here," Olaf says, his voice low and full of wonder. "We'll have further evidence by nightfall, of course. But if even you can sense them, Thrain, if even you can admit what they are – then there can be no mistaking it."

Ivar reaches to grab his brother's shoulder, and they share an eager, boyish smile. They've had to contain themselves so far, and I can see how eager they are to celebrate as they congratulate one another quietly. This is the end of a very long journey for them. They've spent years on this hunt, years speculating over the finer details of the myths and ballads that hinted at where the Vanirdøtur might be found.

But they are not dream-like creatures whose existence is mere smoke and poetry. They ride ahead of us now, voices rising and falling, appearing as perfectly normal women to all who would encounter them and not scent their strangeness.

"We cannot do this," I mutter, trying to piece together my thoughts, but even as I begin to express my objection I know it is too late. Princess Tamsin is ahead of us, courting her betrothed. So is Princess Eormen. The Queen oversees this transaction, this selling of young women. It has all been approved of.

All of our plans hinge upon this courtship.

"What?" Ivar asks me. "What can't we do?"

"They are *Vanirdøtur*," I hiss at him.

"Yes," he says with a laugh. "Yes, and I believe you owe me a rather large portion of your armoury to settle our wager."

I glance at Olaf, hoping to at least find some sense in the eldest of my brothers. He is the reasonable one among us three – he has long acted as mediator when we fall out.

"We are wedding that one to Aedan. *Aedan*," I growl at him.

Olaf sighs. "Yes. To capture many, we must sacrifice a few."

"Capture?" I echo. "You speak as though they were hares running into your nets. You are the ones who have studied them so closely. How can you speak of them in that way? As though you were merely trapping prey?"

They're both looking at me curiously. Ivar is the one who speaks.

"What would you have us do, then?" he asks. "Leave them here in the hands of the Christian king? He is the one who agreed to the matches. He does not care that his daughter and niece will wed unworthy men. If you ask me, they will be well rid of him once he's overthrown."

"And you think they will be happier in our hands?" I hiss at him. "After we show nothing but violence towards their kin—"

"Brother," Ivar interrupts, a warning in his voice. "Keep your voice down."

I breathe out slowly, eyes on the riders ahead of us, and fall silent.

Our horses pick their way through the mud of the vast Briton forest that lines the river Clyde. We pass old ruins and stone edifices, large round shapes that belie ancient structures.

There is such a wealth of history here. It's curious to see this place and associate it with them – finally affix a real forest, a real scenery to the legends we have all grown up with.

"I understand your reaction," Olaf mutters to me. "You did not believe in them. You are only just realising what it means for them to be here. But Ivar and I have given this a great deal of thought. We can speak of this again when we're alone."

ᚦᚱᚨᛁᚾ

Our order gets jumbled up by the roads we cross and the speed of our steeds. Domnall and Aedan end up abandoning their princesses, preferring the company of the young Briton princes who've accompanied us. The four Vanirdøtur all ride at the head of our line. It's fascinating to watch the four of them interacting, casually claiming their space in this very real noisy forest.

Domnall reveals an unexpectedly genial side of himself. He brings up the pace and the volume of the conversation until the ride loses its earlier sedate aspect. Soon the princes are shouting their banter as they trot through the thickets. They ride ahead of us in their striped yellows and blues, thick as brothers as they recall details of battles between their forefathers, playful jibes now rather than insults that would call down war between them.

Eventually we exit the forest. And the sight that greets us stops us all in our tracks.

Ahead, the path slopes down to a quaint village of thatched roofs and colourful hanging laundry. The squat little houses seem oblivious to the monstrous green snake that rises from the river and cuts right through them, its humongous body curling away across the fields until it disappears into faraway forests.

"Come on," calls one of the Briton princes. "It's even more impressive close-up!"

My brothers and I glance at one another. For a moment I know we've all had the same thought. If we found the Vanirdøtur here, then who's to know what else lurks in these green lands? Again I want to reach for my axe handle, though I know I'm not wearing it.

As we make our way down to the village of Old Kilpatrick, we realise the snake is in fact a gigantic wall, built of raised earth and stone. In places it's been torn down entirely, the old snake's spine punctured with holes.

We follow a shallow canal of the Clyde until we've reached a clearing. Ahead looms the first section of the wall, the tail tip of the snake. Queen Beatha leads us around an ancient oak tree that occupies the centre of the clearing until we're nose to nose with the wall, tiny figures against the turf giant.

The wall looms over us, tall as a cliff. A chiselled stone plaque is set into its side, depicting a naked woman who holds a wreath in her arm. Her features are so weathered by time that she is more an idea than a woman. All around her strange runes have been carved into the plaque, doubtlessly declaring something of high importance.

The guards stand by Queen Beatha's horse as she dismounts. Her family follows suit. Glancing at one another, my brothers and I follow the Britons' lead.

"I have brought you to this ancient place so that we may reflect together on the significance of our meeting," Queen Beatha intones, holding her golden head up as she addresses us all. She opens her hand towards Lady Catriona and the Alban men. "Do you recognise this wall? Do you know its purpose?"

"I have heard of it, yes," says Lady Catriona. "But we surely do not know the tale as well as you do."

She's graciously offering the queen the opportunity to make her speech regardless of what the Albans know. I'm glad for it – I have no idea who erected that thing, nor how it could possibly be maintained across so many miles. Queen Beatha inclines her head, then turns to her fair-haired daughter.

"Eormen, my darling. Would you explain to our guests the significance of this wall?"

By now the guards, princes and their steeds have all spaced out in a half-moon to form an audience around Princess Eormen. I turn to scope the rest of the clearing and spy several children on the outskirts, hidden behind bushes. They're surely villagers, come to stare in awe at the Strathclyde royals.

Eormen smiles as she steps up to the plaque, falling into her role as orator. Domnall smiles back at her with that genial air of his. Clearly of both matches, theirs is the most functional so far.

"This wall was built by the Roman Emperor Antoninus Pius," she says in a clear, unwavering voice. "Seven hundred years ago, our Celtic ancestors faced the largest invading army they had ever known. Twenty thousand cursed Roman soldiers marched through these lands. Their emperor ordered for this wall to be erected so that we might be controlled, taxed and subdued."

She pauses for dramatic effect. I try to imagine the numbers. I have heard of this ancient empire before, but never in so much detail.

"Sixty miles of turf and stone fortifications spread from here into Northumbria," Eormen goes on. "Except at the time, there was no Northumbria or Strathclyde. These lands were tribal and disunited. While they remained so, they couldn't face the invasions.

"After years under Roman control, our ancestors decided that they could no longer suffer the presence of the invaders. The disparate tribes came together to form the Celtic confederation of the Maeatae.

"They ran off Emperor Antoninus's men. Then when the next emperor sent an even bigger army, forty thousand strong – the confederation still held. Emperor Septimius was even more bloodthirsty than his predecessor. He ordered every man, woman and child to be slaughtered so he might avenge Rome's previous defeat. These were his words."

Eormen takes a breath, eyes glazed.

"Let no one escape sheer destruction, not a single soul. Not even the babe in the womb of the mother, if it be male; let it not escape sheer destruction."

The breeze shivers through the high grasses in the silence that follows. Goosebumps have pricked my skin as I listen to her tale. Forty thousand men? What kind of man wields enough authority to lead such humongous numbers? I find myself torn between flattery that we Vikings might be compared to such a man – as seems to be the purpose of her story – and sheer horror at the idea of the carnage he must've wrought.

"But even as war ravaged the lands, the Maeatae still held. They led the Romans out to the bogs until they all fell sick from the fumes and poisonous water. Legend has it that it was Clota herself who led Emperor Septimius to his death. He followed her through the mists until he fell head-first into the bogs. And when he opened his eyes, he saw the white faces of all those women and children whose deaths he had ordered. He's still there now, trapped in the peat, cursing himself for his mistakes. For he knew that the Maeatae were bound by more than contracts or greed. The Maeatae were bound by their sacred oath to protect these lands. To keep them safe from those who would seek to ravage it."

Queen Beatha beams at her as she concludes. So do the Briton princes. It is a tale well told, and Eormen's cheeks are quite flushed with her performance.

"I trust you understand why we are here, relating this tale to you," Queen Beatha says. "Only through unity can we keep our claim on these ancestral lands. Whatever our past disputes may have been, now is the time to set them aside. Now is the time to show strength in the face of the Viking threat. And I cannot tell you how proud and humbled I am to welcome you to our land at last, as friends."

Lady Catriona comes forward to grasp Queen Beatha's hands. They bow to one another. The theatrics are somewhat sickening to watch. Catriona's smile is so very convincing even as she clasps the hands of the queen she seeks to betray.

"It is a good tale," Domnall says. Then he turns to the audience himself and raises his voice: "Brothers! I am honoured to follow in the footsteps of our ancestors. Let us be bound as they were!"

The Briton princes afford him a charitable cheer.

A thin drawl arises next: "I knew the story somewhat. And you tell it quite well, Princess." Aedan is walking towards the royals, hands hooked in his belt. "However, if I may, there is a question I'd like to ask. I know of your Clota of course, but only by name. It interests me greatly to hear her appear in this story. Who exactly is she?"

Queen Beatha nods and stretches out her hand again, though this time not towards Eormen. We follow where she's pointing until we've all turned to Princess Tamsin, who is standing by her stallion and running her fingers through his mane. She hasn't seen the summons. She's staring out at the river beyond, wearing a grieved expression. When she realises a hush has fallen over the clearing, she turns to find all of us staring at her.

Immediately her whole face turns red, engulfing her freckles.

"Oh," she says faintly. "I'm not much of a story-teller, Aunt Beatha. Eormen can tell it."

At this Eormen smooths her hair and steps forward, all too happy to continue her performance. But Queen Beatha turns to the purse-lipped woman who's journeyed with us and smiles wanly.

"Such a humble child," she says. The other woman only raises her eyebrows. "Humility is a great virtue, Tamsin, but I know you're just as gifted with words as Eormen. I'm sure Lord Aedan would very much enjoy hearing the tale from you."

Still blushing, Tamsin lets her gaze bounce from the queen to her betrothed. Then she decides the audience is too large to sweep through and turns back to the river, surely thinking of an opening line.

I already allowed Eormen's otherworldly beauty and singsong voice to capture me. Now I find myself focussed entirely on Tamsin. There is something profound about her, like the darkness of a deep still lake. Perhaps it's that sadness of hers.

"Clota was a wisewoman of the pagan tribe that lived here," Tamsin says quietly. "The Damnonii. When Emperor Septimius launched his massacre, the Damnonii chieftain was slain. So Clota took over leadership of the tribe. She ordered all her warriors to protect the Rock – the high ground where Dumbarton fort now stands – and made it into a sanctuary for all the women and children fleeing the Roman legions.

"The Maeatae cut down many Romans as the war went on. Eventually Emperor Septimius became enraged that he was losing so many men. He decided to have his revenge on the easiest target he could find, and sent his men to surround Clota's sanctuary."

Tamsin pauses. Again a chill runs through me as I picture the scene, how my brothers and I plan to encircle them in just the same way. I can't help but think that one day, a young woman will stand by the river and speak of us in this way.

"The Roman soldiers followed their Emperor's directive of destruction," Tamsin says. There is a hard edge to her voice now, like quiet anger. "One night a group of cursed soldiers came into Clota's room, fresh from their carnal pursuits. They promised not to harm her if she did not struggle. She closed her eyes to pray, and reached for her dagger." Tamsin's hand rises as though reaching for the knife herself. "There were five of them. She knew she would die if she struck one. But her courage prevailed over fear. In one quick strike, she slit one of her assailant's throats. And as they all clamoured to avenge him, the Romans found they could not pass the line of blood she had spilt on the ground.

"It was the first of Clota's miracles. Seeing that, she understood her purpose at once. God had answered her prayer, filled her with strength, though as a pagan woman she did not quite understand it. She armed as many women as she could, and as they spattered the blood of Romans all around the Rock, so it became hallowed ground. No man could climb up onto the Rock without being struck down by God's will."

Tamsin's eyes rest for a moment on the river. In the silence that follows she leaves us in that distressing scene, a bloody carnage full of groping hands and glinting daggers. I wonder at her own ease in conjuring such images, the way her voice turns to steel as soon as she mentions the suffering of her kin.

"When the morning came, the sun revealed scorched lands, caved-in granaries. The Damnonii knew they would have to leave this place or starve. Devastated, Clota made her way down to the river to look upon its waves. It had turned red with blood. She opened her arms and stepped into it, this river that had sustained her tribe for centuries. She walked into its waters, and there she performed her second miracle. All around her, the water cleared. The further she waded into it, the further the water turned clean and grey as glass.

"Thanks to her, the Damnonii were able to stay and rebuild. She tilled Roman blood into the soil and made it fertile again. All throughout the lands of the Maeatae, word of Clota's miracles abounded. Women came to the Rock seeking Clota's wisdom, and she placed her hands on their bellies to heal them of their barrenness. Like the river, she cleared their bodies of all their bad memories."

She's still staring out at the river as though she's completely forgotten her audience. She might be recounting the tale to her horse, for all she cares of our reactions. Slowly she brings her hands to her own belly and concludes the tale.

"The daughters of Clota are the descendants of those she touched. Both blessed and cursed to hold memories of chaos.

For we must not forget that the soil must be tilled, and the womenfolk protected."

I had not thought that the Britons' own tale of the Vanirdøtur would be so drenched in gore. Compared to our stories, theirs is a grim picture of war and all its ugly consequences. I can almost smell the charred devastation she has painted in my mind, the scents of bodies broken open for the crows to feast.

In the silence that follows her story, the men appear rather uncomfortable. Domnall swoops in to save us from all these solemn contemplations.

"Such are the women of Strathclyde," he says, "and so I have always heard of your kind. You have always inspired deep respect in those who know of you. I daresay it is a warning to any man who might approach with ill intent." He gives a laugh. "I only hope I may keep my throat intact on my wedding night."

Several of the Briton princes smirk, and Queen Beatha gives a gracious laugh. Eormen goes to him wearing a reassuring smile, and the tension is dispelled.

At least on the surface.

There is a thinly veiled threat in the Briton women's attitudes, their choice to recount those tales to us here, now. They do not trust the Albans. They want it to be clear, even under all the smiles and politeness, that they are only allies out of convenience.

I see then a terrible knowledge in the women's postures, the patience with which they entertain their guests. They do not trust men, whether Alban or otherwise, and especially not the "cursed". I wonder again about those flower-clad soldiers who have been ever-present around us ever since we landed. Are they diminished somehow? Drugged or castrated? Perhaps that is the only way they tolerate the presence of Vyrgen in their lands – stripped of all potential danger.

Knowing this, it's incredible that they might still be willing to risk this alliance. They shake hands with the Albans and entrust them with their girls without knowing how the Albans truly operate. Clearly they fear that we Vikings will bring carnage to their shores that will rival Emperor Septimius's efforts.

The reason for Tamsin's deep sadness is suddenly painfully

obvious. Her mind bears all these bloody stories of violence and daggers in the night. I doubt she holds any pleasant illusions about her marriage at all.

It is all I can do to stay silent and mount my horse again, trying to quiet the warring thoughts in my mind.

Chapter 12

TAMSIN

DAY 6 OF THE WANING MOON OF MAY

T HAT EVENING IN the great hall, wine flows freely and music brightens everyone's spirits. My mind is sunk in the bleak darkness of the dungeons below us as couples get up to dance, royal princes from both kingdoms roaring with laughter together over mead and venison.

Aedan is still ignoring me. Domnall has chosen to regale my cousins with tales of their historic battles against the Vikings, and Aedan chimes in sometimes to bring corrections. My cousins make an easy audience for them, laughing and gasping at all the right places.

It's hard not to like Domnall's boisterous manners. Eormen and her sisters are all but fawning over him, which only spurs him on in his exaggerated tales. He's delighted to have won the attention of so many royal princesses. Aedan doesn't seem to mind it either when he butts in. I hang back, eating my food listlessly next to my mother, listening as Domnall's voice rings across the flagstones.

"… and with that, the warlord was turned to stone!"

My younger cousins gasp and cry out, but this time Eormen

isn't fazed.

"My darling, all your tales are full of giants and talking foxes," she says with a smile. "How are we meant to believe anything you say?"

"You talk like they don't roam your own lands," Domnall says. "Yet I think I've seen a few bright eyes and bushy tails around here."

"I'm not denying that there's strangeness in this country," Eormen says obligingly. "Only, we don't depend on the magic of woodland creatures to solve our issues. We have political advisors for that."

"Are you telling me there aren't a few bright eyes among your king's councilmen?" Domnall says, making my older cousins scoff. Leaning closer together, they start referring to a few of Uncle Arthgal's advisors who might indeed be hiding a tail beneath their cloak.

"Come, tell us a real story," Eormen commands. Then, eyes flicking between me and Aedan, she changes tack: "Lord Aedan. You're more sensible than your dear cousin. Tell us something worthwhile."

"Oh, I'm really not..."

"Ha! See how suited you are to Tamsin! You blush just as she does," Eormen says. She's making such painstaking efforts to get us to interact. "Come now. Let me give you more wine. Tamsin makes a fine story-teller when she puts her mind to it – I'm sure you are the same."

She lifts a finger for a servant girl to come and top him up. I can't help but glare at her. She's effortlessly managing the conversation, forcing me to pay attention to Aedan now that he's been put on the spot.

He holds up his goblet for the servant girl to pour. While staring at that stream of deep red wine, inspiration strikes. "All right. I know just the thing." He looks around the table. "The tale of our battle against the three wolves of Dublin. You want to hear it?"

Domnall seems surprised. He lifts his head to scan the hall as though worried they might be overheard. But before he can say anything, Eormen and her sisters all nod vigorously.

"All right." Aedan sips his wine and settles into his role. "Earlier this year, we were to face the oncoming threat of the most vicious Viking warlords we have ever met. The three wolves of Dublin. They have long tormented the High King of Ireland, Màel Sechnaill. After they successfully drove him to his death, they turned their eyes outwards. To our own lands.

"The youngest among the three has the bloodiest reputation of them all. Thrain Mordsson. His very name spells murder in the Nordic tongue. Six feet tall, hair long as a witch's, eyes the same deep red as the fires of Hell. Face so distorted and ugly that just one look would stop your heart in your chest. He and his brothers hail from a cold hellish heartland way up north, where no man could possibly survive. Miles and miles they travelled overseas, following the scent of blood. They established Dublin as a slave market where they could sell their Christian war prisoners to their heathen kin. And now, their path of desecration has led them to our last strongholds on the isle of Islay."

The princesses are all leaning over their platters now, enrapt. Aedan has such a chilling way of setting the scene that even I find myself putting down my knife, eager to hear more.

"Picture the windy cliffs of Dál Riata, a rocky coastline battered by the waves. We've rallied armies from all over our mainlands and southern islands to face them. Our scouts tell us where they've landed, and the sights they speak of are enough to chill a grown man. Wide red sails on turbulent seas, longboats as huge as the trees they felled to build them. Hordes of barbarians tall as giants, armed to the teeth, spilling onto the sand."

"Aedan," Domnall mutters, a warning in his tone, but Aedan only raises his voice and goes on.

"When we arrive at last, we meet them in battle. Head on. I'm standing face to face with Thrain Mordsson himself. The air turns to ice as he breathes, and he swears he will have my head by day's end. But as we face one another in the heart of the storm… something happens that none of us could've foretold. Something ungodly. Quite possibly unfit for the ears of delicate Briton princesses such as yourselves."

"You must tell it!" Eormen says excitedly. She's practically on the edge of her seat.

Like all men who've sat face to face with my cousin, Aedan is far too pleased with her interest as well as the plunging view she's giving him of her cleavage. I find myself vaguely annoyed, before remembering that there should be no rivalry when I don't even *want* to wed the man.

"All right, Your Grace," he says, savouring his own suspense. His voice has carried enough now to capture Lady Catriona's attention, who sits a little way away. Strangely enough, Aedan forsakes Eormen in order to stare straight at his mother before continuing. "I pointed to the beast and I said, I told him – you will not make slaves of us. You may have come to expect that all the lords and ladies of these isles will spread their thighs for you, but it will not be so for us."

"Aedan," Domnall warns again, but Aedan is too riled up to stop now.

"You have taken enough of our Christian kin to make slaves of them, and you will not do the same to us. We are a proud people – and we will not stand for your godlessness!" He slaps the table here, making my cousins jump. Several Britons around us shout *aye* in approval. Both Lady Catriona and Domnall look distinctly uncomfortable.

"And Thrain Mordsson laughed," Aedan goes on. "That ugly heathen bastard laughed. But my words were heard by others that he had long since forgotten about.

"The wind shrieked in our ears. At first, we thought that was all it was. But then – and I swear to God, this is the truth – we saw them. Over the waves they came, hundreds of banshees clad in torn black cloaks, trailing the chains of their servitude all the way from Dublin. Their wails were enough to turn a man's blood to ice.

"They swarmed the Vikings and sought out Thrain Mordsson and his brothers. I swear by the holy texts, they put the fear of the Almighty even in the heart of that monster. It was enough to make them turn tail and leave with their whole army."

He sits back, replete with satisfaction as my cousins all cry out and acclaim his tale. Domnall smiles gingerly and pats him on the back, as though indulging a small child. His embarrassment is palpable, though I can't understand why he seems so put off by a tale of bravery and resistance.

I know it can't all be true, but even I find myself chilled by Aedan's story. I can see the scene so clearly. A jagged landscape, alive with wailing ghosts. The sea all around, iron-grey and choppy as it crashes against the cliffs and the hulls of Viking ships.

When I wed him, that will be my home.

Eormen gives me a pointed look. I should be asking Aedan more details, taking the opportunity to talk to him. The prospect of Dál Riata and its turbulent histories should be exciting to discuss. But it's not. Without my brother, the thought of leaving Strathclyde scares the life out of me.

I pick up my knife again, staring down at my roasted pheasant marinating in its bloody juice, my heart banging painfully hard in my chest.

Somehow, even though we've spent the whole day with them, it's only now that the reality of our situation is really sinking in.

They're here. They're going to take Eormen and I away with them.

And there's nothing I can do about it.

↑ᚼᚤ�928ᚼ

After we've finished eating, couples begin trickling onto the dance floor to join in with the traditional Briton dances. I'm light-headed from wine, barely repressed panic, and the wound in my chest that gets ripped afresh every time I remember that I cannot go to my brother, neither for comfort nor to save him from his fate.

Tomorrow. Tomorrow he's going to the bogs.

I want so badly to go down to the dungeons again. Threaten Emrys until this time he lets me through. We've argued so much over the past few days that he won't even let me talk to him any more. Tonight, though... I can't stand sitting here doing nothing, listening to these idiots and their fairy-tales while my brother awaits his fate in the dark.

"May I be excused?" I ask my mother. She looks at me like I just spat on the table.

"You can't just disappear in the middle of the feast. They've been with us all day and you've barely even talked to Lord Aedan yet."

From the look on her face, she knows exactly where I'm planning to go. I sigh. It's useless to point out that Aedan's ignored me thus far. I need to at least fulfil my quota of chatter so I might be allowed to get out of here. Never mind that he might prefer Eormen, as Mother can plainly see. They all prefer Eormen.

I just need to playact for a little while. Then I can leave. Holding onto that thought, I get up and sidle over to Prince Aedan. He glances up at me in surprise, breaking away from my young tittering cousins.

"Can I tempt you to a dance, my lord?"

He stares blankly at me. Annoyance flashes across his face as he realises he can't exactly refuse me in front of everybody. His annoyance only fuels mine. What, did he think I'd disappear if he ignored me?

Eventually he gets up. "Lead the way, princess."

Eormen smiles up at us, delighted that we're finally speaking to each other. She's trying so hard to encourage me. It's strange for her to put on her big sister act for me — she's always left me alone, seeing me as the odd cousin who's too busy tramping knee-deep in horse manure to bother with royal etiquette. But I was chosen for Aedan instead of one of her younger sisters, so she's sweeping me under her wing.

I would've loved receiving so much attention from her when I was younger. But this, now — making sure we're both behaving adequately as brides-to-be — I'd rather she go back to ignoring me altogether.

Aedan and I march to the dance floor. I step back to give him room as we cross other couples. Every sign of respect I give him seems to take me a huge effort, as though I were moving boulders. I remind myself: *just do this, then you can go.*

Once again I think of what I promised Rhun back in the dungeons. That I'd enlist the Albans' help to get him out of there and smuggle him to Dál Riata. Ice fills my body as I think of the hours I've wasted today, shying away from Aedan, letting myself be intimidated by him.

I have to try, I *have* to. But how in God's name am I meant to persuade him to help me in one evening? He hates me for reasons I'm powerless to change.

Aedan's cold, bony hand closes around mine as the song begins. We sweep around the dancefloor, performing a drab revision of dance steps we've both learned for this occasion.

I raise my chin. The moon must be rising – even on Aedan's arm, I can feel the stirrings of heat in my belly as the exercise warms us. As the dances wear on and the moon rises higher still, I find myself breathing through my mouth, trying to focus on the steps. Aedan's own posture has relaxed, his grip on me tightening further than the polite embrace we'd been sharing.

An idea forms in my mind.

I know Aedan is a normal man, that these last days of my heat cannot affect him like it would a cursed man. He can't scent me, he doesn't have that deep-seated drive to claim me as a cursed man would. But I know that all men are weak to the wiles of young women, regardless. Perhaps… perhaps there is a way to make the most of this situation.

The moon is almost at its last quarter. I know I can keep my head tonight regardless of how much I stoke the heat. It disgusts me to think that even a ferrety little man like Aedan could stir my desires, but then, such is the fate of a daughter of Clota; anyone will do when in the throes of the full moon.

I let him take me by the waist as we begin the next dance. I know he sees my flushed cheeks, my glazed eyes, my parted mouth. There is cold curiosity in his clear grey eyes as he gazes down at me.

"I'm sorry," I tell him, trying to appear dizzy. "It's just, the way you're holding me… my heat is starting. If you find it inappropriate, we can stop here."

He says nothing for a moment.

"We can continue," he says at length. "I don't mind."

Oh, he's definitely interested.

I cling close to him as he sweeps me around the dance floor again. His body heat envelops me. Eventually I can feel his rigid interest against my thigh as our legs brush together.

My pulse pounds to have such intimate contact with him already. He only encourages it, his grip on me growing tighter still.

"Is there any truth to it?" he asks after a while. "Your heat?"

"What do you mean?"

"Isn't it just a way of excusing your desires? So you can be exempt from responsibility over your actions? All women have desires, so how can you claim to be any different from them?"

It barely surprises me that he would hate everything about me, even down to my heat. But I can feel his excitement beneath his tunic. His mouth is spouting disdain while his body seems all too glad to take advantage of my vulnerabilities.

"We are not exempt from responsibility," I tell him. "We're taught to correct ourselves. We do not let the heat take over our minds."

"Is that so."

I grit my teeth as he guides me rather forcefully. There is something in the way his bony hands close over me... God, why was my body made to be responsive even to dogs like this? The shame that creeps through me is genuine this time.

He watches me. The sight of me flushing only excites him more. When he spins me away from him and holds me again, there is a renewed strength in his grip.

I've captured his loins, at least. Now I need to capture his head.

"I'm sorry that you dislike me," I tell him. "I wish there was something I could do to make this easier for the both of us."

He pauses a moment and then says, "I'm sure we can work through it together."

Well. That hardly took any effort. Clearly he likes it when I act ashamed and submissive. The heat will help in that regard; I lean into it as we dance more intimately still. If I close my eyes

I can pretend he's someone else, a pretty prince from one of Domnall's stories.

He smells of bitter ale and burnt wood. I press my thigh against his and say, "This coming week… I'd like to get to know you properly. If you'll permit me to."

He keeps our close contact, slowing the dance to better appreciate it. He must know I can feel his erection pressing into my dress.

"That is the purpose of our visit," he says, his voice husky with arousal. "If you truly are what your king promises, then I would be a fool to spurn you. He does us a great favour."

It's working. He's yielding to me.

Now to bring up the subject of the bogs somehow. I rack my mind for some topic of conversation as my heat clouds my thoughts, pulling my focus down to that wildly inappropriate point of contact between us.

"My king is entrusting us to you," I tell him. "I hope what you were saying about the Vikings earlier is true. Did you really earn a truce with them thanks to vengeful ghosts?"

"Well," he says with scoff. "The rest is politics, which I'm afraid doesn't make very good table conversation."

"I've nothing to fear then, when you bring me to your shores. They won't be returning to such a haunted place."

He seems wistful then. "If all it took were vengeful ghosts to dissuade the Vikings, there would be nowhere they could dock their boats."

"So you told a fanciful lie at the dinner table?"

"No lie. A simple embellishment."

"What's the real story, then? What did it take for Thrain Mordsson to leave your shores?" He seems to grow pale when I say that name. It's intriguing. I need to be alone with him if I'm to continue this conversation and eventually steer it towards my brother. When we step through the next phase of the dance together, I smother his erection again. "Or are there some things that I can't tempt you into?"

"Mmm," he purrs. "That depends. To tell a story like that, I believe I would need a good deal of tempting."

"The corridors are dark, my lord. And I am soon to be yours. Surely it would be no sin to indulge early."

That incenses him. His eyes glint with eagerness, bony fingers greedily crooking into my flesh. "Much as I appreciate your boldness, Tamsin, I would not dream of insulting my hosts in that way."

"Really? Even when your hosts have already dealt you many grievous insults in the past?"

"Have you no fealty to your king, girl?" he sputters.

"What is the fealty of a woman worth? When we are but bartering chips for those who wear the crown."

The way he looks down at me brings my heat to a new intensity. It hurts as much as it delights - it is equal parts longing and disgust.

He pulls me across the dance floor, letting a charged silence hang between us as we dance our way across the hall. Stone archways lead off into the darkness of the corridors beyond. As we approach one, I glance over my shoulder at the table where my mother and cousins are sat. None of them are looking at me.

But someone is. I catch Emyrs's eye – he is standing guard behind my mother. There is an anxious look on his face as he watches Aedan take me by the hand and lead me away.

I turn away from him.

It is all too easy to slip away into the darkness.

Chapter 13

TAMSIN

DAY 6 OF THE WANING MOON OF MAY

SOMEWHERE AT THE back of my mind, I know Rhun would be horrified to know what I'm doing.

But much more present in my mind is the fact that soon, if I don't do something, he will no longer have any opinions about anything. And that simple knowledge makes me spin out of control.

Aedan pushes me up against the cold stone wall, his rough hands drawing up my pretty red skirts. His breath is hot and sour on my lips as he leans in to kiss me.

I have never been kissed by a lord before. I discover that it is mostly wormy wetness, my mouth trapped in uncomfortable angles. It isn't very enjoyable until his tongue snakes against mine, sending a streak of unwanted pleasure right through my core. I hold onto his tunic, moaning helplessly as my heat takes hold of me.

"Tamsin," he mutters. "I thought you would hate me."

"I do hate you. I hate all of you."

He grins against my mouth. "What is it that you want, then, if you'll suffer the touch of my hand? A story about the Vikings?

Or something else?"

As he speaks, he buries the stiffness of his desire into my crumpled skirts. I tilt my head back. It's almost too much to keep my mind on the task at hand.

It makes me forget there even was a task beyond utter self-destruction.

His mouth skims my neck while he shoves one hand between my thighs, the layer of my skirts bunching between us. The rugged contact has me sighing mindlessly.

"You do not seem to be suffering much, girl," he says. "Perhaps this is what you wanted after all?"

"No, there is something," I gasp. "There is something."

I'm trying my hardest to stay focussed even as the flush of the heat overwhelms me. I can feel the bunched skirts between my thighs growing damp with my own arousal as he rubs me there.

Aedan speaks into my hair: "Tell me, then."

"There is a boy in the dungeons. My twin brother. He's sentenced to die."

He lets out a cold laugh. "You would have me break a criminal out of your dungeons while we are guests in your house? I don't think that would bode well with your king."

"Do you really care?"

He smirks at me. "Of course I care. What makes you think I wouldn't?"

My thoughts are jumbled from the heat. I glare at him, trying to think of some way to persuade him to do my bidding. There was something about that story he told... something I could twist into an accusation.

"For a savage, bloodthirsty warlord, Thrain Mordsson seems rather easily defeated. If you could chase away the three wolves of Dublin yourselves, then why would you need us at all?" I gauge his expression as I go on with the story. He seems surprised. And there's that stricken expression again when I mention that name. "Unless you never defeated them at all. And you come here as their agents to destroy us with their help, because you could never manage it alone."

"What a wild imagination," he mutters, before leaning closer with a smile. "So you wish to blackmail me? I give you your brother, and you don't go to your king to sow discord between us?"

"That's exactly right."

He chuckles. "You are too clever for your own good, Tamsin."

There is a dull *thunk*.

Aedan stills in my arms. In the next second he is wrenched away and falls unconscious to the floor in a heap.

Emrys stands over him, sword in hand. He must've knocked the man out with the pommel. He sheathes his blade and looks at me with alarm as I lean against the wall, panting, trying to navigate the roaring disappointment of the cold air around me after those groping, hungry hands. I should be relieved, but the heat ravages all good sense like a forest fire, suffocating me.

"Your Grace." Emrys takes my arm to pull me from the wall. I bite my lip so I might not whine with sheer need. "Are you all right?"

I frown down at Aedan's unconscious body, trying to remain in the moment, trying to hold back from begging Emrys to pick up where Aedan left off.

I hate it. My body. My heat. I thought I could keep it under control, but the excitement of law-breaking, the proximity of the dancers beyond this dark corridor, and the hatred I bear for that man – somehow it has added a potent fuel to my heat that I cannot douse by sheer strength of will.

Emrys stabilizes me as I straighten my skirts. I can only imagine how strong my scent must be for him. When he sees how I lean into his grasp, he pinches my chin and tilts my face up so he might look at my eyes.

My pupils must be dilated as wide as the mouths of Hell. His gaze grows heavy with judgment.

"What in God's name were you doing?"

I open my mouth to reply, but can think of nothing to defend myself.

Emrys lowers his voice. "I think you should go to the chapel. I'll wake our guest and explain the misunderstanding."

I shake my head. The shame is overwhelming, as is the urge

to refresh the welts that run across my back. "No, there was no misunderstanding. He knows what I am. I tempted him and he accepted."

"Let me guess. You gave him terms involving your brother's safety?"

It seems so foolish now. He would never have accepted. "I had to try."

"And so you lured him into an agreement that could've placed everything into jeopardy."

"That's not what I wanted. Please don't say anything. I don't want to ruin Uncle's efforts."

Emrys's gaze is hard. "I won't. But we can only hope that your betrothed will keep this to himself, too. I know you are unhappy, princess, but — you *cannot* take risks like this."

"I know. I'm sorry. I'll — I'll go to the chapel."

Swallowing past the lump in my throat, I give my skirts one last pat and hurry away down the corridors towards where my salvation lies.

Chapter 14

THRAIN

DAY 6 OF THE WANING MOON OF MAY

I WALK THROUGH THE castle's winding layout as the evening's
festivities continue, keeping my back hunched so as not to
draw suspicion. Alban monks do not have the stature of a Viking.
The brown robes I am wearing barely reach my ankles.

The week we will spend here as per the Albans' courtship
traditions will allow us to appraise the complexity of the place
and the height of the prize that awaits us. Already in this short
day, we have seen much that pleases the eye.

As we rode back to the fort from Old Kilpatrick, we took a
higher road through the village's surrounding countryside. We
spied farmers tending freshly-planted crops, foresters traipsing
through their wakened woods. Fishing vessels roamed freely
along the river Clyde, pulling up bountiful nets.

No map could reveal the true beauty of this place. It's no
small wonder that the Vanirdøtur might've bloomed in such
fertile and inviting lands.

But the mere fact that they are here at all... I can still barely
believe it.

After the ride, I spoke with Ivar and Olaf for a long time. They were both so confident that the Vanirdøtur are ours by right, only mislaid for centuries and caged by rigid Christian customs. Listening to them both, one would think these women have just been sitting in this castle waiting to be saved. I cannot help but disagree entirely. As Tamsin and Eormen both told us, they are very aware of their own histories, and they involve themselves actively in the fate of their kingdom. They hold onto their stories of war and invasion as cautionary tales, a way of informing their present-day choices.

'Don't our legends warn against mistreating them?" I asked my brothers. "Will we not lose them again if we try to catch them against their will?"

We argued this point for a while. Neither Olaf nor Ivar could deny that after we claimed Strathclyde, it would take a long time for the women to acclimatize to our occupation. And they wouldn't all stay here, either. My brothers have plans to ship them out to Ireland and the northlands – Gofraid wants a number to reside in the Southern Isles, too.

My brothers made plans regarding how to divide the Vanirdøtur and care for them on their trips to their different destinations. But they had not counted on the sheer numbers that we would find here. The sweet honeyed scent never left us as we rode around their farmlands. From the poorest to the highest-ranking families, they are everywhere.

"This is their home," I said. "They will not come quietly."

"Of course they won't," Ivar snapped. "But our people are scattered, and we've been given many favours and made many promises. Plenty of the Jarls who helped us in Ireland only did so because they hoped to be blessed with a sacred spouse by the end of our endeavours."

Olaf nodded. "It's the same for the Southern Isle Jarls who've allied with us for the siege."

"So our Vanirdøtur are to be given away as repayment for old debts," I muttered. "It does not bode well to treat them as such. We would be invoking Freya's wrath."

Olaf slapped a hand on my shoulder. They both commiserated over the fact that it was a gamble, and that they would have to compensate to regain the gods' favour. But then Ivar asked me to imagine it – those women living among us, breaking bread with us. And I cannot deny that a part of me was delighted by the idea.

The Vanirdøtur, our wives, our wisewomen, our daughters. It is like a dream to imagine them meshed into our lives. But the prospect of winning them over, however we go about it, will be an even bigger challenge than the taking of this fort.

ᚦᚱᚾᛁᚾ

My brothers and I agreed to hold ourselves apart from the locals while the moon still affects us. But I couldn't resist looking in on their evening meal.

The royal Vanirdøtur are amassed in the great hall, their glorious scents mingling together. It makes such a poignant bouquet now that night has fallen that I must keep myself at a distance so as not to go mad from it.

It's so *strong*. My blood pounds in my temple, fingers curled into fists as I withstand it even from my secluded corner.

Their dances have strict choreographies I've never seen before. With their glittering robes and jewelled headdresses, it is like peering into another world. It is still so uncanny to see them moving around, fully in control of their movements even as the moon rises and calls us to chaos.

Some are standing in quiet conversation, casually sharing wine and gossip. I try to bring to mind the details of the legends, but I cannot reconcile them with these straight-backed Christian women. There is no mistaking the heady scent of them, and yet they appear no different to the deeply religious women I've known in Ireland.

I can only admire the level of self-mastery they have attained. If the legends are correct, they are all prey to their heat tonight.

The corridors grow darker as I stray further from the main hall. Thick wooden doors bar the way to the rooms of those families who live here. Everyone is gathered in the hall save for a few who take to the corridors for private conversation. Lords and ladies fall silent and nod as I pass, unaware of whom they pay their respects to.

The heat scents are making my head spin. I find a red-painted door that is crowned by their martyr's cross; a chapel no doubt. I push my way inside, searching for respite.

I thought I could handle myself, but this is getting dangerous. Daggers of unspent desire are spearing through my guts, making it difficult to walk. I understand better now why the only Vyrgen they'll allow in these lands are tempered by suppressants – no man could stand in a room full of heat-struck Vanirdøtur without going berserk.

The room is dim, lit only by torchlight. Alcoves on either side host tombstones and stone saints who wear kingly attires.

I dither in one of the alcoves, breathing out slowly to calm my thudding pulse. The place is drenched with gold and silver. The smell of all that precious metal is a feast for the senses, and a welcome relief from all those tantalizing perfumes of flesh and sweat.

Something of the heat-struck woman still lingers. At first I think it's some aftereffect, some scent that's clung to me.

Then I realise I am not alone.

There is a Vanirdottir in here.

My loins tighten as I look around myself. I should go, leave the castle entirely and seek the quiet darkness of our sleeping quarters. But that scent… I know it, I'm sure of it.

Quietly I advance through the chapel, around the pillars that block the nave from sight.

Ahead, at the foot of the altar, a fiery-haired woman is kneeling on the flagstones. She is undoing the laces at the back of her gown. Once they're loose, she pulls away the red wool to bare the soft white shift beneath it.

As I watch, she pulls her arms from the sleeves of the undergarment and strips it down to her waist, baring herself to her god.

I take in a sharp breath. Her back is lacerated, covered in old scars and mottled with purple bruises.

There is some kind of instrument on the floor beside her. She picks it up by the handle. It spills long leather strips as she holds it up.

It's some sort of small leather flogger, the kind we might use on animals.

Her arm moves. Leather flashes across her back, biting into her flesh. The sharp slap of it reverberates in the chapel. She whips herself a second time, over the other shoulder.

I hear her breathing hard as she pauses.

Then she does it again.

Slash. Slash. And a third time.

Her back is red with it as she kneels there. But she continues. My mouth parts as I watch her inflicting pain upon herself. Of all the strange customs I have seen in these isles, I have never found one as repugnant as this.

She is of such precious lineage. The gods themselves have blessed her and her kind. So why in Odin's name would she be pushed to do something like this?

Eventually the pain builds enough to make her whimper and stop. She's breathing with a strange languor, as though she relishes it.

I cannot bear to let her continue.

"Girl," I call out to her in the Gaelic tongue.

She gasps and immediately scrambles for her linens. Holding them up against her chest, she glances over her shoulder at me.

It's Tamsin. The king's niece.

My whole body tenses at the sight of her freckled face. I'm intruding on her – Aedan's betrothed, naked to the waist, a sight entirely forbidden to my eyes. She stares at my monk's robes and sits there open-mouthed, just as lost for words as I am.

"F-Father," she greets me eventually. "I didn't realise you were here."

Father? Why would she – oh. Of course. That term is used as an honorific here. That she would call me that only makes the situation stranger.

I should go, leave her well alone while the scent of her heat drifts around us.

I should go now, *now*, instead of staring at her freckled shoulders and those wide green eyes. Tear tracks shine on her cheeks. She looks so sad, just like before.

With enormous effort, I turn away so I might stare at a stone sarcophagus instead of her nakedness. Everything in me screams at me to leave, to not compromise the situation by straying in the company of this girl while the moon is rising.

But if I leave... I can't just let her resume beating herself.

"You're that monk," she says at last. "You're with the Albans."

Linen rustles in the silence as she pulls the sleeves of her shift up her arms again.

"Yes, I am." Mindlessly, I reach for what a monk would say. "I would not normally interrupt prayer, but... that was no prayer. You should not inflict this on yourself."

That sobers her somewhat. "With respect, monk, you have no say in how we do God's bidding here. Our customs are not the same."

Though she speaks quietly, her tongue is surprisingly sharp for one who has just whipped herself. I chance a look at her and find her covered again in her shift, knots neatly tied at either shoulder. She's coaxing the red sleeves of her gown up her arms, but her body is hunched as she does it, as though the movement pulls at her inflamed skin.

She needs help. I take one step across the flagstones.

No. *No.* Stay away from her.

"Are you all right, princess?" I ask her stupidly, just to excuse my lingering presence.

"I'm fine," she says, but her hands are shaking as she reaches back to tighten the gaping laces of her bodice. She can barely pluck at the criss-crossed pattern.

It is torture to watch her fumble.

"Let me help you," I hear myself say.

She pauses, considers this. She seems just as surprised as I am that a religious man would offer to dress her. Of course no man of my station would offer such a thing. *Idiot.* Her heat makes me stupid as a dog straining to be of service to her somehow.

"If you would," she mutters. "That would be kind of you."

My heart lurches. I want to tell her, *don't let me near you, don't give in to me,* but instead I find myself kneeling behind her before

I have even given my body the command.

What am I doing. Odin, what am I *doing*.

Her scent is as sweet and musky as elderflowers as I draw closer to her than modesty would permit. She allows me to start on her laces, though she tenses to feel me so close.

"Thank you," she murmurs.

Goosebumps prick her skin as the red wool bodice closes over her. I wonder if she senses me despite the deterrents I wear. Perhaps she doesn't realise what it is she's sensing. Perhaps this is the first time she has strayed for very long in the company of an undiminished Varg.

Gods, that scent. It is a feat to dress her with all the chastity of a monk whilst I sit in the mire of it. She is untouchable, I remind myself, absolutely untouchable. There can be no mistakes while we're out here.

To distract us both, I ask her, "Why do you do this?"

"It is how we repent."

"What are you repenting for?"

She lowers her chin. For a moment I wonder if she's even going to answer me. Then she shakes her head, reaching to wipe the tears from her cheeks.

"While the moon still has us... we do things we regret."

Well. I certainly have an idea of what she means. But it seems so cruel that she might punish herself so violently for something that is in her very nature.

"It is only human to have desires," I tell her. "Surely yours do not warrant such cruelty."

"It isn't cruelty but self-correction. Though I understand you Albans give a different type of council to those who stray from God's path."

I try to bring to mind what I know of Alban customs as I pull her laces as tight as her sore back will allow. It is wonderfully bizarre to be trusted like this just because I wear the monk's robes.

"We suggest prayer and self-exclusion," I tell her. "A man must commit a very grave crime before any violence is dealt. And I don't believe a girl like yourself might've committed such a crime."

She breathes softly as she takes in my words.

"You're wrong," she murmurs.

I pull her last few laces together, trying my hardest to concentrate on what she's saying rather than what her scent is doing to my body. "What is it that you've done?"

"You know what we do to our cursed boys, don't you?"

"I do not."

Her hands are still trembling as she holds her bodice against her breasts. She pauses, as though wondering whether she's permitted to tell me her people's customs.

"Well... they're in the dungeons now," she says. "My brother Rhun is among them, and... I can't bear for him to be taken away with the rest."

"What is their crime?"

"Only that they are born with the devil's mark. And though my brother bears it too, everyone knows he's a good boy. He's never hurt anyone in his life. But he failed the wolfsbane trial, and now... now..."

My hands slow as I try to piece together what she's saying. The devil's mark... that is their god of worldly pleasures, which they deny themselves so thoroughly. And the wolfsbane, I know to be a powerful suppressant. I realise with a pang – that is the flower that those guards wear on their tabards.

I see now that their "cursed" boys, their Vyrgen boys, must pass some kind of trial involving the suppressant. And if they fail...

"What is your brother's fate?" I ask her.

"He is to be taken to the bogs tomorrow. To be sacrificed."

My breath catches in my throat.

They would *execute* their own Vyrgen boys?

"I know it's a sin to conspire against my king and the rites of the church," she goes on. "But I would do anything to save my brother. And tonight... tonight I went too far. That is why I repent."

Her laces are done up. Her dress is drawn tight over her slim body. She turns to look at me, and the fairness of her face is almost painful to look upon.

She's achingly beautiful. To see her eyes rimmed with red only deepens my anger.

"I will speak to Lady Catriona about it," I tell her. "There must be a way to save him from such a bleak fate."

Save him indeed. I want to find their dungeons myself and run their guards through with my own blade.

How *dare* they treat young men of my ilk with such disregard?

Not to mention, he is a prince of royal blood. I'm sure the Albans would agree that taking a boy of such lineage could be useful to us while we draw up our schemes for the coming siege.

Her amber-green eyes fill with hope. I realise she's close enough to see my face under my hood – the scar that runs down my cheek, the distinctly un-Dálriadan slopes of my face.

Whatever assumptions she makes about me, she doesn't seem to care. Instead she takes my hands in hers.

The touch of her soft skin sends a streak of primal recognition through me.

Vanirdottir.

Mine.

Surely she must feel it too. She blinks, frowning. But she is still swept up in the gratitude of my offer, so she must think the nascent song in her bloodstream stems from that.

"Thank you, monk," she says. "I don't know if you'll succeed, but... thank you."

I wait for her to move away. But she doesn't. She seems stuck there, heavy-lidded eyes fixed on our joint hands.

It takes all my willpower to pull myself out of her grasp. I want nothing more than to bask in this sensation, wonder at the ancient magic that is waking in us both. As though we had waited all our lives to meet at last.

Every movement I make is carefully controlled. I bow to her, stand up and break away from her, each step a forced effort. When I pass through the red-painted door, I lean against the stone frame, trying to calm the thudding blood in my veins.

Tamsin. The king's niece.

Bless all the gods that the moon has lost most of its potency.

If this were the first night and my rut less manageable… I don't even want to think about what might've happened if we let that sensation cloud our minds.

I will help her, but I cannot let her touch me again.

Chapter 15

Tamsin

Last Quarter of May

T HERE'S SOMETHING ABOUT that monk. An awesome presence I felt in my bones. I had no idea that men of God could inhabit a room like that. He embellished everything around him with the strength of his spirit.

It gives me hope. If he speaks for me, then maybe... maybe Rhun stands a chance.

I twist and turn in my bed all night long. In just a few hours, the cursed boys will be hauled onto horses and led out to the bogs, accompanied by those priests and elder daughters of Clota who are to carry out the rites.

Our guests are not invited to watch. They aren't meant to know that it's happening. Uncle organised games in the King's Garden, challenges involving archery and falconry. We're all meant to play and feast together while our cursed boys file out from the dungeons and head to their death.

I don't get a wink of sleep. My belly is hot with unwanted heat, my back stings from the lashing, and a whirl of nightmarish images keep spinning in my mind. Outside my window, the sparkling constellations progress across the night sky. When the pale blue light of dawn finally emerges, I feel sick with exhaustion and fear.

I push myself up. Maybe I can run down to the dungeons while the boys are being let out. Just so I can see what's going on, whether the monk managed to make anything happen.

I'm meant to wait for Hilda to come wake me and lead me down to breakfast at sunrise. But by then who knows where Rhun will be? No, I'm going down there now. Let Emrys try and stop me.

I stride to my coffers, yank one open and pull on a dress over my shift. I'm halfway up the laces when I hear my door creaking open.

My mother looms in the doorway.

I've never seen her so angry. My insides tie themselves into knots as she stares down at me. She's beyond furious — her face is drawn, her gaze sharp and heavy as steel. She's all but holding me at sword point as I kneel there in my half-laced dress.

I open my mouth, trying to explain why I'm dressing myself in the dark. But she sweeps into the room and the words fall out of my head. I get up, back away to the wall.

She slaps me so hard across the face that I fall against the stone bricks, crying out in pain.

"How dare you," she seethes. "How *dare you*. Do you have any idea what you've *done?*"

Clutching my cheek, I stare up at her, throat tight. I'm too bewildered to understand what she's even talking about.

"Emrys told me about your depravity last night," she hisses. "You convinced Aedan somehow, didn't you? You convinced him to save Rhun. I won't even ask what you did to secure his safety—"

Rhun.

The monk's promise. He must've spoken to Lady Catriona right after meeting with me.

Hope rushes through me. Desperately, I blurt out: "What do you mean? Was he taken out of the dungeons?"

Mother looks as though she's about to tear the skin from my face again. I recoil into the wall, dread and hope tangled together.

"The dungeon guards were corrupted," she says. "Last night Lady Catriona met with them and asked that Rhun be let out on the assurance that I was the one to have issued the order. They were paid handsomely for their trouble. Do you know what this has caused, Tamsin?" Her forehead is veined and craggy with worry as she carries on: "They came to me right after they had smuggled Rhun out. They knew I could not have issued such an order. But they could not refuse Lady Catriona for fear of spoiling our alliance."

She pauses, letting me take in what she's said. But I don't care about their politics – I want to jump with joy at the idea that Rhun has been freed. I want to ask where he is, but she's far from finished.

"Do you know how fragile this alliance is?" she continues. "Now that it's done, I can't protest Lady Catriona's actions. It would affect our relationship very negatively if I accused her of corrupting our men and colluding with our prisoners. You have tied my hands behind my back, Tamsin, you have betrayed your *king* – and for what? Some short-sighted idea of mercy?"

That makes me break my silence. "For what? For *what*? Isn't that obvious?"

"I know you love your brother!" she shouts back. "You think I feel nothing for my own son? But there are larger powers at hand, Tamsin! You know that! God chose to place him among the martyrs. And now you have decided to thwart God's own will!"

"What does God care that the numbers aren't exactly right? What does He care that there's one less boy than there should've been? We're already killing off all our childhood friends – can't He be happy with what He's given?"

Mother looks as though I've sprouted horns. She slaps me again and this time I brace myself against the wall, taking it with a grunt.

"I explained it to you," she seethes. "Time and time again. If these rites are not respected, then why should God protect us? Why should He answer our prayers when we openly disrespect Him?"

I glare at her. I could let out the words that are on the tip of my tongue – that if God wants Rhun to die, then He is no God of mine – but I know they're only half true, and definitely not what Mother wants to hear.

"If anything happens," Mother says, her voice thin and trembling, "if this alliance falls apart and we are defeated after centuries of glory – then you know who is to blame."

The enormity of her words takes me a moment to decipher. "Me? You want to blame me if the Albans turn traitor? Or if we lose against the Vikings?"

"Who else!" she shouts. "Who else conspires with the enemy and betrays our most ancient rites!"

My heart is racing with anger and fear.

She's wrong. It's all superstitions. The success of our armies isn't based on whether or not a specific set of boys died that year. She has no right to place that kind of accusation on me.

Still. The idea is paralyzing. If she's right, if my actions set off some kind of cataclysm – but no, no, she can't be right.

"I have tried my best to find a suitable candidate to replace him," she says. "So that perhaps your misguided actions might be pardoned."

"A suitable candidate?" I stammer. "What do you mean?"

"What else could I do?" she snaps. "The sacrifice must be made. Now that Rhun has been freed, all we can do is hope to appease God by replacing him with another. That is the position you have put us in."

I shake my head, horrified. "But there were only forty who failed the trial. Who—"

"We took a boy who succeeded his trial. You left us no choice. We had to pick one who most resembled Rhun."

My head keeps tilting left and right, *no, no, no.*

"You will come with us," she goes on, her tone imperious. "So you understand how serious this is."

Usually no one is allowed to attend the rites, except the priests and elders who preside over them. I don't even know what the sacrifice itself entails.

I only know the bogs are full of corpses, curled up in their cradles of peat. Romans, Damnonii, early Christians, Strathclyde boys. They say the mists that hang over them are really the spirits of the dead drifting there, waiting eagerly for visitors. Once you set foot in the bogs they drape around you, whisper in your ear until you go mad.

"Finish dressing yourself," Mother commands. She chucks me a black cloak. "Wear this. Once you're ready, meet me at the passageway behind the Cavaliers' tower."

ᛏᚼᚥᛊᛁᚼ

The sky is still a muted kind of blue when I emerge into the courtyard. Servants and villagers are milling around the barns and houses beyond.
Heart in my throat, I cast a look at these people going about their morning like it's just another day.

There are families among them who're going to lose a son today. Some of them stop what they're doing to stare at me. It seems unfair suddenly – that Rhun might've been spared but the others are still being marched away. I could've helped more of them. Why didn't I think of that?

I shake the thought away. There's nothing more I can do now.

I pull up my hood, grab my woollen skirts by the fistfuls and rush along the inner wall, skirting behind the fort's many roundhouses and buildings. The Cavaliers' tower bulges out of the wall, voices already ringing within as the fort garrison wakes. A few steps beyond it, Mother's waiting by a little gate, several Cavaliers with her.

The gate opens with a whine. Within, a roughly hewn spiral stairway burrows down into the foundations of the wall, and further still into the ancient rock itself. We climb down into the damp darkness, hands skirting gritty volcanic rock, until finally we reach the bottom. Another gate, another key turning in a lock – and we're spilled out into the forest. Mother leads us through the maze of moss-covered boulders and trees.

Eventually we step out into the sleepy village. A black-clad group of riders await us in the empty street. Mouth dry, I let my mother lead the way to the pair of horses that were prepared for us, fumbling a little as I mount mine.

Seagulls wheel overhead. Woodsmoke is sweet on the air, the villagers still enjoying the warmth of their hearths at this early hour. I stare at the figures of the condemned, morning fog draped around them like ghosts beckoning them on.

A whole cohort of Cavaliers flank the cursed boys to dissuade anyone from escaping. Several of our priests are watching from the side-lines, seated on a horse-drawn cart that bears a collection of earthenware pots. Heading the procession are five elder daughters of Clota, waving us over.

A sudden thought flashes through my mind. How am I to know that Rhun isn't among these boys? Mother's indignation is good enough evidence, but I need to see them, I need to make sure.

We trot past them and I peer under their hoods, scrutinizing their faces one after the other. They're all pale, bruised and bloody from their stay in the dungeon.

Rhun's not there. I count forty of them, but Rhun's face isn't among them.

I wonder which of those faces is the boy who's replacing my brother.

We set off as a group, the Cavaliers staying at our flanks while the priests tail us. I crane my head to observe the procession of boys. They're all keeping their heads down and their reins slack. What does it feel like to be in their place? Do they think it's unfair? Or do they believe in the necessity of their sacrifice?

How many would run if they were given the opportunity?

ᛏᚼᛉᛋᛁᚼ

The journey to the bogs takes the entire morning. Eventually we're so sunk in mist and ancient gnarled woods that it becomes impossible to tell the time.

We venture deeper into these dangerous lands, following the waystones that mark the path. Sometimes there are red scarves fluttering from the branches of the trees, leading the way. I wonder how old this tradition is, who might've placed those scarves. Whether they were on their way to sacrifice someone they loved.

The cursed boys haven't all been following without protest. Arguments have broken out along the way, shouting matches and attempts to flee on horseback, all prevented by the guards. We have one break to relieve nature's call, and two boys try to run for it again. They're dragged back to our rest stop covered in muck, stern-faced Cavaliers holding them steady.

I've stopped by the priests' cart while the incident is handled. They've all climbed down and drifted away to watch. All save one, who stands by the horses.

He's very tall.

I wonder. Could that be… no, surely it can't be him. My mother would never allow strangers to look in on such a private and sacred Briton practice.

He turns to face me as I come nearer. I take in that beard, that mouth, familiar now after the unlikely evening we spent together.

It's him. It's the Alban monk.

Mother and the women are all occupied with the cursed boys. No one's watching me. I step right up to him so that we might speak more discreetly.

"What are you doing here?" I mutter.

"Lady Catriona wanted to have eyes on the ordeal," he tells me.

My mother's shouted words resound in my head again. By asking him for help, I've betrayed my king, I've betrayed my own people. I've handed the Albans power over us. But I can't bring myself to feel guilty.

"Where's my brother?" I ask him, voice pressed with urgency.

"He waits for us on the river Leven. Lady Catriona took him to our ship. He is setting off with us once the courtship is done."

Relief rushes out of me. I can feel heat prickling my eyes.

He's safe. He's safe.

I find myself gazing up into the face of this strange monk. Just like last night, the gratitude I feel towards him threatens to overwhelm me.

I don't think I've ever felt so strongly towards someone. I'm suddenly glad that he's standing so close, that I can almost feel his warmth enveloping me.

It isn't proper. But right at that moment, I don't care.

"I don't know how to thank you," I manage to say.

"No need," he mutters. "But princess, with all due respect – what are *you* doing here? Whatever this sacrificial ritual entails, I don't see why they would bring a young princess to witness it."

I hang my head. "My mother made me come. She... she replaced Rhun with another boy. I think she wants me to see it."

"To punish you," he says. It isn't a question.

I nod.

From the way he breathes out and glances over at the elder women, I can tell he's appalled by my mother's actions. The strange kinship I feel towards him only blooms stronger at this protectiveness he's showing me.

But he's powerless to shield me from what's coming. He's only here as a spectator.

"Tamsin," comes my mother's voice. She's summoning me back to my proper place.

The monk gazes down at me again, his face still half hidden in the shadow of his hood, the glint of his eyes meeting mine. I still have so much to thank him for. But fear of the imminent ritual eclipses the rest.

"Take care of yourself," he tells me.

"Thank you. I'll try," I whisper. "I – I have to go."

Chapter 16

THRAIN

Last Quarter of May

WE RIDE ON through the misty marshes. I observe the interactions between Tamsin and her mother, who seems to be the head of the elder Vanirdøtur.

I wouldn't have expected to find such merciless protocols in these lands. They are a hard, steely people. But perhaps this is what allows them to keep strict control over how they regulate their population, especially regarding the safety of the Vanirdøtur.

I wonder if those elder women spend every full moon self-flagellating, too. I wonder how many loved ones they have lost to these rituals. How many sons, cousins, brothers.

How they rationalise it to themselves, to put their daughters through the same pain.

Something looms out of the mists beyond. A great dark oval, eerily growing closer. As we approach, we discover a huge stone statue of a woman. She's holding out her hands as though in welcome, her body lacking detail owing to the sheer age of the statue. Spiral patterns have been carved into her curves, a style that reminds me of ancient Irish stonework.

At her feet, a ledge of solid beaten earth steadily gives way to a large circular pool. The surface of the water is milky and stagnant, emanating a foul stench of decay.

The priests I'm accompanying halt the cart. They busy themselves distributing the pots all around the stagnant pool. In front of every pot, a boy is forced to kneel by the Cavalier guards.

The women watch the procedure from the foot of the stone statue. They pull down their hoods, revealing long grey hair fashioned into plaits. Tamsin's mother is younger than the others, but her royal lineage clearly hands her the authority. Tamsin stands beside them, wide-eyed and fearful.

Her mother turns to the statue while each boy is held in his place by a guard.

"O Clota," she intones, and then continues in Brittonic, barring me from whatever spell they are weaving. I recognise the word they use for their Christian god, and as their invocations continue, I feel a strange pull in the mist, as though the air were growing heavier, wetter, waterlogged with intention. Shivers run down my body as they enter into conversation with whatever forces inhabit this place.

They turn and walk slowly around the circle of kneeling boys, touching each one on the head in passing. Blessing them, perhaps thanking them for their sacrifice. I wonder at what power a Vanirdottir holds in her hands – I had not expected their deep knowledge to extend into the realms of death.

But then, it isn't so bizarre. One who is knowledgeable in the creative powers of life itself must learn to walk the boundaries between worlds, and guide the condemned to secret places.

Once the blessings are given, the guards each slip braided leather ropes around the boys' throats.

Then they begin to choke them.

I watch, mouth parted, as these young boys struggle as best they can. Some chuck their shoulders around as they try to escape the noose – others accept their fate, only for their bodies to jerk and twitch once their lungs begin to protest.

They are unwilling.

I am watching forty unwilling sacrifices die. Forty unwilling Vyrgen boys.

My hands ball into fists. My throat burns as I stay rooted to my spot. If I move even a muscle, I know I will launch myself at the guards, all forty of them, and tear out their throats without further thought. It is daytime and yet the urge for violence is as strong as it has ever been.

Breathe out. Count to ten.

The boys are going to die in the time it takes me to calm down.

One after the other they each fall still. They seem to have fainted – the guards let the nooses go once the boys are slouched over their earthenware pots. If the guards had wanted to kill them, they would've kept choking them for longer.

I frown. This isn't the full ritual. Something else is coming.

The elder Vanirdøtur begin to walk around the circle of prostrate boys. They step up behind them, lean over them, and reach for the boys' throats.

For a moment I wonder if they're removing the nooses.

Then I see blood. Pouring like so many fountains from the boys' necks. Collecting below in the earthenware pots.

The women stride between the boys, leaning over each one to slice their throats. By then I have stopped breathing, cold shivers running through me as I feel the steel against my own neck.

They would've done this to me, had I been born here. Had my body rejected the wolfsbane.

Each boy slumps further against his pot as his body regurgitates every last drop of blood it contains, his heart pumping each spurt from his sliced flesh. The Vanirdøtur complete their task and re-join at the foot of the statue. Only one boy remains uncut, kneeling unconscious over his pot.

Tamsin stands there, staring, shaking. Her mother presses a dagger into her palm.

The implications are loud and clear. Again I have to repress the urge to step forward and command them to leave her out of this. She's so scared – I'd wager she has never killed a man in her life. Why would they involve somebody so completely unprepared in such an important ritual?

She looks to her mother, her eyes pleading. But there is no room for any protestation. Her mother points to the final boy, the one who has taken Rhun's place.

More punishment. More of their strange idea of repentance.

But this is no Christian custom. This is far more ancient. Perhaps that's why there is so much blood.

Tamsin is pushed forward by the elder women. They guide her until she's leaning over the ginger boy who is not her brother, who could've been her brother, who's dying in his stead.

I want nothing more than to pull her away, shield her from the cruel lessons of her elders. Surely one cannot properly contribute to this type of ritual if their presence there is punitive, if their actions stem from fear.

But these are their customs – I am here to observe, not interfere.

She's sobbing. It's easy enough to understand the gist of what she's saying.

I can't, I can't, please—

The elders encourage her, their tone firm.

My heart thuds in my chest to hear the fear in her voice. Gods, if I could only break out of this damned stasis – she needs my help, she needs someone to pull her out of there!

The women don't let her escape. Tamsin tries to focus on her task but she keeps slipping, she's trembling so hard. She holds herself over her victim, frowning in concentration, trying to force herself to do the deed. But her body doesn't seem to be heeding her commands.

Her mother leans over her to guide her more closely still. The woman's hand closes around Tamsin's and moves with deadly precision. They cut the boy's throat together.

Blood gushes over their fingers. Tamsin drops the knife once it's done. It sinks into the bog, sending a red curl of blood into the stagnant water.

I can only watch as Tamsin staggers away from her victim. She falls down on the floor, unable to stop staring as the boy slouches over his pot. Her panicked gaze flicks between him and her bloody hands. She holds them up in front of her, ogling at her reddened fingers.

The Vanirdøtur each go to the statue of their Clota and press their bloody hands into her giant stone palms. Tamsin's mother picks her up off the floor and guides her to the statue so she might do the same. They each say something in a language I don't recognise as they do this – Clota's hands grow red with fresh blood as they make their offerings.

Their role in the ritual seems to be finished. While they face their stone ancestor, the priests pick up the blood-filled pots and stow them in our cart. The guards push the bloodless boys forward so that they keel into the pool, one by one, a slow fall into their milky grave.

And it is done.

ᚦᚱᚾᛁᛪ

The priests expect me to help them heave the pots into the carts. Each container is stoppered by a cork lid, but I can still see the blood in my mind's eye, sloshing around in there.

I wonder why this blood is being kept, how it's going to be used. Thinking back on Tamsin's story, the women cut the Vyrgen boys' throats just like Clota did. This blood… perhaps they'll spread it around the perimeter of their lands, just like in the story. Perhaps they'll till it into the soil to better repel us and bring us bad fortune.

Even now the potency of their ritual presses around me, the air grown thick and difficult to breathe. By helping the priests with this task, I'm helping them to guard their lands against us. The idea of handling the blood of unwilling sacrifices already repulses me, my body recoiling at the idea of picking up these pots.

I grit my teeth and do what I have to do.

Much harder to ignore is Tamsin, the hunched figure she makes in the corner of my eye. While the others mount their horses and ready themselves for the journey back, she stands by the bog, staring down at the water.

Her mother drapes an arm over her shoulders in a comforting sort of gesture. There are hushed words, a gentle tone meant to soothe Tamsin's fear.

I doubt that woman can be of any comfort to her daughter whatsoever, seeing her role in this ceremony.

Tamsin lets herself be steered away from the bog. The elder Vanirdøtur help their youngest back to her horse and then disperse to mount their own. I turn back to my own task of securing the pots in the cart.

My hands are shaking. If even I feel this sickness in my chest, I can't imagine how Tamsin must be taking this.

I glance back at her once the cart's ready. She hasn't mounted her horse. She's standing there wringing her hands as though trying to get every last smudge of blood off them.

The elders are engaged in discussion with some of the guards. They aren't paying attention to her.

Damn it all. I can't just leave her there like that.

I hop down from the priests' cart and stride over to her. She's breathing hard through her nose, her eyes fixed sightlessly ahead of herself. When she senses my presence she jerks her head around as though waking from a dream.

"Princess." I take out a waterskin from my inside pocket and uncork it. "Here. Hold out your hands."

She does as I say. Her fingers are crooked like talons, as though they had ceased being a part of her body. I splash water over them and wipe them with my burlap sleeves, careful not to touch her skin.

"It's done," I tell her. "It's over."

Her mouth opens but no voice comes out.

"You had to do your duty. It's all over now."

Feebly, she says: "But... that boy... if it weren't for me—"

"If it weren't for you, that boy would've been your brother."

She watches me clean her hands silently for a moment.

"We have all done regrettable things for the people we love," I mutter.

Her reddened eyes meet mine. "Surely you haven't *killed*—?"

"Yes. I have."

She stares. "But you're a monk."

"I wasn't always." I reach her wrists, wiping away reddish residue there. "And I'm sure even a religious man would do his best to protect those he loves."

Her hands are clean now. She seeks me out beneath my burlap sleeves, finds my bare hands and holds onto them without warning.

Gods. It's like she's pulled me against her. I let out a breath as that profound joining shimmers through my veins as before.

She closes her eyes as it envelops her, too.

She needs it. I let her hold onto me a little longer, trying to push down the light-headedness that's creeping through me.

"This is the first time for you," I murmur. "I know it feels like it has changed the core of who you are. But it hasn't. You will get up on your horse, ride back to the castle. And everything will keep going as before. You'll meet with your brother once the courtship is up and you'll be glad and happy again. You'll see."

Glad and happy, indeed. I know what awaits her far better than she does. It pains me to offer her false comfort like this, but perhaps it will appease her to imagine good things ahead.

"How?" she whispers. "How can I do that? That boy – how could I just go back to my life when he—"

"That boy served his purpose," I tell her, reaching for their logic. "Just like all the rest of them. This sacrifice was necessary for the good of your country. I'm sure he understood his role. He had his duty, just as you had yours."

She chews her lip as she mulls over my words. I know we should part – the others will be ready soon, I shouldn't linger here with her.

"You're going to be all right, princess," I tell her again. "You'll see. Think of what awaits you while we ride to the castle – a good hot meal and the warmth of the hearths. Don't dwell on this."

She nods, though she looks far from convinced. I know she'll dwell on every detail of this ritual in the hours it'll take us to reach Dumbarton fort.

I step away from her, but she holds on.

"Monk," she whispers. "Will you meet me at the chapel tonight? After supper?"

Her offer takes me off-guard. She stares at me imploringly and I think of all the warnings I have given myself.

It'll be the last night of my rut. I shouldn't risk it again. But, that sadness of hers… I can't leave her like this.

"I will," I promise her.

Chapter 17

Tamsin
Last Quarter of May

THE COURTSHIP IS meant to last a week. It's tradition, and it also serves my uncle, so that he may gather the troops that he's sending with us to Dál Riata. The armed envoy is meant to protect us on our journey over the Firth of Clyde, and to serve as the first gesture of solidarity between Strathclyde and Alba.

A whole week. It's unbearable. To think I must spend so many days eating and traipsing around the grounds with this stone in my belly and Rhun waiting all alone on the river. And Aedan, God, Aedan – having to face him again after all that's happened!

I know the monk meant well, but I have nothing to look forward to. Nothing to be eager about. Perhaps just the thought of my brother now that I know he's safe – but his face blurs with the innocent boy's, and I feel my hands grow hot and clammy with guilt.

This evening marks the last night of my heat. We have another feast, punctuated by music and dancing and tales of our forefathers' glory. Mother tries to be gentle with me, but her reminders to stop looking so wild-eyed and haggard don't do much to make me feel better.

I can't believe she presides over those rituals. I can't believe she's been doing that all these years. I can barely look at her without wanting to vomit.

Aedan's acting cold and aloof again. I would be thankful for it if he didn't send me these strange sly looks from across the table. Clearly he's wondering whether another opportunity will arise for him to scrabble at my skirts again.

His obvious interest would be mortifying if I still cared about our relationship at all. My mind is full of mist, my hands beginning to itch horribly. I keep scratching them under the table until my mother stops me.

I can't wait to see the monk. I've reached for the healing of holy men before, but never has anyone had such an effect on me as he has. Perhaps in Alba they achieve a higher peace than here, a higher degree of holiness, growing rugged and world-wise as they travel among pagan Picts and Vikings.

When Aedan finally plucks me off my seat and takes me to dance, everything feels unreal. Couples and buffet tables lurch around me in a slanted carrousel. I step on Aedan's toes, amble woodenly around him until even he notices something's wrong.

Eventually he stops us, annoyed at my poor manners. "Your Cavalier gave me ample apologies and explanations for your behaviour last night," he says. "You don't have to be ashamed."

I want to laugh. As if our little corridor drama had any importance now! As delicately as I can, I push away from him. "I feel unwell," I tell him. "I think I'll go to the chapel, if you don't mind."

He seems amused by my discomfort. "The *moon* still governs you, does it?"

He says it like he still doesn't believe my heat is real, like I'm just overcome with whorish lustful feelings. It's amazing that he can't tell the difference between heat-stupors and genuine distress.

The moon is still low; my heat is a gently glowing coal engulfed in the wild storm of anxiety that inhabits me. I don't want to dignify his drivel with a response, so I nod. He opens his mouth as though to make some lewd proposition but thinks better of it.

"Of course, Your Grace," he says with a bow. "Take all the time you need."

I stoop into a curtsey, hating the intent in his gaze as he watches my every movement. He seems delighted that I am so discountenanced.

I turn away from him and stride decisively out of the hall.

ᛏᚼᛃᛋᛁᚼ

The corridors are peacefully quiet. I trail my hands across their cool stone walls as I make my way to the chapel. The cracks and nooks remind me of the treasure hunts we would go on with my brother. We would stuff secret notes in the interstices between the stones, leaving clues for one another. Even now, a childish part of me hopes to find a small wad of inked cloth waiting for me, bearing a coded message only I can decipher.

Our old rituals are long gone now. And he is far away on the river, destined for Dál Riata just like I am.

When I see the red-painted door of the chapel, a lump starts forming in my throat.

How will I ever be able to tell Rhun what I've done?

Where should I even start? There's so much to say.

The Albans. The monk. Mother's long bloody history as ritual master.

That boy... God, who was he? I don't even know his name.

I stand in front of the chapel door, looking at the flaws in the paint and the copper door handle. I'm not sure how long I stand there until I remember the monk must be inside already, waiting for me.

I open the door and step across the threshold. He's lit several torches and candles around the chapel so that a soft golden light fills the place. I find him standing before an ancestor's tomb, hooded as always, gazing thoughtfully up at the cross that hangs over the stone sarcophagus.

The sight of him is familiar now. The dark brown of his robe, the way it falls in layers over his broad shoulders, cinches at the waist, then falls all the way to the floor. The slack, pointed hood, the hands tucked into his sleeves. It's funny, when he's among others he's always stooped. Now he's standing at his full height and the hem of his robes are hitched up his ankle, revealing laced leather boots.

Though he's Alban, though he's part of the crowd who will whisk me away soon... he is the only one among them that I'm glad to see. He is the only one who knows the extent of what I've been through these past two days, and helped me through it.

He helped Rhun. He saw... he saw what I did. For my brother.

And yet he did not judge me for it. He didn't look at me like I was monstrous.

My throat is burning as I look at him. I think of how his touch reverberates through me in a way that I can't explain. Like I am touching divinity through him.

I need that again. I need his friendship more than ever.

I march across the chapel towards him. He hears me, turns his hooded head. He seems surprised that I show no sign of stopping. Then he understands my mute request, because he holds a hand out in an invitation.

I all but collapse onto that outstretched hand. My fingers close around it, two shells adhering to solid rock. His bare skin is warm and rough with callouses. I slide over them, shaking until my fingers lock around his and clasp us together.

I sigh and close my eyes as relief ripples through me. Tension seeps from my shoulders until I'm almost hunched over that point of contact. He's standing close enough for his scent and body heat to wrap around me. Already that peculiar scent of his is comforting to me – it's like he's sewn dried herbs into his robes.

"Thank you for coming," I mutter.

"Of course."

Where there was tension, now there is only a frail scaffolding holding me up. I catch the iron-wrought fence next to us, trying to keep from falling. But my knees are crumpling like sodden parchment.

"I'm sorry," I mutter as I lean more heavily still against twisted black metal, all but sliding down. The monk follows me down until we're both kneeling there in front of the fence, hidden in the shadow of the stone sarcophagus.

"Have you had something to eat? Drink?" he asks. I nod.

"I feel so sick," I tell him. "I don't know what to do with myself."

"You don't have to do anything," the monk murmurs. "You should rest tonight."

I stare down at that hand I'm still holding, the way his palm is turned up for me. He has all sorts of scars slashing across it. I turn it over, observe his salient knuckles, the weathered look of his skin.

I wasn't always a monk, he told me.

"The person," I start, pushing the words past the lump in my throat. "The... the first person you killed."

He waits as I try to get the rest out.

"How... did you do it?"

He thinks for a moment, perhaps lining up the words. Then he sighs.

"I was young," he says. "I thought, because I had seen other men do it, that it would be easy. That it was just a question of moving your hand in a certain way. Wielding the knife in a certain way."

With the way we're seated, the torchlight doesn't reach any part of him, not even his beard. I stare into the deep shadow of his hood as he speaks.

"My mother," he mutters. "She was vulnerable for a time. Men sought to take advantage. So I protected her."

"So the person you killed – he deserved it?"

"I would say he did," he says. "But I still felt the same sickness as you. The first time you see death, the afterimage of it haunts you."

The cold of the flagstones is seeping through my skirts like bog water. For a moment it almost feels like talking to Death himself, with the way his face is plunged in utter blackness.

"In Brittonic we call him the *Ankou*," I murmur. "Death. I feel like I donned his robe today. And now I don't know how to get rid of it."

He grips my hand tighter and then offers to pull me up.

"First," he says, "you come back into the light."

I take a breath, holding both him and the metal fence. With a little effort, I manage to haul myself back up onto my feet. Torchlight glints on the curve of the monk's lip, touching enough of his face for me to see that he's wearing a soft smile.

"You must give it time," he says. "There was powerful magic in that ritual. Your elders made an exchange. Blood for protection. Trading death for the continuation of life. It is the oldest prayer there is. Anyone who deals with ancient magic of that kind must take time to recuperate. You must eat, live, walk in sunlight. Then the cape of the *Ankou* will gradually fall away until you wear none other than your own."

I fiddle with the metal points of the fence, heart thudding. He has a way of talking about it that makes it sound less horrendous somehow. Once imbued with purpose, the boys' deaths seem less tragic. It's what my mother has been trying to teach me, to accept that they must die.

The monk eases out of my grasp, steps back and inclines his head, inviting me to walk. I fall into step beside him as we wander away from the tomb and further into the small chapel, taking in the peace of the sanctuary.

"You must allow yourself time to heal," he says. "Like that bruising on your back, this will fade eventually if you give it time."

A pang runs through me at the reminder that he witnessed my flogging. It is a strangely intimate thing to have experienced with someone else, especially someone who doesn't understand it. Now that he's seen even more of our customs, I wonder just how insane he thinks we are. Then again, judging by his calm and benevolent attitude, I'd say the pagan tribes of Alba must have desensitized him to the vagaries of faith and enduring customs of our ancestors.

We've come to the altar. A golden cross stands in the centre, glowing in the candlelight.

"Do you treat that bruising at all?" he asks quietly.

"Not really. It's nothing serious," I mutter. "Mostly I just let it heal by itself."

"You should use a comfrey poultice. It's good for bruises and broken skin."

Clearly he won't let up until I promise to take better care of myself. "I don't know if our priests grow that. I'll have to ask them."

He nods. "I've seen the chapel gardens outside, they do grow it. If you'd like, I could make you some."

I sigh. "Fine, fine."

He considers me a moment. "You shouldn't treat your ailments lightly, princess. For tonight, I'd also advise a strong infusion of valerian and honey. And wine, too."

I can't help scoffing at that. "I should've taken advantage of the buffet in the hall. Oh – wait."

I know there's some good restoratives in here. Turning away from the monk, I kneel in front of the altar and flip the tablecloth up, revealing a set of carved wooden doors. Inside are candles, goblets, and many dusty wine bottles.

The monk lets out a laugh. "So that's why you come to this chapel often."

"The ones at the back are imported from Francia," I tell him as I reach inside. "West Francia, now. The vineyards of Aquitaine." As I place one onto the top of the altar, I glance at the monk, suddenly realising his station. "Unless you find it offensive to drink from the priests' stash?"

He steps up to the altar, intrigued by the squat wax-sealed bottles I'm unearthing.

"Surely not," he says. "I'd be a fool to turn down good wine. But, princess – I'm not sure this is a good idea."

"The priests never notice anything. They aren't too holy to keep from drinking between ceremonies."

"No, I meant… wine would do you good, but not *ten bottles* of it."

"I'm not going to drink all of them," I tell him with a tired smile. "There's still so much of the courtship to get through. I'll need to keep some for later. I just can't remember which ones are the good ones."

I fiddle with the cork of a half-empty bottle. He arranges the earthenware cups for me, looking thoughtful.

"What do you think of Aedan?" he asks.

"Well," I say as the bottle pops open. I pour deep black wine into two cups, then hand him one. "How would you feel if you had to marry that man?"

He takes the cup. For a moment I see something like guilt or shame flash through his face, his brow furrowing, eyes searching the table. But he schools his expression as always.

"I'd probably drink fine wine from West Francia."

"Well, there you are then." I lift up my cup, only too glad to not linger on the subject. I clink my cup against his. "We say *yec'hed mat.*"

He repeats it solemnly: "*Yec'hed mat.*"

His face is still so shadowed as he lifts his cup to his lips. The earlier impression of speaking with the Ankou endures, sending chills through me. I know I'm not drinking with Death himself, but some lingering superstition makes me gesture at him with my cup and say, "You can't drink with me and keep your hood up. That's just bad manners."

He considers me a moment. It might be some Alban custom of modesty or some such, but he hasn't minded the boldness of my requests up till now. And I can't help but be curious to discover the face of the one Alban who's been kind to me.

Finally, he sweeps the hood down. Candlelight touches the contours of his face.

I stare at him openly.

His eyes are deep-set and a piercing blue colour. His cheekbones are wide and well-defined, underlined by a well-trimmed blond beard. It follows the square line of his jaw, leaving space for his shapely mouth.

His hair is very long for a monk, drawn up in several braids over his skull before being set loose again over his neck. The lengths of it disappear into his robes.

What stands out the most is the mark on his left cheek. A cross, like the mark of a branding iron, covers his cheekbone. The old scar reaches up to cut across his eyebrow. It's a small wonder he isn't blind in that eye, if he was branded in such a crude way. Strangely, though it evokes violence and pain, it only adds to the rugged elegance of his face.

He... does not look anything like a monk.

I am suddenly and quite rudely reminded that my heat is not over. I may be on the seventh and last day, but the mere sight of him is enough to stoke what I thought were smoking embers.

I look down at our cups as colour rises to my cheeks.

He might not look like one, but he is a man of God. It is inappropriate to feel that way towards him.

I dig my nails into my palms and repeat it to myself.

I am in control.

I am in control.

"*Skål,*" he says, visibly amused by my reaction, and clinks our cups again.

We drink.

"Oh," he groans after draining his cup. He's squinting as the wine fills his mouth. "This – how old did you say this was?"

I grab the bottle, glad for the distraction. The inkwork is smudged and faded with time. I hold it closer. "It looks like... eight-hundred and twenty-two."

He laughs. "You're giving me wine that's almost fifty years old? I thought the point wasn't to poison ourselves."

"Oh no, I thought it was still good! The Francs call them – what was it – *vin de garde,* wine that matures with time."

"Mmhmm. You can show off your language skills as much as you like, princess. This is still foul. It has black crumbs at the bottom."

"All right, all right." Smiling, I reach for another. "Here. How's this one. Still West Francia, looks like it's... ten years old this time."

"I'm trusting you," he says, offering me his cup.

Chapter 18

TAMSIN

LAST QUARTER OF MAY

W E TRY THE wine and comment on the quality. For a
blissful moment there is only the acrid taste of wine in
my mouth, his deep voice in my ears, our laughter ringing off the
high ceiling. The world is tucked away behind the chapel door.
Tonight it can do without us.

We move around the altar, lighting all the candles on the table
so that it glitters. The flagstones are cold under our shoes, so we
unroll one of the sheepskin rugs on the floor, the monk kneeling
there first. He holds up a hand for me – covered in burlap, I
notice – and I lean on him, making an effort to not stagger on
my way down.

"Careful," he says. "We wouldn't want to stain the sheepskin."

"I'm not *drunk,*" I protest. "I'm just tired. A reasonable level
of inebriation is necessary at this point."

He knows what I mean. He has the tact not to bring up
everything I've endured over the past few days again. Together
we sip from the East Francia vintage that we've discovered, a
sweet young wine that blooms in the mouth.

The moon is rising. I can feel it. I know better than to drink too much, even if this is my last day. As soon as the heat begins to grow more intense, I'll leave.

"I don't mean to spoil a rare vintage with this subject," he says, "but it still saddens me to hear that your betrothal is... dissatisfying."

Just thinking of Aedan makes me take a large sip of wine. "I never expected a satisfying betrothal. I don't think it's rational to have high expectations when you're destined to a man you've never met."

"Eormen seems to be content with her match."

"Eormen is a good actress. We both know marriage is more about endurance than anything else."

He stares into the red ripples of his cup. "Endurance," he echoes thoughtfully. "A fitting descriptor for the people of this kingdom."

"Is that the impression we give, then?" I ask him. "You're sure it isn't more along the lines of madness and the smell of bogs?"

He scoffs indignantly. "Far from it. This is a beautiful place."

"Hmm. I'd say it traps you with its beauty. I've been longing to leave for years."

"Is that so?" His deep, smooth voice is giving my body reason to rise against my will. I smother the heat firmly. I'm going to have to leave soon.

But I don't want to leave. It's so cosy in this chapel, this enclosed sanctuary I've known forever. And he makes such a good drinking partner. Conversation should delay the heat, so I throw myself into it. "I always knew it was my fate to be wed to some foreign noble. But I never took it seriously. I thought I'd be long gone by the time I turned eighteen."

"What made you stay?"

It would take too long to go through all the convoluted conversations between Rhun and I on the subject. I finger the rim of my cup and summarise: "I suppose I was just afraid of being alone out there."

"Mm. I understand. I come from faraway lands, too. When you are removed from the place you grew up, where all your old habits and rituals were... it is no small feat to find happiness among strangers."

I frown at him. "Faraway lands? I assumed you were Dálriadan."

"I am from further north."

"Pictish, then?"

He smiles down at me. "It matters not. It is in the past. Like you, I was destined to go further than comfort dictated."

"I suppose there is some similarity between monks and princesses, then. Both of us are moved by higher powers. Neither of us can be masters of our fates."

He seems intrigued by the thought. His blue eyes roam over my face. I realise too late that I'm staring at him, that I'm letting the uncanny beauty of him capture me.

"What would you do, if you were master of your fate?" he asks me.

I smile back at him. "Funny you should ask. I always wanted to travel, actually. Only, I would go to places of my own choosing. My brother and I... we had a plan to travel all over Ireland and then the coasts of Francia in the south."

"You wouldn't go north?"

"To the realms of the Vikings? If we were armed with some invincibility cloak, why not," I say with a laugh. "I would go everywhere, see everything if I could. But it is a child's dream."

"It is no child's dream. It is the spirit of a great adventurer that inhabits you. Dál Riata will be the first stone in your edifice."

I can't help the rush of affection I feel for him as he comforts me. He always seems to find the right words. I glance down at his hands, curled as they are around his cup, trying to quell the desire to take them in mine as before.

"You're kind to say so. But we both know I will never taste that kind of freedom."

"That depends only on you."

As he says it, he is the one who reaches between us. He takes my empty cup from me and his fingers brush mine.

My desire for him surges in an irresistible wave. I blink, feeling suddenly as though I had drunk too much wine. The roughness of his skin, the warmth of his palm... God, why does it fill me with such longing? The rest of my body aches to feel that warmth against it.

The moon must've risen to its apex already if I'm responding like this. I should go.

"You must fight for what you desire," he says. "No one can know what the Norns have in store for them."

I have never heard that word before. It must be some Gaelic turn of phrase. But I am far too distracted to ask him about it. Even as he gets up to place our goblets on the altar, it is like all of my soul is still focussed on the tingling in my fingers.

How those craggy knuckles fit around mine. How our fingers thread naturally together before he broke away. It had to be intentional.

I feel it as though he had slipped his fingertips between my legs. My pulse there throbs so insistently that it is all I can do to keep from rubbing my thighs together to relieve the need. Even when Aedan kissed me, it didn't affect me as much as this tiny, insignificant contact. It's incomprehensible. I'm growing slick with arousal, my cheeks flushing as I wonder if he meant something by it.

God, no, he is a *monk*.

I push myself to my feet. He's lingering near the altar, arranging the cups and bottles, oblivious to my struggling. I shouldn't approach him – but I can barely hold myself up straight. I step beside him, intending to lean against the altar. It seems suddenly a long way away – my hand catches in his robes as I steady myself.

He grasps my shoulder to stabilise me. "Princess," he says, and I stare stupidly at the folds of his hood, his beard, those wine-stained lips. "Perhaps that's enough wine for tonight."

"Mmm." He's so close. Heat pulses through me as I stand there, revelling in his presence, the warm weight of his hand on my shoulder. He moves slowly and his fingers find my bare neck, sending pleasant shivers down my spine. The words *I'm not drunk* leave my mouth but I barely hear them, barely register my own mouth moving to form them.

He's so close.

I can't think any more. All that exists is that point of contact. His fingers sink into my hair as I lean closer, his nose coming against the crown of my head, breathing me in. It hardly lasts a second – he gently pushes us apart again, reining himself in.

"The moon is rising," he murmurs. "We should go."

There's a tremor in his touch as his hands curl around my shoulders, poised to peel me off him. But his fingers are digging into my shoulders almost possessively. I try to wade through the thickness of the heat as I dare myself to explore what pulls us together, to enjoy it.

It's strange. He makes me feel like I could do anything. It's the first time in a very long time that I haven't felt quite so impotent and powerless. I dare myself to hold his gaze longer than I should, and his eyes darken as he realises my intention.

Desire glimmers in my veins as I feel his grip tighten. He decidedly does not look away.

"Stay," I whisper.

Both of us are poised to push the other away, but instead we're holding one another, mindlessly appreciating this heady proximity. He rubs his thumbs against my shoulders and I utterly melt into his touch.

"I can't," he says, trying to sound firm.

I watch his mouth form the words. I could not command my body to break away from his if my life depended on it.

I think of what it was like to kiss Aedan. How much better it would be to kiss a man I want. How shapely his lips are, how soft and well-trimmed his beard looks. And his scent... earthy herbs and rich red wine.

I'm pulling at his robes, lifting my chin, making a demand of it.

His gaze is fixed on my mouth, looking at me with naked hunger. His breath has gone shallow as he considers the outrageous proposal.

"I can't," he says again, without much conviction.

His face seems to be coming awfully close.

I can feel his breath on my mouth. We're far too close now for propriety. This is not how a monk should behave. Nor is it how a royal princess should behave. But God, I want this – I have wanted it since he first took down his hood.

We both act against our better judgment.

He brushes his lips against mine. Limp with heat, I can do nothing but moan with the relief of it. It isn't anything like what Aedan did – his mouth moulds mine irresistibly as he deepens the kiss, his tongue filling me like a primal claim.

I forget that he is a monk, that I am betrothed, that everything about this is wrong. I hold onto him, the burlap rough and prickly against my fingers. He kisses me until I am dizzy with it, until I feel there is nothing else I would want to do than this – lose myself in the texture of his lips, the sharp edges of his teeth, the hot wet curl of his tongue.

There is no understanding the belonging I feel as he kisses me. I can only revel in it. Like I have come home at last.

Chapter 19

THRAIN
LAST QUARTER OF MAY

S HE TASTES OF wine. Rich, red, dripping. The roundness of her lower lip guides my tongue, invites my teeth. I bite down upon it, open her mouth, penetrate it.

It is all a blackness of breath and desperate desire. It sucks me in like the horizon at night, like the deep black sea.

She is so vast. Her hunger is all around me, her body all I can touch. My fingers glide down her neck, into her hair, cup the curve of her skull.

Like woodsmoke, her heat grows stronger and more suffocating still as I breathe upon her, enrage the fire inside her. Like woodsmoke, it draws out the wildling in me just as surely as the sight of blood might.

She wants to be mated. I can see nothing else than that invitation, that darkness, the sweet-smelling smoke that curls within it and lures me by the nose.

Catching her waist, I lift her up and sit her on the altar amidst the many lit candles. Her thighs open around my hips, her whimper ringing in my ear as I wedge myself between them.

When I kiss her again, she winds her arms around my neck

and sinks her hands into my hair, pulling me further against her. Her body fits against mine so perfectly. We both belong in this unity, her hands in my hair, my mouth joined with hers.

There is so much of her to feel. Her soft cheek, peach fuzz against my fingertips. Her hair, guiding me down in twisting turns, swallowing my fingers until they're lost in a curling lamb-soft labyrinth. Her neck.

Her neck.

My mouth opens against it. Here, her scent grows prickly, sharper, more defined. More *her*. I touch my tongue there, trail down that long white track, taste it, taste her. Plant my teeth in a shallow ridge so I might swallow more of it.

Mine. She's mine. She's *mine*.

The claim rumbles in my throat as I bite harder, pull her closer. The low growl vibrates in my chest and in hers too, surely, she's all but part of me now – her legs wound around mine, her arms attached to my back like ivy.

She moves, pushes. Detaches. Her voice is as a susurrus of water sliding between us.

"Monk."

No, she can't break this, can't break away from me. We'll both fall apart. We'll both break to pieces if the light finds us outside of each other, outside of the darkness.

I cling; she pushes harder.

"Monk, please."

I blink.

The growl ceases. My throat and chest are oddly empty without it. Too wide. Cavernous.

Her moss-green eyes are on my face, pupils blown wide. Her mouth is swollen, puffy, half-open. Why is she looking at me like that? Why is she separate from me? Why...

Oh.

Oh, Loki's *cock*.

I was kissing her.

I'm standing between her thighs, holding her face, my forehead tipped against hers. Kissing her. Touching her in ways that are far removed from what's appropriate.

"You growled," she murmurs. "Are you... are you cursed?"

She clings to me, so supple and warm in my arms. Cursed, she says. Cursed by the devil. But she doesn't seem afraid of the concept. Kissing a cursed man. Even as she says it her eyes are heavy-lidded, her breaths slipping between those parted lips in shallow, excited bursts.

"Yes."

The confession hisses between my teeth. Dimly, in this moment of clarity, I remember I should not say so. It's vital that we keep the secret. Weave herbs into our robes. Else the Britons will suspect.

But she is beyond suspecting. She wears my bite-mark on her neck, my saliva on her lips, my scent on her clothes, her hair, her breath.

She knew even as she asked me.

Another question: "Do you take the wolfsbane, in Alba?"

She knows the answer to this one, too. If I took the wolfsbane I would not be wedged between her thighs, delirious at the mere sight of her, inhaling the potency of her heat.

"We don't take it," I tell her. I'm only too aware of the irony as I say the next words: "We practice self-discipline."

Her gold-dust brow arches, pulling up a net of freckles. There's a hint of a smile playing around her lips.

"Self-discipline," she echoes.

Even as clarity endures and brightens my mind, I still can't break away from her. My forehead leans against hers again, heavy as a rock, fitting itself in its rightful lodge. To stop and suffer this sudden awareness is intolerable. All of me aches to sink again into her delicious darkness.

"I'm sorry," I tell her. "I'm not... I never lose control. But, your scent... you... I can't resist you."

She lifts her chin, makes a soft noise. She's taking it as a compliment rather than an admittance of weakness.

Painful, painful clarity holds onto me, plants hooks in my mind to prevent me from falling into her.

"We should stop," I tell her.

"No," she whispers. "I want this."

Those words. Those *words*. I push them away and they seep between my fingers, cover my hands in ink, swallow my arms. I can't resist her. I can't. Why should I resist her?

"The moon governs you," I remind us both. "Like it governs me."

"The moon readies me for anyone," she whispers. "But I am choosing you. I would choose you even in daylight."

"No you wouldn't," I tell her, a whimper, a whine. She has me – all I can do is delay. "Not a cursed man. You know how this could end."

"I know. I've heard." That mouth, so close to mine again. Wine on her breath. "I want it."

She doesn't mean that. Can't mean it. Stop taking her seriously – stop, stop this ballooning warmth in my chest, this staggering pride that a woman like her would choose me beyond all good sense. But it is the highest victory imaginable – who needs any other accomplishment than this, her words feather-light against my mouth, her approval, her desire—

No. She doesn't know me. She doesn't know who she is choosing.

"You want this?" I ask her. This – what we both refrain from naming, what I cannot, *cannot* give her.

The thought allows my mind to stay afloat. But she pulls me against her, and my body moves by itself. I draw up her skirts, wool and linen bunching over my forearms. My fingertips skim the tender skin of her inner thigh. She takes a breath, sharp and shuddering.

"You want this?" I drop the words into her open mouth.

My hand finds the moist juncture. Her nether lips are sticky with arousal. My fingertips slide easily between them.

Her eyes are locked onto mine, heavy-lidded, dilated pupils black as night. I trace the outline of her inner lips, brushing against the sensitive bud that tops her entrance. Her thighs quiver around me as I explore her contours, knuckles sliding over her wetness.

"Yes," she sighs. *"Yes."*

Gods. The feel of her. I'm lucid enough to remember that I

cannot give in to the impulse of burying my aching cock inside her and mating her. That would be pure madness, given the situation.

But neither can I pull away from her. Not now. Not when she is holding me so close and whining her need in my ear. Perhaps she is like me, her heat confined to the same limitations as my rut. Perhaps if I give her release... she will recover enough lucidity to save the both of us.

I slide two fingers into her. She tenses in my arms to feel me stretching her, burrowing inside her. The pad of my thumb finds her engorged bud, rubs against it. Before long she is grinding against me, her hands caught in my hair, her mouth against my ear sighing her pleasure.

I hope to Freya that she will recover after this. Because the way she's clenching around my fingers... *gods*, no man could touch her like this and keep his sanity.

She leans back, pressing a hand down flat against the altar top to take her weight. The angle lets me drive deeper into her. Her eyes squeeze shut, head tilting back, baring her throat to me. Distantly I hear something clatter, a metallic ringing in the air. The golden cross lies askance among the wine bottles.

Neither of us care.

Her body tenses, and she arches her spine as the climax overcomes her. She clenches all around my fingers, holding me in a vice-grip, and I can only watch her and take in every last detail of this scene; her neck, her red hair strewn over her shoulders, the sweat-slick domes of her bosom straining against her bodice. Her open mouth. Divinity shining through her as it explodes from my fingertips.

"Oh my *God*," she moans, and I grin to hear her invoke the one we are so blatantly disrespecting.

I cup her mound with my palm, fingers curled inside her, moving in time with her hips as she rolls them against me. Her breaths come in ragged gasps, and then they start to catch in her throat as the climax wears itself out.

She leans against me, recovering. Her breaths turn to something else; shivering, tearful gasps. I slide out of her and hold her around the shoulders as she comes down from the high. Those gasps are beginning to sound like sobs.

She's crying.

This isn't right. This isn't good.

Clarity shines upon me like the full force of daylight at the sound of her weeping. I cradle her against me and she buries her face in my neck, her tears smudging against my skin.

The vestiges of my rut are making my mind hazy. I try to retrace the steps, see if there was anything I did that might've hurt her.

Maybe she regrets it already. I should never... ah, Freya help me, I should never have touched her.

Perhaps she didn't want me after all. Perhaps she only wanted to break herself against me. After everything that happened earlier ...perhaps this is her alternative to self-flagellation.

"Tamsin," I murmur, drawing back so I might look at her face. She's tucked in her chin, her mouth raw and swollen, freckled cheeks shining. Her eyelids are lowered, pale lashes spiked with tears.

"I'm sorry," she hiccups. "I don't know what... there was just... a lot."

I lean in to kiss her eyelids. It's been a very long day. After everything we discussed, it's hardly surprising that her climax might've brought other feelings to a head. "I didn't hurt you, then?"

"No." Her dewy eyes catch mine. "No."

She all but snuggles against me, so I drape my arms around her shoulders again, careful not to touch her bruised back. Though she's hauled me out of the moon-craze at last, it's still a feat to manage my rut in the thick scent of her climax. I breathe in and out slowly, concentrating on the details of our surroundings to fix my attention elsewhere than that gorgeous, tantalizing nectar that clings to her.

The lit candles all around us are burning low. We've knocked over several empty bottles, and the altar cloth has purple blotches on it from wine spills. Our cups are off on the corner of the table where I put them, one of them knocked onto its side.

What a mess.

I allowed this to happen. How could I allow this to happen? We didn't even drink that much. This girl... I shouldn't have underestimated the pull she would have over me. I should've left after the first sip of wine, after the conversation had unwound into laughter and familiarity.

Ah, gods... Olaf and Ivar are going to skin me alive if they hear of this.

"We really should leave now," I tell her. "While we're lucid."

"Should we?" she mumbles. "If we just stay here, maybe no one will notice. Maybe they'll go to Dál Riata without us."

"Mmm." The prospect of staying here with her is absolutely not good to pacify my rut. I force myself to be realistic. "Princess... once we leave this chapel, we'll have to avoid each other for the rest of the week."

She draws away, frowns down at my chest as she takes the full meaning of my words. "I'm... I'm sorry. I didn't mean... I didn't want to lose your friendship."

For a moment I'm lost for words. I almost ravaged a daughter of the gods and she thinks she's the one at fault. For wanting me.

Again that pride of being deemed worthy surges. Again I strangle it.

She would not deem me worthy of her if she knew who I was. What I planned to do.

"You haven't lost my friendship," I tell her, the words a string of barbs. "But you shouldn't be around me during your courtship, whether you meant what you said or not. Now that this has happened, it wouldn't be prudent."

Her eyes flicker up to mine. A touch of embarrassment lingers in her face, but she still holds my gaze. "I did mean it."

I brush tear-slick curls from her cheeks. "Princess. You don't know me."

The rebuttal makes her frown. "I know you're a decent man. I know you're the one person in Dál Riata that I'll be glad to have as a friend," she mutters. "There is little else that makes me glad about the coming weeks."

I take her words and stow them carefully away, knowing that

soon she will want to take them back. Once the heat no longer rules her. Once we set everything into motion. But for now... I let them warm me as they sit like embers in my chest.

As I slick back her hair, I uncover a faint bite mark on her neck. I run my fingers along the reddened grooves, equal parts appalled and thrilled to have placed that on her.

"Do you have a collar or scarf you can wear?" I ask her. "To hide this?"

She smiles, bringing a hand up to feel the mark. "I do."

We both linger there, staring stupidly at one another. I hold her face in my hands, thumbs following the curves of her cheekbones.

To think I will have to reveal myself to her.

It will hurt her so much more now that this has happened. Now that I've allowed her to grow close to me.

Bang bang bang.

Both of us jump. Someone is knocking on the door of the chapel.

Princess! Princess Tamsin? Are you in there?

Tamsin swears, jilted into a more alert state. She groggily shoves me away so she can slide off the altar, then takes my hand and pulls me after her. "There's an exit behind the pulpit – just over there, come on."

I let her lead me out into a cramped unlit corridor. We paw our way through absolute darkness until the corridor spits us into a larger hallway. This one has windows, at least. Moonlight filters in, slicking a silver outline over us. Tamsin leans by the small door we've just exited, listening for whoever interrupted us.

"Cavaliers," she says. Then adds in a mutter, "They'll put out the candles."

She closes the door and turns to me.

I gaze at her beautiful flushed figure. Her dress is a crumpled mess, her eyes still glazed from climax, her lashes jewelled with tears.

"Where do you sleep?" she whispers.

"Outside the castle, at the leatherworkers' house."

She nods and points into the darkness. "You'll have to go that way."

"Where do you sleep?" I ask her, and the corner of her lip curls up.

"I'm not sure I should tell you."

That smile of hers... it's very dangerous. She's right to keep certain things to herself. I drift towards her despite myself, so she presses her back against the wall.

I know I will never be able to let this happen again. It's only by sheer strength of will that I have kept from claiming her at all – and it's vital that I don't further compromise our alliance with the Albans. Not now, not when everything has gone smoothly so far.

But the knowledge that I will have to keep myself away from her only makes this parting more difficult.

She's panting already as I lean closer to her. When my palm comes against her cheek, she closes her eyes, leaning into the contact.

Mine. The claim sings through my veins. *My Vanirdottir.*

She clasps my wrist with both hands. "I can't just avoid you," she whispers.

"You'll have to," I hear myself say, hating our situation, hating that she is not mine.

She smells of wine and sex and rich black earth. I'm close enough to kiss her one last time. I catch her lower lip between my teeth and she moans, forgetting where we are as I plunder her mouth with my tongue.

When she breaks off I hold onto her tighter, furious that this night must end, furious that I can't follow where she's headed. That I can never touch her again.

"We should go, they'll come and check this corridor," she says. "*Go.*"

And in a flurry of linen and wool skirts, she's slipped away into the darkness.

I take in the last of her glorious scent and turn to march in the direction she pointed.

Idiot.

Idiot.

Chapter 20

TAMSIN
Waning Moon of May

IT'S LIKE I'VE stepped through a veil and am wandering through the land of the fae. Everything is tinged with gold, and my insides have turned to freshly sheared wool.

After a flogging, the heat is usually crumpled enough by pain to no longer be an issue. That is how I have always defeated my deepest heat-stupors. But now… it's as though the surge of heat has burnt itself out in a triumphant blaze, leaving me soft and tired and content, eyes bleary and out-of-focus in the aftermath. I'm still blinking slowly and moving through the castle as though tearing my way through long translucent curtains.

My legs can barely carry me. Little jolts of pleasure spark in my belly as I take one step after another.

What *is* this?

It's like he's unlocked something within me, something I had no idea my body contained. A deeply buried treasure that once opened, drenches everything in gold.

It takes all my concentration to arrive at the staircase that leads to my room. The Cavaliers' steps echo in the hallways — they're headed my way.

I try to force my legs to climb the steps faster. I wonder what they will make of my fae-touched state if they catch me. I can barely feel anything other than dizzy satisfaction.

I've just reached my door when the torchlight reaches me. Emrys and Kelwynn appear in the curve of the stairwell.

"There you are, Your Grace! Your lady mother wanted to know where you were," Kelwynn says. Then he abruptly stops and frowns at me. "Are you alright? The chapel… we feared there may have been intruders."

With a pang, I realise that both he and Emrys can sense how strong my scent is. This climax has made it noticeable even to me. Emrys glances at my bedroom door as though he might want to check for intruders.

"I was just going to bed," I mutter, too frazzled and bone-tired to think of anything better to say.

I wonder if he knows what to make of the scent I bear. Perhaps before making their vows, some cursed boys learn about this – *thing* – with the farm girls they tumble into the hay. I know Rhun has never told me about anything like this. But Emrys…

From the look on his face, I'd wager he knows the exact reason behind my flushed cheeks and languid posture.

"What happened in the chapel, princess?" he insists. "You were there. I know you were there. Your scent was all over the place."

It's so hard to concentrate on him. My heart thuds heavily in my chest at his implications.

"There were wine bottles," he goes on. "The altar cloth was rumpled."

"What do you think, Emrys?" I snap at him, reaching wildly for a way to word things that won't incriminate the monk. "I was drinking. Do you want to go and tell my mother that I was drinking? I think she won't be too surprised to hear it. Why don't you ask her where she dragged me today?"

Emrys seems too astounded by my behaviour to say anything. Kelwynn glances at him and then speaks more gently; "We know where you went today, princess."

"Well then." I push the words past my tight throat. Everything is on the surface, my soul shimmering on my skin. "Maybe you could show yourselves to be understanding for once." I open my bedroom door in a burst of inspiration. "Do you want to look inside, Emrys? See if I'm hiding Aedan under my bed? Or can I go and sleep?"

"That's — that's not necessary."

"Grand. Well then, good night."

I shut the door in both their faces.

ᛏᛁᛦᛋᛁᛏ

I lay in my bed that night, unable to control my whirring thoughts. I keep feeling the monk's mouth on mine, the hot slippery contact making my mind swim. I close my eyes, thinking of my flogger that lies in one of my coffers. I know the correct thing would be to fetch it and apply it to cleanse myself.

But… the fae glitter still clings to the walls around me. For the first time, I'm beginning to question why we would shun such a thing.

Even in prayer, I have never felt so filled with belonging. There was something sacred about our joining, like I was swallowing light from his lips.

My hand wanders down my body as I lie in my bed. I let my fingers sink between my thighs and trace the paths he took.

I find a round, swollen bud, like a pebble lodged in rain-slick petals. When my fingertips skim over it, it sends ripples of pleasure through me.

I snatch my hand back. No, it's… it's not right.

Pleasure must not be chased. I know that. I've always been taught that.

It is not my place to question the teachings of our Lord.

Ha! Says the girl who just had a monk's fingers shoved up inside her.

And not just any monk. A cursed monk. An Alban who does not take the wolfsbane.

I think of him carrying me away like in the stories, bundling up his prize for a night of sinful indulgence. What should serve as a cautionary tale only stokes the brazier in my belly. My body arches, mouth parting as my fingers linger where they should not.

Self-discipline. His own will was all that kept him contained. I would've found it hard to believe if he hadn't demonstrated it, pausing when I asked him to, staying alert to how I was feeling. He is a fully-grown man, his curse as potent as the devil meant it, and yet he was completely capable of holding himself apart from me once I stopped begging to be touched.

My hand stills. I begged him. That's what I did. I lost all control. I... God, I sat there and kissed him and *insisted* even after he asked to stop.

I bury my face into my pillow, fighting between shame and the overwhelming satisfaction of climax. Even now my fingertips set off sparks with each new step they take across my body, tiny fairies skipping across a freshly bloomed flowerbed.

I wonder what he thinks of me now. If he regrets what we've done. I'm the one who made him do it. I insisted until he cracked.

Perhaps Aedan was right. Perhaps I use the heat as an excuse when in fact I am just a greedy, whorish woman. Who else would've waylaid a monk – a *monk* – and dragged him down into debauchery in God's own house? That's what Mother would call it. *Debauchery.* Emrys recognised it in me too, from the look on his face.

I think of those daughters of Clota who are shunned for indulging in sin, who live outside of the villages in dilapidated stone huts. Whores and witches. Everyone says so. Whores and witches who turn the heads of honest men. They are what every mother tries to protect their daughters from. *Take the flogger, stay on God's path. You don't want to end up like them.*

With a frustrated sigh I turn over and wedge both hands under my pillow, determined to ignore the insistent heat. The monk told me we'd have to avoid one another but really, he must be the one who wants to avoid me at all costs. He must regret giving in to me. He'll think I'm whorish now, just like Aedan does. I gave him every reason to think so.

Once dawn comes... I'll have to apologise to him somehow. And then return to my duties.

ᛏᚾᛉᛃᛋᛁᚾ

The sun rises at last, announcing the end of my heat. As the days of the courtship succeed one another, I'm terrified that people might know what happened. Especially Aedan. Surely it's written all over my face – I must be wearing some vestigial blush, some redness in my lips plainly indicating the kiss that still lingers there. I style my hair so that it might hide the bite-mark until it fades – those few days have me hyperaware of my neck, the long column of it, how visible it is when I move my head a certain way. But Aedan sees nothing. He loses all interest in me after my heat is over. I constantly find him too occupied with Arlyn or my other royal cousins to talk to me. We both remain cordial towards one another when circumstances thrust us together, but our conversations are stiff as always.

He can't possibly know. No one knows. But the sheer stress must be why our conversations keep failing – I can't concentrate, I can only stammer vapid pleasantries and hope against hope that he doesn't bring up the monk.

I throw myself into the games and social gatherings that Uncle Arthgal has organised, trying my best to fulfil the role that's expected of me. Thankfully, all this agitation allows me to keep my mind off the bogs, the cursed boys, the chapel – all of it. Mother drifts around me, encouraging me to socialise, showing her approval when I make an effort. She's forgiven me, it seems; she clearly thinks my role at the bogs has set the balance straight again.

Lady Catriona is all too happy to fill her son's absence and stay by my side to talk with me. Though she never mentions the business with Rhun, I can't help but feel it has tied us closer together. She excuses her son's behaviour, telling me that he's always preferred the company of men, that he's too brutish to appreciate good conversation. She makes a joke of his manners, absolving me of all fault.

Her gentle kindness allows me to breathe at last. If she knew about that night in the chapel, she would not be so friendly towards me. And I know her son wouldn't have kept such a thing from her, had he something so grave to share. It's all the reassurance I need to stop mindlessly fretting over it.

So many secrets already, and this is but the start of my life with them.

ᛏᚼᛉᛋᛁᚾ

Mercifully, the monk makes himself scarce just as he promised he would. He only contacts me once, and he does so indirectly.

He goes through Hilda. She's been fussing over me quite a bit ever since the day of the bogs. Mother warned me not to tell anyone that Rhun is still alive – but I couldn't lie to Hilda, I just couldn't. I endured her shining eyes and brave smiles for all of one evening before it tumbled out of me.

"You can't tell anyone," I told her even as she burst into happy tears and hugged me tight. "You have to promise. No one can know."

As far as I know she's kept her promise. But she still can't quash the quiet glee that inhabits her as she potters around my quarters, preparing my clothes, bringing me cups of valerian. I insist on the secrecy of it every time I see her and she only ever says *yes, poppet, I know,* and resumes her jubilant pottering.

One evening after supper, she helps me out of my gown and then fetches a bundle of white cloth. Without saying anything about it, she sits with me on my bedside, clutching it in her lap.

"So," she says. Curiosity radiates from her, but she keeps her tone curt. "I received this today. On my way back from the washhouse. A monk came to deliver it to me personally."

Instantly, my cheeks burn. God, let her not see it!

"One of the Albans," she goes on. "I didn't get his name. I asked, but he wouldn't give it."

That makes me blink and stare down at her bundle. I never got his name either. How could I have kissed the man and never even got his name?

"He said this was a poultice for you," she goes on. "Comfrey. For your back."

I wring my hands in my lap. Hilda gazes at me sternly.

"Are you hurt, love?" she asks. "Did something happen?"

"No, no," I say quickly. I don't even want to hear her theories. I can't admit to her that he saw me half naked. "I... I just. I corrected myself during a heat night and it hurt more than usual. I got to talking with him and he mentioned he was good with medicine. He noticed I was hurting, so... he must've wanted to do me a favour."

Her eyebrows arch up. "Let me see." She's pulling at my shift in the next second. I can't do anything but let her untie the knots and pull down the back so she might see my bruises.

She sees the state of my back all the time. I'm always bruised from corrections – after a full moon she knows to expect fresh purple marks. Usually she only gets concerned if I break skin or if the bruising is particularly extensive. She runs a cold hand down my spine, making me twitch.

"You look all right to me," she says. "You feel all right?"

"Yes, I feel fine," I assure her. "A bit achy, maybe. But no more than usual."

"Well," she says with a sigh. "He prepared it for you. I took a look at it and it all seems fine. Do you want to try it? He said to wear it overnight."

She holds up the bundle so I can see the pulpy green purée in there. I take a sniff and wrinkle my nose.

"Smells like horse feed," I say, and Hilda laughs.

"Won't be any change from your usual perfume, then."

I lay down and Hilda winds it around my back, securing the poultice with long linen bandages. They hug my torso, applying a comforting sort of pressure while the comfrey tingles on my back. I hug my pillow as I lay there, thinking back on that evening, how this almost feels like he's embracing me from afar.

My heart lifts as I ponder the gesture. Perhaps this means he doesn't hate me for making those advances on him.

I catch Hilda before she leaves. "Hilda, will you tell him something for me? If you see him again?"

Bowls and bandages in hand, Hilda turns to me patiently. "Yes?"

"Can you thank him for me? And can you... can you tell him I'm sorry?"

"Whatever for?"

"He'll know what I mean."

From the way she narrows her eyes at me, I can tell she's bursting to ask more questions. But it's nighttime, and she's got to get herself to bed too.

"You girls," she says, shaking her head. But she promises to do so, and leaves.

ᛏᚼᛇᛋᛁᚼ

She has his answer by the next day. She comes to my bedside to help undo my gown, and after talking about the infinitesimal advances of my courtship, she looks at me with that twinkle of curiosity in her eye.

"I saw that Alban monk again," she says. I turn to her a little too eagerly.

"And?"

"He said you have nothing to apologise for. And that he hopes the comfrey did you some good."

Heart pounding, I nod and try to appear nonplussed. My hand is itching to touch my neck, though I know his bite mark is no longer there.

He forgives me, then.

"You're smiling," Hilda says. "What is going on with you and that monk? You ought to be careful, Tamsin."

"Nothing's going on," I tell her with a nervous laugh. "He's a monk, Hilda. What do you think could happen?"

She cocks her eyebrow and gives me a world-wise smile. "There is a man under every monk's robe, girl. You would do well to remember that."

ᛏᚼᛇᛋᛁᚼ

As the days wear on, my thoughts stray more and more to Rhun, all alone out there on the river. I can't bring myself to ask Lady

Catriona about him when she's been carefully avoiding the topic. I know my monk might be able to tell me how he's faring. But clearly he's taken this perilous attraction of ours seriously.

He and his fellow monks vanish entirely for days at a time. I can only appreciate the diligence with which he holds us apart. When I do see him on the outskirts of a crowd or from afar, the rush of reminiscence is almost too much to bear. I find myself thinking of the simple pleasure of his company, the ease of conversation, and the deep respect he had for me even as I pulled him into sin. If he strayed longer around me, I know I'd succumb to the temptation of secluded conversations again.

He's protecting us both. I'm grateful to him, though it doesn't come without frustrations. Especially regarding the question of Rhun.

Only once do I willingly stray into his company again. During an evening feast towards the end of the week, we pass one another in the corridors. He slows and acknowledges me, letting his fellow monks continue on their way.

"Your Grace," he says with a bow. His hood is up again, his expression hidden from me.

"Monk."

Palpable tension hangs in the air between us. I need to ask my question and leave him be.

"Is he well?"

Instantly he understands my meaning. "He is. He eats and sleeps with our crew who keep him hidden. Everything is fine."

It infuriates me that he might be so laconic about it, but there is no other way to evoke this thing we've done. I can barely even grasp how deeply I've betrayed my own uncle by conspiring to save Rhun like this.

But I don't care. I only want to see him. Even the prospect of leaving my home forever is secondary to this yearning. With the courtship almost up, I should be thinking about Aedan and the journey that awaits me – instead I'm only glad that each passing day brings me closer to seeing my brother again.

"Thank you," I tell him.

He bows again and leaves without another word. As he passes

me, I catch a hint of herbs, linseed oil and red wine. I breathe in, close my eyes.

Then I go on my way.

Chapter 21

TAMSIN
NEW MOON OF JUNE

THE FINAL EVENING comes at last.

This is the last time Eormen and I will feast in these halls. Come morning, we will sail to Dál Riata with our new family.

I never really prepared myself for this moment. I never thought it would finally come. But that evening, I'm restless for entirely different reasons.

Only one more sleepless night to bear, and I'll be able to see Rhun. Despite the trust I have in my enigmatic monk and Lady Catriona, I won't be able to rest until I can see him again with my own eyes.

I dance with my betrothed that night, and manage to smile as my cousins throw petals on us to bless our union. We'll be wed at Dunadd fort, the Dálriadan stronghold that I'm headed for.

Eormen is the one with the most important union. She is the centre of attention, with her crown of flowers and the gold-embroidered Alban dress she's wearing.

My cousins dance with her in turn and group around her to weep for her departure. She holds onto them and makes a great show of how she'll miss them.

I'm glad for my own lesser importance. I don't want everyone to judge my performance of grief and gratitude. With everyone's eyes on Eormen, I can sit with Hilda and Cinnie and talk with them. They are the ones I will miss most fiercely. They hold me when I take to my own weeping, and I inhale their fragrances, trying to commit them to memory.

It's not quite real yet, the idea that I won't see either of them for a very long time.

The next morning, they take all the time they can to ready me for the journey. But after a while there are no more broken stitches to repair, no more ribbons to tuck away. I hug them both against me one after the other, a giant ball in my throat. My hands are trembling. It's like saying goodbye to my own mother. It's *worse* than saying goodbye to my mother. Hilda and her daughters – they're my family, my true family.

Eyes shining, Hilda gives me one last smile, one last cheek rub. Cinnie ties a ribbon around my wrist. She has my red Hunter's Moon dress folded over one arm; her face is wet with tears.

"Be brave, sweetheart. We'll write to you."

I turn away at last. I have not cried like this since I thought I was losing Rhun forever. To live so far away from the woman who raised me, from the girls I grew up with… how am I meant to bear it?

How does anyone?

ᛏᚼᚤᛋᛁᚼ

We line up in the courtyard for our last public goodbyes. Prince Domnall embraces Uncle Arthgal, and Lady Catriona thanks Aunt Beatha for the gracious welcome. I gaze on the faces of my royal family, stiff and numb as I say my own goodbyes.

When I get to my mother, she clasps my hands and gives me a solemn nod.

She's no stranger to the duty of marriage. She's from the erstwhile kingdom of Rheged, the one that was engulfed into Strathclyde thanks to her marriage. She had to leave her home behind when she wed my father. The sight of her drawn face reminds me of the lessons she's diligently drilled into me over this long week. Have dignity. Bear a woman's role with grace.

I don't know how to feel as I look at her. She's done too much to me, she's hurt me too deeply for me to feel anything but confusion and vague guilt for not feeling more.

I nod back at her.

Then our hands fall away from one another, and I'm forced to turn away.

Eormen and I mount our steeds. I'm only too glad that I can take Cynan with me; Lady Catriona graciously allowed it, telling me with a smile that she would not dream of parting a Briton from her horse. We set off with the Alban royals, accompanied by traps that carry our coffers. The three monks direct the Galloways that pull the traps, riding ahead of us. The sight of my monk's drawn hood brings me salutary warmth.

Surely once we're out there in Dàl Riata, I'll be able to talk to him again.

I ride alongside Eormen. She's pale and regal as she holds her chin up and tries to embody the strength of her status. As the eldest of the king's daughters, it's her duty to uphold a façade of confidence. Especially now that she's stepping into the unknown with me.

We're both alone among our new allies. Whatever might've separated us before, we only have each other now. And Rhun of course, but she doesn't know that yet. We share a glance, and Eormen smiles at me. She's trying hard as always, but that smile gives her away; she's more frightened than I've ever seen her, but she's determined to keep it tucked away.

Duty first.

Uncle Arthgal's troops are waiting outside the walls of the fort, spaced out in the King's Garden. They've drawn quite a crowd as they stand together, resplendent in the green and gold stripes of Strathclyde. They accompany us with great fanfare down to the river Leven, making a show of our kingdom's might.

Cheering crowds await us on the riverbanks. We have to ride in front of them, dismount as gracefully as we can and display ourselves for all to see. I keep my head down, keeping close to

Eormen. She is the one who is most acclaimed – she smiles and waves to the masses like it's no hardship for her to be so avidly watched. It used to annoy me to no end that she had such natural ease and confidence – it made her seem pompous and arrogant. Right now though, I can only be glad of her strength. I'm discovering that it's a very useful shield that she shelters behind. I duck behind it gladly.

Our fleet is docked along the length of the Leven. Our soldiers climb aboard their own ships, leading several Galloways onboard those that are built to take horses. I watch anxiously as one of the soldiers comes to take Cynan from me.

"Cover his eyes if he gets nervous," I tell the soldier, who grins.

"I know, princess. We'll take good care of him."

We head for our Dálriadan vessel. My breath hitches when I see it. It's a deep-bellied contraption with two-dozen oars and a single white sail. The scarlet panels of the forecastle flap softly in the wind.

My brother must be in there somewhere.

I expect to see him rush out and lean over the bulwark to greet us – but of course, they would've warned him to remain hidden. As soon as our group starts up the gangplank, I run up the flimsy wood, my skirts bunched in my fists.

The crewmen greet us cheerfully, pushing off their benches so they can stand to attention for us. They laugh as I pass them, pretending to catch me and calling after me in heavily accented Gaelic. I indulge them with a smile and dive into the forecastle.

Rhun isn't there. It's empty save for plush furs and a single large crate, surely provisions for the journey.

When I step out again, several crewmen have gone down to help the monks with our coffers. They greet one another with excessive familiarity, even slapping the monks on the back and laughing with them, breaking the solemnity of their office.

Strange. They must keep very different customs in Alba.

I watch them heave the wooden crates up the gangplank and towards a trap door at the rear end of the ship. That trap door – it must lead to the hold! I've never been on a deep-bellied ship like this one, I hadn't expected there to be a hold. They must be keeping Rhun down there!

Eormen calls out to calm myself as I rush to follow the crew. I hear her sigh and excuse my behaviour to Prince Domnall as I push past them again. He laughs at my enthusiasm, grabbing my arm to stop me.

"What's gotten into you? River bug crawl up your dress?"

"I need to see him," I blurt out. He must know about it. If Lady Catriona sanctioned it, then surely they all know. He raises his eyebrows.

"You'll see him soon enough," he mutters. "We need you up here so your people can enjoy the sight of their lovely princesses a little longer."

So he knows. I bite back my childish pleas and tuck in my chin. That's right. I have a duty, just like Eormen does. And I owe this family a great debt now that they've all contributed to my brother's safety. I grudgingly follow Aedan to the bulwark and wave to the crowds as they bid us all farewell.

ᛏᚼᚤᛋᛏᚼ

Our impressive fleet opens the way for us as we head down the river Clyde. The sight of Dumbarton fort retreating behind us is not unfamiliar – I've taken plenty of trips down this river before. But it's difficult to look at the fort on its hilltop and convince myself that this is it.

We're leaving.

Perhaps not forever, perhaps we'll be able to visit – but we will never call that place home again.

I'm too preoccupied to feel as nostalgic as I should. Home, to me, has always been where my twin and I can roam and explore and curl up together around hot cups of honey-milk. Right now, the hold of this ship tugs at my attention far more than the steadily retreating fort.

At last, once we are far away enough, Aedan frees me from his side. Eormen demands to know what all the fuss is about, so I tug her after me, heart pounding against my ribs. She won't be pleased, I know it. She'll ask how I accomplished such a thing, and I'll have to parse out what I can say and what I should omit.

Right now, all that counts is Rhun, seeing him after this interminable courtship.

Aedan comes with us to help open the trap door. While he holds it, I clamber down the ladder and hop down into the darkness of the hold.

The room is low and dim. It smells overwhelmingly lived in. I have to hunch over to move around, shuffling between thin shafts of sunlight that peak through the cracks in the planking.

Crates and coffers line the walls. At the back, sunlight catches on steel and studded leather. Squinting, I manage to make out huge round shields and stacked blades. Strange. Why would there be shields and weapons on a transport ship? Perhaps the crewmen are meant to act as our guard now, and those shields belong to them.

A door leads off to a small cabin. Discarding the shields and the foreboding in my chest, I run to it and knock on the sturdy wood.

"Rhun! Rhun, are you in there?"

"Tamsin? Is that you?"

It's his voice. God, it's his voice. Laughter rushes out of me at the sound of it.

"You're here," I say giddily. "I was so worried—"

"Tam, you need to go back to the castle *now*."

My hands are flat on the door as though it'd help to feel closer to him. "We're on the Clyde, Rhun. You're safe now. We're setting off to Dál Riata, you and me and Eormen. Aedan's going to let you out—"

"Tam, you don't understand. The crewmen aren't who they say they are. You've got to go. Jump ship. Swim back to the fort. For God's sake, *run.*"

Stomach lurching, I turn around to find Eormen climbing daintily down the ladder. Her long blond hair sways as she finally sets foot on the groaning planks. Above her, the trap door squeals shut.

Both of us stare up at that little square of wood. That foreboding feeling comes back in full force as darkness closes in around us.

"Did they just lock us down here?" Eormen frowns up at the door, and then over at me. "What's going on? Who are you talking to?"

"Tam," Rhun says urgently. "The Albans lied to you. They lied to all of us. They made a deal – *they're with the Vikings.*"

Chapter 22

TAMSIN
NEW MOON OF JUNE

I EXPLAIN RHUN'S PRESENCE to Eormen quickly as we stride to the ladder. She only shakes her head, too distracted to chastise me – her attention is still on the trap door.

We knock civilly at first. Then less civilly. But no amount of banging on the door yields any response from above. The ship rocks and lurches as we continue on our journey down the Clyde. We both know we're far away enough now that no one on the banks can hear us screaming for help. We can do nothing but sit in that dark and dismal hold, trying not to despair as our hopes slowly splinter away.

Rhun tries to explain what he knows of our situation. As soon as Lady Catriona brought him onboard the ship, the crew quickly revealed themselves to him so they might threaten him into silence. They kept him locked down here to safeguard both his life and their lies.

"I should've yelled for help," he tells us through the door. "They told me they would kill me if I made any noise. But I should've done it anyway. I should've warned everyone—"

"No," I tell him, choked by his defeated tone. "Rhun – don't torture yourself like this."

"It can't be true," Eormen mutters, still clinging to her scepticism. "Why would a raggedy band of Vikings have come to Strathclyde in secret? Surely they wouldn't risk their own hides like this and sail with a fleet of one thousand Briton soldiers just to get a look at the place."

"I've been with them the whole week, cousin," Rhun insists. "You have to believe me. Here, listen to them. Just listen."

We sit there for a moment, quiet as mice as footsteps creak across the ceiling. Voices ring out above us. I recognise the Gaelic tongue, but... there is another language being spoken up there.

One I am all too familiar with.

"That is the Norse tongue," Rhun tells us from behind his closed door.

"You can't know that for sure," Eormen insists. "It could be some obscure Pictish dialect."

"Think, cousin," Rhun says. His tone is growing harsher by the minute. "The Vikings already conquered Alba's outer isles. They've been neighbours with King Causantin for a long time. And Causantin has been thirsting to come down upon us ever since Uncle Arthgal burned down Dunblane."

"Our weddings were meant to serve as a pardon for that."

"Your weddings mean nothing. You have to face the truth. The kingdom of Alba joined forces with the Vikings in order to overwhelm us. They came to Strathclyde to map out the place and take hostages, and that's why they've locked us down here. They must be leading us straight into a trap. Us and all of our men."

"No," Eormen breathes out. But she's breaking at last. I can see it in the taut lines of her face. "No, you're wrong."

My heart is racing as I try to envision what Rhun means by a 'trap'. We might already be sailing across the Firth of Clyde. Beyond, where the Firth spills into the Atlantic, the waters have always been infested with all sorts of bandits that the Irish try to keep under control. Our fleet was meant to protect us against any stray threat, but...

God. What if Rhun is right? What's going to happen to us?

There is a clank of metal and a groan of wood. Light floods the darkness of the hold as the trap door is lifted at last.

Eormen and I jump around to find several burly crewmen climbing down the ladder. Eormen reaches for me instantly, drawing me against her as though to protect me from them.

They grin at us, genial as always, as though they aren't aware of the horrible threat they pose to two solitary girls. As if they haven't just helped our Alban suitors to betray us all.

I've got to do *something*.

I scramble to my feet. Eormen lets me go, unable to do anything but gasp my name. My pulse flaps deafeningly in my ears as I try to squeeze between the men.

"Princess!" They laugh as they place their great paws on me. "You stay down here. You don't want to go up on deck right now."

Their words only heighten the frantic urge to escape. Something's going to happen. Rhun's right – we're headed for a trap, and they know exactly when it's going to be sprung.

More men file down as my own captors hold me, bearing my kicks and bites with nothing more than laughter and fond words, as though I were a hissing cat. Eormen watches mutely as the crewmen carry their shields and weapons out of the hold with chilling nonchalance.

The hold is emptying. Soon they will lock the door again. I have to go. *I have to do something.*

With a mighty push and twist, I manage to extricate myself from their grip. They shout after me as I leap for the ladder.

I scramble out. The men around me clutch at my ankles, pull at my dress – but somehow, perhaps by the sheer strength of my panic, I manage to eel my way out of their grasp.

I stagger onto the deck, haggard and dishevelled from their ill-treatment. They're shouting after me as I run to the bulwark and try to ascertain where we are.

It's been at least a few hours since we left the port of the river Leven. The wind whips at my loose hair as I take in my surroundings. All around me, the crewmen are either rowing or fitting their shields around the sides of the ship, their bare arms thick with sturdy muscle. The Alban royals are ahead on the foredeck, calmly seated in their tent, as though they hadn't just taken us hostage and shoved us in their stinking hold. The scene is so jarringly peaceful, I feel like I'm going mad.

From the look of the clifftops around us, we're sailing past the island of Bute and our own Great Cumbrae. The isle of Arran lays beyond, marking the end of our seas and the start of the westward Irish wilderness. Thankfully we aren't heading there. We seem to be heading north.

"Princess. I take it you wanted some air?"

Aedan is coming towards me. He looks wary, as though about to pounce on me at any sudden movement I might make. As he approaches, the Viking brutes turn away from me, going back to their ship-arming process.

Panting, I try to think. What can I do? What can I *do?*

I stare ahead at our Briton fleet, the proud line of vessels sailing ahead of us in a protective arrowhead formation. That at least brings me some comfort. I stare harder at the striped sails, trying to convince myself that it's going to be all right. They know what they're doing. Whatever traps the Vikings might've set, the might of Strathclyde with prevail.

"You betrayed us," I say to Aedan. I want it to sound menacing, but all that comes out is a whimper. "You betrayed all of us."

The look Aedan gives me is one of pity. "There are many things we had to keep from you," he says. "What amazes me is that you guessed it from the start. And yet you still accepted to come along with us and give us the benefit of the doubt."

I stare at him. I guessed it from the start? What does he mean?

There is a roar of laughter from behind us. I glance over Aedan's shoulder at the forecastle.

Three richly attired strangers are sitting there with Prince Domnall and Lady Catriona. In my panic, my eyes had bounced off them before. The men seem thick as brothers, patting each other on the shoulder to congratulate one another for whatever jest they just shared.

One of the strangers has long blond hair. And that mark on his cheek…

It's unmistakable.

My mouth goes dry.

He's wearing wolf fur around the shoulders and a long cape. Underneath, a gold-embroidered tunic, cinched at the waist by a tied-off leather belt. A decorated seax hilt juts out from beneath his cape, the scabbard surely lying across his lower back – many of the crewmen have buckled on their own in the same fashion. His trousers bunch at the knee, tucked into tightly-wound bindings and leather boots.

He has everything of the warrior. And nothing at all of the monk.

When he looks over at me, it is suddenly so obvious, so transparent that this is who he is. Those piercing eyes, that wind-chafed skin, and the way he seeks out his desires with not a single ounce of remorse...

If I had not been stupid with heat, I would've noticed it straight away. As clear as I see it now.

"Viking," I gasp.

"Yes," Aedan concurs, his hand closing over my arm. "All will be revealed to you in due time, princess. It's all right, don't worry. You and Eormen will be perfectly safe. But you have to go back down to the hold now."

I can't help thinking of the story Aedan told. Those vicious warlords who alighted in Dál Riata. The very same that they supposedly chased from their shores.

Three wolves of Dublin.

Three tall monks.

I don't want to believe it.

"Who is that one?" I demand. "The monk with the marked cheek? And his brothers? Who did you bring with you?"

"Princess, come now—"

"*Who is he?*"

With a sigh, Aedan follows my gaze. "You have guessed it already, haven't you?"

He confirms it for me in one breath. It is them. Olaf and Ivar are the two laughing brothers. And Thrain... Thrain Mordsson is the one who wears that mark.

The one who kissed me.

My hands clap over my mouth without me even giving the conscious command. I don't want to believe it. My monk in the wolf furs looks from me to Aedan as though guessing our conversation, and pats Prince Domnall's shoulder again. This time he seems to be excusing himself.

He gets up and turns towards us.

Christ Almighty. I let him touch me.

I was so *blind.*

I pull away from Aedan with all my might and lean over the bulwark, eyes on the Briton fleet. My hands curl over the wood as I gaze at the nearest ship. Surely they're within shouting distance. Surely if I warn them, they could descend on both Vikings and Albans before it's too late.

"HEY!" I yell at them, waving frantically. "HEY!"

Several pale faces appear at their decks. My heart lifts upon seeing them – but Aedan grabs me around the waist and pulls me back. He's waving too, as though to deter the concern of the soldiers. Perhaps he wants them to think that the princess is just having a tantrum.

He's going to force me back into the hold.

No. *No.* I struggle madly in his grasp. If I don't warn them now, then we're all doomed. Once the wolves of Dublin take control, who knows what they plan to do with us? They have no honour or code of conduct.

They are savages. And we are at their mercy.

I wrench away from Aedan, take one last breath, and leap overboard.

Chapter 23

THRAIN
New Moon of June

I WATCH IN UTTER bewilderment as the girl throws herself into the waves. Silence settles over the ship as everyone hears the splash. Then the men roar with laughter.

"So, Thrain! Your charm isn't working like it used to?"

Ivar joins me as I hurry to the aft deck, yelling a command to the men who tilt their oars and engage a halt. We stop beside the idiot lordling who is leaning over the bulwark.

"She's gone under," says Aedan. "I haven't seen her surface yet."

"And you could not prevent her?" Ivar snaps irritably.

Aedan shakes his head. He doesn't seem particularly inclined to save her. Perhaps he doesn't know how to swim. As always his incompetence astounds me. I push him aside and look to the waves myself.

The blue expanse rolls and heaves under the midday sun. I spot the last snow-white ripples of her impact, drifting away. Then I see her. Tamsin's cutting a path through the water with the vigour of the damned. But she's struggling against the cold sweep of the fleets' backwash, repeatedly pulled under by its relentless churning.

I loosen my cloak. Prince Domnall and Lady Catriona arrive beside us as I pull off my belt and tunic.

"You're going in after her?" Domnall asks me, clearly concerned. We've almost passed the island of Bute – soon, it will be time.

"I'll be quick," I promise him.

"If you aren't, we'll have to begin without you," Ivar says. As always he makes a challenge of it, pretending not to care for my health. I smirk at him.

"You'll need the head start," I tell him. Rubbing my hands, I ready myself mentally for the cold of impact. And I jump.

The water greets me with all the amiability of a block of ice. It shocks the air from my lungs. I drag myself through the cold darkness until my head breaks the surface.

The air I rake into my lungs is sharp as daggers. I take it in regardless and swim towards our runaway princess.

The sight of her bobbing ginger head guides me until it disappears completely.

She's gone under again. I take a breath and dive in after her.

The salty water stings my eyes as I open them to the darkness. I dart forward, looking all around myself. Gods, she had better be holding her breath. Do Briton princesses even learn to swim in deep water?

There. A misty swirl of white. I propel myself towards it.

It's her, drifting in the cloud of her dress. I plough through the drifting fabric with one arm until I find the solid warmth of her body. She yields to the pull of my arm as I lock her against me.

When we break the surface together, she gasps and sputters for air. Her arms skid against me, finding their strength again as she tries to push me away. She's blinking water from her eyes, barely able to open them with the salty sting.

I clamp her against me, enduring her struggles and the sharp nails she drags across my skin. She kicks and rasps as I drag us both back to the boat. My men welcome us with a bout of exaggerated cheer. I give them a foul look as I come to the side of our ship.

Ivar and Olaf chuck us a length of rope. Both look far more concerned for Tamsin than the rest of our crew. I wonder if it's because they have ascertained what she is while the crew has not. Though they might have taken our word for it, they haven't experienced those royal halls full of flushed Vanirdøtur under the full moon. They cannot scent her now, so they do not respect her status yet.

We are heaved aboard. The men plunge their oars back into the water with renewed vigour to make up for the lost distance. Aedan pushes past my kinsmen and helps me pull the girl across the creaky planks of the ship, holding her wrists so she might stop swiping those claws at us both.

We deposit her on the aft deck, leaning around her to bar her from view. Aedan pulls at the laces of her dress while I pit my weight over her legs – she's trembling with the cold, still blinking seawater from her eyes as she tries to fight us off. Behind me, Ivar calls to the men in Norse, commanding them to look away so as to safeguard the princess's virtue, which has them all laughing. The sound of their jibes sets a scowl on my face.

We strip her of the wet, ice-cold dress. I do it mechanically, trying not to look at her, trying to ignore the fact that I'm betraying her, that I've already shattered her trust into a thousand pieces by showing her who I am. But it's necessary, else the cold will seep into her lungs.

She yelps, tries to hold onto her dress as we pull it up. I wrench it easily from her fingers. Her soaked shift clings to her every curve, outlining her breasts and stomach. Once the dress is off, she crosses her arms over her chest and squeezes her eyes shut. The vulnerability of near-nudity makes her go very still, like a prey animal scenting her own demise.

Aedan looks at her with interest while I hurry to cover her with my discarded cape. He says something to her – *I didn't think you could be prude, wife* – and for a split second I'm all but ready to throw him overboard.

As I wrap her in the thick fur-lined wool cape, I'm infinitely glad that she smells of nothing but salt. She doesn't need the interest of my men piled on top of the crassness of her own betrothed.

"Give her mead," I grunt at Aedan. He leans closer over her, boxing her in so that not a single breath of warmth can slip away. With one hand he fiddles with the skin on his belt, fumbling to uncork it.

She is trembling like a leaf as I rub warmth into her tightly crossed arms. Her teeth chatter a senseless rhythm, her lips covered by her own wet hair. I pluck it from her face, slicking it back over her head.

As soon as I pulled off the monk's robes, I dreaded the moment she would see me like this. We've shared so much in such a short time. Part of me is enraged that I might incite the desire to flee in her now, rather than to come running.

But this is how it must be.

We were never meant to share anything at all. I've no right to mourn what could've been.

Tamsin starts muttering *no, no, no*, refusing the restorative as she pushes at Aedan's chest. I grab the waterskin from Aedan's useless grasp, nudging her mouth with it. "It's mead, princess. It'll warm you."

Her eyes open at the sound of my Gaelic. She stares straight at me with all the crimson intensity of Fenrir.

She takes some of the mead and then spits it right in my face.

Aedan laughs as I reach to wipe it from my cheek. "I think she takes issue with you, Viking."

If it were just her and I, I would accept the repudiation – but Aedan's mocking laughter makes me see red. I grab him by the clasp of his cloak, yanking his face close to mine. His nose is right there, thin and breakable, it would barely take a bump of the forehead to—

"Oy!" Ivar's boots creak across the deck towards us. "None of that! Thrain, release him. Lord Aedan, her dresses are in the hold, take her down there to change."

Aedan sneers at me as I let go of him. It takes all my strength to stand up and turn away from him, fingers still flexing angrily around thin air as I follow Ivar away from them both.

"Here, Thrain," Olaf says as he joins us, handing me my tunic and belt. I take both items, yank the tunic over my head and buckle on the belt while we march to the prow. One glance over my shoulder shows me Aedan pulling Tamsin up, still wrapped as she is in my wolf furs. She's shivering, leaning against him while he rubs her shoulders, hushing her.

Gods, I don't even know that girl beyond the pair of evenings we shared together. So why do I feel this stabbing jealousy as I watch her betrothed hold her in his arms? He was always meant to have her.

And yet... in a way I know her more intimately than I rightly should. She's allowed me to see parts of herself that I doubt Aedan will ever discover. Though I'm sure she regrets it now.

I watch Aedan steer her towards the hold. She grudgingly accepts to follow him, but not without glaring straight across the aisle at me.

Even with this distance between us, I can feel the heat of her hatred.

It is all I should expect from her. From the moment her hand first touched mine, I had an inkling that things would get... complicated. But I can do nothing about it while the revelation is still fresh.

"SAILS!"

The shout comes from the Briton ships ahead of us. The voices are faint – many of them are yelling it at the same time, warning the ships behind them. Surely they expect us to turn around and flee with our royal charge.

"It's time!" I call to the men.

A roar of delight rises from them. They pull harder at their oars, eager to not be left out of the fray. Olaf hands me my axe, and I relish its weight in my palm as I stare straight ahead.

The line of Briton ships is slowing down. We're rapidly overcoming the distance between us. Ahead lies a small island just off of Bute, which serves as a cover for our own welcoming party. Slowly they come into view beyond the striped sails of the Britons. The wind fills out the sails of many massive longboats as they encircle us with the slow grace of giants. I know there are forty of them in total. Twice the size of the Briton fleet.

"VIKINGS!" come the panicked yells. "VIKINGS!"

Excitement rushes through my body at the sound of their fear. Ivar and Olaf ready their shields on either side of me, grinning. Prince Domnall strides to meet us, his own sword hanging heavy at his belt.

"Lady Catriona is safe in the hold?" Olaf asks him, to which he nods.

Without thinking I glance back to check on Tamsin. To my dismay, she's still on the aft deck, both her and Aedan staring white-faced at the oncoming ships.

"Aedan!" I roar at him, sparing no time for formalities. "Get her down there *now!*"

He jumps to attention and drags her down through the trap door, heedless of her screamed protests.

Chapter 24

TAMSIN
NEW MOON OF JUNE

S AILS. VIKING SAILS.
So many of them.

I bang at the trap door, yelling for Prince Domnall, ignoring Aedan and Lady Catriona's insistence that I calm myself. Eormen and Rhun keep shouting at us to explain what's going on. Everything is chaos until Lady Catriona pulls me forcibly from the ladder and bids me sit down beside Eormen, using the imperious tone of a queen.

"Viking ships," I tell my cousin as she grasps my hands. "I saw at least two dozen. They're coming straight for us."

Eormen stares at our Alban captors. Her face is white with fear and rage. "You knew about this, didn't you?" she seethes. "You and your family allied yourselves with the Vikings and plotted against us."

Lady Catriona sighs as she sits down and drapes herself over one of our secured coffers. Aedan joins her side. "There's no time to discuss this now. Be quiet and brace yourselves."

"Brace for what?" calls Rhun from his cabin. "What have you done?"

Yelled commands reach us from above. Soon the planks of the ship groan with the weight of many feet as the Vikings stir. Eormen and I frantically wedge ourselves between our coffers and each other, staring up at the bright interstices above our heads.

The ship groans around us as the Vikings manoeuvre it. Backwash sloshes against the sides, the ship rocking perilously. Then—

CRASH.

I can't hold back my scream as impact shivers across the wooden walls of the hold. There is a sickening brushing sound, wooden seams creaking and groaning in protest, as though we were dragging along the hull of another ship.

Dull thunking sounds punctuate the continuous creaking. I'm panting in terror as I stare at the ceiling. Are we being boarded? Or are the Vikings throwing out our own grappling hooks to hold our neighbours close?

Many voices rise beyond the cacophony of colliding ships and sloshing waves. Men are yelling from every direction. At first it seems to be war cries and shouted orders.

Then the screams of fear and pain begin.

I can't breathe as I sit in that hold, unable to do anything except stare around us like a frightened animal. I can't even summon the strength to pray. My mind is screaming too much for that. Eormen is clinging onto me so hard that I feel she'll break my fingers.

There's no knowing how long we wait down there, listening, jumping each time a heavy body splashes into the water around us. Our own ship seems deserted at first – perhaps they've all gone to invade the ones we are grappled against.

But then several feet thump over our heads again. They seem to step across my own spine as they venture from starboard to port. Metal clashes messily against metal. Grunts of effort follow in their wake. Then, a fatal slash, a drawn-out gasp – and a body crashes overhead, blocking out a chunk of light, making us cry out.

Blood plinks down from the planking. I stare in horror as the droplets form a dark pool on the floor of the hold.

Eormen stirs at last. She shakes her head, wrenching her eyes from that ominous stain.

"One thousand Briton soldiers came with us," she says. "Many of which are Cavaliers. We'll overwhelm them."

"No we won't." Rhun's despairing voice rises from the cabin. "The ships make narrow and uneven battlegrounds. Many will probably sink if the Vikings squeeze around them and lash them together as roughly as this. And – how many sails did you see, Tamsin?"

I've been panicking too much to think of a potential outcome. I think back on that horrid sight. All those strange sails on the horizon.

"I don't know how many there were," I mutter.

"If they planned this from the start then they will have planned to overwhelm our numbers," Rhun says. "The men that sail with us were meant to form a vanguard against stray, disorganised attackers. But one thousand is a small number, Eormen. We will not hold if they swarm us."

"No," Eormen mutters. "No, no, no." Tears are streaming down her face, though she doesn't seem to notice it. "Tamsin," she adds suddenly, renewing her grip on my hands. Her teary eyes seek mine. "You must pray with me. The Lord will give our men strength."

I bow my head and try to join her in prayer. But still there is that ringing in my mind, fear making me seize up. I concentrate on the feeling of my cousin's hands on mine, grit my teeth, and try to endure with her as the battle rages all around us.

ᛏᛘᛙᚼᛁᚼ

Our heads are bent together for a long time.

I don't know whether to be glad or fearful when the screams and shouts and thunking arrows finally dwindle. Overhead, footsteps thud across the planks of our ship again. Horrid dragging sounds rush across the floor as bodies are hauled away. Voices ring out, their tones cheerful.

They speak Norse.

My eyes blink open. Eormen stares back at me.

Defeat then.

The concept remains distant. While we are down here, the world above surely cannot be so different from the sunny world that I saw barely a few hours ago. I can't accept it until I've seen it for myself.

I get up from the coffers, ignoring the Albans' insistence that I stay seated. Yanking Thrain Mordsson's fur-lined cape closer around myself, I stride to the ladder, climb to the trap door, bang against it and shout for somebody to open up.

"They will not come, Tamsin!" Aedan roars at me. "They will organise crews for the ships they won and stow away their prisoners. We will stay down here until we reach port."

I keep banging. The pain of my fist against the hard pinewood is somehow more comforting than the idea of sitting down there doing nothing. Eventually Aedan has to come and heave me off the ladder himself, though I kick and scream at him.

We sit together again, we Briton and Alban royals. Enmity boils between us. Lady Catriona decides to diffuse the tension by explaining the situation in that calm, deep tone of hers.

She tells us things that we already know. That the Vikings overtook the isles on the western coast of Alba, thirty-odd years ago after they sacked the chapel of Iona. We knew they had eaten away at the northern coastlines of the country ever since, driving the Pictish tribes downwards and into the waiting arms of Strathclyde and Northumbria.

What we didn't know was that the many Viking settlements now form a makeshift kingdom, which they call the Kingdom of the Southern Isles. One Viking warlord, Gofraid, calls himself king of those isles. He is father to the three lords of Dublin, those very Viking lords aboard our ship. It is with him that King Causantin negotiates regarding who controls which coastlines.

Gofraid demanded that Dunadd Fort be ceded to his three sons. It was one of the last strongholds untouched by Viking settlement. But the sons of Gofraid could not be refused. They did not seek to settle there, anyway; they wanted to use it as a strategic launching point. First to scout the area; then as a base for their vast armies.

Because they were ultimately aiming for Strathclyde.

"So these weddings," I stammer, staring at Aedan. "They're a sham. They've always been a complete sham."

Aedan stares straight at me, his hooded eyes cold.

"But we've both been betrothed for years now!" Eormen protests. "Have you been planning this betrayal for that long?"

"No," Lady Catriona says. She sounds strangely sad. "There was a time when we sincerely thought an alliance between our kingdoms might be beneficial. But your father insisted on aggravating us, souring any possibility of forgiveness. Meanwhile the Vikings grew in strength and number with each passing year."

"So you told the Vikings of our betrothals, and they decided to take advantage of them."

Lady Catriona nods.

Eormen continues angrily; "You say that my father insisted on aggravating you. But he only ever crossed your borders because you provoked him!"

Aedan scoffs. "Is that how he puts it? I fail to see what provocation brought his wrath down upon Dunblane."

I shiver into the cape I wear. I still haven't changed, so the cold wet linen of my shift clings to me. With everything that's happened today, I feel like I'll never be warm again.

My brother strikes the door of his cabin, making us all jump. "You bastards," he seethes from his small prison. "You fucking traitorous bastards!"

"Can you let him out?" I snap at Aedan. "Why is he even locked away when we aren't?"

Aedan shrugs. "It's orders."

"And you just do the Vikings' bidding now? Like their servant boy?"

He glares at me from under his brow, his face an ugly grimace of anger.

"You will not speak like that to me. I have met the Vikings on the battlefield. There is... there is no possible victory against them. It is pointless to try and resist them." The words are strangely choked as he forces them out. I would pity him if he hadn't just stuck a knife in all our backs.

"Those are the words of a coward," I spit at him, fire raging in my chest. "Is that why you skulk down here with the women and prisoners?"

"Tamsin, please." Lady Catriona reaches for me as though to shield me while Aedan glowers with barely contained rage. "My son is right. Your people have not faced them. You don't know what they're capable of."

I know I'm still riding the high of fear that the battle stoked in me. There's so much shame, too, that I might not have been able to warn our kinsmen in time. And that I... did what I did in the chapel that night. With *him*. But I cannot repent, not in this dingy hold, not when I'm already half-frozen to death. So I'm forced to exorcise it somehow, and my *new family* is the perfect target to take my frustrations out on.

Lady Catriona goes on: "When your only choices are sacrificing your pride or facing annihilation, you must accept to opt for the former."

"Indeed. That is generally how one defines cowardice."

"Tamsin, stop," Lady Catriona commands. "This solves nothing."

I dig my hands into the ample folds of the cape, searching for warmth as I seethe in silence.

"So... what will happen to us?" Eormen demands. "Are we still going to go through with the weddings at all?"

"Your weddings will still serve an alliance," Lady Catriona tells us. "Just not the alliance that you were expecting. They will symbolise the union between King Gofraid and King Causantin. Therefore yes, you will still be wed."

I stare at Eormen. She looks like she's on the verge of tears, but the concentration required to piece together our situation is just about holding them at bay.

"Don't worry," Lady Catriona adds. "All will proceed as though this were a regular marriage for you both. You'll see, your lives will not be so different. Domnall and Aedan will be your protectors, and no other man will touch you. You will live with us in the fort while the preparations take place."

No other man will touch you. For a moment I realise the amplitude of that statement.

Eormen and I will be the only daughters of Clota for miles, in a fort controlled by cursed Vikings. And our only protection against the masses of cursed males under the full moon will be this pair of cowardly Alban men.

From the look on her face, I can tell that Eormen is realising the same thing. She looks like she's about to crumble, but she's holding back for my sake.

"Tell me something," I manage. "Why did you allow the wolves to dress as *monks?*"

Aedan sighs impatiently. "They wanted to do some reconnaissance."

"It is blasphemy to claim an office given only by God."

"I know. And I will pray for forgiveness until the end of my life."

"That will not be enough to save you, *wretch.*"

"I told you already, Tamsin," he snarls. "You will not talk like that to me. I am your—"

I slap him around the face before he can say what he is. My betrothed. This stinking traitor is meant to be my sole guardian in a savage land.

He strikes me back. Pain erupts across my face, and I crumble to the floor before I even realise that he's done it. Eormen screams.

"Tamsin? Tamsin!" My brother's banging on the door. "If you hurt her, you son of a whore – I will make you regret it!"

In moments, Eormen has bent over me protectively. Rhun is yelling more insults, but Aedan ignores him as he gets to his feet, drawing himself up to his full height.

"There's no need for violence," Lady Catriona states angrily. "Sit down."

"Look, I've been patient with her," Aedan snaps back. "But I will not constantly turn the other cheek for her! This is the situation we are in, and we must learn to deal with it. All of us. She should have the maturity to handle herself. Isn't that what you told me?"

"She's just a girl, Aedan!" Lady Catriona shouts. "If you hit her again I will have Domnall drag you out there to scrub the blood from the decks."

He stands for a moment in front of his mother. Bewilderingly, I wonder if he'll hit her too. He's bristling with violent intent. Even she recoils a little, as though this were not the first time he'd threatened her this way.

Still, she holds her ground, glaring up at her son. "Sit. *Down.*"

Moodily, he breaks away from her and does as she commands.

Eormen shuffles me across the planks until we're curled against Rhun's door. She tends to my face, wiping blood from where Aedan's rings caught my skin. After a moment of this stunned silence, the ship lurches around us as it detaches from our neighbours.

We're moving again. I can only stare blindly at our coffers lining the wall of the hold.

Little boxes full of home.

Chapter 25

TAMSIN
NEW MOON OF JUNE

I FEEL AS THOUGH we spend an entire week in that cramped hold. Eormen helps me into a dry dress, both of us taking far longer than we normally would because of how much we're shaking. After that, I'm barely aware of what my body is doing. Between crying, sleeping, and staring listlessly at nothing, time ceases to have much meaning.

At long last we come to a stop, presumably at the port of Dunadd. The trap door is flung open, deep golden light spilling in. Prince Domnall comes down, strides between Eormen and I without acknowledging our existence, and opens the locked door of the cabin. When my brother spills out, all scruffy and dirty-looking, we both throw our arms around him. I'm so senselessly happy that he's here with me, even though I might've just doomed him a second time.

Together we follow the Alban royals up the ladder and through the trap door.

The sight that greets us steals my breath away.

I blink in the vivid light of sunset as we step out onto the blood-spattered deck. The Dálriadan docks are teeming with masts and rolled-up sails, both our Briton stripes and the Viking reds and blacks. Beyond, the waters of the port are infested with even more of those horribly intimidating longboats.

So many ships.

So many dead.

Prisoners are streaming from many of the Briton boats, heads hanging as they follow their captors ashore. Galloway horses whinny shrilly and fight their handlers as they'd led down the wooden docks. The sight of Cynan rearing against his own handlers brings one small burst of relief, but it's short-lived. I can't stop staring at the dozens of bloody ships, empty now, our men either decimated or chained together.

Rhun is by my side, holding my hand. If it weren't for him, I would've crumpled onto the deck.

Eormen drifts to the bulwark. The wind lifts her resplendent blond hair, snags at her gown. I think of how her mother must've had that gown specially made for this day. How her servants must've taken time to twine that thin crown braid around her head, so that the cheering crowds might find her as lovely as Strathclyde's darling should be.

She holds herself still as she looks at the aftermath of the carnage. I can hear how shallow her breaths are coming. Domnall goes to fetch her, and when she turns around, her expression is as pale as a ghost's.

She pulls something from the folds of her dress.

Metal sings as she unsheathes the dagger and points it straight at her fiancé's neck.

Several voices cry out at once. It's only then that I realise we are surrounded by our Viking crew. They approach Domnall, perhaps trying to remind Eormen of what awaits her if she goes through with her threat.

"My dear," Domnall says. "If you harm me, you will only bring harm upon yourself."

Eormen blinks tears from her eyes. Then she draws back the dagger and presses it against her own throat.

"Eormen!" Rhun and I shout at the same time. "Don't – please – *don't!*"

She's gasping for breath as she stands there, steel against her throat, every bit the noble martyr. I break away from Rhun and rush to her side.

"We can survive this," I tell her doggedly. "Together. We'll survive it. I need you to stay with me, cousin. Please."

She closes her eyes. Takes a deep shuddering breath.

I reach for the dagger, and she lets me take it from her.

Immediately Domnall grabs her arm and forces her to follow him. She staggers after him, caught between him and the wolf with white-blond hair, Olaf, as they initiate the descent from the ship. The crew follows them down onto the dock in a long line.

When I turn back to Rhun, I find two brutes taking him roughly between them. One of them has that shaved and tattooed skull, his long black hair braided to form a crest. Ivar. My heart lurches as they pull Rhun away among the Viking crew.

"Tamsin!" he calls. The fear in his voice pulls my feet across the planking, heedless of Aedan's calls that I should stay by him. I don't make it far until a large man bars the way.

I look up into familiar blue eyes.

Thrain Mordsson.

His face is blood-spattered. It makes him look like such a wanton predator that for a moment I feel utterly frozen to my spot.

Without a word, he holds out a hand.

I realise I've still got the dagger. Patiently, he waits.

I breathe slowly as I stare into that bloody face. Shame threatens to engulf me as I remember what happened between us. The trust I had placed in him. The yearn for his presence. How right it felt when he... when he kissed me.

He orchestrated this massacre, he and his brothers. He deserves to be run through more times than all the martyrs of Iona put together.

I see myself plunging the dagger into his chest. My eyes roam over his body, looking for weak points. Surely he sees me looking and knows my intention.

Still, he waits.

He thinks I will not do it. He thinks I cannot.

Blind rage surges through me as I stare at his outstretched hand. It is the same hand that he touched me with.

I grit my teeth, and plunge the blade into his palm.

He yells in pain, clutching his wrist, eyes flying wide in surprise. The world crowds in on us – several remaining crewmen approach us both, concerned for their chieftain, but Thrain barks at them in Norse, a growl rattling in his chest. They dither, none of them approaching me, though there is bewilderment in their gazes as they stare at me.

"I'm fine," Thrain grumbles in Gaelic as he slides the dagger sickeningly from his hand. "She missed the bones. I'll live. Now get off your damned arses and take the coffers from the hold."

Thrain turns away from me without a second glance, tucking the dagger in his belt and holding his injured hand against his chest. "My lady," he throws carelessly over his shoulder as he passes a pale-faced Lady Catriona. "Please escort the princess to the docks."

Once the others turn to follow him, Aedan grabs me by my girdle and pulls me firm against him.

"Much as I want to see that man hurt, you are endangering me and my family by acting out your wild fancies," he mutters. "I am your keeper now. You will *not* act without my consent."

"What makes you think I care what happens to you and your family?" I snap at him.

"Tamsin," he seethes. "You will not be exempt from his wrath if you do something like that again. That is *Thrain Mordsson.*"

"I don't care."

His brow furrows. "Are you touched in the head?"

"Maybe I am," I tell him, drawing close enough to see the sweat beading on his wide forehead. "But at least I'm not a coward."

Aedan's indignant grimace returns. My heart is pounding hard and slow, the determined beat of righteous rage that pushes aside all fear. His palm flies up – pain erupts across my face again, making me spin and crash to my knees. Roars and heavy footsteps fill my ears. No thought exists in my mind – I can only cringe in anticipation of more blows.

This is it. They're going to kill me.

I'm not the important one. Eormen is. I'm dispensable.

At least I will have made both of those bastards hurt.

There is an incomprehensible scuffle. Planking creaks and groans as men shift around me. When I next look up, Thrain Mordsson stands guard in front of me, one deadly sharp axe brandished. Aedan is standing with his hands open and empty, the sharp edge of the axe wedged under his chin. He's holding his head up, barely breathing as the thin slice of metal presses into his throat.

"My lord," Lady Catriona stammers. "My lord. Please."

Thrain takes a moment to calm down. Then he growls, "Touch her again and I will open you from your groin to your chin."

Aedan blanches. I wonder if he's seen Thrain perform such a thing. From the look on his face, he probably has.

"Lady Catriona," Thrain says again. "Escort the princess."

Lady Catriona seems faint as she approaches the warlord. She skirts around him and hurriedly bids me to get up. Thrain lowers his axe, and Aedan brushes himself down, trying to regain some form of dignity.

"You threaten me when she is the one who maimed you?" he snaps.

"Aedan," Lady Catriona says sharply. "Come."

Rather than dignify Aedan with a response, Thrain simply turns away, giving my betrothed leave to move past him and answer his mother's summons. Aedan does so, scowling, paler than ever. Once he's by my side again, we walk across the deck in silence.

Thrain's low voice rises from behind us: "She was simply righting the balance."

Lady Catriona glances at me in confusion, while Aedan pretends not to have heard.

Righting the balance. I realise that those words are only meant for me – only I know what he refers to. I'm infinitely glad that I'm walking away from him, that I might not have to meet his eyes.

Without another word, Lady Catriona steers me down the gangplank to meet my fate.

ᛏᛰᚥᛋᛁᛰ

A welcoming party awaits us ashore. Most are curious Dálriadan folk from the fishermen's village that curves around the loch. Among them stand raucous groups of cheerful bearded men. Several are wrapped in sumptuous patterned wools and a great deal of jewellery. It is all too easy to pick out the Vikings - only thieves and bandits would wear their wealth so gaudily. There is much clapping on the back and congratulating one another in their gravelly Norse tongue as they meet their victorious Viking brothers.

It grates me to no end as I walk alongside Lady Catriona. These wretched Vikings and their golden brooches, their silver belt buckles, their stolen riches. When the three wolves greet them all, it's like they are kings greeting their noble court, but a perverted heathen version of it.

Lady Catriona leads us towards a horse caravan. Absently I'm glad for the authority she wields over both the heathens and the local Dálriadans hailing her return; we're given a wide berth as we follow her. Ahead, a group of ponies have been prepared for us, far smaller and scrawnier than our Galloways which the Vikings are still struggling to subdue.

I sit astride my own steed while our crewmen stow our belongings onto two rickety traps. Aedan brings his own pony next to mine. The gesture clearly states that there will be no more freedom to move around and clutch at my family. Eormen is slotted beside Prince Domnall, and Rhun beside Lady Catriona. We sit and wait for the three Viking lords to break from the crowd and lead us to the fort.

I can't tear my eyes from the docks. The sheer amount of ships is astounding. Not to mention the number of Vikings who stream from them. No wonder we were overwhelmed.

Many of the men are staring insistently at Eormen and I. Ivar is regaling them with some tale that leads them to cast wondering glances at us.

Perhaps they know what we are.

Perhaps they hunger for us already.

I shiver to see such large packs of men. I wish they would hurry up. Better to be imprisoned than gawked at out in the open like this.

A flash of gold directs my eye to Cynan's palomino coat. He's still fighting and rearing, his frantic neighing pulling at my heart. Those two damned men who're holding his lead rope are yanking at him without any finesse – they're hurting him, pulling at his head, chucking a whip at his hindquarters to punish him each time he rears.

God, if I were trained in combat – I would rip right into them.

A voice calls out. As I watch, the cursed silhouette of Thrain Mordsson in his wolf furs approaches the men. Several onlookers follow his progress as he takes Cynan's rope from the handlers.

I grit my teeth. I want Cynan to strike him down, to lean into his own strength instead of submitting to ropes and halters. He's so much heavier and stronger than the man who tries to control him – if only he could realise his own strength.

Thrain leaves the rope loose, holding it in his right hand, his injured hand still tucked against his chest. Cynan goes wild, throwing his hooves out, twisting in the air. Thrain never pulls him down, only gives him enough slack to express himself. At last, once Cynan understands that he will meet no resistance, he takes an interest and calms somewhat. Thrain takes the opportunity to send him out on a circle.

My pulse pounds deafeningly in my ears as I watch him.

He's emulating me. Doing what he watched me do in the courtyard. That was him back then – asking me what a Viking warhorse was doing in Strathclyde, and how I knew Norse.

Why hadn't that seemed strange to me? Why hadn't I guessed it then?

Eventually, Cynan winds down to a more receptive state. Thrain reaches him, holds up a wad of fabric, lets Cynan sniff it before wrapping it around his head to cover his eyes. Cynan chucks his head up in protest – Thrain strokes his neck until he accepts it, taking his time, letting Cynan sink into the comforting dark of blindness.

My throat's growing tight as I look at Cynan's wrapped head.

It's enviable, in a way. A simple blindfold and he forgets what he's afraid of. If he can't see what's surrounding him then surely it doesn't exist. I suddenly wish I could close my eyes on all this and feel the same sense of relief, as though I were drifting in a great dark lake, the noisy shores far away.

Thrain joins his brothers again, Cynan clopping along behind him as they march to our caravan. While Ivar and Olaf mount their own steeds, Thrain keeps walking, heading in my direction. I feel him approach as though he were a blizzard, my body overtaken by ice.

I can't look at him. Undeterred, he has the gall to brush his hand against my thigh so that I might take Cynan's lead rope. Wordlessly I pluck it from him, making sure I avoid touching him. Cynan scents me and gives a soft nicker, raising his head and bumping his nose against me. I'm holding back tears as I scrub Cynan's head.

"It's all right," I tell him in Brittonic. "You're all right, boy. I'm here."

Thrain turns away. When he mounts his steed and follows his brothers to the front of the line, he still holds his bloody hand against his chest. It's trembling, though he pretends not to notice. His mouth moves around the syllables of their incomprehensible tongue as he and his brothers talk, and it seems so obvious now that the strange accents in his Gaelic came from Norse.

God, why couldn't I see who he was?

Why hadn't any of us seen it?

ᛏᛘᚼᛂᛋᛂ

It is several miles to Dunadd fort. The three cursed lords accompany us across rocky uneven farmlands, trailing a great company of blood-spattered cursed men. I ride beside Aedan, trying to remember the maps I had pored over back at Dumbarton fort in the security of my history lessons.

Technically, we could regain Strathclyde over land. I know that much. From the look of the wide round dock, we arrived at Loch

Gilp. From here there aren't so many miles to the borders of Strathclyde.

But of course, we would have to pass the ancient Pictish strongholds, repurposed Roman walls and watchtowers that have been fortified and rebuilt over the decades. And the open land is striped with lochs and rivers and swamps. If we were to plan an escape, we'd have to diligently avoid detection and try not to get lost. And we'd have to somehow get out of the fort, first. Which looks to be no simple task.

As we plod our way up the land, I take in the wilderness around us. The sunset slants peacefully over fields and farmsteads. Dunadd fort is perched on a hilltop, a high mound that stretches up out of this beautifully jagged countryside. Overhead, seagulls caw and wheel around the walls of the fort.

It's difficult to think of it as a prison. But that is what it is. Thick stone walls, ironclad gates, crenellated parapets for guards to keep a constant watch. To escape that, we'd need a disguise of some kind. It would take meticulous planning. And I have no idea if we'll even stay together at all, once inside.

Night falls as we follow the path around the outside of the hill, steadily climbing up until our ponies are toeing thin, stony ridges. When we're through the first wall, I watch them close the doors behind us, my heart heavy in my chest.

I am a hostage here.

They're shutting us away for good.

ᛏᚽᛉᛋᛁᚾ

We ride into the courtyard of the castle proper. We're met by servants, several of whom take our horses to lead them to the fort stables. All around us stand a host of richly attired men alongside their spouses, and finally the two masters of the household.

One is tall as a giant, has tattooed arms and wears a long white beard caught in several braids. He must be Gofraid. King of the Southern Isles, indeed. What a farce. He's flanked by what I take to be nine Viking chieftains, all of them brimming with the vigour of warriors, though they aren't all particularly young. Some have their wives alongside them, staring curiously at Eormen and I.

The other master is far more formal. He commands a cold and kingly presence in that courtyard. My eyes roam from the golden crown perched atop his neatly combed grey hair, to the sumptuous midnight-blue robes and jewelled belts he's wearing. Behind him stands a council of wise old men who prefer to observe the proceedings from a distance.

I gawp at him.

Is it him? King Causantin? My uncle's dreaded enemy?

Olaf comes forwards and throws out an arm to the two expectant men.

"O mighty kings! The Allfather has blessed us on this day, for we bring you the spoils of victory. Lend an ear, and you will hear the singing of Valkyries as they lead our fallen to Valhöll!"

Gofraid's great moustache curves into a smile while his men cheer at Olaf's words. One of our rickety traps is brought forwards as Olaf goes on with his eulogies. Thrain and Domnall both heave a crate from the cart and carry it to the feet of the kings.

Thrain can only use one hand to manoeuvre his metal handle whilst Domnall uses his two good hands. The crate is lopsided between them. I watch their progress, trying to see some small victory in his struggling.

Then they upturn the crate, and a horrible metallic clatter fills the courtyard as they pour an endless stream of bloody swords onto the flagstones.

And even that smallest of victories dies.

"A thousand worthy adversaries," Olaf goes on. "We will drink to their honour tonight. And those who survived, we will welcome in the halls of Dublin!"

"And a fine welcome you will give them, no doubt," Gofraid rumbles with affection. I see Olaf smile, overcome like any son who hears pride in his father's tone.

That smile fills me with dread. It takes me a moment to realise why. According to Aedan's stories, Dublin is a great slave market – so why does Olaf speak of it as if it's something to take pride in? Do they really intend to ship the survivors off so they can be sold, as a final insult?

Lady Catriona comes forwards next.

"Your Graces, King Gofraid, King Causantin," she intones. "Let me introduce you to the newest members of our household."

She opens an arm towards us, beckoning us forwards. I glance at Eormen, but she is too deadened by grief to respond to me. She walks as a wraith might, limply accepting Domnall's hand when he offers it.

Aedan grabs my hand and pulls me roughly after them. I keep my eyes trained on that pile of bloody steel as we're brought to the centre of the courtyard.

We are part of the spoils.

We stand in a line, bow and curtsey, as though these two kings had not sanctioned the slaughter of one thousand of our kinsmen this afternoon.

"Ravishing," Gofraid says as he devours us with his eyes. "Sons of mine! Are these women what we hoped for?"

"They are," Ivar says. There is a possessive caress in his tone. "Strathclyde holds a very rare plunder indeed."

A strange intensity appears in Gofraid's expression then. When the old whitebeard Viking looks upon Eormen and I again, it is with vigorously renewed interest. The same change operates in all the faces of his men – they stare at us with rapt curiosity, so many eyes watching from the darkness.

I curl my fingers into fists.

Causantin observes us with cool indifference, apparently not caring that we may be true daughters of Clota. Then for the first time, the King of all Alba speaks.

"Welcome, princesses, to our humble fort of Dunadd. Please don't be afraid. No harm will come to you now that you are under our protection." His calm drawl sends ice down my spine. He turns his head a fraction, catching Lady Catriona's attention. "Tell me, sister; who is that lad standing by Ivar's side?"

"An unexpected refugee, Your Highness," Lady Catriona tells him. She gestures at Rhun who comes forwards warily. "Princess Tamsin's brother. Nephew to King Arthgal."

The way King Causantin leers at my brother makes me want

to rip out his eyes.

"I see," he says. "Be welcome, then, prince of Strathclyde. We'll be sure to find a place for you."

"Yes, welcome, welcome!" Gofraid booms as he steps forward. "We have prepared a feast for the victorious returns. You'll all soon be warm and glad again. Ivar! Step out from the shadows. Come where I may see you, my three sons. Come."

There's movement, a schism in the courtyard as the Viking chieftains break out of their assigned places. The three wolves of Dublin go to their brethren, nodding and smiling to acknowledge the shouted greetings. They bow before their king, and then embrace him in turn, switching easily to Norse as they greet one another informally.

Causantin doesn't seem impressed by this break in protocol. The Alban side of the courtyard decides to keep to their own rigid customs. We come forwards, but Domnall doesn't look like he's about to go thump his father on the back.

"Please," King Causantin says, opening his arms to us. "You will ignore the crass manners of my friend and ally. I have joined him here recently and discovered that he has no notion of proper etiquette." His casual admittance of their alliance chills me to the bone. He shows neither remorse nor deference to the other man. Plainly they are working together as co-conspirators. "While you are our guests here, you will be treated with all the respect owed to persons of your high birth."

He nods to Eormen and I.

"Princess Eormen, Princess Tamsin. The weddings will take place at the full moon, as per the traditions of your people. That is in two week's time. Until then, you will have to keep close quarters in order to avoid any unpleasantness. As you can see there are not many women here, and your kind are of particular interest to my allies. I will leave it to the staff to help you settle into your rooms, where you will be safely guarded until you are wed."

He gestures and the flock of waiting servants come to separate us from our suitors. They all look the same to me as they crowd around us, grim-faced women in grey-brown robes, shuffling around their new charges. Their grip is surprisingly strong as they bid us follow them towards one of the squat towers embedded in the inner walls. Eormen lets herself be steered, holding up her chin. I glance wildly over my shoulder as we're divorced from the men. The two monarchs begin to lead the crowd towards the main doors of the fort. My brother stares after us with wide eyes as they march him away.

"Tamsin!" he yells.

"No! Rhun! *Rhun!*" Panicked, I shout at the Albans, "Where are you taking my brother?"

"Don't worry, princess!" Domnall calls after me. "You'll soon be seeing him."

ᛏᚼᛦᛤᛁᚾ

My room is downstairs from Eormen's in the tower. It's painfully obvious that this place is usually used to stow away important prisoners. There is a single shuttered window in my room, from which I can see the silvery curl of the river Add and the farmlands around us.

I ask the servants if there is a chapel somewhere in the fort. An old Irishwoman called Eilidh tells me yes, that surely I saw it when I arrived as it's accessible from the courtyard. I just stare blankly at her. I have no recollection of a chapel. My mind is full of the metallic cascade of swords on the flagstones and Rhun's panicked face. She clicks her tongue and goes on to tell me that I won't be allowed to go to the chapel until I'm wed. I'll have to spend two weeks in this prison cell, biding my time until I can live in Aedan's quarters and gain the freedom to move around our prison.

After setting up my washing station and shooing the others from my cell, she takes pity on me. She grasps my hands in both of hers and says with those musical Gaelic notes of hers, "Trust me, princess. A beautiful young girl like you should not roam this place unguarded and unwed. You and Princess Eormen will be safe here. My staff and I will personally see to it."

She waits, perhaps for me to thank her for this empty

reassurance. When she realises she won't get anything more out of me, she clicks her tongue and leaves me to my own devices, bolting the door behind her.

I take in my surroundings. Four stone walls. A bed, with wool and linen to ward off the night chill. A copper bedpan, earthenware washing equipment, folded linen towels. My coffers sit there in a corner, deceptively familiar in this foreign environment.

I go to them, lay a hand on the first trunk. Opening it, I find familiar patterned dresses of the most impractical kind – long sleeves that trail to the floor, embroidered decorative bands following every hem, delicate white veils that my mother would punish me for ripping.

Do you have any idea what you've done?

I hear her voice as clearly as if she'd spoken in this room.

Why should God protect us? Why should He answer our prayers when we openly disrespect Him?

I sink to my knees by the trunk, staring down at the dresses without seeing them. My hands are beginning to itch again, except this time the itch gains my forearms, my chest, my whole body.

If anything happens, then you know who is to blame.

My breathing is coming short as I picture the carnage at the loch, those bloody decks, those lines of prisoners with their heads bowed.

It's my fault.

My fault we were betrayed.

My fault so many men died.

For love of Rhun, I invited God's wrath. And He came down upon us just as my mother had warned. I sabotaged our sacred rites and this is my punishment.

It's all my fault.

Chapter 26

THRAIN
WAXING MOON OF JUNE

G OFRAID HAS ONLY our word to go on, regarding the lineage of those princesses. Now that they are no longer in heat, they had the scent of regular women when they entered the courtyard. But he seems ready to believe us. He is curious, at the very least. He and the others need only wait for the full moon to reveal whether they are what our legends promised.

We spend that first night together in the great hall, our Vyrgen washing themselves and digging into their well-deserved feast. My brothers and I sit with Gofraid by one of the great hearths, enjoying the relative privacy of it. Ivar cleans my injured hand while Olaf regales his father with details of the sea battle.

Gofraid keeps turning back to me, asking me to tell him again how I got that foolish wound in my hand. He seems endlessly amused that I might've evaded injury whilst teetering on a battlefield of boats against a thousand Briton men, but one angry girl could've somehow bested me.

Ivar is rubbing the last of the blood and grime from my wound. I can't speak for the incapacitating pain of it. He resumes for me: "Thrain opened his hand to a she-wolf with a dagger and a death-wish. He was entranced by her during our whole stay in Strathclyde." Here he glances at me pointedly. "She draws him into irresponsibility."

I scowl at him. I told neither him nor Olaf about what happened between the princess and I in that chapel. But Ivar noticed how closely I had tailed her those first days. And how diligently I avoided her afterwards. And of course, the scent that clung to my robe that night, though I endeavoured to wash it off. He suspects something, though he has not gotten it out of me yet – and he never will, if I can help it.

Gofraid guffaws. "Sometimes I'm glad that you are not my true-born son, Thrain. My true-born son would get a beating for such a lapse of judgment."

I grind my teeth as Ivar places my hand on his thigh so he might wrap it up in bandages. The firelight glimmers on the ugly edges of the wound. I observe it drily. While the distraction of our homecoming lasted, I could keep the throbbing waves of pain at bay. Now they roll through me as keenly as the red-tinted water of the Firth of Clyde.

"Good thing you aren't left-handed," Ivar says. "Oh, wait! You are!"

"You know I use both hands," I snap at him. He should know it's not the time to jest. But I do the same to him when he's foolish enough to drag himself home with some easily preventable wound hanging open.

And it isn't their judgment I feel as I sit there. It is Tamsin's, sitting heavy as a mountain in the crook of my palm.

Olaf goes back to his story-telling, this time detailing the fort of the Britons to a keenly interested Gofraid. I sit and wonder whether my hand will ever feel like a hand again rather than a red-hot lump of coal while Ivar pulls linen strips close around it.

"I'm almost envious," Ivar admits to me. "I haven't dared to stray as close to a promised Vanirdottir as you have. But then, you've always been far more reckless than I."

I scoff. "I've told you time and again, Ivar. I did not stray as close to her as you seem to believe."

"Eh. Even if it gets you a blade through the palm, I expect the pain is well worth it."

I shake my head at him. "I'm not going to hear the end of this for a long time, am I."

"Not likely," he agrees with a grin, tying off the first layer of bandages. He takes out his pot of numbing salve and adds dressing so that it might seep through the linen. "There's a good deal of swelling. I think she shattered some bones in there. You've probably lost your last two fingers."

"Well then, I can still pluck a harp. No harm done."

Ivar smirks. "You aren't angry at her at all?"

"What is there to be angry about? She acted as I would've acted, had I been in her place. In fact she was far more merciful than I would've been."

Ivar's black eyes bear knowingly into mine. "Whatever you might say, you *are* taken with her," he says. "Deny it all you like, even Olaf can see it."

I shake my head at him. "Can you please concentrate? I'd rather not lose more than two fingers."

He goes on smirking as he adds another bandage. My thoughts are already bent on Tamsin – he needs not direct them any further. She's alone in that cold tower. I keep seeing that pale and bereaved face of hers when she called after her brother in the courtyard.

I am no stranger to the holding of captives. It shouldn't be so difficult for me to bear the idea of her enforced solitude. But… it's *her,* trapped in that tower, trapped behind that bolted door. *My Vanirdottir,* says the dormant beast inside me. *Mine.*

I need only ignore Ivar's jibes and I hear her voice again, talking with me in the dark, choosing me, praising me. I cannot bring myself to regret that night, that sacred moment we shared. But those words now weigh in my palm – those praises I did not deserve drip down my forearm in blood-red lines.

I imagine her locked up in that rabbit cage of a room and my mind supplies more memories, more images to torture me. That wistful tone of hers when she spoke of her aspirations of travel. How she smiled… and how she held onto me that night.

How she trusted me.

So far she has borne the hardship of the journey as best she can. She showed astounding bravery back on the Firth when she leapt into the waves. But now that she is shut away... I understand my brothers' reasoning behind it but gods, she's done nothing to deserve such treatment. She will wither away in there until the moon releases her.

I think of those bruises criss-crossing her naked back and grind my teeth. With nothing to do in that locked room, she'll undoubtedly keep up that reviled custom that remains her sole source of solace.

I want so badly to go to her, see that she has all the comforts she needs, perhaps even take the flogger from her. But Gofraid made it very clear that no one but their husbands-to-be may approach them while they're in the tower. And she'll very likely never want to see my face again, much less take my council regarding self-punishment.

For now... I cannot interfere.

ᚦᚱᚢᚾ

The boy Rhun intrigues Gofraid. I hadn't yet thought of the potential role he could play in our plans once he arrived here. Gofraid invites him to our council chamber where he and Causantin host our military discussions, as though he were an honoured guest rather than a captive.

All of us have been bent over the challenge that the fortified kingdom of Strathclyde poses. On the table are several maps that our Alban allies dug out of their archives. Carved statuettes and sticks of coal litter the table from previous strategising.

Now that the Alban princes and we three have explored the castle from the inside out, we have additions to make to our plans. Rhun stays still and silent by Gofraid's side as I add to our maps, following my own memory and the directives of my brothers. Causantin often breaks in to cast doubt on our affirmations, which only strengthens the clarity of our joint memories.

While we work, servants bring in wine and refreshments. Gofraid pours our captive prince a generous amount before serving himself.

"You were set to be sacrificed, then?" the old man asks Rhun. "Causantin tells me your Briton people have little regard for cursed men, as I believe you call yourselves. You must be happy to be a free man again."

Rhun stares into his goblet.

"Come boy," Gofraid says genially, slapping him on the back. "You may speak plainly here. You are among friends. We are all cursed here! Aren't we boys?"

"Aye!" My brothers and Gofraid's own Southern Isle Jarls laugh as they lift their goblets and drink. The Albans don't seem impressed by our enthusiasm.

"You are no friends of mine," the lad says quietly.

"Hmm? Really now. You would feel more kinship towards your executioners in Strathclyde?"

"You wouldn't understand," Rhun says. His jaw is almost too clenched to allow speech.

"Ah, but that is why I've brought you here, my lad," Gofraid says. "So that I may understand. Why do your people send cursed boys to their deaths when they are not even men yet?"

"It's necessary. We're a threat."

"Indeed," Ivar says, slamming down his cup. "And the kingdom of Strathclyde will regret how they've treated our kin."

Several Vikings rumble in agreement. The Albans seem to grow even quieter. They are barely any better than the Britons in their treatment of Vyrgen men. But then, I have come to understand over the years that it is a rare kingdom that decides to educate its Vyrgen rather than send them to their deaths, whether prematurely or on the frontlines.

I watch Rhun curiously as his hands ball into fists on the table. He's staring into space, clearly distressed.

"You have no fear of God," he says quietly. His gaze lifts to spear into Causantin's. "None of you do. That's why you do not understand."

Quiet as his voice is, the underlying reverence of his words is enough to catch the men's attention again. Causantin silently bears the hatred in the boy's gaze, looking merely curious.

"What utter strangeness," Gofraid says. "You are among the most powerful of men, and yet you would let fear govern you? Surely your god didn't give you this strength so you might turn it upon yourself." He gestures at Causantin. "Look at your Christian neighbours. You worship the same god, do you not? And yet Causantin doesn't send his cursed to be sacrificed."

"Causantin sends his cursed to die in battle," Rhun says. "He knows that this strength is perilous if it cannot be controlled."

"Ah. I see. They have taught you to fear yourself rather than to govern yourself."

"I do not fear myself!" Rhun exclaims. "I... I only fear what I may inflict on others."

"Indeed." Gofraid opens his hand in offering. "You need not fear, my boy. You are among your own kind. We will have you placed with... well, I could find no finer men than those around this table. Who among you has time for a royal ward?"

The men mutter among themselves. Tactfully perhaps, none of the Albans offer their tutelage. They sit back and observe, as though intrigued to see how we cursed Vikings go about our business. Orokia, one of Gofraid's Jarls, stands and bows.

"If Your Grace does not mind hard work and the smell of fish," he says, making several others laugh.

"Perfect," Gofraid says. "This will be your home until the next full moon, my lad. You need not fear us. I count you as one of my guests at this table, and a ward of the Kingdom of the Southern Isles. Of course, you are free to contest such a title, if you don't care for the privilege of our company. Seeing the quality of the men around this table, however, I would encourage you to accept it."

Several men drink to that, grinning at the excessive flattery. I watch Rhun struggling. He sees the maps and meticulous planning on the table. He knows it would serve him much better to accept Gofraid's offering of friendship. I don't even know what Gofraid has planned as an alternative. Surely he wants to pick the boy's brains about Strathclyde, and prefers to do it under the guise of friendship. There are other ways to obtain information from the boy, of course. Rhun must understand this.

He sits there stiffly for a while. Then he stands, and bows in turn to Gofraid and Orokia. Amusingly enough, he does not offer Causantin the same respect.

"I thank you for your generosity," he says, and adds rather clumsily, "Your Highness."

Gofraid's laughter booms around the room.

"Very good! Come, sit down, my boy. You haven't yet touched your wine."

ᚦᚱᚾ�

Slowly we piece together the contours of our target. It's maddening to think that such a tantalising fruit dangles in our hand, ripe and full, yet we are so far from plucking it. There is much planning to do, many provisions to organise, and many men to keep informed throughout the coastlines of Dál Riata and the Southern Isles.

As we continue preparations, bright summer sunlight falls upon Dál Riata. The soft drift of it in this peaceful landscape reminds me of Illskarheim and the hall where I grew up, far away in the Northlands. How short the summers were when they graced us. Like here, they might've been bright and cheerful, but the winds stole away their warmth.

I find myself missing home quite terribly.

It has been years since I've set foot there. And yet, while we spend our days enjoying the camaraderie of hunting and fishing and provision-planning, that old yearn to see the fjords of my homeland sparks again.

Still. It is not all domestic occupations. We must also continue to defend ourselves against the backlash of the Pictish tribes who contest Causantin's alliance with us. Like a plague they eat away at his territories, and he disappears for days at a time with our Vyrgen to accompany him. While the King of all Alba busies himself reclaiming his lands and relaying our plans to his own warlords, we spend long days working, feasting and telling tales of battle.

The moon waxes on, not quite a perfect circle yet. The siege of Strathclyde looms ever closer, and yet still it feels distant and formless. Planning has become a never-ending routine, sending out envoys to the surrounding isles, setting meat to dry, repairing our damaged ships. With my injured hand, I cannot be as useful as I'd wish. My brothers set me to the tasks I can feasibly accomplish, and I hate their deliberately careful treatment of me, as though I were some invalid. They thump me on the back come dinnertime and ask me if salting the fish did not sting my wound too much. I try to refrain from giving them a face-full of the table.

It's hard not to think of Tamsin as the moon approaches fullness. We organise the full moon feast ahead of time, inviting Vikings and shieldmaidens from the environing lands to fill the fort with merriment once it hangs full in the night sky. It continually aggravates me to know that she is alone in her rooms, awaiting the predicament of her marriage, certainly miserable.

I hear from the servants that she punishes herself. Aedan confirms it too. Apparently she refuses to stop even when he visits her. He paints garish images of her kneeling on her mat, Latin litanies falling from her lips while she flogs her bruised back.

Aedan tells us of the prayer she intones night and day. *Mea culpa, mea culpa.* The repentance of sinners who ask God for forgiveness. Knowing her, she must blame herself somehow for what happened. While I agonise over the impossibility of visiting her while she is mired in her spiritual pain, Aedan decides it isn't worth his time to continually be rebuffed and stops going altogether, content instead to mock her.

"Strange customs they have in Strathclyde," he tells his councilmen over dinner one night. "Though perhaps there is some genius to it. You don't have to beat your women if you teach them to beat themselves."

It gets a laugh from the older councilmen. Most still haven't forgiven him for Lady Catriona's white eye, however, and they wear a pinched sort of look as they continue talking. Aedan sits there looking smug and proud of his little joke.

I stare at him from across the table, sinking my cutting knife deeper into the wood, breathing through the nascent rage.

How he will treat her once they're married? Does he realise that he would never even have the *permission* to touch a woman of her kind if it weren't for this alliance?

I know we all agreed on their prize. I know we accepted to give sacrosanct women to ignorant men who might not give them the respect they deserve.

I pluck my cutting knife out of the table and stare at the whetted blade. I know there is still a way to break their arrangement, though it wouldn't bode too well with our diplomatic relations.

But when the time comes, if he is not worthy of her, then I will break it myself.

Chapter 27

THRAIN

WAXING MOON OF JUNE

T HE FULL MOON looms ever nearer. One night, my brothers
are out at the docks enjoying the rewards of a long day
spent hammering at ship hulls and winding rope, giving me some
much appreciated peace and quiet. Gofraid and I eat with the
Albans and they thankfully retire early, disappearing to their
quarters. Gofraid lays a hand on my shoulder, bids me goodnight
before disappearing too.

I am blissfully alone in the great hall with several servants
cleaning and Gofraid's Jarls sleeping in their panelled sections.
It's such a rare thing, this quietude. I pour myself some mead and
sit by the main hearth, intent to relax.

I barely get a few moments of peace until someone calls my
name. Glancing up, I find Eilidh rushing across the hall towards
me. I straighten at once. She's one of Tamsin's assigned servants.

"My lord," she says. "Beg pardon, but Lord Aedan does not
want to be disturbed. Permission to bring Princess Tamsin to the
chapel?"

"Why, what's happened?"

"She's… she's fainted, my lord. She hasn't been eating, and

her wounds... she does not let them heal, we're afraid they'll fester."

I push myself to my feet.

"Take me to her."

ᚦᚱᚨᛁᚾ

When I get to her room in the tower, I almost recoil at the smell in there. It stinks of cooped up animal, like the lair of a wolf who dragged in a kill. The only window seems to have remained shuttered ever since she was first brought in.

The girl is kneeling on the rug in the middle of the floor, holding herself up with both arms. Her worried servants sit on either side of her. She seems only just returned to consciousness. Her shift is yanked down to her waist, and I breathe in sharply as I see the wreck of her back.

Immediately, I order the servants to get up and straighten up the place. They are to open the window, bundle away the dirty laundry, and bring in flowers to chase away the bad smell. To Eilidh, I give the task of finding me hot water and clay for the wounds.

I go to Tamsin myself, pick her up off the floor and lead her to her bed. She whimpers as my arm presses against her fresh wounds. Her blood seeps into my own clothes as I help her to lay down belly-first on the linens of her bed.

She's still groggy as she lays there, breathing softly in the steadily growing cold of the room. I slick her hair away from her back, taking in the new gashes. Bright red blood traces contrasting lines over older brownish patches. It is as though she set to hacking at herself without even stopping to clean herself up.

I go to her wash basin, pour some cold water in it, then sit by her side and set to cleaning the muck from her skin with a clean washcloth.

"Don't touch me," she sobs into her pillows. "Please don't touch me."

"I don't particularly want to, Tamsin," I tell her softly. "But you leave me no choice."

"My servants can take care of me."

"Your servants clearly haven't given you the type of care you should've been receiving. Or, you have not let them near enough to do so."

She hisses as I scrub at the dry blood between her shoulder-blades. Anger thrums in my veins as it always does when I'm reminded of this disgusting custom. But now I have the words of her own betrothed to fuel it, too. I try hard to stay gentle as I rub patches from her nape.

"Thrain," she says at length into her pillows. The sound of my name in her mouth sends an unexpected thrill through me. "Thrain Mordsson."

"Yes."

"You know, Aedan told me a story about you," she says weakly. "He said that when you arrived here, you were chased away by the ghosts of all those Christians you enslaved."

I frown down at her scarred back. "I suppose he was trying to gain your trust with some fanciful tale."

"You mean a *lie*. You all stood in our halls and won our trust with bare-faced lies."

I always knew this was coming, and yet to confront her misery is unbearable. I focus on wiping the blood up without aggravating her wounds, racking my mind for an answer.

"Aedan did resist us when we arrived here," I tell her. "There is an agreement between Gofraid and Causantin, but Aedan is the one who rules this fort. He had some noble idea that he should at least put up a show of strength to protest his uncle's orders. But in so doing, he tested the loyalties of his armies, who do not trust his leadership. Once the lady arrived to call back their men, they all easily stood down so that we could consolidate our alliance."

Her chest bobs against the bed as she gives a mirthless laugh. "And Aedan told it like some self-aggrandizing tale of victory."

I'm scowling as I imagine how Aedan might've framed it. Of course he would turn it in his favour. I wonder how far he took the lie just to build himself up. "The whole ordeal has affected his standing quite profoundly," I tell her. "Perhaps he wanted to impress you while he still could, while you were still ignorant of the realities of this place."

She stays silent as I give her wounds a final stroke of my blood-soaked cloth.

"I hate him," she whispers at last. "I wish he would die."

I'm surprised to hear such words from a devout Christian. Then again, it is with the same sentiment that she drove that knife through my palm. With my good hand, I rinse my cloth in the basin that I placed on the bed, trying to pick apart my racing thoughts.

"You would be in quite the predicament without him."

"I don't care."

"Tamsin, there is a difference between bravery and lacking consideration for your own survival."

Eilidh comes back at last with the materials I need. I bid her prepare the clay, and she mixes vigorously until it's of the appropriate consistency. I watch her deft movements and envy her the coordinated strength of her hands. *It'll come back,* I tell myself for the hundredth time. I thank her, and she bows out of the room. The other servants follow her out, holding bundles of linens. One of them has rolled up the rug and carries it out to pat the dust from it.

We're alone. I place Eilidh's tray on the bed beside Tamsin's slight body, then lay a thin strip of linen over her back. Once I've covered her, I start dabbing clay over the linen, following the dark outlines of her open gashes.

She twitches and sighs as I go on placing the clay. After a while, she grumbles, "Since when does a warlord like you know so much about healing?"

"A warlord is constantly surrounded by the sick and wounded," I tell her. "I wouldn't be much of a leader if I couldn't help to heal my own. Though it is not easy now that I'm one-handed."

I can't help the evocation, especially now that I'm forced to work the clay in this clumsy and imprecise manner. She says nothing to that. Once I've finished applying it, I let it sit, telling her that she'll have to stay still for another hour or so before she can be rid of it. She breathes softly against her pillows, lost in thought.

"Your hand isn't healing, then?" she asks after a while. Her tone betrays nothing of her feelings. I wonder if it would bring her joy to know that it continuously smarts and stings as though caught in a wolf's jaw.

I decide to be laconic: "It is healing. But it's a slow process."

She falls silent again. I get up to stow away the bowls on her washing station. When I come back to the edge of her bed and sit there lightly, she seems contemplative.

She settles more comfortably against the cushions. When she next speaks, her voice is softer than before. "Can I ask you something?"

"Please."

"Why did you come seeking me out during my courtship? Of all the girls in heat in the castle, a lawless man in disguise could've had his pick. Why not Eormen herself, the king's daughter? Why be content with just the niece?"

However quiet her tone, it is still full of accusation. I can only be glad that she isn't wishing my death like she did for her betrothed.

"I was never meant to befriend you," I mutter. "When I met you in the chapel, I found it intolerable that you might hurt yourself. So… I suppose I wanted to protect you."

She turns her head. I see a glint of green over her naked shoulder as she glances at me.

"It is God that moves my hand," she says.

"Then I would protect you from him."

She scoffs. "You're an arrogant fool, Thrain Mordsson."

"Perhaps."

Silence follows. I stare down at the clay-covered expanse of her back, the freckled skin of her shoulders, her long slender arms as they disappear under her pillow. Even they bear faint purple marks. I cannot help but hate her god for placing those bruises all over her.

Then she mutters in an angry, wounded voice, "I wish I had never met you. I wish you had just left me alone. You had no right to – " Her voice breaks and she says no more, hugging the pillows closer to her.

I bow my head. "I know."

She wipes her face with difficulty. "You just took what you wanted," she goes on in that horribly broken voice, "you pretended concern only to lay me bare and then gloat to your brothers about it—"

"No one knows what happened that night," I contradict her. "I do not wish to share that memory with anyone but you."

She swallows, letting another pause drift between us.

"Don't pretend to care about me," she whispers. "Don't. I might've fallen for it once but I won't believe your lies a second time."

"I am not lying," I urge her. "As long as we are under the same roof, I will protect you. If you ever need help against one of the men here, or even against Aedan himself, you can come to me."

She's silent for a moment.

"And you would want something in return, of course?"

Her cynicism is inevitable. Gone is the girl who would reach for my hand and pull me closer, the one who believed my intentions could be pure. She is wiser now, mistrustful. I know it will serve her well, but her words still cut deep.

"There is nothing I want in return," I manage to grumble. "Except perhaps that you stop this self-punishment. Your skin is torn open – you must let it heal or you risk illness."

"I don't make deals with savage warlords."

This time I can only smile, though there is no mirth to it.

"You have nothing to punish yourself for, princess," I tell her softly.

"You understand nothing," she seethes through a tight throat.

I get up, search the room. Finally I find the leather handle of her flogger, discarded on the floor near her trunks. I march over to it and pick it up.

"No," Tamsin breathes as she sees me slide it in one of my belt loops. She starts to push herself up and then stops, remembering her nakedness. "No, please! Leave it."

"I will not," I snap. "And don't you dare find a substitute."

"Please," she says, staring at me beseechingly with eyes full of tears. "Please leave it."

She distinctly reminds me of those men who drown themselves in ale and turn violent when the barrels are taken from them. I wait for her to start shouting at me, and she does just that.

"You don't understand! You don't understand *anything,* you're just a pagan – hairy savage *bastard!*" Angry tears run down her reddening face. "You're the devil! I asked you to help me and you did, and it's because of you that the ritual was sullied – and I betrayed my king, I betrayed my *God*—"

"Your god only asks to be betrayed if he forces his subjects to treat themselves this way," I say coldly.

She lets out a disbelieving scoff. "Don't you see it? Are you *blind?*" she shouts. "It's because of my selfishness that God turned His face away from my kingdom. It's all because of me that a thousand of our men died, and that many more will die in the siege to come. So you will leave the flogger, you'll leave me at least the means to repent if you *care* for me so much—"

I stare at her. I knew she would have some form of guilt but to shoulder the entire enterprise of Gofraid and Causantin herself?

"Last I checked," I tell her, "it was my axe that was wet with the blood of your Briton soldiers. And last I checked, you were glad for your brother to be alive."

She pants in the ringing silence that follows, still looking at me with those reddened eyes, that ashen, aggrieved face.

"We are not your agents," I tell her. "Gofraid and Causantin plotted together long before you saved your brother. The trap was laid already when we arrived. You have absolutely no business shouldering this burden. You have done nothing. We planned to overwhelm your men, and I assure you, they could not have been saved even if your god descended from the sky."

"You know nothing of our God," she seethes.

"If he willingly lets a thousand of his loyal followers die to punish one girl, I doubt he is worth knowing," I bite back.

She frowns at this. She angers me so much with her misplaced guilt, but gods, that face she wears – I want nothing more than to sit by her, give her warm spiced mead, comfort her rather than shout at her. But she would not tolerate such gentleness from me right now, that much is obvious.

"Give it back," she says again, this time in a pitiful croak. "Please, Thrain. *Please.*"

I go to the door, call for Eilidh. She comes in. Ignoring Tamsin's continued pleas and sobs with difficulty, I give the servant instructions so she may more efficiently peel away the still-wet clay from Tamsin's back. Then I excuse myself, bidding the princess goodbye.

"Wait," Tamsin calls weakly. "My brother. Eormen. Are they—"

"They're fine," I tell her. "You will see them soon. At the wedding, I expect."

Tamsin nods, exhausted now, her lips pressed tight together. Then she lays her head on her pillows again, staring ahead into nothingness as she lets the old Irishwoman finish the treatment in silence.

ᚦᚱᚨᛁᚾ

On the eve of the full moon, the princesses' joint wedding ceremonies are prepared. They're to take place in the privacy of the fort chapel without any Vyrgen in attendance. That way they might conform as much as they can to their own Christian customs even under Viking occupation.

I feel my body grow restless with anticipation as the full moon looms. It is the first time in centuries that we Vyrgen might share the moon with Vanirdøtur. I'm acutely aware of their presence in the fort, even locked away as they are, as my blood begins to run hotter and hotter. For the first time I am fiercely glad that they're protected behind bolted doors – all my pack must be feeling the same way.

I help my brothers and the servants to prepare the main hall for our seven-day feast. The staff are far better prepared now that it is their second moon accommodating our needs. I make my visit to the kitchens and find Mugain just as busy as always, this time less chaotically so as they have planned their supplies much more efficiently.

Though I try to banish Tamsin from my mind, I cannot help but imagine the night that awaits her. Her back hasn't even had much time to heal. I told Eilidh to make sure she didn't aggravate her wounds, but those slashes must barely be scabbing over. I imagine that scaly, yellowish mess hidden under the glamour of her bridal garb. Will Aedan even take care not to hurt her?

Aedan. Just imagining him touching her at all is enough to make me want to pierce him through the heart with the spear I stilled. She will lie under him and he will take from her with no regard for her own desires.

I station myself at the window of my quarters, watching the courtyard so I might see the proceedings. Crowds of people throw petals into the air as Eormen is led first into the open doors of the chapel. Then... Tamsin arrives on Aedan's arm.

Her gown is a deep forest-green, embroidered with gold and gems. Both sleeves trail all the way down to the floor, completing her elegant silhouette. Her ginger hair is loose and falls down her back, covered by a sheer white veil that is held in place by a golden circlet. Aedan walks beside her in matching green attire.

I press my fist against the window frame as I stare down at them. For the breath-taking beauty of her gown, it's laced far too tight, decorative belts cinched close around her torso. She must be in a lot of pain. I wonder if she wears bandages beneath. Perhaps they chose that deep green colour so any blood seepage wouldn't be seen.

"Freya protect her," I mutter.

"Thrain," comes Ivar's voice from my doorway. "Are you coming?"

Scowling, I push myself away from the window. I can't let myself dwell on it. Such was her fate as soon as she stepped aboard our ship.

I have to let her go.

ᚦᚱᚨᛁᚾ

As before, musicians fill the great hall with the sound of lutes and drums. There is roaring laughter and chatter as men and women come together. Soon, the wolf pelts will be overtaken by frenzied bodies, the tables will be weighted down by couples pinning each other onto the mead-sodden wood.

I stand by one of the entrances of the great hall, a goblet of wine in hand, staring unseeingly at the revelry.

By now she is being led to Aedan's quarters.

I cannot stop torturing myself with images of them in their bedchamber. Will he even know how to touch her? Will she wind her arms around his neck and plead with him to stay, and make her satisfied?

Or will he hurt her? Will she recoil from him as she did on the ship?

I see her again, pouring wine for us both in the privacy of the chapel. A sardonic smile on her lips. *Marriage is more about endurance than anything else.*

Her mouth open against mine. Hot breath, wine-stained and intoxicating. *I would choose you even in daylight.*

I drink deep from my goblet. I will get no satisfaction from this feast, not if she is unavailable to me, not if I know she is somewhere in this castle and I cannot reach her.

It must be this pain that Olaf feels as he holds himself apart from the revelry. I swore never to feel this, never to subject myself to this weakness, this *pining* for an unattainable woman. But I know that laying with strangers will only remind me of the one I cannot have. It is supremely ironic that I might suffer now as though Tamsin were my Vanirdottir, stolen and about to be ravaged by another man, though she is not mine and never was.

I should try to do as Olaf does; drown myself in wine and forget her.

Chapter 28

TAMSIN

FULL MOON OF JUNE

I KNEEL THROUGH MY wedding ceremony with a stony face. The bishop who blesses our union smiles forcibly at me to try and get me to at least show some joy on my own wedding day.

The only thing that brought me a modicum of solace was the sight of Rhun when I first came in on the bishop's arm. He was sitting in the pews, guarded by a single heavy-set Dálriadan man. It was the first time I caught a glimpse of him since being locked away in the tower. My heart leapt to see him healthy and rosy-cheeked. His hands gripped the back of the pew as he stared back at me. He was not wearing shackles.

If he's here at all, then it means that whoever monitors him at least gave him some leeway to move around the fort. We could only stare hopefully at one another as I was walked down the aisle by the bishop, and then he disappeared behind me as I knelt in front of the altar.

I try to hold onto the knowledge that my twin is here with me, watching over me, to give myself courage. Diligently I take from the flesh and blood of Christ. When I turn to face my betrothed, Aedan wears a smug sort of smile. Self-satisfaction radiates from him. He's claiming his prize at last.

"You are now husband and wife," announces the bishop. "Tamsin, you may rise as our Lady of Dál Riata."

Aedan helps me up, then presses his wormy mouth against mine in an attempt to kiss me. He smells overpoweringly of meat and spoilt fruit.

This is my lot. And I must suffer that stench for the whole night.

Everyone sitting in the pews rises as we walk down the aisle together. I find Rhun's face in the crowd again. He gives me a firm nod, his expression heart-breakingly grave. I want to cry just looking at him. Where is he staying? Is he all right? I want to shout the questions at him. But protocol dictates that I stay silent, and I don't want him to get into trouble for my sake. I stare at him until it hurts my neck too much to turn it, and follow Aedan outside.

A crowd of people wait outside to cheer and throw down flowers for us. Eormen and Domnall were wed just before we were; the courtyard is already choked with crushed bouquets. Aedan leads me between the cheering crowds and towards the main doors of the fort. He's to lead me all the way across the corridors to our quarters, where we are to consummate the marriage.

I feel sick at the mere thought of it. My heat has returned, but it seems to be rolled up in a tight ball in my belly, quivering with disgust every time he looms nearer.

I can't bear to feel my heat in a place like this. I can't bear the betrayal of it. I know that once the moon rises and Aedan starts touching me, he will unravel it and make my body demand more. I know there is nothing to be done but last through the night. Survive.

But God, I wish it could be different. I wish I could be like one of the other girls, not enslaved to my heat cycle, not craving proximity even with men like Aedan once I've sunk deep enough into the heat-stupor.

My breaths get shorter and shorter as we make our way through the main doors and into the corridors of Dunadd fort. I crave more air, more sky, after the full fortnight spent shut up in the tower. But we sink into the claustrophobic stone passageways and skulk towards the quarters belonging to the lord of the fort.

Servants are waiting there, holding the doors open for us. Aedan smiles down at me and invites me to go in before him.

The woollen bed covers are all lined with sumptuous silver-thread embroidery. I'm to lay back, drag up my skirts, and close my eyes.

But I can't. I *can't*. Everything about this marriage is a lie. Surely I have no true obligation towards him. Not when he brought me here under false pretences.

The doors close. Aedan loosens the ceremonial cape from his throat and lets it slide to the floor. The rumple of fabric makes my breath catch in my throat.

"I can't do this," I blurt out.

"What, consummate our marriage?" he says with a laugh. "Come, now. I'll be gentle, I promise."

I shake my head. "No, Aedan, I... I can't do it. I don't want to."

"It's normal to be afraid," he croons. "Lay back, take your time. We have all night."

His words pull at the heat in my belly. I want to throw up as I feel it filling my body with its usual first-day intensity.

"There's nothing legitimate about this wedding," I tell him, staying by the doors. "You wed me so that you could have me without breaking any rules. But God sees you for the liar that you are."

"Tamsin," Aedan sighs. "Do you remember what I told you on our way out here?"

"That I shouldn't test your patience?" I thrust up my chin. "What, are you going to hit me again?"

His expression darkens with annoyance. "You think I wouldn't do it?"

"I think you're perfectly capable of hitting your bride on your wedding night."

For a moment I expect him to lash out in anger. But he does something far worse.

He smiles. That horrid, sneering, self-satisfied smile.

Without any warning, he grabs me by my hair. I yelp in pain

as he yanks me around hard, forcing me to the bed. He gives one merciless pull and I fall onto the bed, air knocked from my lungs by the impact.

He straddles my hips, kneeling over me. Before I can crawl out from underneath him, his fingers curl tightly around my wrists, pinning me there on the mattress. He leers down at me, candlelight shining on his receding hairline and those delighted, insane eyes.

"Do you know how little I care for your comfort?" he murmurs. "You ask me to respect you, when your people took my father from me? I've been waiting for this night a long time, Tamsin. You can struggle all you like. It'll only make it sweeter."

The menace in his tone crackles down my body. I stare wide-eyed at the ceiling as he leans down to slobber on my neck, one hand unbuckling my decorative belts. Pain spears along my back as he pulls them from me, each belt raking horribly against my wounds through the dress.

He pulls my skirts up next in quick tugs. Time stretches, nightmarish, as I try to unglue myself from his persistent snake-like arms, kicking and pushing with what little strength I have left. Heat throbs between my legs and the betrayal of it makes me want to cry.

He smirks at me as he takes in my panting, dishevelled state.

"If you truly are what King Arthgal promised," he purrs, "then you'll beg me for it, even if I hurt you. Won't you? You'll let me do exactly what I want with you, and you'll even ask for more."

My heat glows hotter at his words, and hotter still as he thrusts my skirts up between my thighs, bunching them up against my slick centre. He rubs me roughly through the fabric, pleasure blooming as he touches me down there. I blink desperately through the growing haze of it. I have to stay lucid. *I have to.*

It horrifies me that he's right. Just the touch of his hand in the right places and my heat reacts already. Even if he hurts me – my heat will still shiver and rise to his slightest encouragement.

I have to get out of here.

He kisses my mouth as he goes on igniting me with his hand.

I bite down hard on his lip. He groans and bites back. Pain flashes, blood trickles down my chin. I manage to wrench away from him, whimpering, pushing myself up into a sitting position only to realise he's letting me do it. He's grinning at me as though this were some sick game. Then he grabs my hair again and forces me down on my front.

Pain erupts through me. He's pressing one hand down on my back. I'm temporarily blind with pain. I can feel my skin splitting.

"Do you think you've repented enough?" Aedan whispers in that mad, eager voice. "I don't think you have. How about we continue your prayer?"

That hand stays on my back as the other unbuckles his own wedding attire. Sight comes back to me slowly as I breathe through the horrid pain. A washing station stands next to the bed, sporting a ceramic jug and washing basin. I stare at it, trying to hold onto my conscious mind as pain writhes through me.

"Say it," he whispers. "The mea culpa." He begins the prayer in Gaelic. "O God Almighty, who desires that all men be saved, who commands us to cleanse ourselves and be purified... go on, princess. Repent."

His belt clatters to the floor. I frown at the wash station, eyes wide. "You're insane," I whisper. But he presses down harder, making me gasp in agony.

"Repent!" he orders.

"Thou... Thou who bids us to reject all malice from our hearts," I stammer, translating haphazardly into Gaelic. "We shall take up endeavours that are pleasing to Thee; thus we shall be whiter than snow, we who have sinned..."

A strange sound adds itself to the silence as I pant and try to focus on translating. It's like... skin on skin, soft slapping behind me, but I can't see what that madman is doing.

"O my master, please invoke upon this sinner, Thou unworthy servant... the promise of forgiveness Thou made to Thine most faithful..."

Slap, slap, slap. He's groaning now, panting as he does whatever it is he's doing.

"*Mea culpa, mea culpa... mea maxima culpa.*"

He groans again, this time so overtly sexually that I realise with a jolt what's making that sound.

He's touching himself. While I say the *mea culpa*.

Horror fills my body. He's insane. Completely mad. Why in God's name would a Christian lord do that – *why* – I can't lay here and let him do that, I *won't*. It's too horrible.

Days of barely eating anything have made me damnably weak. I know I can't overpower him. Not unless he's distracted.

I can only go on saying the litany, focussing on how his grip on my back weakens as he goes on masturbating to the sound of my repentance.

"O my God, who reads our hearts, I come to Thee now in utmost sincerity and subordination. I regret all my faults and in future I will renounce all sin and shameful acts. I will spend my days in deepest obeisance of Thine sacred commandments—"

"*Uggn,*" Aedan moans. He's almost let go of me. Holding my breath, I check over my shoulder. His eyes are closed as he goes on frenetically masturbating. He's not looking.

"*Mea culpa…*"

Heart thumping, I fix my eyes on the washing station.

"*Mea culpa…*"

I reach. My hands close around the wash basin. The heavy earthenware is coated with a blue ceramic glaze.

"*Mea maxima culpa.*"

He gives an ugly high-pitched whine as he reaches climax. I turn around and smash the basin so hard over his head that it breaks into a hundred pieces, pouring down his body and clattering on the floor.

He yells and falls sideways, cradling his head. I scramble away and push myself off the bed, panting and whimpering like some wild wounded creature.

Aedan staggers and slumps to the floor. He's curled there, his penis poking out of his robes, arms over his head, the picture so grotesque I can barely believe what I'm looking at. He seems unconscious – I don't stop to check. I run for the door, almost falling against it.

The handle is so stiff. I throw my weight at it until it creaks down at last.

I bolt right out.

ᚾᚼᚤᛋᛁᚼ

I'm holding my bridal dress in bunches as I run across the corridors, half-blinded by the throbbing pain that spans my back.

There's nowhere I can go for help. Not even the chapel – they'll know I should be consummating my marriage, they sanctioned this whole farce. Perhaps if I knew where Rhun or Eormen were staying – but there is no way of knowing that right now.

Dimly, I remember words spoken in a moment of weakness, I remember the sombre tone they were spoken in. I might not be able to trust him, but… he did say he wanted to protect me. And so far, he has done nothing untoward, even whilst having full access to my room in the tower.

I must be mad to go seeking a vicious Viking warlord under the full moon. But I'm torn between pain and the overbearing urge to keep away from Aedan. It's my only immediate solution, abysmal as it is.

I run towards the music and revelry. Perhaps I'll find him there.

There are Vikings in the corridors on the way to the hall. They smell me, even engaged as they are with each other or the women who've come to the feast. Their heads come up, and they snarl as they watch me pass.

I am throwing myself into a den of wolves. I must be out of my *mind*.

He's got to be here somewhere.

I stop in the colonnaded walkway that lines the hall. Inside, it is as though Lucifer himself had orchestrated a hellish ball. There is a feast of food and drink and flesh. People are coiled together in couples and groups, caressing, pleasing, moaning and sighing.

Hell. I am in Hell. Perhaps I drowned when I leapt from the ship and Thrain pulled me up into another plane altogether.

The wounds on my back should've banished the heat – but it returns with a vengeance as I stand there and stare. There are *so many people.* So many cursed men, their scents mingling in the air, drawing me in by the nose. My body doesn't care about any moral codes I might be clinging to, nor that Aedan caged me against his bed only moments ago. The sights in front of me are triggering my heat to unprecedented heights, so much so that I can barely even feel the pain in my back any more. It's unbearable to hold myself apart from it all.

I make myself look for blond hair. Faces turn towards me, eager and hungry. Dimly I'm aware that it's not a particularly brilliant idea to make myself so visible and available to this horde of cursed men. I must look a sight too, with my split lip and dishevelled hair.

With the growing fog of the heat-stupor, I see their sculpted bodies, their beautiful faces, their tender gestures. If only for a moment, I want nothing more than to throw myself in their midst. There is beauty to this pagan gathering, and the Other Tamsin recognises it. I teeter as though standing on the edge of a cliff, seduced by the void ahead of me, filled with the strange urge to let myself fall.

A hand finds my shoulder, and I am abruptly pulled behind a pillar into relative seclusion.

Thrain is there, still dressed and cloaked, looking like he's barely even touched the heathen extravaganza all around him. His eyes rake over my bridal garb, and then focus on my split lip.

"What in Odin's name are you doing out here?" he says. "It's far too dangerous for you here. What happened? Why aren't you with Aedan?"

I shake my head. I can barely get the words out.

"Did he hurt you again?" Thrain growls, and the threat in his tone makes me senselessly afraid. He angles my chin up to better observe my split lip. "Did he do this?"

"Please," I say, and I can't help the sob that bubbles out of me. "He's insane. He's insane."

Thoughtlessly I reach for the monk, the friend I used to have, the one who would hold my hands in the dark and comfort me. He lets me grasp him and our familiar joining shimmers through me, reaching through the chaos that inhabits me to touch my soul.

"Tamsin," he rumbles. A growl is building in his chest as I lean against him.

"You said you'd protect me," I manage. "Can you take me somewhere safe? Where he won't find me?"

He breathes out sharply, and nods.

"Come with me."

Chapter 29

TAMSIN
FULL MOON OF JUNE

T HRAIN TAKES ME to what I can only assume are his own
quarters. It's all sunk into darkness while the hearth remains
unlit; moonlight drifts in from the window, offering only a dusty
outline of the place. He closes the door behind us and strides in
to light the readied pile of kindling in the grate.

I lean against the closed door, catching my breath, watching
as the fire slowly builds in intensity. Thrain blows upon it and
an orange glow illuminates the room as the flames grow. A large
bed sprawls before me, plush with furs. One tired-looking table
occupies the length of the wall to my right, while the wash station
is off in the corner. His own paraphernalia is strewn everywhere —
leather pouches and coins on the table, sheathed weapons leaning
against the corners of the room.

It smells of linseed oil in here, as well as the unmistakable scent
of a masculine host. Be it the sweat, the musk, the leather... I can't
quite explain it. I only know that I am in his lair, and my body is
achingly alert because of it.

Thrain comes back to me, his face drawn with concern. He
touches my shoulder so I might turn, then hisses through his

teeth as he sees my back.

"You're bleeding," he says. I wrap my arms around myself as cold realisation seeps through me. Aedan hurt me – really hurt me. "I mean no indiscretion, but – are you wearing bandages?"

"Yes. Under the shift."

"We'll have to change them. Wait here a moment, I'll be right back."

He leaves, closing the door behind him. I sit down on the bed with a sigh. My legs are shaking so much, I don't know if I could even stand up again.

He comes back soon enough. "A servant will come with salves and linens," he says as he bolts the door behind him.

I sit there for a moment. I don't know what to say. Though I'm here with Thrain I still feel pinned against Aedan's mattress, reciting prayer with that awful slapping sound in my ears. I have to get the scene out of me.

"He told me to say the mea culpa," I tell Thrain. "He told me to pray and he was excited by it. Me asking for forgiveness. He… he was excited by it."

Thrain sits on the bed beside me, his own wash basin in his good hand. I stare down at it, remembering the weight of cold ceramic in my palms. He soaks a rag in the water, frowning in bewilderment as he tries to find an answer.

"Why?" I ask him. My voice sounds high, despairing. My heart's still banging in my chest. "Why would he do that? He blames me for his father's death. I thought that's what it was about at first. But it was as though… as though he were equating himself with God. As though God Himself would take that kind of pleasure in hearing His subjects pray to Him."

Thrain looks up at me for a moment, eyes flickering between mine. "You are the one who knows your god best," he says. He reaches to wipe the blood from my chin.

Recognition streaks through my veins again at the touch of his hand. I close my eyes. It feels so purifying after Aedan's oppressive insistence.

"God made Man in His image," I mutter.

"Mad and perverted, then?"

The blaspheme is enormous and yet, somehow, exactly what I need to hear. Someone who agrees that this is too much – too horrible. Just thinking of picking up my flogger again makes me feel sick. I know God should be beyond such things, but the question blares in my mind and will not leave me alone. In all the scriptures, statues and chapels, He is male.

"Do your gods feel sexual attraction?" I ask Thrain. He smiles faintly at the oddness of the question.

"Yes, of course. Doesn't yours?"

"He's not... supposed to."

"Hmm." I expect him to go on criticizing our Lord as he seems to enjoy doing, but instead he says, "Whatever the true nature of your god, I'm not sure Aedan's madness is anything to go by. That boy is in his own realm entirely."

He lets go of my chin. I smile faintly at him, grateful for his calm patience, the benevolence that still seems to emanate from him even now that I know who he is. Somehow I understand him better than Aedan – he is a cursed Viking, his culture pushes him to bloody violence in battle, his pagan faith explains his lack of remorse when it comes to food and sex. Warfare is one thing, political squabblings over land and riches an understandable evil. Aedan's perversions, however, as a Christian man who is not cursed... they're far harder to understand or justify.

"Would you like the servant to bind your bandages when she arrives?" Thrain asks. "I can step out and guard the door."

I nod. Realisation hits me suddenly – it's the first night of my heat, and he's been able to scent it since I first barged in here. I can't believe I've been sitting here not even aware of the efforts he's making to control himself. "I'm sorry to impose—"

"Don't apologise," he says. "You can sleep here tonight. This door can be bolted shut, but there are a lot of Vyrgen men in this fort tonight, and you gave them all a taste of your scent when you went to the hall. I think many of them are going to be seeking you out. I'll stand outside and make sure no one bothers you. Especially Aedan."

There is a familiar look in his eye, a darkness underlying his own feelings towards me. "I know you aren't impervious to my scent either," I stammer.

He holds my gaze. "I will not touch you, princess. I'm used to spending sleepless nights under the full moon."

I sigh and bow my head. Then something he said sparks a red light of worry in my mind. "Aedan," I mutter. "I… I smashed a bowl over his head."

Thrain represses a smirk. "Do you want me to check if he's still alive?"

"If you could. I'd appreciate it."

A knock comes. Thrain gets up and goes to the door, letting in the servant girl who is half buried in a pile of linens. He nods over at me before leaving. "I can come back with some food, if you'd like."

"Oh, yes please."

"You'll stay here?"

"I will."

Once he leaves, the servant girl picks up the wooden bolt and slides it on the door pegs. The sound of it fitting in its pegs makes me feel truly secure for the first time this evening.

Still, my heart knocks a nervous rhythm against my ribs as I wonder if this was the best course of action.

Locked in the private bedchambers of Thrain Mordsson.

Shaking a little, I let the servant girl fuss around me. We unlace my dress together, and the pressure falling away makes me wince. Once it's off I stare at the blood blackening the back of it. What Mother would say if she saw this! My shift is probably wrecked, too. The servant girl pulls it down to my waist, much like Hilda used to do. I sit up straight on the edge of the bed as she pulls every last bit of linen from me, squinting as the scabs and torn skin smart horribly.

After it's all taken care of and my torso is wrapped again in large linen sheets, the servant girl offers me a fresh shift to wear. She sits by the door, waiting to be dismissed.

"Do you mind staying until he gets back?" I ask her. She smiles at me.

"It'd be my pleasure, my lady."

She's been quiet and empathetic throughout the whole

procedure. I wonder what she thinks of me, as a guest in her master's fort. Technically I should be lady of the fort by now, had I consummated properly. Perhaps she shows me deference because she assumes I have risen to the position.

I've never felt further from any type of lady or figure of authority. I pull on my shift and let myself sink into the pillows, finally free to relax my rigid posture. The scent of Thrain is all over the linens. I close my eyes, allow myself to appreciate the heady masculinity of it. There is precious little that feels familiar or safe here, and all I know is that his scent harkens back to that night we spent in the chapel, the private glittering world he led me into. It gives me a fleeting impression of comfort, so I cling to it, however impossible such a thing might seem.

I wrap myself up in the covers and furs, and try to relax.

ᛏᚼᚹᛌᛁᚠ

Loud music and sounds of revelry reverberate from the great hall, keeping me on high alert regardless of my efforts to shut off my mind. Laughter and screams of pleasure ring in the night. Sometimes there is the smashing of crockery against flagstones, accompanied by the yelling of men perhaps fighting over a partner. Dimly, I wonder if Thrain has had to go up against Aedan in my honour.

The thought is difficult to believe. A Viking warlord, defending my honour… it seems so bizarre that I would seek the protection of the worst of the barbarians against my own betrothed.

If my uncle only knew what a terrible place he's thrown us into.

Savagely, part of me is happy that soon his castle will be overrun with Vikings. It'll serve him right for putting us in this position. Selling Eormen and I for a sham of an alliance.

He must've known something was wrong. He must've had some inkling. I know he has spies all over Strathclyde and Alba. It's impossible that he didn't get any word about this alliance between Causantin and the Vikings.

Someone knocks on the door.

The sound sends a thrill down my spine. I jerk up, staring at the wood that stands between me and whatever lust-crazed assailants are beyond. The servant girl looks alarmed.

"She's in there, I can smell her!"

"Princess! Are you all right? They say you fled from Lord Aedan's chamber."

"Thrain's going to get an earful for stealing Aedan's bride on his own wedding night."

"Ha! It was bound to happen. Those Albans wouldn't know the first thing about laying with a Vanirdottir anyway."

"Did he really steal you, princess? Do you need rescue?"

God, there's a whole group of them. Their voices are slurred with alcohol. My whole body tenses when they knock again, the hail of fists making the door tremble in its hinges.

"Princess! We know you're in there. Don't be frightened!"

"No! No, I don't need rescue!" I call to them. I must be out of my mind to be replying to them at all. "I'm fine right here."

"We can help you," one of them says. "It's the full moon. You shouldn't be all alone."

"Please," I stammer. "Don't concern yourself with me."

"But we are," another says, and I can hear the smile in his voice. "Very concerned."

"What in Hel's name do you think you're doing?"

Thrain's voice booms over the rest. I find myself sighing with relief at the sound. He chastises his men for crowding his door, and chases them away with a few well-chosen words. When they laugh and tell him that Gofraid will have his hide for breaking their covenant with the Albans, he curses them in his own tongue.

The servant girl bows to me and rushes to lift the wooden bolt. Thrain comes inside, lets her out and turns immediately to shut the door again.

We're alone. Safe.

Well, as safe as I can be in the company of Thrain Mordsson.

"Is he alive, then?" I ask him.

"Oh yes," he grumbles darkly. "Very much so."

I'm not sure I'm relieved to hear it. He's silent as he hands me a platter of food and then moves away to seat himself at his table. He diligently looks away from me; it takes me a moment to realise I'm wearing naught but a shift and bandages. Flushing, I focus on my food. The panic has carved a hole in my stomach – I devour the bread and cheese and apple pie he's given me. Another glance at Thrain shows me that he's unwinding the bandage from his injured hand.

He notices my attention and says, "I don't mean to linger. Only, I have to change this."

The lines of his face are tensed with pain, more so than earlier. I wonder for a moment if he might've hit Aedan with that hand.

I shake my head. I almost want to laugh. "Your turn to change your bandages, is it?"

He smirks. "Let's say we are both a little worse for wear."

"I should've asked the servant girl to stay and help you."

The moment feels like a dream as I sit there with this notorious villain, trying to ignore the sight of him struggling with his one-handed bandaging effort. There's something so strange and pitiful about seeing such an imposing man struggle with a handicap he's not accustomed to yet.

"Did you hit my husband?" I ask him.

"Might've done," he grunts.

Fierce delight surges through me. I put down my apple slices and wander over to him.

"Here," I say as I sit on the second stool beside him. "Let me bind it."

He stares at me in surprise, leaning back to keep a formal distance between us. He decidedly keeps his eyes off me, both of us focussed on his hand that's lying on the table. Heat swells in my belly as I watch him walling himself up in his self-control.

"Is my scent too strong?" I murmur.

"I can handle it," he says gruffly. "For now."

"I'll be quick." I reach for his bandages and unwind the bloody mess.

I breathe in sharply as I uncover the scar. The edges of the gash are red and sore. Fresh blood has seeped from it. His fingers tremble as he holds his hand open for my inspection.

I don't know enough about healing to ascertain how well he's recovering. All that registers is how painful the injury looks. I wonder for a moment at his stoicism, how he has never tried to seek reparation for this, even when he had full liberty to seek me out during the past fortnight.

I clean it carefully with one of the fresh rags and the water bowl left over from the servant's treatments. He twitches, his last two fingers stuck together and moving jointly when I begin to bind his hand. It's difficult to believe that he might've been able to operate this hand so decisively before.

I think of the chapel, first. A blush steals across my face.

Then I think of the Firth of Clyde. The axe that this hand wielded.

The silence is growing charged. I can feel Thrain's eyes on me as I work. I'm lost in the dissonance of my affection for him, the friendship that is still very present between us and so easy to fall back into, and the constant reminder of who he is. What he's done.

My captor. I have many captors; King Causantin, Aedan, and God perhaps, if Thrain were to add to the list. But he is also on there somewhere.

"Are you going to make a full recovery?" I ask him sheepishly.

"I don't think so," he says.

"Oh."

He betrays his cool façade by wincing at the tightness of my binding. I try to be more gentle as I tie the linen and pin it. My heart thumps against my chest as we lean together over the table.

"I'm the one who invited you to touch me that night," I murmur. "I shouldn't have cut you. I'm sor—"

"Don't," he says sharply. "Don't apologise. For mercy's sake, stop putting the blame on yourself. We both know I shouldn't have accepted the invitation."

I let him go to signal that I'm finished. Thrain doesn't move. Breathing in, I meet his gaze at last. His heavy-set brow is dented in a frown, blue eyes glowing golden in the firelight as he observes me. At long last he lifts his good hand and strokes my cheek, pretending to be brushing away a strand of hair.

"I'm the one who should apologise," he says. "For wearing the disguise. For lying to you."

My mouth parts. Sorrow hangs heavy in my chest, but I barely feel it for the heat that swells in me at the touch of his fingers. From the way he stops breathing, I can tell he's noticed the spike in my scent. He removes his hand but I clutch it, keeping it against my cheek. There is such simple mindless pleasure in the act of burrowing against his palm, just like that timeless night.

"Tamsin," he sighs. He leans closer until his forehead is pressed against mine, his breath hot on my mouth. He strokes my bare neck, letting his hand linger there as we both savour this closeness. "I'm going to go outside. We can continue this conversation in the morning."

"Is it my scent?" I mutter.

"It's you," he says. He seems about to elaborate, but decides against it. My whole body is growing limp as the heat-stupor takes over, and when he presses a kiss against my forehead I give a quiet needy whine. God... if he could only stay and stoke this delicious mindlessness. "Thank you for the bindings," he murmurs against my hairline. "Call me if you need anything."

"All right."

He diligently goes to the door. I follow him so I might bolt it behind him. He glances at me one last time before the door closes, his gaze full of tenderness.

The spell of his calm, soothing presence lifts as I bolt the door. Miserable contemplations eat away at the temporary delight of his company. I go back to the bed, trying not to think of the future and what awaits me when Aedan finds me again. I am wed to him, whether I like it or not. And there are still so many days of this damned heat to endure.

I finish my food, chewing hard and nervously. The more I think of what awaits me as Lady of Dál Riata, the more my mind becomes a jumbled mess. I'm thinking of how it felt to wield that dagger back on the ship, how it felt to slice the throat of that poor boy. How this time I would love to puncture Aedan's inescapable bulk like one punctures a swollen waterskin.

What a blow it would be to him if I did lay with Thrain.

The thought is too wicked to consider. I catch myself delighting in it, and try to reason with myself. I am probably already facing some type of punishment for running away on my own wedding night. If I insult him even further... Domnall's chilling words come back to the forefront of my mind.

By harming me, you harm only yourself.

I finish my food, tasting none of it. As I pull back the covers and recline against the cushions, I stare at the door, imagining Thrain standing out there like a loyal guard hound. It's such a bizarre image. I wonder if he'll be able to stand there all night while the revelry goes on all around him.

The thought of the revelry, and the sounds that ring from the hall... my heat-stupor finally takes over and crushes all other preoccupations. I remember those naked pairs and groups I saw while the moans and shouts punctuate the night. Now that I've taken such cares to dress my back, it would be stupid to search for my flogger among Thrain's belongings to try and banish the heat. He's right, my back has never been as bad as it is now. I need to let it heal.

I sigh through my nose. It won't be the first night that I endure the intensity of my heat and try to sleep through it.

I slide under the covers, close my eyes, and breathe in Thrain's heady, reassuring scent.

Chapter 30

TAMSIN
FULL MOON OF JUNE

I CAN'T SLEEP.

The noise isn't diminishing at all. Sometimes music adds itself to the chaos, other times particularly spirited revellers try to make their pleasure known to the whole of Dál Riata. Every so often, Thrain's deep voice wards off curious people who approach the door.

It was all frightening and outrageous at first. After several sleepless hours it's just an utter annoyance. The constant moaning doesn't allow my heat to subside enough for sleep – on the contrary. Mindless desire fills every nook of my body until I am twisting in the covers, pulling them between my legs, sighing irritably against the cushions.

If they could only be quiet. Then this damned throb between my thighs would go away. Sometimes the music overtakes the noise and I drift, my body hot and heavy in the mattress, before being jerked awake again.

I sit up in bed, then pad across the room to knock on the door.

"Thrain? Are you still there?"

"Princess," comes his muffled voice. "Is there something you need?"

"No, it's just… is this going to last all night?"

"It's the first night, so I'm afraid it might last quite some time."

I sigh, leaning back against the door. The wood is cool and smooth against my shift. Even just the feel of the bolt against my lower back brings satisfaction to the aching heat. I close my eyes, trying to ignore what it's doing to me to stand in Thrain's room in nothing but my shift, holding myself apart from all those revellers shamelessly enjoying one another. If it drives me this close to madness, then I can't imagine how it must affect Thrain.

"You're really going to stand out there all night?" I ask him.

"I vowed to protect you, princess."

I find myself smirking, safe enough behind this door to goad him. "Are you not frustrated?"

"Absolutely not."

He's trying so hard to stick to that noble façade of his. The recklessness of the full moon makes me want to poke holes in it. "You're lying. There's no way I'll believe that you are the one Viking in this fort who has achieved perfect self-mastery."

"Why do you need me to admit my frustration?" he asks. "Would you prefer if I left this door and acted on it?"

Stricken, I hold the wooden bolt as though it were his own arm. "Please don't. I'm sorry. It's just – I can't sleep and all of this noise is aggravating me to no end."

"You and me both," he says. I can hear the smile in his voice.

One of the louder female voices starts up again. I recognise the style of it. I tilt my head against the door and wonder incredulously whether she's really going to climb that crescendo for the third time.

"I swear I heard that one barely an hour ago," I moan. "Please, not again."

Thrain laughs. "Honestly I'm surprised she doesn't shatter the windows."

"Is there a perimeter around her so the others might keep from going deaf?"

"They probably block their ears. Or she only chooses the deaf to please her."

She climbs, and climbs, and screams, and I can't help the boiling anger and jealousy that surges in me at the sound of her pleasure, how she can simply enjoy herself whilst I am here in the dark, wed to a Christian mongrel and frustrated out of my mind.

"Congratulations!" I call out in my annoyance. "Now chuck her out, for the love of God."

Thrain's laughing again. "Surely she is sated by now."

"Let's hope so."

We stand there on either side of the door like a pair of fools for a while longer. I let my hands play over the texture of the wood, feeling the lines of its grain with all the heightened clarity and interest of the heat. I'm yearning so badly to touch warm skin rather than this cold unyielding wood.

All I can think of when I close my eyes is what Thrain looked like, that night at the chapel. The way his eyes roamed hungrily over my face. The feel of his mouth... so hot and wet against mine. And his hands... just to think of that sensation he gave me is enough to make my pulse throb wantonly. Surely it would take just the brush of his fingertips again to unwind all this tightly wound tension.

I'm going mad. I'm going utterly mad. I should go looking for something sharp, something to break the tension with force and pain rather than the touch of my enemy's hand. It's what I should do. It would be the proper thing to do.

But nothing about this wedding night has been anywhere near proper.

"Thrain," I hear myself say.

"Princess?"

He sounds wary. I wonder if he can hear the yearning in my voice.

"If... if I let you come back inside—"

"No."

"I haven't even finished speaking!"

"Your scent is as strong as the first day of spring. If I step through that door, it won't be to sleep quietly next to you."

I stand sullenly, trying to persuade myself that this soaring disappointment is only a result of my heat, that his careful refusal is saving me from further shame.

"You could control yourself at the chapel," I mutter. I don't even know what I'm asking for. I'm just angry and aroused and miserable, and he is the only target I have to vent it all onto.

"It was the last night of your heat," he says. "And already it was difficult. I don't... know if I could trust myself tonight. Please," he adds, "don't tempt me any further. It's late. You should try to get some sleep, at least while that screaming woman is satisfied."

I smirk. "You're right. Now is probably the best chance I'll get." With a heavy sigh, I push away from the door. "I'm sorry. I'll leave you alone."

I stalk to the bed, ram my traitorous body under the covers, pull them tight over me.

If he can bear his own desires, then I must be just as stoic as him. I will not be the one to tempt a cursed man. Nails biting into my palms, I close my eyes and breathe out as I try to relax.

I am in control.

I am in control.

Maybe... if it's that climax I seek. Maybe I could give it to myself. I was so blissfully adrift afterwards. I remember sleeping like a log that night. Surely it would be safer to just... administer it to myself, so that I can spare both Thrain and I the complication of opening that door.

I slide a hand between my thighs, and try to chase that glittering fae magic.

Chapter 31
THRAIN
FULL MOON OF JUNE

I HAD NOT ANTICIPATED the sheer effort of restraint I would have to uphold as I stand guard by the door. There was such longing and warmth in her voice. It's driving me mad to keep this distance. I praise Odin for the small mercy that the door bolts from the inside. So far she's had the strength to keep the bolt firmly in its pegs.

I can only hope her self-control holds. If it's becoming as frayed as mine then we're both in danger of doing something very, very foolish.

I stare sightlessly at the wall ahead of me and fix my mind on images of the boat-fixing from this afternoon. I manage to drag myself through the problems we encountered, until I'm focussed enough by the calculations to not think of Tamsin, lying undressed and languid with heat in my own damned bed.

The sound of creaking and brushing wood draws my attention.

My eyes blink back to reality.

The bolt is being pulled out of its pegs.

"Princess," I mutter, heart pounding as she removes that salutary barrier between us. "What are you doing?"

That quiet, breathy voice emerges from the silence: "Thrain... come back inside."

Her words send a shiver of desire down my spine. I curl my fingers into fists. Boats. Think of boats. Wood wax. Stinking barrels of salted fish.

"Bolt the door, princess. You should tend to yourself."

She sighs. "I – *can't*. I can't do it."

"Can't do what?"

"What you did," she says, almost annoyed now. "At the chapel."

I try to stop the smile from pulling at my mouth. I imagine her lying in my bed, her hand wedged between her thighs. My groin tightens all the more and I can't help the soft groan that escapes my throat.

"Why must you do this to me," I mutter. "It's already hard enough."

The door opens a sliver. It's such a slight opening and yet the scent that curls out to greet me is insufferably strong. I can feel my cock filling with hot blood as I sense her blatant arousal on the air.

She's there beyond the door. She isn't looking at me. I gaze upon her pale profile as she frowns down at the floor.

"I'm going insane," she mutters, rubbing her forehead with a shaking hand. "I shouldn't have... it was tolerable before I... aggravated it. And now, I need... I need..."

She trails off helplessly. From the sound of her voice, her frustration is bringing her close to tears. I breathe out, trying to control the surge of lust at what she's suggesting. My erection is stiff and heavy as it twitches beneath my tunic, aching for stimulation.

We both know what she needs.

If I give even a little rein to my desires, I know I might not be able to stop myself.

Not when the air is gorged with the golden scent of her arousal. If I could just... satisfy her, whilst leaving my own ardours untouched. Like at the chapel. Then she would leave me be.

"Go to the bed," I tell her. "Let me collect myself. I'll show you how to do it, then I'll leave you to sleep. You will not touch me, and you will not ask me for any more than that. Is that understood?"

She lingers there for a moment. I take in her slight shoulders, the messy ginger braid that's spilling down her front. Then mutely she nods, and disappears into the room.

I stare at that sliver of darkness. The temptation of the open door.

It's madness to give in to this. I have no idea if I can truly control myself once I step into that room. But she is the one who opened the damned door. She is the one who plays with both our fates.

Either she's trusting me a great deal, or her heat truly has driven her to madness.

I breathe out sharply, trying to gather my wits. I promised her I would protect her from any who may harm her. Apparently that includes herself. I need to protect her against the potential consequences that await us both tomorrow morning if this goes any further than her own release.

I make sure no one is watching, then push the door open.

Step inside. Turn around, and bolt it shut.

ᚦᚱᛏᛁᛉ

Tamsin is lying on the bed with her back to me, curled up on her side, breathing softly in the darkness. She's wearing naught but her bandages and shift, folding artfully over the curves of her body. From the stiffness of her shoulders, I can tell she's got a hand between her thighs again. I wonder if she chose this position out of modesty, so I might not see her blatantly splayed out and touching herself upon coming in.

I try to ignore the leap of excitement at the sight of her, at the mere idea that she's inviting me into her intimacy. I take in the messy spill of her braid, the delicate ridge of her spine that's visible through the gaping collar of her shift.

I sit on the edge of the bed and meticulously unlace my leather shoes, forcing myself to take my time and control each movement. Then I turn and crawl closer to her, trying not to alarm her. Her breathing is already shallow with anticipation as she feels me draw nearer. I lie beside her, make sure not to let her body touch mine as I lean on one elbow and curl around the shape of her.

My good hand follows the line of her arm, fingertips ghosting over her skin. Goosebumps prickle her flesh as she accepts the touch.

She opens her thighs a little more to make room for me. My fingers slide between hers, and we both sink into the slick curves of her nether lips.

I blink groggily as her scent drifts around us, overpowering now. I try to lock her fingers in the correct place, and move them in a small circle.

"There," I murmur, my mouth just above her ear. "Like that. Be firm, but light."

Her eyes are closed as she feels her way through the exercise. I guide her hand through circle after circle, until I am basically helping her climb to the peak. She gives no indication that she wants me to stop, instead growing limp and leaning back against my chest as she lets me pleasure her.

It's torture. Plain torture to be encouraged like this, with the full expectation that I might control my own desires.

"Princess," I murmur. "You have the gesture now. I'm going to stop."

She shakes her head. Then – she slides her hand from under mine, and presses me into her swollen, slippery contours.

"Don't," I growl at her even as my fingers fit naturally around her clit. "Don't encourage me. Do it yourself."

"Please," she sighs, and presses me further against her wetness. "I'm so close, I can't bear it."

I sigh into her hair, and draw her against me properly. I hiss as my cock presses against the backs of her thighs through the layers of tunic and shift, the contact more frustrating than relieving. She's warm and supple in my arms, and my self-control is dangling by a thread.

I rub her clit in circles until she tenses against me, until her spine arches and her nails bite into my arm. When she comes at last, she laughs with the sheer relief of it, and then melts against me irresistibly. I bite her neck and nuzzle her hair as she lets herself go in my arms, completely mindless, and completely *mine*.

Her entrance is veiled with slick. I push my fingers into her waiting depths, and she gives a mewl of pure need.

I can't stop now. I need to have her.

"Tamsin," I whisper in her ear. I'm growing delirious with how much I want her. She turns, kisses me in the darkness, my moan losing itself in her mouth. Her arms snake around my shoulders, her leg curling around my waist as she pulls me closer. Our clothes have ridden up with her movements, and my bared cock fits naturally between the slippery grooves of her centre.

I pant against her mouth, her shift bunching between my fingers as I hold her by the hips, trying to keep myself from ramming into her. It is like holding a bull by the horns.

"Tamsin, please," I beg her with the last of my self-control. "You aren't mine."

"I'm not his, either," she whispers savagely. "I don't belong to anyone."

"If we do this there is no going back. You understand?"

She rubs herself against the head of my cock, reckless with need. Mercifully, it's never the right angle for me to slide into her.

"If we do this, and I lose control… I'll invoke the pair-bond," I tell her.

"What's that?"

"It is the bond between your kind and mine," I murmur. "Like sealing a pact. I will be yours forever. And you'll be mine."

She stills her hips, blinking up at me through the haze of her arousal.

"That's just Viking superstitions," she says. "A cursed man doesn't become pair-bonded with the first servant girl he lays with. There's no such thing."

"You are no servant girl, Tamsin," I tell her. "You are Vanirdottir. Daughter of Clota. Surely you've already observed such a bond, where you live."

"No," she insists. "If it's love you speak of, it only blooms rarely, and sometimes not for very long."

I gaze down at her face in the darkness. Her eyes are glazed with the heat, her lips swollen from where she bit them. I rub my thumb against her cheek and she nuzzles my hand again irresistibly, searching for more contact.

"Just this once," she sighs. "Please. Just this once..."

The answer suddenly appears to me. Of course she's never witnessed the pair-bond. They kill their Vyrgen men. They can never enter into such a bond when their Vanirdøtur are always paired with human men.

I've only ever heard of it from our legends, myself. But I can't allow myself to test the theory, not when this is her wedding night, not when she's out of her mind with lust.

I kiss her deeply, drawing sweet moans from her as I cup her face and allow myself this last indulgence. Then, mustering all the self-discipline I can, I pull away from her, sitting up in the bed and breathing through my rampant desire.

"Thrain," she protests, but I push her seeking hands away.

"No," I growl at her. I get up and stagger to the door, lifting the bolt with trembling hands. I cast it away on the floor in frustration and it crashes loudly on the hardwood, making Tamsin cry out. "Lock yourself in," I tell her gruffly over my shoulder, and then slam the door shut behind me as I march out into the cool air of the corridor.

Chapter 32

Thrain

Day 1 of the Waning Moon of June

T AMSIN AND EORMEN were meant to be taken to the great hall the following morning, fresh from their consummated marriages, accompanied by their new husbands. They were to be shown to our people, their awakened scents as proof of their lineage, a taste of treasures to come.

Evidently it's going to be more complicated than that.

I haven't gotten a blink of sleep. Ivar found me in the early hours of the morning as I went for water and refreshment, noticed how I trembled and sweated with unspent desire. My presence at the door of my own chamber was noticed by everyone at that feast, of course – it became the running joke of the evening. My Vyrgen passed by first out of hunger for Tamsin's scent, then simply to goad me and try to tempt me from my post.

Ivar was more serious about it. Perhaps because he knows how much that girl weakens me, and what's at stake if any of us give in to the temptation she poses. While I gulped water and ate cold remains of venison, he asked me to swear on my life that nothing irreversible happened between us. I swore it to him and he accepted it, perhaps swayed more by my irritable and dishevelled state than my words.

With the dawn rising, I should send her back to Aedan so they may enter the hall together as planned. Thank the gods that Causantin is away in Alba. Whatever stupidity befalls us this morning, at least he won't bear witness to it.

I push myself off my bench with a sigh. I chose a spot to rest where I could see my chamber door. Wisely, Tamsin hasn't opened it since I slammed it shut, even just to peek out and ascertain whether the feast was over.

My tunic is soaked with sweat. Clearly my body doesn't understand how I might've lain with a Vanirdottir without ravaging her. Thankfully though, the exhaustion of a sleepless night and the light of the morning have all but withered my frustration away to a limp sort of grumpiness. I go to my chamber door and knock.

"Princess? It's me."

I have to knock again before I hear her respond. She calls that she isn't decent. I smirk and go back to the hall to give her time. When I sidle back to the door to knock again, it's with a platter of feast leftovers that I gathered up before the servants could begin their vast clean-up effort.

The bolt lifts from its latches. I breathe in, give her a moment to retreat from the door, and enter the room.

Wisely she's left the small window wide open and beaten out the sheets to dispel her scent. She's fully dressed in her bloody bridal garb, standing by the foot of the bed and folding up the bedsheets. Her heat still lingers on the air, but nowhere near as heavily as last night.

"Good morning," she says stiffly. She hasn't looked at me once.

"Morning." I pass her and place her breakfast on the table. "I thought you might be hungry. The servants will put out the morning meal in about an hour."

She makes a small noise of acquiescence and goes on stripping the bed of the last layers of linen. As I watch her swift movements, I notice her bridal gown isn't properly laced at the sides. She probably hurried to prepare herself and straighten up the room all at once, eager to erase any trace of what happened last night.

Despite the ghoulish black stains on the fabric, the cut of her dress outlines the curve of her waist beautifully. I watch her, understanding only too well the frantic energy that possesses her.

"Princess," I tell her softly. "The servants will take care of that. You may take the time to lace your dress."

She stills. Her hand comes around to feel her sides, as though stricken by the idea that she might appear half-dressed before me in daylight.

"I'm sorry," she says. "I just... I'm not myself this morning."

Indeed. I half expect her to say she wasn't herself last night, either. I get up and approach her so that I might at least help her to accomplish one task among the many she's thrown herself into.

I pull at her laces. She staggers a little and then stills as I start methodically tightening them. As I progress down one side and shift to the other, the stiffness gradually leaves her shoulders. She stares down at my bared bed as she lets me help her. As I work, my gaze lingers on her bare snowy neck, the brilliant contrast that her red-gold hair creates.

It's difficult not to think of the reason why her braid is so dishevelled.

"Thank you," she says at length. "For... last night."

From the way she says it, I know she doesn't mean the climax. She's thankful that I left her well alone, once the craze of the heat had waned. I push the reminiscence away, the feeling of her leg gripping my waist, how hot and slippery she had been with need.

"We both played with fire," I tell her gruffly. "It was foolish."

"I know."

I sit at the table, drawing out one of the stools for her again. Warily she comes to sit with me, resuming our positions from yesterday as if there had not been a mad interval of pent-up lust in between. I give her the goblet of cider I prepared for her and she takes it, staring down at the golden liquid thoughtfully.

I rip up the bread, helping myself to some of it while silence settles between us. She reaches for the goat cheese, slathering a generous amount on her bread. She leaves me half, but seeing how thoroughly she seems to enjoy it, I let her have the rest. With relish she goes on slathering her bread slices with the creamy white paste. She's clearly ravenous, but her upbringing forces her to keep her movements measured and elegant.

Somehow this peaceful morning feels like even more of an intimate thing to share than yesterday's grasping hands and desperate pleading. I try to keep my eyes off her, enjoying the simple privilege of sharing a meal with her without any reminder of our differences to spoil this moment.

"Is this what you do at every full moon, then?" she asks at length. "Music and revelry?"

"It's a safe setting to let our desires run their course," I tell her. "We limit the chaos to one room, one group of people."

"And did you... partake in it? After you left?"

"I did not."

She wonders about that for a moment. "You were also holding yourself apart from it when I ran into you."

I rip the bread into unnecessarily small chunks.

"Why?" she insists. "Do you never partake in it at all?"

I try to find a way to word it without letting my own possessiveness of her too apparent. "I... could not find peace of mind, knowing you were in Aedan's hands."

She mulls over my words for a moment. The longer she stays quiet, the more her expression turns pale and hounded.

"I'm going to have to go back to him, aren't I," she says, lowering her bread to the table. "I've been thinking about it all morning. Whether he was allied with Vikings or not changes nothing about our marriage. The insult of Dunblane was always going to stand between us. He was always going to hate me."

Her gaze shifts to the two sheathed daggers that lay across the table beyond our platter. My breath hitches as I imagine what she leaves unsaid.

"He would always have treated me like this," she goes on quietly, as though to herself. "And yet my uncle still agreed to the match. Never mind Gofraid and Causantin. My own uncle sent me here to be with that... that..."

I pour more sweet cider for her. "If it's any consolation, I did come quite close to killing him when I first arrived here."

Her bloodshot eyes meet mine. She asks me to elaborate so I recount the tale, how Lady Catriona had prevented me at the last minute. The humiliating handshake we had shared.

It's very interesting to see how bent she is on the details. She seems to be chasing a thought as she stares absently at her cup of cider. There is something almost translucent about her this morning, whether it's the way the dawn touches her skin or her own misery.

"What would've happened? If you'd killed him?" she asks.

"Well, you must take into account the context," I tell her. "He initiated the fight. I acted in self-defense. Causantin could not have faulted me for the act." I gaze at her, ragingly curious to discover what point she is driving towards. "I have only prevented myself from planting metal in his back all this time because he agreed to stand down. To kill him now would spell mutiny on my part."

She looks down into her cider, ponders the golden ripples for a while.

"Don't you think it's unfair that the innocent always seem to die first?" she says at last. "Why do the guilty get the privilege of continuing to live? Are politics really a worthy reason to let them survive?"

I'm amazed to hear those words. She was so traumatised by the idea of having potentially caused the deaths of a thousand men.

"In Strathclyde," she goes on, "we mark the cursed as guilty, as you know. Always guilty. Guilty by nature rather than by any particular action. But now I know that a normal man can far outrank the cursed in terms of vile, disgusting behaviour. And I know the cursed can be decent if they're taught to be, which I had always believed to be true."

I remain quiet. She seems to have done a lot of thinking while I stomped around the hall in my morning torpor. She takes a swig of cider, gripping the cup so hard that the tendons in her hand stand out.

"Whatever you might say," she murmurs, "I have caused the death of many innocent men. I've caused the death of men who never laid a finger on their wives, nor blasphemed against God. From where I'm standing, I already wear the cape of the Ankou." She turns her hard gaze upon my sheathed blades again. "So if I'm to bear the weight of it, why not cause the death of at least one deserving man?"

Her words send pleasurable shivers down my spine. She speaks as a Valkyrie, gliding in the white shafts of sunlight that illuminate the dead, no longer shying away from the gruesome duties that lay before her.

"I can't consummate my marriage," she tells my daggers. "And I see no other way of getting out of this."

"Princess." The word tumbles out of me, a eulogy, an exclamation of just how much I admire her. She has chosen to protect herself rather than to bow to a man who would abuse her. If there were one worthy cause she could lay before me to justify mutiny against Aedan's continued existence, she could not have chosen a better one.

She's apparently unable to look at me. "I know it might make me seem repugnant to you—"

"On the contrary." I lay my good hand over hers. The whisper of magic connecting our skin makes her look up at last. "I would expect nothing less of a daughter of Clota."

She gazes at me a moment. Her face has lost its worried pinch as I show her my approval. "Clota was not really a Godly woman."

"Perhaps she wasn't. But she survived."

She nods. Slowly, her fingers fit between mine. They're trembling, but her face is set as she ponders the conversation. At last she asks, "What is it that you call our kind? Vanirdottir? What does it mean?"

"Daughter of the Vanir. In our stories, you are the lost daughters of our goddess Freya, who hails from the beautiful realm of Vanaheimr."

She frowns. "So we are daughters of gods to you?"

"Yes." I gaze into those amber-green eyes, chest swelling. "You are sacred to us."

"And yet your King Gofraid would lock us in a tower and wed us to disgusting villains."

The accusation is just as sharp as I anticipated. "The betrothals were a means to an end. Gofraid and my brothers have always been obsessed with your kind. They would've hunted you down to the ends of the earth."

She arches her brow. "But not you?"

"I didn't believe the Vanirdøtur really existed before I met you."

She considers me a moment. "Is that the reason you were drawn to me, then? I was a legendary creature?"

I smirk at her. "A legendary creature with an extraordinary taste in wine. And horses."

She smiles at last. I rub my thumb along her knuckles, ignoring how my wounded hand still aches and stings as I keep it in my lap. I can't help but grieve that I will never be able to touch her properly with that hand now.

Dawn light still gilding the crown of her head, she asks me, "Can you help me, Thrain?"

"You forget, I have already promised Aedan retribution," I tell her. "I would only be too glad to make good on my promise with your blessing."

She beams at me. Feeling I should seal the promise, I bring her hand to my lips. She has no rings to kiss, so I kiss her bare knuckles instead. A faint blush rises to her freckled face as she watches me do it. It makes me smile to see that timidity return after her rampant hunger last night.

"Thank you," she says. "So... what happens now?"

I proceed to tell her how the morning should go. I should lead her back to Aedan's quarters so that they might enter the hall together as they were meant to. Her and Eormen would be officially paraded before everyone. The formal presentation would serve to cement their unavailability to all the men, and to prove their status as Vanirdøtur.

She scoffs at that last part. "I think your men already know what I am," she mutters. "Is it really necessary for me to go back to Aedan and pretend I slept with him? Everybody knows that I did not."

"It would be the safest option, if you'd like to take some time to plan this," I tell her. "I can convene with Gofraid and persuade him to act as though everything is in order."

She shakes her head. "But it would be such a farce. To stand before everyone and celebrate a union that wasn't consummated."

"Do you have an alternative solution in mind?"

She says nothing. We sit there for a while longer, finishing our food and contemplating the situation. I look at the redness around her temple, her split lip, the gory dress.

"I think I have an idea," I say. "I know that when Gofraid and my brothers see that bloody dress… they won't like the idea that Aedan lifted a hand to a Vanirdottir. As you say, I know Gofraid has been unfeelingly pragmatic in his treatment of you and Eormen. But you are still sacred to him and all the pack. If you stood before them wearing proof of last night's abuse… then I think there's a strong chance that the pack will encourage mutiny."

She blinks at me. "Mutiny?"

"We have our own laws when it comes to notions of honour," I tell her. "We can provoke Aedan. I'll walk you into the hall as the first insult. Then the men will protest his treatment of you. If he is built like a man then he will want to duel to save face. And then the deal is done."

She balks at the simplicity of the plan. "Surely Causantin wouldn't sanction it."

"No, he wouldn't. Especially with rumours circulating that you spent your wedding night with me." I smile. "But Causantin isn't in the fort today."

Her breaths are coming faster, shorter. "I didn't think we could come to a solution so fast."

"If you come into the hall on my arm, you must be prepared for it to be taken as a provocation already," I remind her. "This would be a way of taking advantage of the situation."

She nods, her face serious. She doesn't speak up again for a long time, so I decide she isn't about to opt for the trip back to Aedan's quarters. I fix my mind on Gofraid, trying to persuade myself that he'll be reasonable. As she isn't moving from her spot, I go to rummage in my coffer for my things. She gazes up at me as I run a bone-carved comb through my hair. She reaches for it in a request to use it, but I shake my head.

"Stay as you are," I tell her. "You're perfect like this."

She twists her long ginger hair anxiously between her fingers.

"What happens after he dies?" she asks suddenly.

I'm puzzled that she hasn't guessed. Or perhaps she's checking to see if we're on the same page. "My vow to protect you still holds. If you'll accept me as your guardian."

"My guardian," she says with a nod. "I can accept that."

That and nothing more, her tone clearly implies. There can be no room for disappointment when she is already showing me a great deal of trust to be making deals like this. I turn to pull the door open, trying not to smile as I remember words spoken in rage.

I don't make deals with savage warlords.

She must've decided that Aedan was the savage one out of the two of us.

She takes a deep breath, readying herself for whatever pandemonium we're about to unleash. Then, with all the dignity of a captive queen, she leads the way out.

Chapter 33

TAMSIN

DAY 1 OF THE WANING MOON OF JUNE

I T'S A FEAT that the servants might've cleaned up the great hall
for the occasion, after the madness of last night. There are
fresh spring wreaths on the walls, the long tables are swept, and
bunches of candles add light to the darkness of the room.

Eormen is only just arriving on Domnall's arm, stepping up
to the raised dais where Gofraid and his Viking lords are sat. My
heart skips a beat as I see Rhun sitting right by Gofraid's side, the
place usually reserved for a son. He's spent two whole weeks with
the Vikings – I can only wonder what he's been through. He
hasn't seen me yet, deep in conversation as he is with the great
whitebeard.

Prince Domnall is looking rather grim as he leads Eormen
past Gofraid's sons to the space beside Lady Catriona. My gaze
crosses my cousin's, and it's shocking to see how thin she looks
even with the rouge she's added to her cheeks.

On the other side of Lady Catriona sits Aedan. When I see
the furious look on his face, I almost want to run back to Thrain's
room. He gets up as we walk through one of the hall's many
entrances.

"Ah, there she is!" Gofraid booms a welcome, getting up with his arms outstretched towards us. Rhun meets my gaze. He looks so worried and confused as he watches me walk in on the arm of Thrain Mordsson.

The boy from the bogs already spoils my gladness to see my twin. Now this assassination I'm planning with Thrain adds its weight on top of the rest. I manage to nod at him, hoping he'll see some confidence in the gesture.

Many of the warriors seated at the tables leer at me insistently. Their attention is divided between me and Eormen, their chatter filling the hall as they wonder openly about us.

We smell of the heat. And this room is filled with cursed men who are undiminished by wolfsbane.

I meet Eormen's gaze from across the hall. She looks just as alarmed as Rhun upon seeing my companion. If she knew what I sought to do... well. I'm sure she'd be glad to be rid of her own traitor husband.

"Please, come in, be seated," Gofraid says.

"To our king of Dublin!" one of the warriors shouts, lifting his goblet to Thrain. "He who makes maidens run from their own weddings just to spend a night with him!"

The silence erupts into jeering and fists banging on the tables.

It's started already. To my horror, Aedan walks around the high table and steps down from the dais. It's going too fast. His face is full of murder as he points a finger in Thrain's direction.

"They speak the truth, sire!" he announces to Gofraid. "This scum – your warlord, Thrain – he took my bride for himself last night! He even came to me to gloat about it!"

"What? And you did nothing to get her back?" the Viking warriors roar back at him.

"Cowardly runt! Not even capable of keeping his woman!"

"A woman that *we* had to secure for him, no less!"

"Silence!" Gofraid bellows at his warriors. "I'll not have our friends insulted in their own hall. What is the problem here, exactly?"

Prince Domnall comes around the table to stand beside his cousin, placing a hand on his arm in a clear request to calm down.

He seems to be telling him not to make a scene. But Aedan pulls away from him savagely.

"Have the girl examined!" he shouts. "If she is no longer a virgin – I demand reparation!"

"She is untouched," Ivar calls from the dais. "We all saw my brother standing guard by her door last night."

Several Vikings attest to it, shouting their agreement. My face is burning with shame. I can't believe they would discuss my virginity like that, in a room full of leering men.

"And why would I trust the word of a savage like you?" Aedan snaps at Ivar. That man's black gaze shines dangerously as he looks upon the mad lord.

Thrain is the one to growl his response: "Perhaps if you did not beat her on her wedding night, she would not have felt the need to escape your bedchamber."

Several Viking warriors hiss at this new information. I hear some of them refer to the incident on the ship. Now is the moment. Breathing in, I close my eyes and turn around to let them see the state of my dress.

Howled indignation rises from the crowd. Aedan looks taken aback, uncomprehending that I might be siding with the Vikings. No amount of yelling *she did that to herself* appeases the baying of the wolves.

"What is it to you, anyway?" he shouts at last. "You would really try to shame me, when your people are known for raping every woman and child you meet after stealing their lands from them?"

I clap my hands over my mouth. He has completely doomed himself with barely any help from us.

Viking warriors spring to their feet under a renewed clamour. Lady Catriona is white-faced with shock that her son might've provoked his guests so badly. Gofraid has to bang his fists on the table to regain control of the room.

I want to run to Eormen and Rhun, pull them out of the way of this horde of angry men, hug them against me for comfort. But Thrain's hand is on my forearm, holding me there next to him, his grip so tight that it's beginning to hurt.

"Holmgang!" some of the Vikings start shouting. "Holmgang!"

After a while, Gofraid manages to quiet the crowd. He lifts his hand to Aedan.

"Aedan mac Causantin, prince of Alba and lord of Dunadd Fort. Are you challenging my vassal, Thrain Mordsson?"

"Like Hell I'm challenging him!" Aedan rages. "Let's have it out right here!"

"No!" Prince Domnall booms. "No prince of Alba is challenging a Viking to a holmgang."

"You do not speak for me, cousin," Aedan snaps. "The lord of Dál Riata has spoken! The challenge holds!"

"Thrain Mordsson," Gofraid says, turning to my protector. "Do you accept the challenge?"

This must be the Viking duel that Thrain mentioned. Panic ripples through me as I grasp the reality of Thrain's proposition. He will fight Aedan to the death, and insodoing he'll risk his own life. As a favour to me.

Images of him bloodied to the hackles on the Firth of Clyde come to mind. I know he has abilities that a pampered Dálriadan lord probably does not have. Not to mention, his curse allows him preternatural strength. But his hand is maimed – he'll be fighting one-handed against an uninjured adversary.

Heart thumping, I look up at him. He's smirking as he holds Aedan's gaze.

"I accept the holmgang," he intones.

He seems confident enough regardless of his wound. A thrill of icy delight fills me as I realise this power he's lending me. It's as though he were the blade I was holding to Aedan's neck. I gaze across the hall at Aedan, finding no remorse whatsoever at the sight of his taut, ferrety face.

He deserves everything that's coming to him.

I touch Thrain's arm as he passes me. He turns his head, his eyes flitting between mine. *Good luck,* I want to tell him. *Keep yourself safe.*

He nods at me. He's understood.

ᛏᚼᚤ�510ᛏ

The Vikings push the central tables to the sides of the room and roll up the cow-hide rugs to uncover a square of beaten earth floor. Rhun comes to fetch me, looking horribly worried as he leads me to the raised dais.

"You all right?" he mutters. "What the Hell happened?"

"I'm fine. I'll tell you later. You?"

"I'm not the one wearing the banshee's dress, am I?" he says. The warm clammy feeling of his hand in mine makes my soul sing. At last, at *last* we're side by side again, though it's bound not to last.

We stand near Eormen and Lady Catriona. My cousin looks as terrified as I feel as she reaches to clasp us both. Mutely, we all watch the two men step into their improvised arena.

"What's a holmgang?" Eormen asks Lady Catriona, who is observing the events with wide panicked eyes.

"It's a type of duel," she tells us. "It is not always to the death. It… depends on how vindictive the participants are."

From the look of rage on Aedan's face and the pure bloodlust shining in Thrain's eyes, it's obvious that neither of them are about to let each other off easy.

Aedan throws the cape from around his shoulders and unsheathes his sword with a high-pitched ring of metal. Thrain stands there, his maimed hand very visible with its clean white bandages. Many of his men are offering him their shields – he plucks one from them with his good hand and calmly assumes his position, knees slightly bent, his weight evenly distributed.

I don't understand. He's unarmed – he hasn't taken out the seax that lies across the small of his back. But he seems so sure of himself. Perhaps he's waiting for the opportune moment.

Several Vikings hand Aedan their round wooden shields, jeering at him. He scowls at them, as though wondering whether they mean to disadvantage him by giving him battered ones. At last he picks one of the more prettily decorated ones and takes his position.

Aedan seems to be more encumbered by his shield than anything. Still, he holds it up as they both prowl on either side of the arena, waiting for the other to engage.

"They have as many chances as they have shields to wield," Lady Catriona tells us. "Normally they're given one or two more if they're disarmed. The first to fall out of the perimeter loses."

Aedan is the first to lunge. He hits the studded edge of his shield against Thrain's with a dull *thunk*. Thrain holds out against him, feet firmly planted on the ground even as Aedan hammers against that solid wooden barrier. Then, quick as a snake, Thrain presses the flat of his shield against Aedan's and *twists,* forcing Aedan's down flat, trapping his sword beneath it. Thrain darts across the distance, throwing his elbow hard into Aedan's face.

Howls of delight rise from his men. My heart's thumping so loud I barely hear them. Aedan's nose is broken and bleeding down his face.

They face one another again, shields at the ready. Clearly Aedan doesn't know the art of shield-manoeuvring like Thrain does. Aedan slashes angrily with his sword at that solid red circle, but as before Thrain easily stands his ground.

Then, almost dancing, Thrain traps Aedan's sword again and *rams* into Aedan, shoulder against chest. Aedan gives a loud *oof,* staggering backwards.

He teeters on the edge of the perimeter, grasps Thrain's tunic to wrench himself back into balance. They breathe in one another's faces, staring pure hatred at one another. Aedan pushes his opponent away with a grunt of effort. Thrain lets him do it.

He's grinning.

"I've never seen this combat style before," Rhun mutters next to me. "Thrain Mordsson uses his shield almost like a weapon. I thought Aedan would have the advantage, but... that damned Viking's toying with him."

I watch Thrain's movements eagerly. I can see it now, the bloodthirsty warlord that Aedan first spoke of when he told that story about the three wolves of Dublin. I see it in his shining eyes, the predatory curl of his lip. I see it in the graceful movements of his body, how he swings his shield as though it were an extension of his body.

He's as terrifying as he is beautiful.

It doesn't take long for Aedan to lose his first shield. I don't

even see how Thrain does it – he eels around his opponent
again, wood brushing against wood, Aedan's sword arm twisted
uselessly beneath. A loud bang erupts in the hall as one of the
shields falls to the floor.

A grinning bearded man hands Aedan his second shield. They
continue with their spar. Aedan tries his best to stab Thrain
over the edge of his shield but constantly gets deflected. His
annoyance at being unable to best a wounded unarmed opponent
is making his gestures wild and erratic. In another move that's
too fast to register, Thrain wedges Aedan's second shield in a
diagonal against the floor, Aedan's sword arm twisted beneath
it as before. Then he rams his foot down against it until it splits
with a loud CRACK.

"Oy!" shouts the bearded man who offered it.

"I'll make you a new one, Finngeir!" Thrain calls back, drawing
laughter from his fellows. They're in high spirits to see him so
easily brushing away Aedan's efforts.

The Vikings standing around them refuse Aedan a third shield.
He has to fight with nothing but his blade now. He slicks back his
hair with his free hand, glaring at Thrain who is still holding his
first shield by his side.

"Get him!" Shouts start up as they prowl around one another.
"Come on! Get him!"

The Norse exclamations all around us evidently mean the
same thing. A steady chant builds: *blòd! Blòd! Blòd!*

"Now he'll have to unsheathe his seax," I mutter to Rhun. He
stirs next to me.

"Who, Thrain? I don't know. He might not even need to.
Imagine the edge of that shield against your throat, with *his*
weight pitted against it." I shiver as I feel the ghostly pressure
against my own neck. Rhun leans closer to mutter in my ear.
"We'd better hope Aedan has some trick up his sleeve. What'll
happen to you if he loses this fight?"

"Don't worry about me," I tell him. "I'll be just fine."

I can feel him staring at me.

"You made a deal with Thrain Mordsson?"

As always, he guesses without me even needing to explain.

"Better the devil than Aedan mac Causantin," I say through gritted teeth.

"Tam—"

I grasp his arm. I'm growing light-headed from stress. "Not now. I'll tell you everything later."

Thrain hides behind his shield, taking Aedan's attacks. Aedan slashes and slashes at him from every angle imaginable. That round red wall meets him every time. At last Aedan lets out a cry of sheer rage and throws himself bodily against the shield. He grabs it, wedges his elbow around it and yanks it from Thrain's grasp.

Thrain's pulled forward. I gasp as his arm twists painfully. He lets the shield go at last and it clatters on the ground. Yelling in triumph, Aedan swings the length of his longsword in the air between them, deadly close.

I can't breathe.

The tip catches Thrain's thick leather belt, cuts into it. Thrain staggers to the edge of the perimeter. Blood trickles down his tunic from beneath the belt. He drapes an arm around his waist, bending as though in pain. His men come to him with shields, but he refuses them.

I clutch Rhun closer. No, no, no. He's wounded. Why is he doing this? Taking risks like this? He should take all his chances to win. He's a lord of Dublin, a wolf, a chieftain, he's...

He's my friend.

He can't lose.

"Yes," breathes Lady Catriona, eyes trained on her son. "Yes. Come on. You have him now."

Perhaps it's Rhun's presence by my side that makes me reach for a familiar name, a familiar desperate prayer. *Clota,* I think as I watch. *You know my pain. You know what it is to lay with beasts. Guide Thrain's blade as though it were your own.*

Aedan lifts his blade for a final killing blow. Cheers follow him as he all but runs at Thrain, all notions of perimetres forgotten. He swings down with a cry.

Thrain has nothing. No blade to parry. No shield.

Incomprehensibly, he lunges forwards into the attack and

throws up his maimed hand. The flat of Aedan's sword catches against Thrain's metal-studded bracer with a clang. He all but sweeps the blade aside and dives into Aedan's defenseless posture.

A thin hiss of metal accompanies the seax that Thrain unsheathes.

I barely even see it happen. One moment they're engaging one another in a messy clash of metal – the next they're standing still, legs planted wide apart, both of them frozen in the middle of their arena.

Thrain has stuck his seax deep in Aedan's belly. The next time he moves, it's to drag it up.

I will open you from your groin to your chin.

He makes good on his promise.

I'm clinging to Rhun, gasping for breath. A cry rings out in the hall. Someone shouts – there's movement at our table, men rising from their seats and rushing to the arena. Blue-clad Dálriadan guards whose presence I hadn't even noticed emerge from the outskirts of the hall. Lady Catriona calls out to them as she runs to her son.

Thrain doesn't seem to care. I look with wide eyes as he continues eviscerating my would-be husband in the middle of this chaos. I can't rip my eyes from the sight. A hysterical kind of glee is spreading through me, tangled with icy horror.

Aedan's voice thins to nothing as Thrain's blade runs higher up his body. The spattering sounds of blood hitting the floor in uneven gushes make my throat stopper up with disgust. I lean against the table, closing my eyes to try and quell the urge to throw up.

When I next look up Aedan is on his knees, his torn clothes drenched black. His belly is gaping open horribly, his guts hanging out of him. Light glistens on the red and purple spill. His lips are parted soundlessly, his clothes strewn with pearls of blood.

Lady Catriona is standing on the edge of the perimeter, one hand covering her mouth, the other held out to halt the Dálriadan guards that have surged forwards. Clearly she tried to get close to her son but couldn't bear to come too close to that gaping cadaver. Ivar and Olaf have a hold of Thrain who's holding his head low, a snarl on his face, eyes red with bloodlust. He's never worn his wolf moniker as well as now. Even in daylight the moon-craze seems to have taken hold, making him struggle against his brothers as though he would've wanted to rip Aedan apart with his bare hands.

The Dublin Vikings all roar and cheer for the victor, banging their goblets on the tables. Gofraid's bunch are silent and staring in shock. Thrain breathes, getting a hold of himself while Aedan kneels there, staring into nothing.

My heart beats like a drum in my chest. I can't believe it could've happened so fast.

Eventually Aedan keels over, crumpling onto the beaten earth at last.

Chapter 34

TAMSIN

DAY 1 OF THE WANING MOON OF JUNE

"GOFRAID!" PRINCE DOMNALL roars at the Viking king. "You – what – what have you *done!*"

Gofraid turns to address the pale-faced Alban royals. He gives a little bow to Lady Catriona first, who doesn't see it. She's collapsed onto her knees, bent over and covering her face with both hands.

"The lady should have been spared such a gruesome sight. For that I apologise," he says. Then, to Prince Domnall; "You will agree, I'm sure, that it is Prince Aedan who dealt the first injury. Therefore the challenge was honourable and the outcome appropriate."

I sigh with relief as Gofraid takes our side. I can't believe I didn't anticipate that this would affect their alliance so badly.

"*Honourable?*" Prince Domnall all but yells. "Explain to me what this injury is that you think Aedan dealt!"

"If you would but look at Princess Tamsin," Gofraid says, gesturing to me. "You would see it yourself."

I can only cringe under the murderous glare that Prince Domnall slams upon me.

"What goes on between a man and his wife is his own business!" he froths. "I don't see how it insults anyone else!"

"You have no respect for the daughters of the gods," Gofraid intones, his voice grave. "You scarcely believed in their existence when we first approached you with this alliance. Even now, I know you doubt our claims. You are not a Varg, so you cannot sense what they are. The crime of striking a woman who bears the mark of the gods themselves would have invited punishment, be it from Thrain's hand or my own."

"You – your man *gutted my cousin* on the floor of his own ancestral hall!" Prince Domnall yells. "Only the lowliest of criminals could possibly merit such – such—"

"Please," Lady Catriona croaks. She's tight-lipped, her eyes glued to the disgusting sight in the middle of the hall. "Domnall, stop. Aedan is dead. We may speak of reparation once he is removed from this place. I cannot... I cannot bear to see him like this." With the help of one of the terrified servants, she gets shakily to her feet. "Gofraid, if you would have the mercy to heed me – would you permit me to remove him from the hall?"

"You may of course remove him, my lady," Gofraid says. "We may speak more on the matter at a later date, when your king has returned to us."

"Yes!" Prince Domnall seethes. "Indeed! I would very much like to see what my father makes of this! That you might have sanctioned the murder of his own nephew!"

"You forget, our own laws have been in effect here ever since the alliance was signed," Gofraid says calmly. "There is nothing unlawful about this event. If Aedan did not want to risk his life, he should not have blatantly insulted my people and called our alliance into question right where we stand. Nor should he have treated a Vanirdottir like a common slave. The holmgang was justly called." He pins the Alban prince with a cool gaze. "You may consider the insult repaired."

Prince Domnall's mouth spasms around empty air for a moment. Lady Catriona sweeps to the dais while he stays stuck there in his outrage. She bows to Gofraid, intent on continuing to follow the correct protocol. Clearly she's lost all trust in her

Viking allies and acts out of sheer terror.

I stare coldly at her, trying to quell the squirm of empathy in my chest. It serves her right for choosing such allies. She shouldn't have presumed that she could tame wolves.

"Your Grace," she says. Then she gestures to the servants, who've been lingering on the sides of the hall, staring and muttering among themselves. They spring into action. From the way they move around Aedan's gory body, it would seem like they're used to manoeuvring corpses. They treat him like they would a pig carcass, bringing buckets for his innards, moving his inert body with unfeeling efficiency. I find myself again riveted by morbid fascination.

He is in pieces. He will never tower over me again.

Thrain is still standing nearby with his brothers, fully recovered now. When Lady Catriona approaches, all three of them bow at the waist as though showing contrition. Then Thrain steps ahead and presents Aedan's sword to her.

"He fought valiantly," Thrain tells the lady. "He will enter the halls of his forefathers with pride."

It is a strange peace offering. Gofraid oversees the exchange with a knowing eye, waiting for her response. I wonder if the family of the deceased are allowed to take up the blade and seek revenge.

Lady Catriona is still pale with shock, but clearly she doesn't want to further rouse Thrain's wrath. She takes the hilt of her son's blade and accepts the gift with a nod. Prince Domnall looks on, still wearing his outraged expression, but he decides against criticising the exchange. He turns to Eormen, asks her to follow him in a cordial tone, and leaves the table.

Eormen gazes at Rhun and I, eyes wide with fear. I suddenly realise that if she leaves, we'll be all alone in this hall with all these cursed men, the Dublin pack and those grim-faced warriors from the Southern Isles. Aedan lies dead – I have no formal ties with the Alban family any more. Eormen will stand alone among them now.

Resolutely she takes my hand anyway and bids me to come with her. From the look on her face, she thinks she is saving me from the company of Vikings, that somehow the Albans are preferable. I let her pull me after her a few steps, unable to voice a credible objection.

"Wait," Thrain intones. "There are still some details to account for."

We stop. There is that tenderness in Thrain's gaze again as he appraises me. I take in his imposing stature, his bloody hands, the wolfish hunger that still lingers in his eyes. Perhaps I am just as foolish as Lady Catriona to think I have tamed him. But right then I can only be fiercely glad that he's alive, that he cares for me, that he acts in my interests.

He turns to Gofraid.

"As Lord Aedan rushed into the challenge, he did not take the time to draw up what was at stake were he to face defeat," he says. "Therefore I can claim any or all of his worldly possessions."

"I *protest!*" Prince Domnall shouts. "You will not start bartering whilst my cousin's corpse is still warm. We will wait for my father to return before making such considerations."

"We shall, indeed," Gofraid says, beady eyes glinting over at Thrain as though pondering his true intentions.

"Your Grace, as per the laws of the holmgang, those men and women who are part of the prize may state their own will," Thrain says.

Worldly possessions. That he would include me in such a statement makes me taste bile again at the back of my throat. Rhun stirs at the table.

"Yes indeed, you are quite correct," Gofraid says. Judging by his tone, he's finally understood what Thrain's driving at. I can't tell if he approves.

"My sister is no one's worldly possession," comes Rhun's sudden voice. I cast an urgent glance at him, willing him to stay quiet.

Gofraid only chuckles at him. "My boy," he croons. "You will find that marriage is a binding contract. Insomuch as Princess Tamsin might've 'belonged' to Aedan in that way previously, now it is obviously no longer the case." He inclines his head at me. "Princess. If you would join me."

He lifts a hand. Leaning heavily on the table so that my legs might not give out from under me, I make my way over to the Viking king.

Domnall and Eormen watch from the doorway. Lady Catriona is supremely unconcerned with anything that isn't the clean-up effort surrounding her son. I can't blame her. I'm only too happy to have one less set of eyes on me as I stand before Gofraid. The Viking horde sits transfixed, a strangely reverent silence falling over them.

Gofraid's hand waits in the air. I place mine lightly upon his palm.

"Thrain! Come and stand before us," Gofraid calls. Thrain threads his way through the chaos of milling servants and curious warriors. I watch him arrive at the foot of the dais. From there, he has to tilt his head to look up at me.

I gaze down at his blood-spattered face, wondering at how the drastic sight does not shock me this time. With the spectacle he made of Aedan's body, I feel nothing could shock me any more.

He radiates calm confidence as he holds my gaze with those haunting blue eyes. Almost as though he'd like to channel some of it to me while we stand in the godforsaken mess of this hall. Together we have broken my previous status into pieces – the Albans will soon be gone to tend their dead lord, the lady of the fort completely uncaring of my fate.

I am adrift now. Thrain too, in a sense – his own people's alliance with the Albans has been dangerously rocked. Gofraid is going along with it for now, surely out of filial loyalty, but I can only wonder what he plans for Thrain once this is all over.

"Do you claim authority over this woman?" Gofraid asks him.

Thrain's clear blue eyes pierce mine.

"I do."

His words echo through me. Again, gladness swells in my chest as I look upon my unlikely ally. He killed Aedan for me. He risked his own standing with his king, and with King Causantin, for me. He certainly knew better than I what chaos this holmgang would spark.

And yet he heeded my wishes anyway.

"Princess Tamsin, do you protest his claim?"

I gaze up at the Viking horde seated beyond him, hoping they are all listening, hoping that by this act they will know I am unavailable to them.

"I do not protest it," I say, as loudly and clearly as I can manage.

The room erupts into noise as the Vikings bash their goblets against the tables. Some even have the gall to cheer. Gofraid reaches to clap a hand on Thrain's shoulder. I look over at Eormen again, who is following the grim-faced Albans out of the hall. She stares urgently back at me, looking petrified for me. But there's nothing she can do other than follow her husband out.

"The holmgang is settled!" Gofraid says after the Albans have disappeared from the hall with Aedan's corpse. "We will proceed with the assembly once the hall is back in order."

While his warriors all push the tables back into place, Thrain steps up to the dais to join me. He takes my hand formally as Gofraid did and leads me around the table so that I might be seated with him and his brothers. Rhun watches me from across Gofraid's rotund bulk, still worried as ever.

Ivar smiles at me as I sit, whilst Olaf nods in greeting.

I'm alone with the three wolves of Dublin.

"You crazy bastard," Ivar says to Thrain. He speaks in Gaelic, apparently inviting me into the conversation. "Father is going to rip you a new earhole as soon as he gets you alone."

"I think I may do so right now," Gofraid rumbles. He gives Thrain a sidelong glance, still smiling genially as though he were commenting on the weather. "Explain to me, you son of Loki, why you could not simply push the prince out of the arena?"

"Listen—" Thrain begins, but Ivar cuts in:

"No, Aedan deserved what he got. He should've died on that beach when we first arrived. Princess Tamsin is well rid of that one, we all are. He was a disloyal little runt. I wouldn't have trusted him further than I could throw him."

"Perhaps, but he would've posed an easy problem by himself," Gofraid says, still in that deceptively calm mutter. "Now Thrain has struck a blade in the hornet's nest. King Causantin will not be happy."

"King Causantin is never happy," Olaf says, slapping the table. "Thankfully, we don't need him to be. He'll defer to us. He always does."

"Oh? And I suppose you'll be the one to make him bend the knee?" Gofraid growls. "You forget, son of mine, you are not the one who has spent years coddling and placating the man. He's powerful. Why else do you think we allied ourselves with him instead of crushing him? It's far better to have him as an ally than an enemy, as I have *endeavoured* to tell Thrain."

"What would you have me do?" Thrain snarls, raising his voice for the first time. "Perhaps you did not see the blood on Princess Tamsin's dress. I could not risk Aedan somehow reclaiming the Vanirdottir he so eagerly bloodied once the duel was over. He had to die."

"Hmmm." Gofraid's beady eyes glint as he looks from me to Thrain. "Perhaps," he concedes, finally resting on me. I try not to squirm in my seat. "In any case, what's done is done. We must take measures to repair your mess. We'll speak more on the matter after the assembly. Now, princess," he adds, leaning against the table. "I may have to ask a favour of you."

The whitebeard turns fully to face me, obscuring my field of vision with his wild tangled mane of white hair and beard. Rhun leans closer, mutely struggling to stay involved, wearing an expression of utmost concentration. I wonder if they aren't speaking Gaelic as much for his benefit as for mine.

I stare into the face of one of the three kings who wed me to Aedan. It would've taken a simple word on his part to break the union, I know it. Thrain and I forced his hand and he isn't happy about it. A thrill runs through me to know that we might've thwarted the authority of the king of the Vikings.

"Yes, sire?" I ask. He smiles at the honorific.

"As I'm sure you understand, princess, we will have to show respect to our allies so they might forgive this fault," he says.

Perhaps it's the sight of blood and gore that has squashed my fear. I find myself lifting my chin and saying, "Don't you think you should show respect, first?"

Gofraid looks gobsmacked. Ivar laughs.

"You don't know who you've invited to the table, Father," he says. "The women of Strathclyde are not to be trifled with."

"Of course," Gofraid says, inclining his great shaggy head. "Yes. I must apologise before all else. I had some inkling that Aedan would not be worthy of a Vanirdottir."

"Aedan would not have been worthy of any woman," I say coldly. Rhun watches me, bewildered by my boldness.

"I deeply regret having inflicted him upon you," Gofraid says. "It was diplomacy that moved my hand. It was never my intention that you might suffer."

"Really?"

The word is too pressed, too loud. The afterimage of Thrain's cathartic violence makes me crave the weight of a sword, the physical strength to plunge it into my enemy's belly.

Gofraid observes me coolly for a moment. Warmth closes over my hand, a tell-tale shiver running through my bones. Thrain has lain a hand over mine, warning me to stand down.

I tuck in my chin. I'm riding a strange high. I need to not spoil our victory by overstepping boundaries.

Gofraid takes this as his cue to resume: "I regret to say that I shall need you to fulfill your duty just a little longer before you can be rid of him entirely. I will send a runner to Causantin so he might be informed of what's happened. No doubt he will return shortly. As the bride... the widow, rather, it would be appropriate that he might find you grieving alongside his family."

A chunk of ice drops into my stomach.

"You want me to join them in the chapel?" I ask him. "When I am the reason he died?"

Thrain overrides me, chastising his king in Norse, and they go on in their own tongue, promptly excluding me from the argument. Rhun and I exchange a glance. The thought of being pushed into the Albans' arms again in this context feels even worse than the prospect of marriage.

I stare at the clean-up efforts ahead just to fix my mind on something while the wolves go on snapping at one another in their gravelly Norse. The servants have swept away most of Aedan's remains, but a dark patch still subsists on the beaten earth floor. The Vikings hold back from placing the rugs back over it, leaving it to dry, but they still drag the tables carelessly close to that dreaded spot.

They have no real respect for the Albans. I wonder at how it is pure pragmatics that have led them to join forces. I stare up at Thrain as he argues some ineffable point, taking in the elegant lines of his face, the honey-blond fall of his hair. It is not entirely pragmatics that have led me to the same alliance, but still. I'm operating on the same principle.

The enemy of my enemy...

My brother's fiddling thoughtfully with his goblet. I need to talk to him so badly. There's so much to explain. I can only wonder how we've both come to sit alone at the Vikings' table.

I'm sure he'd understand my actions. At least, I hope he will.

ᛏᚼᚤᛧᛁᚼ

Once the room is back in order, Thrain stands and leads me back to the front of the dais so that everyone can have a good long look at me. He stands close to me, his expression drawn. Clearly he isn't happy at having to force me to this spot. But this was the whole purpose of this assembly, as he told me earlier.

To be displayed.

I can only be glad that Eormen is away with the Albans and spared this crudeness. At least Rhun is with me, though he is too squashed under Gofraid's authority to do much else than observe.

I grip Thrain's bloody hand tighter.

The Viking warriors seated at their tables stare at me in wonder. They have been mired in my scent ever since I entered this hall, but now they are called to focus upon it, this supposed proof of my sacred lineage.

Gofraid speaks to them of the legend of the Vanirdøtur, that after all this time we have been found at last. Ivar and Olaf stand then and attest that Dumbarton fort is full of women like us, trapped by the Christian king, that they saw us with their own eyes. The men's faces light up with greed and lust. They see opportunity in me, surely imagining all the shapes and sizes that their precious Vanirdøtur might come in.

"These are the last days of preparation!" Gofraid booms. "When the moon wanes to its last quarter, we shall depart. We will sail with our Irish brothers to save our Vanirdøtur from the clutches of the Briton king!" This draws cheers from his minions again. "Now, let us feast and give offering, so the gods may bless our endeavours."

I wonder if they're just going to resume the debauchery of last night, right now in broad daylight, when Aedan's blood is still fresh on the beaten earth floor. They seem to have enough appetite for food, at least. They dig in with relish, loud voices clamouring around the hall, servants milling around with more platters and jugs to bring. Those Dálriadan women look pale and shocked that the lord of their fort might've been slain – but they go on with their duties regardless.

"Come," Thrain says quietly. "I should take you to the chapel. Let us part from Gofraid."

"Do you have to?" I mutter. "What will it accomplish? Surely Domnall would sooner stone me than let me near Aedan—"

"I'll accompany you," he says. "We'll see how they react. You know I won't let them harm you."

Heart thumping, I nod. He's played his part in this hare-brained plan. Now it's my turn to do something ill-advised to finally put Aedan behind me and somehow minimize the consequences.

Thrain turns me so we might both face the Viking king. I see him bow, so I follow his lead.

"The Vanir bless you, Thrain!" one of the warriors calls out from the tables. "To be the first among us to win a Vanirdottir! Is she not the first to be claimed proper by Viking hand?"

"That, she is," Gofraid rumbles. His beady gaze follows my movements as I straighten.

"He should introduce her properly to the revelry of a Viking feast," another man calls. "You shall soon be glad, princess! You are among a people who can match your appetites."

"Yes! Come and let her share in the feast tonight."

My blood runs cold. How can they speak so openly of these

things? Then again, judging by their feast nights, they probably don't have much to hide from one another.

Rhun stands before Thrain can react and shouts, "Shut your filthy mouth, Nýr! That's my sister you're talking about!"

A roar of laughter rises from a section of the tables. A man with a ginger beard wild enough to rival Gofraid's throws up his goblet and says, "The pup barks!"

"That is all he does!" says this 'Nýr' character. "He is the one Varg in this hall who is chaste as a neutered dog!"

To my amazement, Rhun spits out a virulent phrase of Norse that has them all roaring again. The ginger mass of hair stands and bows to Gofraid.

"I apologise for my ward, Your Grace. I am trying to teach him manners."

"I'm sure you are, Orokia," Gofraid says with a smile. His calm and commanding tone appeases the hall again. "Princess Tamsin has just lost her husband. She must grieve as per the customs of her Christian people."

"Yes, indeed!" one shaven warrior calls. "And doubtless Thrain leads her away to partake in her grief!"

The men in the hall break into gales of jeering laughter. Thrain throws out something in Norse that doesn't much improve the hilarity.

"They will wear themselves out eventually," Thrain grumbles to me. "Have patience."

It's incredible that they might have the gall to mock my widowhood and Aedan's death like this. Prince Domnall himself has barely even left the hall that they already jeer about it.

"By Loki, I could've cloven that Aedan's skull myself," another shouts. "No disrespect, Thrain – but you only won her by chance and circumstance!"

"Sit down, Vegard," Gofraid breaks in. "If a deer wears Thrain's arrow in her neck, you would not contest his right to claim her. The siege is but a week away – you will all have the opportunity to win the favour of the Vanir."

The parallel snaps me abruptly out of my tentative appreciation of them. This 'Vegard' gives a snort and goes on addressing

Thrain: "Your hunting arrows are among the swiftest, Thrain, as we all know. But I would not need to contest anything, as you always share the fruit of your hunt."

"If we were talking about game, I would readily agree," Thrain says thinly. "However, as you can see, the princess is not a deer."

This draws another rippling of laughter, as though they were simply bandying words between them rather than discussing their right to claim me simultaneously. Gofraid's crass image of a deer suddenly feels horribly appropriate.

"Go, Thrain. Take your princess away," Gofraid says, freeing us at last. "And the rest of you!" he adds in a roar. "Do not think I don't see your minds. Prince Domnall is not to be touched. These are extenuating circumstances. Don't give Causantin any more reasons to come down upon us with his blue-faced army."

Before we can go, Gofraid leans closer to add a private command to Thrain; "Go to the docks and fetch the Jarls on overseer duty. We convene at midday to sort out this mess."

Thrain nods curtly and leads me down from the dais. I squeeze Rhun's arm as we pass him.

"Come see me if you can." I slip him the words in Brittonic. "I don't know how long I'll be out at the chapel."

He nods. "I'll come. Tam – good luck. Clota keep you."

"And you."

The Vikings go on jesting at one another as Thrain and I quietly slip through a doorway. It's not until we've placed a good measure of stone corridor between us and the main hall that I stop, clutching the wall, all strength leaving my body now that I don't have to hold myself up before a crowd.

Thrain stands beside me, leaning one arm against the wall so I feel cocooned there in that small space. I breathe for a moment. His reassuring scent is spoiled by the coppery tang of blood. I glance up at him to find him observing me quietly, his hooded eyes intense.

"Are you all right?" he asks.

"Just about," I manage. "What about you? Aedan cut you—"

"It's shallow. I wanted him to think he had the advantage," he says. I touch the split leather of his wide belt, dark now with his blood. I still want to check the wound just to make sure.

"I can't believe you did it," I blurt out. "I can't believe we managed it."

"Don't speak too fast. Save your joy for after Causantin returns."

I nod. He gently plucks me away from his wound, smearing blood on me in the process. Regardless of the muck that covers us both, that familiar warmth rushes through me as the contact pulls us closer as always.

"Do I belong to you now?" I mutter. "Is it as simple as that?"

He smirks. "You call that simple?"

"Well… you know what I mean."

His thumb runs along my knuckles as he ponders his answer. "I am your guardian, as we agreed," he says. "Anything more would require the proper ceremonies."

I nod. It's so blissfully quiet in this corridor. My fingers fold around his metal-studded bracer, running absently along the dents. His expression is so peaceful after the barbarity of the hall.

"Thank you," I murmur. "Thank you for doing this for me."

He leans in. The kiss he presses to my forehead is light, gentle. I keep my eyes closed after he breaks off, savouring the tingling he leaves in his wake. But the overwhelming scent of blood is still too present to appreciate the moment.

"Come," he says. "We should get you presentable for the chapel."

Chapter 35

THRAIN

DAY 1 OF THE WANING MOON OF JUNE

I LEAVE HER TO change in Aedan's quarters, where her coffers are.
Though she balks at the sight of the place she escaped last
night, it has all been cleaned up, the sheets changed, the bed
made. Perhaps that makes it somewhat more bearable.

Bravely she strides in and makes use of the staff who are
still lingering around, unsure who they should be serving now
that the lord is dead. Even though she clearly hates Gofraid's
directives, Tamsin still embraces her role as widow just so she
can order them to help her. It's strange to see her so authoritative
– since she's been rid of Aedan, she seems to be emulating the
older ladies of Strathclyde and their steely dignity.

I leave her so I might wash up in my own quarters. When I
return, she's sitting on the edge of the bed in black mourning
garb. A dark veil covers her lap. She fiddles with it while one of
the servants runs a comb through her long loose hair.

She looks a sight in all that black velvet. It marks a stark
contrast against her pallor. I wonder at the fact that her family
thought to pack that for her. Surely they couldn't have foretold
that the bridal dress would so quickly make way for the mourning

gown.

"Leave us," I tell the servants. They share glances at one another as they scatter.

Once they've gone, Tamsin smiles up at me and says, "They pity me. They think the great wolf of Dublin has come to claim his enemy's widow."

I smirk as I sit on the bed behind her and resume the servant's work. "Perhaps I should throw you over my shoulder and carry you away as they expect me to."

She affords me a soft laugh. "It'd solve a lot of problems. I'd much rather that than the chapel, for one thing."

My fingers work her long ginger coils into a braid. Both of us remain silent for a moment. The day's events slant through me, joy and frustration clashing. I have won her, but not entirely. She's decided to trust me and enjoy my company again, but she still keeps a certain formality with me.

She addresses the issue herself. "Thrain... we understand one another, don't we?"

My body understands that she's sitting close to me, her scent relaxing my tightly wound nerves, her sheer presence luring me in so that I want nothing more than to sit here with her while the siege preparations clatter on ahead. I have devoured a man for her – the moon and my own instincts roar that she be mine entirely.

Still hazy with the fight and the aftermath, my mind struggles to accept why it cannot be so. I fix my attention on her hair, keeping my mouth resolutely shut.

"I appreciate everything you've done for me," she says quietly as I tie the black ribbon at the end of her braid. "I know... I know you care for me. But I can't... "

"You are a princess of Strathclyde," I finish for her. "A young woman who is far from home. And a hostage in enemy territory."

I run my fingertips along the burnished bumps of the braid, resolutely ignoring the yearn that boils in the pit of my stomach. *Guardian,* she said. *I can accept that.*

"I won't add to your distress by laying my own desires upon you," I tell her. "I will not touch you unless you desire it yourself."

She bows her head. "We understand one another, then," she murmurs.

It is no easier to bear her company as she completes her preparations in silence. We're interrupted momentarily by servants ordered here by Gofraid, who're to take her coffers out to the chapel. Rage thrums through me at the idea that he's forcing her to stay down there potentially several days just for appearances' sake.

But where else could she sleep? Certainly not my own quarters. Not if Gofraid wants to placate Causantin before we leave for the siege – and not if she wants to keep this distance between us.

Once we're alone again she asks, "Is it safe? The chapel?"

"Yes. We have a covenant with the priests. No Viking is allowed in there."

She seems thoughtful as she wanders over to the small window, staring out at the greyish midday sky.

At last, she says, "Gofraid mentioned you were leaving for Strathclyde at the last quarter. That's barely a week from now. What's going to happen to me? And the others – Rhun and Eormen?"

I breathe out slowly, trying to decide how much to tell her.

"We and the Albans will divide into two parties. Gofraid will lead us into Strathclyde by the Firth while the Albans travel overland. Rhun will be coming with us. Eormen will be going deeper into Alba with Domnall to join Causantin's forces."

She blinks rapidly as she takes all this information. "Gofraid is taking Rhun with him? As a hostage of some kind?"

"Put simply, yes. As for you... before all this happened, Lord Aedan and Lady Catriona were meant to stay here in Dunadd. Which meant you were to stay in Dál Riata with them." She glances over at me as I speak, her expression grave. "Now that Lady Catriona has resumed her title of ruling lady of the fort, and you are no longer attached to them—"

"I'll come with you," she says immediately. "I'll accompany Rhun."

Her unwavering loyalty to her brother brings a faint smile to my lips. "I'll have to speak to Gofraid about it when we meet later today. I'll give you the news as soon as I know."

She bows her head. When she speaks again it's in a quiet, timid voice: "But you aren't allowed in the chapel, are you?" she asks. "I'll be alone in there until Causantin is appeased."

She looks so forlorn in that little square of light. I get up, unable to resist her any longer, my body all but summoned to her. I lay my hands upon the jewelled belt she wears at her waist, aching to take her in my arms. Goosebumps prick her neck as I loom behind her.

"I'll come to you," I tell her. "You shouldn't be there long, anyway. I won't stand for it."

She places her hands over mine. I close my eyes to savour the shimmer of her touch. We stand there together for a moment, certainly too close for a guardian and his ward. Her scent draws me in until I am calmer and more centred than I have been all day.

Mine, whispers the beast inside me. *My mate.*

She turns. Her moss-green eyes meet mine and then drop to linger on my mouth. I forget to breathe until finally she breaks away, focussing instead on the woven patterns around my collar.

"You say you won't touch me unless I desire it," she murmurs. "But you know that I do desire it, come nighttime when the heat steals away my reason."

Her words are low, intimate. I try to ignore the effect they have on my body as they evoke what happened last night.

"Then I will respect only those wishes you make in daylight," I tell her. "You have my word."

She nods. An eternity passes as we linger there, both of us trying to pretend we aren't entirely focussed upon the other. Then she steps away, resolutely keeping her eyes off me.

"Would you pass me my veil?"

ᚦᚱᛏᛁᚼ

We step out into the courtyard. She turns her face up to the open sky, the sun already at its zenith. I realise quite suddenly that she hasn't been free to linger outside at her own leisure in weeks. Her spirits seem somewhat eased as she takes several deep breaths, collecting herself while the sun warms her coppery eyelids.

Their Christian chapel is ahead of us. As is Prince Domnall, who is conferring with a group of old hunched councilmen. They stride towards us, deep in conversation.

Tamsin throws her black veil over her face. Prince Domnall glares at the dark figure she makes as he and the councilmen approach. I lay a hand on the hilt of my seax as he passes.

He makes no comment, nor does he even spare me a glance. Once they've entered the fort again the tension drops, as do Tamsin's shoulders.

The wordless encounter speaks volumes for how complicated our situation has become. Tamsin looks straight at the chapel's sun-washed red doors. It's strange to think that only last night she was wed in there.

"One less Alban to deal with," I mutter to her. She scoffs mirthlessly.

"Let's go, then."

There's terrible weariness in her voice. I hate to bring her here and throw her into the wrath of a grieving mother. But bring her I must if we're to emerge from this murder unscathed.

The small chapel door creaks open. A priest appears, turns to us and bows, clearly waiting for the princess to go to him.

Tamsin's face seems even more pale and gaunt beneath all that black lace. Her shockingly vibrant hair defies the mournful garb, windswept ginger curls clinging to her dress. There are no comfortable options ahead of her; she has the air of one who is contemplating the ancient rusty sword she must fall upon.

"Princess," calls the priest. "Please come inside."

He looks pointedly at me as though to remind me of our covenant. Pushing down my annoyance, I turn to bid Tamsin farewell.

"I'll come for you soon," I promise her.

"Please do," she mutters back.

She squeezes my hand one last time and turns away from me.

I watch her stride through the chapel door, all alone. She still has seven nights of heat to endure. She should not spend those nights in a cold church. But clearly Gofraid intends to deny her any unchristian behaviour – and he denies me the pleasure of savouring my Vanirdottir's company, surely unwilling to reward my mutiny.

But we have time. She is under my authority now, and mine in more ways than one. Even if Causantin returns and puts our bond into question, it will hardly matter to me when I have something far more precious than a king's consent.

Her affection. Her consideration. Her trust.

Whatever may happen when the King of all Alba returns, he cannot wrest that from me.

The small red door of the chapel closes behind them. I ask Freya to watch over my fiery-haired ward, and turn back to the fort.

Soon enough, we will be together again.

CAST OF CHARACTERS

The Britons

King Arthgal - King of Strathclyde
Queen Beatha - Queen of Strathclyde
Eormen - eldest daughter of the King
Arlyn - eldest son and crown prince
Princess Aphria - sister to King Arthgal
Tamsin - eldest daughter of Aphria
Rhun - twin brother to Tamsin
Hilda - nursemaid & castle servant
Cinnie - Hilda's daughter & castle servant
Emrys - young Cavalier and protector of the royal family
Kelwynn - young Cavalier and protector of the royal family

The Albans

King Causantin - King of all Alba
Queen Matilda - Queen of all Alba
Prince Domnall - eldest son and crown prince
Lady Catriona - sister to King Causantin, lady of Dál Riata
Lord Aedan - son of Lady Catriona, lord of Dál Riata

The Dublin Vikings

Thrain Mordsson - Jarl of Dublin
Ivar Gofraidsson - Jarl of Dublin, son of King Gofraid
Olaf Gofraidsson - Jarl of Dublin, son of King Gofraid
Kætilví - Thrain's mother & acting Jarl of Dublin
Vírún - Olaf's wife
Armod - karl
Orm - karl
Sigbrand - karl
Nýr - karl
Vegard - karl
Finngeir - karl

THE SOUTHERN ISLE VIKINGS

Gofraid - King of the Southern Isles
Aurvandill - Jarl
Orokia - Jarl & Rhun's guardian

[The story continues in the second installement of the Viking Omegaverse series, **Taming the Wolves**, available now!]

NOTES ON HISTORICAL DETAILS

The term "Briton" is used quite loosely nowadays for any inhabitant of the isle of Britain. But historically, "Briton" refers to a specific population: the tribes that inhabited the entire isle of Britain before the Romans arrived, which Tamsin and Eormen speak of in this book. They were a Celtic population whose culture was distinct from those populating Ireland (known as Gaels). The Britons had to cede their territories to successive waves of invaders: the Romans, then the Anglo-Saxons, then the Danes. These ate away at the main body of Britain, provoking a mass westward exile of the Britons. And so during the time of this novel, the last hubs of culturally "Briton" peoples are in Strathclyde, Wales, Cornwall, Brittany (France), and Gaelicia (Spain). Eventually, centuries after the events of this series, the territory of Strathclyde would be merged with the Gaelic culture of the rest of Alba/Scotland, and thus it has lost its Brittonic roots, making it a tantalising "lost kingdom of the Britons" about which not much information remains.

As I come from Brittany, our ancient Briton past has always fascinated me, but it is shrouded in mystery and quite confusing to disentangle between what is historical, and what is warped cliché. The legends of those Britons who were exiled to the shores of Brittany have survived even a thousand years later: for instance, we have our own "King Arthur's forest" here in Brittany, complete with "Merlin's tomb" and "Morgana's heart". For the longest time I thought the events of the Arthurian legends had happened in Brittany, even though as most British people know, it is actually a Welsh legend.

So, to find out more about my own ancient history, I must look to Britain, and especially Wales. It's become a great interest of mine to try and disentangle what is "Brittonic Celtic culture" and "Gaelic Celtic culture", which is what fuels the research behind this series. In our modern media, there is a tendency to tangle up different Celtic cultures, sprinkle some modern neo-pagan terms in there, or perhaps some reference to Shakespeare, and be done with it. This is immensely frustrating, but only to a tiny amount of people I'm sure - the field of Celtic studies is tiny and hyper-specific, and I'm not sure it'd interest many readers if I went into a long-winded essay about my choice of place-names and historical fudgery here. But in any case, this is why I chose to look into the lost Brittonic kingdom of Strathclyde rather than your more classic tales of "Vikings vs Anglo-Saxon kingdoms" like Northumbria, or Wessex, etc, etc.

As the Celtic roots of Tamsin's kingdom were eaten away by Christianity, the Celtic elements are still subdued in this book. But I want to do my best to put forward truly Brittonic Celtic elements. Clota was a real deity, for instance; she might've been the spirit or personification of the river, which through linguistic shifts became known as the "Clyde." (This would follow the Brittonic tendency to sacralise founts & freshwater sources.) The myths I wrote about her here are purely fictional however, as there is very little information about her; and Tamsin's view of her as an "ancestor" rather than a deity follows what Christianity did to local pagan beliefs; warp and desacralise them, making it difficult to piece together what the old beliefs used to be. Later on, you will find Welsh myths & legends, too, as they seem to be the last repository of Briton culture whose roots run furthest into the pre-Christian past. I hope, as the series progresses, to uncover a whole lot more about the original polytheistic & druidic culture of the Britons.

The Bog Rituals

In case you were wondering what inspired the ritual ceremony in the bogs: the pre-Roman tribes of Britain did partake in human sacrifice, and we have some ideas of how those sacrifices were done thanks to the bog bodies that have been excavated over the centuries. I tried to incorporate several key elements into my fictional ritual with those archeological finds in mind.

ACKNOWLEDGMENTS

Thanks so much for picking up this book! I hope you enjoyed it. I set off to write a simple omegaverse story and it... kind of exploded into something much bigger. I'm pretty sure I'd still be tearing out my hair over it if it weren't for my amazing beta-readers, so some thanks are in order! Matt Gregory first of all, for all the much-needed support and generally keeping me sane. Simon Pressinger for helping me out even if he doesn't read romance and was astounded by the amount of smut (and even more astounded when I mentioned this book is relatively light in the smut department). Nikki Bradley for reading through multiple drafts, discussing Viking combat, being wonderfully blunt and also massacring all of my commas. Breanna Glasse for actually adding commas (who'd've thought?!) and giving precious feedback on pivotal points. And Rave and Darktownart for the awesome enthusiasm!

ABOUT THE AUTHOR

Originally a fantasy/SF writer, I took a sharp left turn in 2020 and got lost in the omegaverse. This probably explains why my smut ends up being pretty plot-heavy, as you can tell by now if you've gotten this far! My writing process is mainly fuelled by cheese (all the cheese), my undying love for historical reenactment, and folk bands that I am currently obsessed with. Thanks so much for reading & come say hello on my social media!

Sign up to my newsletter to keep up with my projects & get bonus material:
https://www.subscribepage.com/lyxrobinsonnewsletter

I love to hear from readers! Feel free to shoot me an email at:
lyxrobinsonauthor@gmail.com.

MORE BY LYX ROBINSON

The Viking Omegaverse
Taming the Wolves (Book 2)
A Meeting of Wolves (Book 2.5)
COMING SOON: The Summer Siege (Book 3)